THE PILGRIM'S PROGRESS

THE PILGRIM'S PROGRESS

DOVER THRIFT EDITIONS

John Bunyan

DOVER PUBLICATIONS, INC.
MINEOLA, NEW YORK

DOVER THRIFT EDITIONS

GENERAL EDITOR: PAUL NEGRI
EDITOR OF THIS VOLUME: SUSAN L. RATTINER

Bibliographical Note

This Dover edition, first published in 2003, is an unabridged republication of the text of *The Pilgrim's Progress* (originally published in 1678), as printed in Volume 15 of "The Harvard Classics Series" by P. F. Collier & Son Company, New York, in 1909.

Library of Congress Cataloging-in-Publication Data

Bunyan, John, 1628-1688.
    The pilgrim's progress / John Bunyan.
        p. cm. – (Dover thrift editions)
    ISBN-13: 978-0-486-42675-4
    ISBN-10: 0-486-42675-0 (pbk.)
     1. Christian pilgrims and pilgrimages—Fiction. I. Title II. Series.

PR3330. A1 2003
828´.407 – dc21
                                       2002035936

Manufactured in the United States by LSC Communications
42675012   2018
www.doverpublications.com

CONTENTS

THE PILGRIM'S PROGRESS

THE FIRST PART

THE SECOND PART

INTRODUCTORY NOTE

JOHN BUNYAN *was born at Elstow, Bedfordshire, England, in November, 1628. His father was a maker and mender of pots and kettles, and the son followed the same trade. Though he is usually called a tinker, Bunyan had a settled home and place of business. He had little schooling, and he describes his early surroundings as poor and mean. When he was not yet sixteen his mother died; in two months his father married again; and the son enlisted as a soldier in the Civil War in November, 1644, though whether on the Parliamentary or Royalist side is not certain. The armies were disbanded in 1646, and about two years later Bunyan married a wife whose piety redeemed him from his delight in rural sport and the habit of profane swearing. He became much interested in religion, but it was only after a tremendous spiritual conflict, lasting three or four years, that he found peace. His struggles are related with extraordinary vividness and intensity in his "Grace Abounding to the Chief of Sinners." In 1655, the year in which he lost his wife, he began to exhort, and two years later he became a regular Non-conformist preacher, continuing, however, to practise his trade. His success as a preacher roused opposition among the regular clergy, and in 1658 he was indicted at the assizes. His writing began with a controversy against the Quakers, and shows from the first the command of a homely but vigorous style.*

With the reenactment of the laws against non-conformity at the Restoration, Bunyan became subject to more severe persecution, and with a short intermission he was confined to prison from 1660 till 1672. Again and again he might have been released, but he refused to promise to desist from preaching, and there was no alternative for the justices but to keep him in confinement. Sometimes lax jailers permitted him to preach at church meetings; he frequently ministered to his fellow-prisoners; and he supported his family, now looked after by a second wife, by making laces. He had apparently abundant leisure, for he wrote in prison a large number of books, the first one of importance being that already mentioned, "Grace Abounding"

3

(1666). "The Pilgrim's Progress" was also written in jail, but probably during a later confinement of six months in 1675.

In 1672 Charles II suspended the laws against Non-conformists and Roman Catholics, and Bunyan was released. He was called to be minister to a Non-conformist congregation in Bedford, and preached in the barn which served them as a church. But his ministrations were not confined to Bedford. He made preaching tours over a wide district, and even to London, and attracted great crowds of listeners. Meanwhile he continued to write. The first edition of "The Pilgrim's Progress" in 1678 was followed by others with additions, and in 1684 by the second part. "The Life and Death of Mr. Badman" appeared in 1680; "The Holy War made by Shaddai upon Diabolus" in 1682. If the works left in manuscript at his death be included, the total of his books amounts to nearly sixty. He died in 1688, leaving a widow and six children, and a personal estate of less than £100. "The Pilgrim's Progress" became at once popular, and has continued to be by far the most widely read of all his works, and one of the most universally known of English books. Though in the form of an allegory, the narrative interest is so powerful, the drawing of permanent types of human character is so vigorous, and the style is so simple and direct that it takes rank as a great work of fiction. The best sides of English Puritanism have here their most adequate and characteristic expression, while the intensity of Bunyan's religious fervor and the universality of the spiritual problems with which he deals, raise the work to a place among the great religious classics of the world.

THE AUTHOR'S APOLOGY

FOR HIS BOOK

WHEN at the first I took my Pen in hand
Thus for to write; I did not understand
That I at all should make a little Book
In such a mode; Nay, I had undertook
To make another, which when almost done,
Before I was aware I this begun.

And thus it was: I writing of the Way
And Race of Saints, in this our Gospel-day,
Fell suddenly into an Allegory
About their Journey, and the way to Glory,
In more than twenty things which I set down:
This done, I twenty more had in my Crown,
And they again began to multiply,
Like sparks that from the coals of fire do fly.
Nay then, thought I, if that you breed so fast,
I'll put you by yourselves, lest you at last
Should prove ad infinitum, and eat out
The Book that I already am about.

Well, so I did; but yet I did not think
To shew to all this World my Pen and Ink
In such a mode; I only thought to make
I knew not what: nor did I undertake
Thereby to please my Neighbor; no not I;
I did it mine own self to gratifie.

Neither did I but vacant seasons spend
In this my Scribble; nor did I intend
But to divert myself in doing this
From worser thoughts which make me do amiss.

Thus I set Pen to Paper with delight,
And quickly had my thoughts in black and white.

5

For having now my Method by the end,
Still as I pull'd, it came; and so I penn'd
It down, until it came at last to be
For length and breadth the bigness which you see.

   Well, when I had thus put mine ends together,
I shew'd them others, that I might see whether
They would condemn them, or them justifie:
And some said, Let them live; some, Let them die;
Some said, John, print it; others said, Not so:
Some said, It might do good; others said, No.

   Now was I in a straight, and did not see
Which was the best thing to be done by me:
At last I thought, Since you are thus divided,
I print it will, and so the case decided.

   For, thought I, some I see would have it done,
Though others in that Channel do not run.
To prove then who advised for the best,
Thus I thought fit to put it to the test.

   I further thought, if now I did deny
Those that would have it thus, to gratifie,
I did not know but hinder them I might
Of that which would to them be great delight.

   For those which were not for its coming forth
I said to them, Offend you I am loth,
Yet since your Brethren pleased with it be,
Forbear to judge till you do further see.

   If that thou wilt not read, let it alone;
Some love the meat, some love to pick the bone:
Yea, that I might them better palliate,
I did too with them thus Expostulate:

   May I not write in such a stile as this?
In such a method too, and yet not miss
Mine end, thy good? why may it not be done?
Dark Clouds bring Waters, when the bright bring none.
Yea, dark or bright, if they their Silver drops
Cause to descend, the Earth, by yielding Crops,
Gives praise to both, and carpeth not at either,
But treasures up the Fruit they yield together;
Yea, so commixes both, that in her Fruit
None can distinguish this from that: they suit

Her well, when hungry; but, if she be full,
She spues out both, and makes their blessings null.
   You see the ways the Fisher-man doth take
To catch the Fish; what Engines doth he make?
Behold how he engageth all his Wits,
Also his Snares, Lines, Angles, Hooks, and Nets.
Yet Fish there be, that neither Hook, nor Line,
Nor Snare, nor Net, nor Engine can make thine;
They must be grop'd for, and be tickled too,
Or they will not be catch'd, whate'er you do.

   How doth the Fowler seek to catch his Game
By divers means, all which one cannot name?
His Gun, his Nets, his Lime-twigs, Light, and Bell;
He creeps, he goes, he stands; yea who can tell
Of all his postures? Yet there's none of these
Will make him master of what Fowls he please.
Yea, he must Pipe and Whistle to catch this;
Yet if he does so, that *Bird* he will miss.

   If that a Pearl may in a Toad's head dwell,
And may be found too in an Oyster-shell;
If things that promise nothing do contain
What better is than Gold; who will disdain,
That have an inkling of it, there to look,
That they may find it? Now my little Book
(Though void of all those Paintings that may make
It with this or the other man to take)
Is not without those things that do excel
What do in brave, but empty notions dwell.

   Well, yet I am not fully satisfied,
That this your Book will stand, when soundly try'd.
   Why, what's the matter? It is dark. What tho?
But it is feigned: What of that I tro?
Some men, by feigning words as dark as mine,
Make truth to spangle, and its rays to shine.
But they want solidness. Speak man thy mind.
They drownd the weak; Metaphors make us blind.
   Solidity indeed becomes the Pen
Of him that writeth things Divine to men;
But must I needs want solidness, because
By Metaphors I speak? Were not God's Laws,

His Gospel-Laws, in olden time held forth
By Types, Shadows, and Metaphors? Yet loth
Will any sober man be to find fault
With them, lest he be found for to assault
The highest Wisdom. No, he rather stoops,
And seeks to find out what by Pins and Loops,
By Calves, and Sheep, by Heifers, and by Rams,
By Birds, and Herbs, and by the blood of Lambs,
God speaketh to him. And happy is he
That finds the light and grace that in them be.

Be not too forward therefore to conclude
That I want solidness, that I am rude:
All things solid in shew not solid be;
All things in Parables despise not we;
Lest things most hurtful lightly we receive,
And things that good are, of our souls bereave.

My dark and cloudy words they do but hold
The Truth, as Cabinets inclose the Gold.

The Prophets used much by Metaphors
To set forth Truth; yea, whoso considers
Christ, his Apostles too, shall plainly see,
That Truths to this day in such Mantles be.

Am I afraid to say that Holy Writ,
Which for its Stile and Phrase puts down all Wit,
Is everywhere so full of all these things,
Dark Figures, Allegories? Yet there springs
From that same Book that lustre, and those rays
Of light, that turns our darkest nights to days.

Come, let my Carper to his Life now look,
And find there darker lines than in my Book
He findeth any; Yea, and let him know,
That in his best things there are worse lines too.

May we but stand before impartial men,
To his poor One I dare adventure Ten,
That they will take my meaning in these lines
Far better than his lies in Silver Shrines.
Come, Truth, although in Swaddling-clouts, I find,
Informs the Judgment, rectifies the Mind,
Pleases the Understanding, makes the Will
Submit; the Memory too it doth fill

With what doth our Imagination please;
Likewise it tends our troubles to appease.

    Sound words I know Timothy *is to use,*
And old Wives' Fables he is to refuse;
But yet grave Paul *him nowhere doth forbid*
The use of Parables; in which lay hid
That Gold, those Pearls, and precious stones that were
Worth digging for, and that with greatest care.

    Let me add one word more. O man of God,
Art thou offended? Dost thou wish I had
Put forth my matter in another dress,
Or that I had in things been more express?
Three things let me propound, then I submit
To those that are my betters, as is fit.

    1. *I find not that I am denied the use*
Of this my method, so I no abuse
Put on the Words, Things, Readers; or be rude
In handling Figure or Similitude,
In application; but, all that I may,
Seek the advance of Truth this or that way.
Denied, did I say? Nay, I have leave,
(*Example too, and that from them that have*
God better pleased, by their words or ways,
Than any man that breatheth now a-days)
Thus to express my mind, thus to declare.
Things unto thee, that excellentest are.

    2. *I find that men (as high as Trees) will write*
Dialogue-wise; yet no man doth them slight
For writing so; Indeed if they abuse
Truth, cursed be they, and the craft they use
To that intent; but yet let Truth be free
To make her sallies upon thee and me,
Which way it pleases God. For who knows how,
Better than he that taught us first to Plow,
To guide our Mind and Pens for his Design?
And he makes base things usher in Divine.

    3. *I find that Holy Writ in many places*
Hath semblance with this method, where the cases
Do call for one thing, to set forth another;
Use it I may then, and yet nothing smother

Truth's golden Beams: nay, by this method may
Make it cast forth its rays as light as day.

   And now, before I do put up my Pen,
I'll shew the profit of my Book, and then
Commit both thee and it unto that hand
That pulls the strong down, and makes weak ones stand.

   This Book it chalketh out before thine eyes
The man that seeks the everlasting Prize;
It shews you whence he comes, whither he goes,
What he leaves undone, also what he does;
It also shews you how he runs and runs,
Till he unto the Gate of Glory comes.

   It shews too, who set out for life amain,
As if the lasting Crown they would obtain;
Here also you may see the reason why
They lose their labour, and like Fools do die.

   This Book will make a Traveller of thee,
If by its Counsel thou wilt ruled be;
It will direct thee to the Holy Land,
If thou wilt its directions understand:
Yea, it will make the slothful active be;
The blind also delightful things to see.

   Art thou for something rare and profitable?
Wouldest thou see a Truth within a Fable?
Art thou forgetful? Wouldest thou remember
From New-year's-day to the last of December?
Then read my Fancies, they will stick like Burrs,
And may be to the Helpless, Comforters.

   This Book is writ in such a Dialect
As may the minds of listless men affect:
It seems a novelty, and yet contains
Nothing but sound and honest Gospel strains.

   Would'st thou divert thyself from Melancholy?
Would'st thou be pleasant, yet be far from folly?
Would'st thou read Riddles, and their Explanation?
Or else be drowned in thy Contemplation?
Dost thou love picking meat? Or would'st thou see
A man i' th' Clouds, and hear him speak to thee?
Would'st thou be in a Dream, and yet not sleep?
Or would'st thou in a moment laugh and weep?

Wouldest thou lose thyself, and catch no harm,
And find thyself again without a charm?
Would'st read thyself, and read thou know'st not what,
And yet know whether thou art blest or not,
By reading the same lines? O then come hither,
And lay my Book, thy Head, and Heart together.

JOHN BUNYAN.

THE PILGRIM'S PROGRESS

IN THE SIMILITUDE OF A DREAM.

AS I walk'd through the wilderness of this world,
I lighted on a certain place where was a Den, The Jail
and I laid me down in that place to sleep;
and as I slept, I dreamed a Dream. I dreamed, and
behold I saw a Man cloathed with Rags, standing
in a certain place, with his face from his own
house, a Book in his hand, and a great Burden
upon his back. I looked, and saw him open the
Book, and read therein; and as he read, he wept
and trembled; and not being able longer to contain,
he brake out with a lamentable cry, saying *What* His outcry
shall I do?

In this plight therefore he went home, and re-
frained himself as long as he could, that his Wife
and Children should not perceive his distress, but
he could not be silent long, because that his trouble
increased: Wherefore at length he brake his mind
to his Wife and Children; and thus he began to talk
to them: *O my dear Wife,* said he, *and you the Children of my bowels, I your dear friend, am in myself
undone by reason of a Burden that lieth hard upon
me; moreover, I am for certain informed that this* This world
*our City will be burned with fire from Heaven; in
which fearful overthrow, both myself, with thee my
Wife, and you my sweet Babes, shall miserably come
to ruine, except (the which yet I see not) some way
of escape can be found, whereby we may be deliv-* He knows
ered. At this his Relations were sore amazed; not no way of
for that they believed that what he had said to them as yet
was true, but because they thought that some frenzy

13

distemper had got into his head; therefore, it drawing towards night, and they hoping that sleep might settle his brains, with all haste they got him to bed: But the night was as troublesome to him as the day; wherefore, instead of sleeping, he spent it in sighs and tears. So, when the morning was come, they would know how he did; He told them, *Worse and worse:* he also set to talking to them again, but they began to be hardened: they also thought to drive away his distemper by harsh and surly carriages to him; sometimes they would deride, sometimes they would chide, and sometimes they would quite neglect him: Wherefore he began to retire himself to his chamber, to pray for and pity them, and also to condole his own misery; he would also walk solitarily in the fields, sometimes reading, and sometimes praying: and thus for some days he spent his time.

Carnal physic for a sick soul

Now, I saw upon a time, when he was walking in the fields, that he was, as he was wont, reading in his Book, and greatly distressed in his mind; and as he read, he burst out, as he had done before, crying, *What shall I do to be saved?*

I saw also that he looked this way and that way, as if he would run; yet he stood still, because, as I perceived, he could not tell which way to go. I looked then, and saw a man named *Evangelist*, coming to him, and asked, *Wherefore dost thou cry?*

He answered, Sir, I perceive by the Book in my hand, that I am condemned to die, and after that to come to Judgment, and I find that I am not willing to do the first, nor able to do the second.

> *Christian* no sooner leaves the World but meets
> *Evangelist*, who lovingly him greets
> With tidings of another: and doth shew
> Him how to mount to that from this below.

Then said *Evangelist*, Why not willing to die, since this life is attended with so many evils? The Man answered, Because I fear that this burden that is upon my back will sink me lower than the Grave, and I shall fall into *Tophet*. And, Sir, if I be not fit to go to Prison, I am not fit to go to Judgment, and from thence to Execution; and the thoughts of these things make me cry.

Then said *Evangelist,* If this be thy condition, why standest thou still? He answered, Because I know not whither to go. Then he gave him a *Parchment-roll,* and there was written within, *Fly from the wrath to come.* Conviction of the necessity of flying

The Man therefore read it, and looking upon *Evangelist* very carefully, said, Whither must I fly? Then said *Evangelist,* pointing with his finger over a very wide field, Do you see yonder *Wicket-gate?* The Man said, No. Then said the other, Do you see yonder shining Light? He said, I think I do. Then said *Evangelist,* Keep that Light in your eye, and go up directly thereto: so shalt thou see the Gate; at which, when thou knockest, it shall be told thee what thou shalt do. Christ, and the way to him cannot be found without the Word

So I saw in my Dream that the Man began to run. Now he had not run far from his own door, but his Wife and Children, perceiving it, began to cry after him to return; but the Man put his fingers in his ears, and ran on, crying, *Life! Life! Eternal Life!* So he looked not behind him, but fled towards the middle of the Plain. They that fly from the wrath to come, are a gazing-stock to the world

The Neighbors also came out to see him run; and as he ran, some mocked, others threatened, and some cried after him to return; and among those that did so, there were two that resolved to fetch him back by force. The name of the one was *Obstinate,* and the name of the other *Pliable.* Now by this time the Man was got a good distance from them; but however they were resolved to pursue him, which they did, and in a little time they overtook him. Then said the Man, Neighbors, wherefore are you come? They said, To persuade you to go back with us. But he said, That can by no means be; you dwell, said he, in the City of *Destruction,* the place also where I was born, I see it to be so; and dying there, sooner or later, you will sink lower than the Grave, into a Obstinate and Pliable follow him place that burns with Fire and Brimstone: be content, good Neighbors, and go along with me.

OBST. What, said *Obstinate,* and leave our friends and our comforts behind us!

CHR. Yes, said *Christian,* for that was his name, because that *all* which you shall forsake is not worthy to be compared with a *little* of that that I am seeking to enjoy; and if you will go along with me and hold it, you shall fare as I myself; for there where I go, is enough and to spare: Come away, and prove my words.

OBST. What are the things you seek, since you leave all the world to find them?

CHR. I seek an *Inheritance incorruptible, undefiled, and that fadeth not away,* and it is laid up in Heaven, and safe there, to be bestowed at the time appointed, on them that diligently seek it. Read it so, if you will, in my Book.

OBST. Tush, said *Obstinate,* away with your Book; will you go back with us or no?

CHR. No, not I, said the other, because I have laid my hand to the Plow.

OBST. Come then, Neighbor *Pliable,* let us turn again, and go home without him; there is a company of these craz'd-headed coxcombs, that, when they take a fancy by the end, are wiser in their own eyes than seven men that can render a reason.

PLI. Then said *Pliable,* Don't revile; if what the good *Christian* says is true, the things he looks after are better than ours; my heart inclines to go with my Neighbor.

OBST. What! more fools still? Be ruled by me, and go back; who knows whither such a brain-sick fellow will lead you? Go back, go back, and be wise.

Christian and Obstinate pull for Pliable's soul CHR. Come with me, Neighbor *Pliable;* there are such things to be had which I spoke of, and many more Glories besides. If you believe not me, read here in this Book; and for the truth of what is

exprest therein, behold, all is confirmed by the blood
of Him that made it.

PLI. Well, Neighbor *Obstinate,* said *Pliable,* I
begin to come to a point: I intend to go along with
this good man, and to cast in my lot with him: but,
my good companion, do you know the way to this
desired place? Pliable
contented
to go with
Christian

CHR. I am directed by a man, whose name is
Evangelist, to speed me to a little Gate that is before
us, where we shall receive instructions about the
way.

PLI. Come then, good Neighbor, let us be going.
Then they went both together.

OBST. And I will go back to my place, said *Obstinate;* I will be no companion of such mis-led, fantastical fellows. Obstinate
goes rail-
ing back

Now I saw in my Dream, that when *Obstinate*
was gone back, *Christian* and *Pliable* went talking over the Plain; and thus they began their
discourse. Talk
between
Christian
and
Pliable

CHR. Come Neighbor *Pliable,* how do you do?
I am glad you are persuaded to go along with me:
Had even *Obstinate* himself but felt what I have
felt of the powers and terrors of what is yet un-
seen, he would not thus lightly have given us the
back.

PLI. Come, Neighbor *Christian,* since there are
none but us two here, tell me now further what
the things are, and how to be enjoyed, whither we
are going?

CHR. I can better conceive of them with my Mind,
than speak of them with my Tongue: but yet, since
you are desirous to know, I will read of them in
my Book. God's
things un-
speakable

PLI. And do you think that the words of your
Book are certainly true?

CHR. Yes, verily; for it was made by him that
cannot lye.

PLI. Well said; what things are they?

CHR. There is an endless Kingdom to be inhabited,

and everlasting Life to be given us, that we may inhabit that Kingdom for ever.

PLI. Well said; and what else?

CHR. There are Crowns of glory to be given us, and Garments that will make us shine like the Sun in the firmament of Heaven.

PLI. This is excellent; and what else?

CHR. There shall be no more crying, nor sorrow, for He that is owner of the place will wipe all tears from our eyes.

PLI. And what company shall we have there?

CHR. There we shall be with *Seraphims* and *Cherubins,* creatures that will dazzle your eyes to look on them: There also you shall meet with thousands and ten thousands that have gone before us to that place; none of them are hurtful, but loving and holy; every one walking in the sight of God, and standing in his presence with acceptance for ever. In a word, there we shall see the Elders with their golden Crowns, there we shall see the Holy Virgins with their golden Harps, there we shall see men that by the World were cut in pieces, burnt in flames, eaten of beasts, drowned in the seas, for the love that they bare to the Lord of the place, all well, and cloathed with Immortality as with a garment.

PLI. The hearing of this is enough to ravish one's heart; but are these things to be enjoyed? How shall we get to be sharers hereof?

CHR. The Lord, the Governor of the country, hath recorded *that* in this Book; the substance of which is, If we be truly willing to have it, he will bestow it upon us freely.

PLI. Well, my good companion, glad am I to hear of these things; come on, let us mend our pace.

CHR. I cannot go so fast as I would, by reason of this Burden that is upon my back.

Now I saw in my Dream, that just as they had ended this talk, they drew near to a very miry *Slough,* that was in the midst of the plain; and they, being heedless, did both fall suddenly into the bog.

The name of the slough was *Dispond*. Here there- The Slough
fore they wallowed for a time, being grievously of Dispond
bedaubed with the dirt; and *Christian,* because of
the Burden that was on his back, began to sink
in the mire.

PLI. Then said *Pliable,* Ah Neighbor *Christian,*
where are you now?

CHR. Truly, said *Christian,* I do not know.

PLI. At that *Pliable* began to be offended, and It is not
angerly said to his fellow, Is this the happiness you enough to
have told me all this while of? If we have such ill be pliable
speed at our first setting out, what may we expect
'twixt this and our Journey's end? May I get out
again with my life, you shall possess the brave
Country alone for me. And with that he gave a
desperate struggle or two, and got out of the mire
on that side of the Slough which was next to his
own house: so away he went, and *Christian* saw
him no more.

Wherefore *Christian* was left to tumble in the Christian
Slough of *Dispond* alone; but still he endeavoured in trouble
to struggle to that side of the Slough that was still seeks still
                                                      to get fur-
further from his own house, and next to the ther from
Wicket-gate; the which he did, but could not get his own
                                                   house
out, because of the Burden that was upon his back:
But I beheld in my Dream, that a man came to
him, whose name was *Help,* and asked him, *What
he did there?*

CHR. Sir, said *Christian,* I was bid go this way
by a man called *Evangelist,* who directed me also
to yonder Gate, that I might escape the wrath to
come; and as I was going thither, I fell in here.

HELP. But why did you not look for the steps? The prom-
CHR. Fear followed me so hard, that I fled the ises.
next way, and fell in.

HELP. Then said he, *Give me thy hand:* so he Help lift-
gave him his hand, and he drew him out, and set him up
him upon sound ground, and bid him go on his way.

Then I stepped to him that pluckt him out, and
said, Sir, wherefore, since over this place is the way,

from the City of *Destruction* to yonder Gate, is
it that this plat is not mended, that poor travellers
might go thither with more security? And he said

What
makes the
Slough of
Dispond unto me, This miry Slough is such a place as cannot
be mended; it is the descent whither the scum and
filth that attends conviction for sin doth continually
run, and therefore it is called the Slough of *Dispond;* for still as the sinner is awakened about his
lost condition, there ariseth in his soul many fears
and doubts, and discouraging apprehensions, which
all of them get together, and settle in this place:
And this is the reason of the badness of this ground.

It is not the pleasure of the King that this place
should remain so bad. His labourers also have, by
the direction of His Majesties Surveyors, been for
above these sixteen hundred years imployed about
this patch of ground, if perhaps it might have been
mended: yea, and to my knowledge, said he, *here*
hath been swallowed up at least twenty thousand
cart-loads, yea, millions of wholesome instructions,
that have at all seasons been brought from all places
of the King's dominions (and they that can tell say
they are the best materials to make good ground of
the place), if so be it might have been mended, but
it is the Slough of *Dispond* still, and so will be
when they have done what they can.

The prom-
ises of for-
giveness
and accept-
ance to life
by faith
in Christ True, there are by the direction of the Lawgiver,
certain good and substantial steps, placed even
through the very midst of this Slough; but at such
time as this place doth much spue out its filth, as
it doth against change of weather, these steps are
hardly seen; or if they be, men through the dizzi-
ness of their heads, step besides; and then they are
bemired to purpose, notwithstanding the steps be
there; but the ground is good when they are once
got in at the Gate.

Pliable got
home, and
is visited
of his
neighbors Now I saw in my Dream, that by this time *Pliable*
was got home to his house again. So his Neighbors
came to visit him: and some of them called him
wise man for coming back, and some called him

fool for hazarding himself with *Christian:* others
again did mock at his cowardliness; saying, Surely
since you began to venture, I would not have
been so base to have given out for a few difficulties.
So *Pliable* sat sneaking among them. But at
last he got more confidence, and then they all
turned their tales, and began to deride poor
Christian behind his back. And thus much concerning *Pliable*.

His enter-
tainment
by them at
his return

Now as *Christian* was walking solitary by himself, he espied one afar off come crossing over the
field to meet him; and their hap was to meet just
as they were crossing the way of each other. The
gentleman's name that met him was Mr. *Worldly
Wiseman:* he dwelt in the Town of *Carnal Policy,*
a very great Town, and also hard by from whence
Christian came. This man then meeting with
Christian, and having some inkling of him,—for
Christian's setting forth from the City of *Destruction* was much noised abroad, not only in the Town
where he dwelt, but also it began to be the town-
talk in some other places,—Master *Worldly Wiseman* therefore, having some guess of him, by beholding his laborious going, by observing his sighs
and groans, and the like, began thus to enter into
some talk with *Christian.*

Mr
Worldly
Wiseman
meets with
Christian

Talk be-
twixt Mr
Worldly
Wiseman
and
Christian

WORLD. How now, good fellow, whither away
after this burdened manner?

CHR. A burdened manner indeed, as ever I think
poor creature had. And whereas you ask me,
Whither away? I tell you, Sir, I am going to yonder Wicket-gate before me; for there, as I am informed, I shall be put into a way to be rid of my
heavy Burden.

WORLD. Hast thou a Wife and Children?

CHR. Yes, but I am so laden with this Burden,
that I cannot take that pleasure in them as formerly; methinks I am as if I had none.

WORLD. Wilt thou hearken to me if I give thee
counsel?

CHR. If it be good, I will; for I stand in need of good counsel.

WORLD. I would advise thee then, that thou with all speed get thyself rid of thy Burden; for thou wilt never be settled in thy mind till then; nor canst thou enjoy the benefits of the blessing which God hath bestowed upon thee till then.

CHR. That is that which I seek for, even to be rid of this heavy Burden; but get it off myself, I cannot; nor is there any man in our country that can take it off my shoulders; therefore am I going this way, as I told you, that I may be rid of my Burden.

WORLD. Who bid thee go this way to be rid of thy Burden?

CHR. A man that appeared to me to be a very great and honorable person; his name as I remember is *Evangelist*.

WORLD. I beshrew him for his counsel; there is not a more dangerous and troublesome way in the world than is that unto which he hath directed thee; and that thou shalt find, if thou wilt be ruled by his counsel. Thou hast met with something (as I perceive) already; for I see the dirt of the Slough of *Dispond* is upon thee; but that Slough is the beginning of the sorrows that do attend those that go on in that way: Hear me, I am older than thou; thou art like to meet with, in the way which thou goest, Wearisomeness, Painfulness, Hunger, Perils, Nakedness, Sword, Lions, Dragons, Darkness, and in a word, Death, and what not! These things are certainly true, having been confirmed by many testimonies. And why should a man so carelessly cast away himself, by giving heed to a stranger?

CHR. Why, Sir, this Burden upon my back is more terrible to me than are all these things which you have mentioned; nay, methinks I care not what I meet with in the way, so be I can also meet with deliverance from my Burden.

WORLD. How camest thou by thy Burden at first?

CHR. By reading this Book in my hand.

WORLD. I thought so; and it is happened unto thee as to other weak men, who meddling with things too high for them, do suddenly fall into thy distractions; which distractions do not only unman men (as thine I perceive has done thee), but they run them upon desperate ventures, to obtain they know not what. *Worldly Wiseman does not like that men should be serious in reading the Bible*

CHR. I know what I would obtain; it is ease for my heavy burden.

WORLD. But why wilt thou seek for ease this way, seeing so many dangers attend it? Especially, since (hadst thou but patience to hear me) I could direct thee to the obtaining of what thou desirest, without the dangers that thou in this way wilt run thyself into; yea, and the remedy is at hand. Besides, I will add, that instead of those dangers, thou shalt meet with much safety, friendship, and content. *Whether Mr. Worldly Wiseman prefers morality before the strait gate*

CHR. Pray Sir, open this secret to me.

WORLD. Why in yonder Village (the village is named *Morality*) there dwells a Gentleman whose name is *Legality*, a very judicious man, and a man of very good name, that has skill to help men off with such burdens as thine are from their shoulders: yea, to my knowledge he hath done a great deal of good this way; ay, and besides, he hath skill to cure those that are somewhat crazed in their wits with their burdens. To him, as I said, thou mayest go, and be helped presently. His house is not quite a mile from this place, and if he should not be at home himself, he hath a pretty young man to his Son, whose name is *Civility*, that can do it (to speak on) as well as the old Gentleman himself; there, I say, thou mayest be eased of thy Burden; and if thou art not minded to go back to thy former habitation, as indeed I would not wish thee, thou mayest send for thy Wife and Children to thee to this village, where there are houses now stand empty, one of which thou mayest have at reasonable rates; Provision is there also cheap and good; and that which will make thy life the more happy is, to be sure there thou shalt live by honest Neighbors, in credit and good fashion.

Christian snared by Mr Worldly Wiseman's words

Now was *Christian* somewhat at a stand, but presently he concluded, If this be true which this Gentleman hath said, my wisest course is to take his advice; and with that he thus farther spoke.

CHR. Sir, which is my way to this honest man's house?

Mount Sinai

WORLD. Do you see yonder high Hill?

CHR. Yes, very well.

WORLD. By that Hill you must go, and the first house you come at is his.

So *Christian* turned out of his way to go to Mr *Legality's* house for help; but behold, when he was got now hard by the Hill, it seemed so high, and also that side of it that was next the wayside, did

Christian afraid that Mount Sinai would fall on his head

hang so much over, that *Christian* was afraid to venture further, lest the Hill should fall on his head; wherefore there he stood still, and he wot not what to do. Also his Burden *now* seemed heavier to him than while he was in his way. There came also flashes of fire out of the Hill, that made *Christian* afraid that he should be burned. Here therefore he sweat and did quake for fear.

> When Christians unto Carnal Men give ear,
> Out of their way they go, and pay for 't dear;
> For Master *Worldly Wiseman* can but shew
> A Saint the way to Bondage and to Wo.

Evangelist findeth Christian under Mount Sinai, and looketh severely upon him

And now he began to be sorry that he had taken Mr *Worldly Wiseman's* counsel. And with that he saw *Evangelist* coming to meet him; at the sight also of whom he began to blush for shame. So *Evangelist* drew nearer and nearer; and coming up to him, he looked upon him with a severe and dreadful countenance, and thus began to reason with *Christian*.

EVAN. What doest thou here, *Christian?* said

he: at which words *Christian* knew not what to answer; wherefore at present he stood speechless before him. Then said *Evangelist* farther, Art not thou the man that I found crying without the walls of the City of *Destruction?* Evangelist reasons afresh with Christian

CHR. Yes, dear Sir, I am the man.

EVAN. Did not I direct thee the way to the little Wicket-gate,

CHR. Yes, dear Sir, said *Christian.*

EVAN. How is it then that thou art so quickly turned aside? for thou art now out of the way.

CHR. I met with a Gentleman so soon as I had got over the Slough of *Dispond,* who persuaded me that I might, in the village before me, find a man that could take off my Burden.

EVAN. What was he?

CHR. He looked like a Gentleman, and talked much to me, and got me at last to yield; so I came hither: but when I beheld this Hill, and how it hangs over the way, I suddenly made a stand, lest it should fall on my head.

EVAN. What said that Gentleman to you?

CHR. Why, he asked me whither I was going; and I told him.

EVAN. And what said he then?

CHR. He asked me if I had a family; and I told him. But, said I, I am so loaden with the Burden that is on my back, that I cannot take pleasure in them as formerly.

EVAN. And what said he then?

CHR. He bid me with speed get rid of my Burden; and I told him 'twas ease that I sought. And, said I, I am therefore going to yonder Gate, to receive further direction how I may get to the place of deliverance. So he said that he would shew me a better way, and short, not so attended with difficulties as the way, Sir, that you set me; which way, said he, will direct you to a Gentleman's house that hath skill to take off these Burdens: So I believed him, and turned out of that way into this, if haply I might be soon eased of my Burden. But when I came to this place, and beheld things as they are, I stopped for fear (as I said) of danger: but I now know not what to do.

EVAN. Then, said *Evangelist*, stand still a little, that I may shew thee the words of God. So he stood trembling. Then said *Evangelist*, See that ye refuse not him that speaketh; for if they escaped not who refused him that spake on Earth, much more shall not we escape, if we turn away from him that speaketh from Heaven. He said moreover, Now the just shall live by faith: but if any man draws back, my soul shall have no pleasure in him. He also did thus apply them, Thou art the man that art running into this misery, thou hast begun to reject the counsel of the Most High, and to draw back thy foot from the way of peace, even almost to the hazarding of thy perdition.

Evangelist convinces Christian of his error

Then *Christian* fell down at his foot as dead, crying, *Wo is me, for I am undone:* At the sight of which, *Evangelist* caught him by the right hand, saying, All manner of sin and blasphemies shall be forgiven unto men; be not faithless, but believing. Then did *Christian* again a little revive, and stood up trembling, as at first, before *Evangelist*.

Mr Worldly Wiseman described by Evangelist

Then *Evangelist* proceeded, saying, Give more earnest heed to the things that I shall tell thee of. I will now shew thee who it was that deluded thee, and who it was also to whom he sent thee. The man that met thee is one *Worldly Wiseman,* and rightly is he so called: partly because he savoureth only the doctrine of this world, (therefore he always goes to the Town of *Morality* to church); and

Evangelist discovers the deceit of Mr Worldly Wiseman

partly because he loveth that doctrine best, for it saveth him from the Cross. And because he is of this carnal temper, therefore he seeketh to prevent my ways, though right. Now there are three things in this man's counsel that thou must utterly abhor.

1. His turning thee out of the way.

2. His labouring to render the Cross odious to thee.

3. And his setting thy feet in that way that leadeth unto the administration of Death.

First, Thou must abhor his turning thee out of the way; yea, and thine own consenting thereto, because this is to reject the counsel of God for the sake of the counsel of a *Worldly Wiseman*. The Lord says, *Strive to enter in at the strait gate*, the gate to which I sent thee; *for strait is the gate that leadeth unto life, and few there be that find it*. From this little Wicket-gate, and from the way thereto, hath this wicked man turned thee, to the bringing of thee almost to destruction; hate therefore his turning thee out of the way, and abhor thyself for hearkening to him.

Secondly, Thou must abhor his labouring to render the Cross odious unto thee; for thou art to *prefer it before the treasures of Egypt*. Besides, the King of Glory hath told thee, that *he that will save his life shall lose it:* and He that comes after him, and hates not his father, and mother, and wife, and children, and brethren, and sisters, yea and his own life also, he cannot be my Disciple. I say therefore, for a man to labour to persuade thee, that that shall be thy death, without which, the Truth hath said, thou canst not have eternal life; This doctrine thou must abhor.

Thirdly, Thou must hate his setting of thy feet in the way that leadeth to the ministration of death. And for this thou must consider to whom he sent thee, and also how unable that person was to deliver thee from thy Burden.

He to whom thou was sent for ease, being by name *Legality*, is the Son of the Bond-woman The bond-which now is, and is in bondage with her children; woman and is in a mystery this Mount *Sinai*, which thou hast feared will fall on thy head. Now if she with her children are in bondage, how canst thou expect by them to be made free? This *Legality* therefore

is not able to set thee free from thy Burden. No
man was as yet ever rid of his Burden by him; no,
nor ever is like to be: ye cannot be justified by the
Works of the Law; for by the deeds of the Law
no man living can be rid of his Burden: therefore,
Mr *Worldly Wiseman* is an alien, and Mr *Legality*
a cheat; and for his son *Civility*, notwithstanding
his simpering looks, he is but a hypocrite and cannot help thee. Believe me, there is nothing in all
this noise, that thou hast heard of this sottish man,
but a design to beguile thee of thy Salvation, by
turning thee from the way in which I had set thee.
After this *Evangelist* called aloud to the Heavens
for confirmation of what he had said; and with that
there came words and fire out of the Mountain
under which poor *Christian* stood, that made the
hair of his flesh stand. The words were thus pro-
nounced, *As many as are the works of the Law are
under the curse; for it is written, Cursed is every
one that continueth not in all things which are
written in the Book of the Law to do them.*

Now *Christian* looked for nothing but death, and
began to cry out lamentably, even cursing the
time in which he met with Mr *Worldly Wiseman*,
still calling himself a thousand fools for hearkening
to his counsel: he also was greatly ashamed to think
that this Gentleman's arguments, flowing only from
the flesh, should have that prevalency with him as
to cause him to forsake the right way. This done,
he applied himself again to *Evangelist* in words and
sense as follows.

Christian
inquires if
he may yet
be happy

CHR. Sir, what think you? Is there hopes? May
I now go back and go up to the Wicket-gate? Shall
I not be abandoned for this, and sent back from
thence ashamed? I am sorry I have hearkened
to this man's counsel: But may my sin be forgiven?

Evangelist
comforts
him

EVAN. Then said *Evangelist* to him, Thy sin is
very great, for by it thou hast committed two evils:
thou hast forsaken the way that is good, to tread
in forbidden paths; yet will the man at the Gate

receive thee, for he has good-will for men; only, said he, take heed that thou turn not aside again, lest thou perish from the way, when his wrath is kindled but a little. Then did *Christian* address himself to go back; and *Evangelist,* after he had kissed him, gave him one smile, and bid him God speed. So he went on with haste, neither spake he to any man by the way; nor if any man asked him, would he vouchsafe them an answer. He went like one that was all the while treading on forbidden ground, and could by no means think himself safe, till again he was got into the way which he left to follow Mr *Worldly Wiseman's* counsel. So in process of time *Christian* got up to the Gate. Now over the Gate there was written, *Knock and it shall be opened unto you.*

> He that will enter in must first without
> Stand knocking at the Gate, nor need he doubt
> That is a knocker but to enter in,
> For God can love him, and forgive his sin.

He knocked therefore more than once or twice, saying,

> May I now enter here? Will he within
> Open to sorry me, though I have been
> An undeserving Rebel? Then shall I
> Not fail to sing his lasting praise on high.

At last there came a grave person to the gate named *Good-will,* who asked Who was there? and whence he came? and what he would have?

CHR. Here is a poor burdened sinner. I come from the City of *Destruction,* but am going to Mount *Zion,* that I may be delivered from the wrath to come. I would therefore, Sir, since I am informed that by this Gate is the way thither, know if you are willing to let me in.

GOOD-WILL. I am willing with all my heart, said he; and with that he opened the Gate.

The gate will be opened to broken-hearted sinners

So when *Christian* was stepping in, the other

gave him a pull. Then said *Christian,* What means
that? The other told him, A little distance from
this Gate, there is erected a strong Castle, of

Satan
envies
those that
enter the
strait gate

which *Beelzebub* is the Captain; from thence both
he and they that are with him shoot arrows at
those that come up to this Gate, if haply they
may die before they can enter in. Then said *Chris-*

Christian
entered the
gate with
joy and
trembling

tian, I rejoice and tremble. So when he was got in,
the man of the Gate asked him who directed him
thither?

CHR. *Evangelist* bid me come hither and knock
(as I did); and he said that you, Sir, would tell
me what I must do.

Talk
between
Good-will
and
Christian

GOOD-WILL. An open door is set before thee, and
no man can shut it.

CHR. Now I begin to reap the benefits of my
hazards.

GOOD-WILL. But how is it that you came alone?

CHR. Because none of my Neighbors saw their
danger, as I saw mine.

GOOD-WILL. Did any of them know of your
coming?

CHR. Yes, my Wife and Children saw me at the
first, and called after me to turn again; also some
of my Neighbors stood crying and calling after me
to return; but I put my fingers in my ears, and so
came on my way.

GOOD-WILL. But did none of them follow you, to
persuade you to go back?

CHR. Yes, both *Obstinate* and *Pliable;* but when
they saw that they could not prevail, *Obstinate*
went railing back, but *Pliable* came with me a little
way.

GOOD-WILL. But why did he not come through?

A man may
have com-
pany when
he sets out
for heaven,
and yet go
thither
alone

CHR. We indeed came both together, until we
came to the Slough of *Dispond,* into the which we
also suddenly fell. And then was my Neighbor
Pliable discouraged, and would not adventure further. Wherefore getting out again on that side
next to his own house, he told me I should possess

the brave country alone for him; so he went *his* way, and I came *mine:* he after *Obstinate,* and I to this Gate.

GOOD-WILL. Then said *Good-will,* Alas, poor man, is the cœlestial glory of so small esteem with him, that he counteth it not worth running the hazards of a few difficulties to obtain it?

CHR. Truly, said *Christian,* I have said the truth of *Pliable,* and if I should also say all the truth of myself, it will appear there is no betterment 'twixt him and myself. 'Tis true, he went back to his own house, but I also turned aside to go in the way of death, being persuaded thereto by the carnal arguments of one Mr *Worldly Wiseman.* *Christian accuseth himself before the man at the gate*

GOOD-WILL. O, did he light upon you? What! he would have had you a sought for ease at the hands of Mr. *Legality.* They are both of them a very cheat: But did you take his counsel?

CHR. Yes, as far as I durst: I went to find out Mr *Legality,* until I thought that the Mountain that stands by his house would have fallen upon my head; wherefore there I was forced to stop.

GOOD-WILL. That Mountain has been the death of many, and will be the death of many more; 'tis well you escaped being by it dashed in pieces.

CHR. Why truly I do not know what had become of me there, had not *Evangelist* happily met me again, as I was musing in the midst of my dumps: but 'twas God's mercy that he came to me again, for else I had never come hither. But now I am come, such a one as I am, more fit indeed for death by that Mountain than thus to stand talking with my Lord; but O, what a favour is this to me, that yet I am admitted entrance here.

GOOD-WILL. We make no objections against any, notwithstanding all that they have done before they come hither, they in no wise are cast out; and therefore, good *Christian,* come a little way with me, and I will teach thee about the way *Christian comforted again*

Christian
directed
yet on
his way

thou must go. Look before thee; dost thou see this narrow way? THAT is the way thou must go; it was cast up by the Patriarchs, Prophets, Christ, and his Apostles; and it is as straight as a rule can make it: This is the way thou must go.

Christian
afraid of
losing
his way

CHR. But said *Christian,* Is there no turnings nor windings, by which a Stranger may lose the way?

GOOD-WILL. Yes, there are many ways *butt* down upon this, and they are crooked and wide: But thus thou mayest distinguish the right from the wrong, the right only being straight and narrow.

Christian
weary of
his burden

Then I saw in my Dream, that *Christian* asked him further If he could not help him off with his Burden that was upon his back; for as yet he had not got rid thereof, nor could he by any means get it off without help.

There is
no deliv-
erance
from the
guilt and
burden of
sin, but by
the death
and blood
of Christ

He told him, As to thy Burden, be content to bear it, until thou comest to the place of *Deliverance;* for there it will fall from thy back itself.

Then *Christian* began to gird up his loins, and to address himself to his Journey. So the other told him, That by that he was gone some distance from the Gate, he would come at the house of the *Interpreter,* at whose door he should knock, and he would shew him excellent things. Then *Christian* took his leave of his Friend, and he again bid him God speed.

Christian
comes to
the house
of the
Interpreter

Then he went on till he came at the house of the *Interpreter,* where he knocked over and over; at last one came to the door, and asked Who was there?

CHR. Sir, here is a Traveller, who was bid by an acquaintance of the good man of this house to call here for my profit; I would therefore speak with the Master of the house. So he called for the Master of the house, who after a little time came to *Christian,* and asked him what he would have?

CHR. Sir, said *Christian,* I am a man that am

come from the City of *Destruction,* and am going He is entertained
to the Mount *Zion;* and I was told by the Man
that stands at the Gate at the head of this way,
that if I called here, you would shew me excellent
things, such as would be a help to me in my
Journey.

INTER. Then said the *Interpreter,* Come in, I Illumination
will shew thee that which will be profitable to thee.
So he commanded his man to light the Candle, and
bid *Christian* follow him, so he had him into a
private room, and bid his man open a door; the
which when he had done, *Christian* saw the Picture Christian sees a grave picture
of a very grave Person hang up against the wall;
and this was the fashion of it. It had eyes lifted
up to Heaven, the best of Books in his hand,
the Law of Truth was written upon his lips, the The fashion of the picture
World was behind his back. It stood as if it pleaded
with men, and a Crown of Gold did hang over
his head.

CHR. Then said *Christian,* What means this?

INTER. The Man whose Picture this is, is one of
a thousand; he can beget children, travel in birth
with children, and nurse them himself when they
are born. And whereas thou seest him with his
eyes lift up to Heaven, the best of Books in his hand,
and the Law of Truth writ on his lips, it is to
shew thee that his work is to know and unfold The meaning of the picture
dark things to sinners; even as also thou seest him
stand as if he pleaded with men; and whereas thou
seest the World as cast behind him, and that a
Crown hangs over his head, that is to shew thee
that slighting and despising the things that are
present, for the love that he hath to his Master's
service, he is sure in the world that comes next
to have Glory for his reward. Now, said the *Inter-
preter,* I have shewed thee this Picture first, be- Why he showed him the picture first
cause the Man whose Picture this is, is the only
man whom the Lord of the place whither thou art
going, hath authorized to be thy guide in all difficult places thou mayest meet with in the way;

wherefore take good heed to what I have shewed thee, and bear well in thy mind what thou hast seen, lest in thy Journey thou meet with some that pretend to lead thee right, but their way goes down to death.

Then he took him by the hand, and led him into a very large *Parlour* that was full of dust, because never swept; the which after he had reviewed a little while, the *Interpreter* called for a man to sweep. Now when he began to sweep, the dust began so abundantly to fly about, that *Christian* had almost therewith been choaked. Then said the *Interpreter* to a *Damsel* that stood by, Bring hither the Water, and sprinkle the Room; the which when she had done, it was swept and cleansed with pleasure.

CHR. Then said *Christian,* What means this?

INTER. The *Interpreter* answered, This *parlour* is the heart of a man that was never sanctified by the sweet Grace of the Gospel: the *dust* is his Original Sin and inward Corruptions, that have defiled the whole man. He that began to sweep at first, is the Law; but she that brought water, and did sprinkle it, is the Gospel. Now, whereas thou sawest that so soon as the first began to sweep, the dust did so fly about that the Room by him could not be cleansed, but that thou wast almost choaked therewith; this is to shew thee, that the Law, instead of cleansing the heart (by its working) from sin, doth revive, put strength into, and increase it in the soul, even as it doth discover and forbid it, for it doth not give power to subdue.

Again, as thou sawest the *Damsel* sprinkle the room with Water, upon which it was cleansed with pleasure; this is to shew thee, that when the Gospel comes in the sweet and precious influences thereof to the heart, then I say, even as thou sawest the Damsel lay the dust by sprinkling the floor with Water, so is sin vanquished and subdued, and the soul made clean, through the faith of it, and consequently fit for the King of Glory to inhabit.

I saw moreover in my Dream, that the *Interpreter* took him by the hand, and had him into a little room, where sat two little Children, each one in his chair. The name of the eldest was *Passion*, and the name of the other *Patience*. *Passion* seemed to be much discontent; but *Patience* was very quiet. Then *Christian* asked, What is the reason of the discontent of *Passion?* The *Interpreter* answered, The Governor of them would have him stay for his best things till the beginning of the next year; but he will have all now; but *Patience* is willing to wait. *He showed him Passion and Patience*

Passion will have all now. Patience is for waiting

Then I saw that one came to *Passion*, and brought him a bag of treasure, and poured it down at his feet, the which he took up and rejoiced therein; and withal, laughed *Patience* to scorn. But I beheld but a while, and he had lavished all away, and had nothing left him but Rags. *Passion has his desire*

And quickly lavishes all away

CHR. Then said *Christian* to the *Interpreter*, Expound this matter more fully to me.

INTER. So he said, These two Lads are figures: *Passion,* of the men of *this* world; and *Patience,* of the men of *that* which is to come; for as here thou seest, *Passion* will have all now this year, that is to say, in this world; so are the men of this world: they must have all their good things now, they cannot stay till next year, that is, until the next world, for their portion of good. That proverb, *A Bird in the Hand is worth two in the Bush,* is of more authority with them than are all the Divine testimonies of the good of the world to come. But as thou sawest that he had quickly lavished all away, and had presently left him nothing but Rags; so will it be with all such men at the end of this world. *The matter expounded*

The worldly man for a bird in the hand

CHR. Then said *Christian,* Now I see that *Patience* has the best wisdom, and that upon many accounts. 1. Because he stays for the best things. *Patience has the best wisdom*

2. And also because he will have the Glory of his,
when the other has nothing but Rags.

Things
that are
first must
give place;
but things
that are
last are
lasting

INTER. Nay, you may add another, to wit, the
glory of the *next* world will never wear out; but
these are suddenly gone, Therefore Passion had not
so much reason to laugh at *Patience,* because he
had his good things first, as *Patience* will have
to laugh at *Passion,* because he had his best things
last; for *first* must give place to *last,* because *last*
must have his time to come: but last gives place
to nothing; for there is not another to succeed.
He therefore that hath his portion *first,* must needs
have a time to spend it; but he that hath his portion
last, must have it lastingly; therefore it is said of

Dives had
his good
things first

*Dives, In thy lifetime thou receivedst thy good
things, and likewise* Lazarus *evil things; but now
he is comforted, and thou art tormented.*

CHR. Then I perceive 'tis not best to covet
things that are now, but to wait for things to come.

The first
things
are but
temporal

INTER. You say truth: *For the things which are
seen are* Temporal; *but the things that are not
seen are* Eternal. But though this be so, yet since
things present and our fleshly appetite are such near
neighbors one to another; and, again, because things
to come and carnal sense are such strangers one
to another; therefore it is that the first of these so
suddenly fell into *amity,* and that *distance* is so
continued between the second.

Then I saw in my Dream that the *Interpreter*
took *Christian* by the hand, and led him into a
place where was a Fire burning against a wall, and
one standing by it, always casting much Water upon
it, to quench it; yet did the Fire burn higher and
hotter.

Then said *Christian,* What means this?

The *Interpreter answered,* This Fire is the work
of Grace that is wrought in the heart; he that casts
Water upon it, to extinguish and put it out, is the
Devil; but in that thou seest the Fire notwithstanding burn higher and hotter, thou shalt also

see the reason of that. So he had him about to the backside of the wall, where he saw a man with a Vessel of Oil in his hand, of the which he did also continually cast (but secretly) into the Fire.

Then said *Christian*, What means this?

The *Interpreter answered*, This is Christ, who continually, with the Oil of his Grace, maintains the work already begun in the heart: by the means of which notwithstanding what the Devil can do, the souls of his people prove gracious still. And in that thou sawest that the man stood behind the wall to maintain the Fire, that is to teach thee that it is hard for the tempted to see how this work of Grace is maintained in the soul.

I saw also that the *Interpreter* took him again by the hand, and led him into a pleasant place, where was builded a stately Palace, beautiful to behold; at the sight of which *Christian* was greatly delighted: He saw also upon the top thereof, certain persons walking, who were cloathed all in gold.

Then said *Christian*, May we go in thither?

Then the *Interpreter* took him, and led him up toward the door of the Palace; and behold, at the door stood a great company of men, as desirous to go in, but durst not. There also sat a man at a little distance from the door, at a table-side, with a Book and his Inkhorn before him, to take the name of him that should enter therein; He saw also, that in the door-way stood many men in armour to keep it, being resolved to do the men that would enter what hurt and mischief they could. Now was *Christian* somewhat in a maze. At last, when every man started back for fear of the armed men, *Christian* saw a man of a very stout countenance come up to the man that sat there to write, **The valiant man** saying, *Set down my name, Sir:* the which when he had done, he saw the man draw his Sword, and put an Helmet upon his head, and rush toward the door upon the armed men, who laid upon him with deadly force; but the man, not at all discouraged, fell to cutting and hacking most fiercely. So after he had received and given many wounds to those that attempted to keep him out, he cut his way through them all, and pressed forward into the Palace, at which there was a pleasant voice heard from those that were within, even of those that walked upon the top of the Palace, saying,

> Come in, Come in ;
> Eternal Glory thou shalt win.

So he went in, and was cloathed with such garments as they. Then *Christian* smiled, and said, I think verily I know the meaning of this.

Despair like an iron cage

Now, said *Christian,* let me go hence. Nay, stay, said the *Interpreter,* till I have shewed thee a little more, and after that thou shalt go on thy way. So he took him by the hand again, and led him into a very dark room, where there sat a man in an Iron Cage.

Now the Man, to look on, seemed very sad; he sat with his eyes looking down to the ground, his hands folded together; and he sighed as if he would break his heart. Then said *Christian, What means this?* At which the *Interpreter* bid him talk with the Man.

Then said *Christian* to the Man, *What art thou?* The Man answered, *I am what I was not once.*

CHR. What wast thou once?

MAN. The Man said, I was once a fair and flourishing Professor, both in mine own eyes, and also in the eyes of others; I once was, as I thought, fair for the Cœlestial City, and had then even joy at the thoughts that I should get thither.

CHR. Well, but what art thou now?

MAN. I am now a man of *Despair,* and am shut up in it, as in this Iron Cage. I cannot get out; O *now* I cannot.

CHR. But how camest thou in this condition?

MAN. I left off to watch and be sober; I laid the reins upon the neck of my lusts; I sinned against the light of the Word and the goodness of God; I have grieved the Spirit, and he is gone; I tempted the Devil, and he is come to me; I have provoked God to anger, and he has left me; I have so hardened my heart, that I *cannot* repent.

Then said *Christian* to the *Interpreter*, But are there no hopes for such a man as this? Ask him, said the *Interpreter*.

CHR. Then said the *Christian*, Is there no hope, but you must be kept in the Iron Cage of Despair?

MAN. No, none at all.

CHR. Why? the Son of the Blessed is very pitiful.

MAN. I have crucified him to myself afresh, I have despised his Person, I have despised his Righteousness, I have counted his Blood an unholy thing; I have done despite to the Spirit of Grace: Therefore I have shut myself out of all the Promises, and there now remains to me nothing but threatnings, dreadful threatnings, fearful threatnings of certain Judgment and fiery Indignation, which shall devour me as an Adversary.

CHR. For what did you bring yourself into this condition?

MAN. For the Lusts, Pleasures, and Profits of this World; in the enjoyment of which I did then promise myself much delight; but now every one of those things also bite me, and gnaw me like a burning worm.

CHR. But canst thou not now repent and turn?

MAN. God hath denied me repentance: his Word gives me no encouragement to believe; yea, himself hath shut me up in this Iron Cage; nor can all the men in the world let me out. O Eternity! Eternity! how shall I grapple with the misery that I must meet with in Eternity!

INTER. Then said the *Interpreter* to *Christian*, Let this man's misery be remembered by thee, and be an everlasting caution to thee.

CHR. Well, said *Christian*, this is fearful; God help me to watch and be sober, and to pray that I

may shun the cause of this man's misery. Sir, is
it not time for me to go on my way now?

INTER. Tarry till I shall shew thee one thing
more, and then thou shalt go thy way.

So he took *Christian* by the hand again, and led
him into a Chamber, where there was one rising out
of bed; and as he put on his raiment, he shook and
trembled. Then said *Christian,* Why doth this man
thus tremble? The *Interpreter* then bid him tell to
Christian the reason of his so doing. So he began
and said, This night, as I was in my sleep, I dreamed,
and behold the Heavens grew exceeding black; also
it thundred and lightned in most fearful wise,
that it put me into an agony; so I looked up in my
Dream, and saw the Clouds rack at an unusual rate,
upon which I heard a great sound of a Trumpet,
and saw also a Man sit upon a Cloud, attended with
the thousands of Heaven; they were all in flaming
fire, also the Heavens were in a burning flame. I
heard then a Voice saying, *Arise ye dead, and come
to Judgment;* and with that the Rocks rent, the
Graves opened, and the Dead that were therein came
forth. Some of them were exceeding glad, and
looked upward; and some sought to hide themselves under the Mountains. Then I saw the Man
that sat upon the Cloud open the Book, and bid
the World draw near. Yet there was, by reason
of a fierce flame which issued out and came from
before him, a convenient distance betwixt him and
them, as betwixt the Judge and the Prisoners at
the bar. I heard it also proclaimed to them that
attended on the Man that sat on the Cloud, *Gather
together the Tares, the Chaff, and Stubble, and cast
them into the burning Lake.* And with that, the
bottomless pit opened, just whereabout I stood; out
of the mouth of which there came in an abundant
manner, smoke and coals of fire, with hideous
noises. It was also said to the same persons, *Gather
my Wheat into the Garner.* And with that I saw
many catch'd up and carried away into the Clouds,

but I was left behind. I also sought to hide myself, but I could not, for the Man that sat upon the Cloud still kept his eye upon me: my sins also came into my mind; and my Conscience did accuse me on every side. Upon this I awaked from my sleep.

CHR. But what was it that made you so afraid of this sight?

MAN. Why, I thought that the day of Judgment was come, and that I was not ready for it: but this frighted me most, that the Angels gathered up several, and left me behind; also the pit of Hell opened her mouth just where I stood: my Conscience too afflicted me; and as I thought, the Judge had always his eye upon me, shewing indignation in his countenance.

Then said the *Interpreter* to *Christian, Hast thou considered all these things?*

CHR. Yes, and they put me in *hope* and *fear.*

INTER. Well, keep all things so in thy mind that they may be as a Goad in thy sides, to prick thee forward in the way thou must go. Then *Christian* began to gird up his loins, and address himself to his Journey. Then said the *Interpreter,* The Comforter be always with thee, good *Christian,* to guide thee in the way that leads to the City. So *Christian* went on his way saying,

> Here I have seen things rare and profitable;
> Things pleasant, dreadful, things to make me stable
> In what I have begun to take in hand;
> Then let me think on them, and understand
> Wherefore they shew'd me was, and let me be
> Thankful, O good Interpreter, to thee.

Now I saw in my Dream, that the highway up which *Christian* was to go, was fenced on either side with a Wall, and that Wall is called *Salvation.* Up this way therefore did burdened *Christian* run, but not without great difficulty, because of the load on his back.

He ran thus till he came at a place somewhat ascending, and upon that place stood a Cross, and a little below in the bottom, a Sepulchre. So I saw in my Dream, that just as *Christian* came up with the *Cross,* his Burden loosed from off his shoulders, and fell from off his back, and began to tumble, and so continued to do, till it came to the mouth of the Sepulchre, where it fell in, and I saw it no more.

When God releases us of our guilt and burden we are as those that leap for joy

Then was *Christian* glad and lightsome, and said with a merry heart, *He hath given me rest by his sorrow, and life by his death.* Then he stood still awhile to look and wonder; for it was very surprising to him, that the sight of the Cross should thus ease him of his Burden. He looked therefore, and looked again, even till the springs that were in his head sent the waters down his cheeks. Now as he stood looking and weeping, behold three Shining Ones came to him and saluted him with *Peace be to thee;* so the first said to him, *Thy sins be forgiven:* the second stript him of his Rags, and clothed him with Change of Raiment; the third also set a mark in his forehead, and gave him a Roll with a Seal upon it, which he bid him look on as he ran, and that he should give it in at the Cœlestial Gate. So they went their way.

A Christian can sing though alone, when God doth give him the joy of his heart

Who's this? the Pilgrim. How! 'tis very true,
Old things are past away, all's become new.
Strange! he's another man, upon my word,
They be fine Feathers that make a fine Bird.

Then *Christian* gave three leaps for joy, and went on singing,

Thus far did I come laden with my sin;
Nor could aught ease the grief that I was in
Till I came hither: What a place is this!
Must here be the beginning of my bliss?
Must here the Burden fall from off my back?
Must here the strings that bound it to me crack?
Blest Cross! blest Sepulchre! blest rather be
The Man that there was put to shame for me.

Simple, Sloth, and Presumption

I saw then in my Dream that he went on thus, even until he came at a bottom, where he saw, a little out of the way, three men fast asleep, with fetters upon their heels. The name of the one was *Simple,* another *Sloth,* and the third *Presumption.*

Christian then seeing them lie in this case, went to them, if peradventure he might awake them, and cried, You are like them that sleep on the top of a mast, for the Dead Sea is under you, a gulf that hath no bottom. Awake therefore and come away; be willing also, and I will help you off with your Irons. He also told them, If he that goeth about like a *roaring lion* comes by, you will certainly become a prey to his teeth. With that they looked upon him, and began to reply in his sort: *Simple* said, *I see no danger; Sloth* said, *Yet a little more sleep;* and *Presumption* said, *Every Fat¹ must stand upon his own bottom.* And so they lay down to sleep again and *Christian* went on his way. *There is no persuasion will do, if God openeth not the eyes*

Yet was he troubled to think that men in that danger should so little esteem the kindness of him that so freely offered to help them, both by awakening of them, counselling of them, and proffering to help them off with their Irons. And as he was troubled thereabout he espied two men come tumbling over the Wall, on the left hand of the narrow way; and they made up apace to him. The name of the one was *Formalist,* and the name of the other *Hypocrisy.* So, as I said, they drew up unto him, who thus entered with them into discourse. *Christian talked with them*

CHR. Gentlemen, Whence came you, and whither do you go?

FORM. and HYP. We were born in the land of *Vain-glory,* and are going for praise to Mount *Sion.*

CHR. Why came you not in at the Gate which standeth at the beginning of the Way? Know you not that it is written, That *he that cometh not in by the Door, but climbeth up some other way, the same is a Thief and a Robber?*

FORM. and HYP. They said, That to go to the Gate for entrance was by all their countrymen

¹ *I. e.,* Vat or tub.

counted too far about; and that therefore their usual way was to make a short cut of it, and to climb over the wall, as they had done.

CHR. But will it not be counted a Trespass against the Lord of the City whither we are bound, thus to violate his revealed will?

They that come into the way, but not by the door, think that they can say something in vindication of their own practice

FORM. and HYP. They told him, That as for that, he needed not to trouble his head thereabout; for what they did they had custom for; and could produce, if need were, Testimony that would witness it for more than a thousand years.

CHR. But, said *Christian,* will your practice stand a Trial at Law?

FORM. and HYP. They told him, That custom, it being of so long a standing as above a thousand years, would doubtless now be admitted as a thing legal by an impartial Judge; and besides, said they, if we get into the way, what's matter which way we get in? if we are in, we are in; thou art but in the way, who, as we perceive, came in at the Gate; and we are also in the way, that came tumbling over the wall; wherein now is thy condition beter than ours?

CHR. I walk by the Rule of my Master; you walk by the rude working of your fancies. You are counted thieves already, by the Lord of the way; therefore I doubt you will not be found true men at the end of the way. You come in by yourselves, without his direction; and shall go out by yourselves, without his mercy.

To this they made him but little answer; only they bid him look to himself. Then I saw that they went on every man in his way, without much conference one with another; save that these two men told *Christian,* that as to *Laws* and *Ordinances,* they doubted not but they should as conscientiously do them as he; therefore, said they, we see not wherein thou differest from us but by the *Coat* that is on thy back, which was, as we trow, given thee by some of thy Neighbors, to hide the shame of thy nakedness.

CHR. By Laws and Ordinances you will not be saved, since you came not in by the door. And as for this *Coat* that is on my back, it was given me by the Lord of the place whither I go; and that, as you say, to cover my nakedness with. And I take it as a token of his kindness to me, for I had nothing but rags before. And besides, thus I comfort myself as I go: Surely think I, when I come to the gate of the City, the Lord thereof will know me for good, since I have this Coat on my back; a Coat that he gave me freely in the day that he stript me of my rags. I have moreover a Mark in my forehead, of which perhaps you have taken no notice, which one of my Lord's most intimate associates fixed there in the day that my Burden fell off my shoulders. I will tell you moreover, that I had then given me a Roll sealed, to comfort me by reading as I go in the way; I was also bid to give it in at the Cœlestial Gate, in token of my certain going in after it; all which things I doubt you want, and want them because you came not in at the Gate.

Christian has got his Lord's coat on his back, and is comforted therewith; he is comforted, also, with his mark and his roll

To these things they gave him no answer; only they looked upon each other and laughed. Then I saw that they went on all, save that *Christian* kept before, who had no more talk but with himself, and that sometimes sighingly, and sometimes comfortably; also he would be often reading in the Roll that one of the Shining Ones gave him, by which he was refreshed.

Christian has talk himself

I beheld then, that they all went on till they came to the foot of the Hill *Difficulty*, at the bottom of which was a Spring. There was also in the same place two other ways besides that which came straight from the Gate; one turned to the left hand and the other to the right, at the bottom of the Hill; but the narrow way lay right up the Hill, and the name of the going up the side of the Hill is called *Difficulty*. *Christian* now went to the Spring, and drank thereof to refresh himself, and then began to go up the Hill, saying,

He comes to the Hill Difficulty

The Hill, tho' high, I covet to ascend,
The difficulty will not me offend;
For I perceive the way to life lies here:
Come, pluck up, Heart, let's neither faint nor fear;
Better, tho' difficult, the right way to go,
Than wrong, though easy, where the end is wo.

The danger of turning out of the way

The other two also came to the foot of the Hill; but when they saw that the Hill was steep and high, and that there was two other ways to go; and supposing also that these two ways might meet again with that up which *Christian* went, on the other side of the Hill; therefore they were resolved to go in those ways. Now the name of one of those ways was *Danger,* and the name of the other *Destruction.* So the one took the way which is called *Danger,* which led him into a great Wood; and the other took directly up the way to *Destruction,* which led him into a wide field, full of dark Mountains, where he stumbled and fell, and rose no more.

Shall they who wrong begin yet rightly end?
Shall they at all have Safety for their friend?
No, no; in headstrong manner they set out,
And headlong will they fall at last no doubt.

A word of grace

I looked then after *Christian* to see him go up the Hill, where I perceived he fell from running to going, and from going to clambering upon his hands and his knees, because of the steepness of the place. Now about the mid-way to the top of the Hill was a pleasant *Arbor,* made by the Lord of the Hill for the refreshing of weary travellers; thither therefore *Christian* got, where also he sat down to rest him. Then he pulled his Roll out of his bosom, and read therein to his comfort; he also now began afresh to take a review of the Coat or Garment that was given him as he stood by the Cross. Thus pleasing himself awhile, he at last fell into a slumber, and thence into a fast sleep, which detained him in that place until it was almost night; and in his sleep his Roll fell out of his hand. Now as he was sleeping, there came one to him and awaked him, He that sleeps is a loser saying, *Go to the Ant, thou sluggard; consider her ways, and be wise.* And with that *Christian* suddenly started up, and sped on his way, and went apace till he came to the top of the Hill.

Now when he was got up to the top of the Hill, Christian meets with Mistrust and Timorous there came two men running against him amain; the name of the one was *Timorous,* and the other, *Mistrust;* to whom *Christian* said, Sirs, what's the matter you run the wrong way? *Timorous* answered, that they were going to the City of *Zion,* and had got up that difficult place; but, said he, the further we go, the more danger we meet with; wherefore we turned, and are going back again.

Yes, said *Mistrust,* for just before us lie a couple of Lions in the way, (whether sleeping or waking we know not) and we could not think, if we came within reach, but they would presently pull us in pieces.

CHR. Then said *Christian,* You make me afraid, Christian shakes off fear but whither shall I fly to be safe? If I go back to mine own country, *that* is prepared for Fire and Brimstone, and I shall certainly perish there. If I can get to the Cœlestial City, I am sure to be in safety there. I must venture: To go back is nothing but death; to go forward is fear of death, and life everlasting beyond it. I will yet go forward. So *Mistrust* and *Timorous* ran down the Hill, and *Christian* went on his way. But thinking again of what he heard from the men, he felt in his bosom for his Roll, that he might read therein and be com- Christian missed his roll wherein he used to take comfort forted; but he felt, and found it not. Then was *Christian* in great distress, and knew not what to do; for he wanted that which used to relieve him, and that which should have been his pass into the Cœlestial City. Here therefore he began to be much perplexed, and knew not what to do. At last he He is perplexed for his roll bethought himself that he had slept in the *Arbor* that is on the side of the Hill; and falling down upon his knees he asked God's forgiveness for that

his foolish fact[1] and then went back to look for his
Roll. But all the way he went back, who can suffi-
ciently set forth the sorrow of *Christian's* heart?
Sometimes he sighed, sometimes he wept, and oftentimes he chid himself for being so foolish to fall
asleep in that place, which was erected only for a
little refreshment for his weariness. Thus therefore
he went back, carefully looking on this side and
on that, all the way as he went, if happily he might
find his Roll, that had been his comfort so many
times in his Journey. He went thus till he came
again within sight of the *Arbor* where he sat and
slept; but that sight renewed his sorrow the more,
by bringing again, even afresh, his evil of sleeping
into his mind. Thus therefore he now went on
Christian bewailing his sinful sleep, saying, *O wretched man*
bewails his *that I am,* that I should sleep in the daytime! that
foolish
sleeping I should sleep in the midst of difficulty! that I should
so indulge the flesh, as to use that rest for ease to
my flesh, which the Lord of the Hill hath erected
only for the relief of the spirits of Pilgrims? How
many steps have I took in vain! (Thus it happened to *Israel* for their sin, they were sent back
again by the way of the Red Sea), and I am made
to tread those steps with sorrow, which I might have
trod with delight, had it not been for this sinful
sleep. How far might I have been on my way by
this time! I am made to tread those steps thrice
over, which I needed not to have trod but once;
yea now also I am like to be benighted, for the day
is almost spent. O that I had not slept!

Christian Now by this time he was come to the *Arbor* again,
findeth his
roll where where for a while he sat down and wept; but at
he lost it last, as *Christian* would have it, looking sorrowfully
down under the settle, there he espied his Roll;
the which he with trembling and haste catched up,
and put it into his bosom. But who can tell how
joyful this man was when he had gotten his Roll
again! for this Roll was the assurance of his life

---

[1] Deed.

and acceptance at the desired Haven. Therefore
he laid it up in his bosom, gave thanks to God for
directing his eye to the place where it lay, and with
joy and tears betook himself again to his Journey.
But Oh how nimbly now did he go up the rest of
the Hill! Yet before he got up, the Sun went down
upon *Christian;* and this made him again recall the
vanity of his sleeping to his remembrance; and thus
he again began to condole with himself. *O thou
sinful sleep: how for thy sake am I like to be benighted in my Journey! I must walk without the
Sun, darkness must cover the path of my feet, and
I must hear the noise of doleful creatures, because
of my sinful sleep.* Now also he remembered the
story that *Mistrust* and *Timorous* told him of, how
they were frighted with the sight of the Lions. Then
said *Christian* to himself again, These beasts range
in the night for their prey; and if they should meet
with me in the dark, how should I shift them?
How should I escape being by them torn in pieces?
Thus he went on his way. But while he was thus
bewailing his unhappy miscarriage, he lift up his
eyes, and behold there was a very stately Palace
before him, the name of which was *Beautiful;* and
it stood just by the High-way side.

So I saw in my Dream that he made haste and
went forward, that if possible he might get Lodging
there. Now before he had gone far, he entered into
a very narrow passage, which was about a furlong
off of the Porter's Lodge; and looking very nar-
rowly before him as he went, he espied two Lions
in the way. Now, thought he, I see the dangers that
Mistrust and *Timorous* were driven back by. (The
Lions were chained, but he saw not the chains.)
Then he was afraid, and thought also himself to go
back after them, for he thought nothing but death
was before him: But the Porter at the lodge, whose
name is *Watchful*, perceiving that *Christian* made
a halt as if he would go back, cried unto him, saying,
Is thy strength so small? Fear not the Lions, for

they are chained, and are placed there for trial of faith where it is, and for discovery of those that have none. Keep in the midst of the Path, and no hurt shall come unto thee.

> Difficulty is behind, Fear is before,
> Though he's got on the Hill, the Lions roar;
> A Christian man is never long at ease,
> When one fright's gone, another doth him seize.

Then I saw that he went on, trembling for fear of the Lions, but taking good heed to the directions of the Porter; he heard them roar, but they did him no harm. Then he clapt his hands, and went on till he came and stood before the Gate where the Porter was. Then said *Christian* to the Porter, Sir, what house is this? and may I lodge here to-night? The Porter answered, This house was built by the Lord of the Hill, and he built it for the relief and security of Pilgrims. The Porter also asked whence he was, and whither he was going?

CHR. I am come from the City of *Destruction,* and am going to Mount *Zion;* but because the Sun is now set, I desire, if I may, to lodge here to-night.

POR. What is your name?

CHR. My name is now *Christian,* but my name at the first was *Graceless;* I came of the race of *Japheth,* whom God will persuade to dwell in the Tents of *Shem.*

POR. But how doth it happen that you come so late? The Sun is set.

CHR. I had been here sooner, but that, wretched man that I am! I slept in the *Arbor* that stands on the Hill-side; nay, I had notwithstanding that, been here much sooner, but that in my sleep I lost my evidence, and came without it to the brow of the Hill; and then feeling for it, and finding it not, I was forced with sorrow of heart to go back to the place where I had slept my sleep, where I found it, and now I am come.

POR. Well, I will call out one of the Virgins of

this place, who will, if she likes your talk, bring you in to the rest of the Family, according to the rules of the house. So *Watchful* the Porter, rang a bell, at the sound of which came out at the door of the house, a grave and beautiful damsel named *Discretion*, and asked why she was called.

The Porter answered, This man is in a Journey from the City of *Destruction* to Mount *Zion,* but being weary and benighted, he asked me if he might lodge here to-night; so I told him I would call for thee, who, after discourse had with him, mayest do as seemeth thee good, even according to the Law of the house.

Then she asked him whence he was, and whither he was going; and he told her. She asked him also, how he got into the way; and he told her. Then she asked him, what he had seen and met with in the way; and he told her. And last she asked his name; so he said, It is *Christian,* and I have so much the more a desire to lodge here to-night, because, by what I perceive, this place was built by the Lord of the Hill, for the relief and security of Pilgrims. So she smiled, but the water stood in her eyes; and after a little pause, she said, I will call forth two or three more of the Family. So she ran to the door, and called out *Prudence, Piety,* and *Charity,* who after a little more discourse with him, led him in to the Family; and many of them, meeting him at the threshold of the house, said, Come in thou blessed of the Lord: this house was built by the Lord of the Hill, on purpose to entertain such Pilgrims in. Then he bowed his head, and followed them into the house. So when he was come in and set down, they gave him something to drink, and consented together, that until supper was ready, some of them should have some particular discourse with *Christian,* for the best improvement of time; and they appointed *Piety,* and *Prudence,* and *Charity* to discourse with him; and thus they began:

Piety
discourses
him

PIETY. Come good *Christian,* since we have been
so loving to you, to receive you into our house this
night, let us, if perhaps we may better ourselves
thereby, talk with you of all things that have happened to you in your Pilgrimage.

CHR. With a very good will, and I am glad that
you are so well disposed.

PIETY. What moved you at first to betake yourself
to a Pilgrim's life?

How
Christian
was driven
out of his
own
country

CHR. I was driven out of my Native Country, by
a dreadful sound that was in mine ears: to wit, that
unavoidable destruction did attend me, if I abode in
that place where I was.

PIETY. But how did it happen that you came out
of your Country this way?

How he got
into the
way to
Zion

CHR. It was as God would have it; for when I
was under the fears of destruction, I did not know
whither to go; but by chance there came a man,
even to me, as I was trembling and weeping, whose
name is *Evangelist,* and he directed me to the
Wicket-gate, which else I should never have found,
and so set me into the way that hath led me directly to this house.

PIETY. But did you not come by the house of the
Interpreter?

A rehears-
al of what
he saw in
the way

CHR. Yes, and did see such things there, the remembrance of which will stick by me as long as I
live; specially three things: to wit, How Christ, in
despite of Satan, maintains his work of Grace in the
heart; how the man had sinned himself quite out of
hopes of God's mercy; and also the Dream of him
that thought in his sleep the day of Judgment was
come.

PIETY. Why, Did you hear him tell his dream?

CHR. Yes, and a dreadful one it was. I thought
it made my heart ake as he was telling of it; but
yet I am glad I heard it.

PIETY. Was that all that you saw at the house of
the *Interpreter?*

CHR. No: he took me and had me where he

shewed me a stately Palace, and how the people were clad in Gold that were in it; and how there came a venturous man and cut his way through the armed men that stood in the door to keep him out, and how he was bid to come in, and win eternal Glory. Methought those things did ravish my heart; I would have stayed at that good man's house a twelve-month, but that I knew I had further to go.

PIETY. And what saw you else in the way?

CHR. Saw! Why, I went but a little further, and I saw one, as I thought in my mind, hang bleeding upon the Tree; and the very sight of him made my Burden fall off my back (for I groaned under a very heavy Burden), but then it fell down from off me. 'Twas a strange thing to me, for I never saw such a thing before; yea, and while I stood looking up (for then I could not forbear looking) three Shining Ones came to me. One of them testified that my sins were forgiven me; another stript me of my Rags, and gave me this broidered Coat which you see; and the third set the Mark which you see in my forehead, and gave me this sealed Roll: (and with that he plucked it out of his bosom.)

PIETY. But you saw more than this, did you not?

CHR. The things that I have told you were the best; yet some other matters I saw, as namely I saw three men, *Simple*, *Sloth*, and *Presumption*, lie asleep a little out of the way as I came, with Irons upon their heels; but do you think I could awake them? I also saw *Formalist* and *Hypocrisy* come tumbling over the wall, to go, as they pretended, to *Zion*; but they were quickly lost; even as I myself did tell them, but they would not believe. But, above all, I found it hard work to get up this Hill, and as hard to come by the Lions' mouths; and truly if it had not been for the good man, the Porter that stands at the Gate, I do not know but that after all I might have gone back again; but now I thank God I am here, and I thank you for receiving of me.

Prudence
discourses
him
Then *Prudence* thought good to ask him a few questions, and desired his answer to them.

PRUD. Do you not think sometimes of the Country from whence you came?

Christian's
thoughts
of his
native
country
CHR. Yes, but with much shame and detestation: Truly, if I had been mindful of that Country from whence I came out, I might have had opportunity to have returned; but now I desire a better Country, that is, a Heavenly.

PRUD. Do you not yet bear away with you some of the things that then you were conversant withal?

Christian
distasted
with carnal
cogitations
CHR. Yes, but greatly against my will; especially my inward and carnal cogitations, with which all my countrymen, as well as myself, were delighted; but now all those things are my grief;

Christian's
choice
and might I but chuse mine own things, I would chuse never to think of those things more; but when I would be doing of that which is best, that which is worst is with me.

PRUD. Do you not find sometimes, as if those things were vanquished, which at other times are your perplexity?

Christian's
golden
hours
CHR. Yes, but that is seldom; but they are to me golden hours in which such things happen to me.

PRUD. Can you remember by what means you find your annoyances at times, as if they were vanquished?

How
Christian
gets power
against his
corruptions
CHR. Yes, when I think what I saw at the Cross, that will do it; and when I look upon my broidered Coat, that will do it; also when I look into the Roll that I carry in my bosom, that will do it; and when my thoughts wax warm about whither I am going, that will do it.

PRUD. And what is it that makes you so desirous to go to Mount *Zion?*

Why
Christian
would be
at Mount
Zion
CHR. Why, there I hope to see him *alive* that did hang *dead* on the Cross; and there I hope to be rid of all those things that to this day are in me an annoyance to me; there, they say, there is no death; and there I shall dwell with such Company as I

like best. For to tell you truth, I love him, because
I was by him eased of my Burden, and I am weary
of my inward sickness; I would fain be where I
shall die no more, and with the Company that shall
continually cry, *Holy, Holy, Holy.*

Then said *Charity* to *Christian,* Have you a
family? Are you a married man? Charity
discourses
him

CHR. I have a Wife and four small Children.

CHAR. And why did you not bring them along
with you?

CHR. Then *Christian* wept, and said, Oh how willingly would I have done it, but they were all of
them utterly averse to my going on Pilgrimage. Christian's
love to his
wife and
children

CHAR. But you should have talked to them, and
have endeavoured to have shewn them the danger
of being behind.

CHR. So I did, and told them also what God had
shewed to me of the destruction of our City; but
I seemed to them as one that mocked, and they
believed me not.

CHAR. And did you pray to God that he would
bless your counsel to them?

CHR. Yes, and that with much affection; for you
must think that my Wife and poor Children were
very dear unto me.

CHAR. But did you tell them of your own sorrow, and fear of destruction? for I suppose that
destruction was visible enough to you.

CHR. Yes, over, and over, and over. They might
also see my fears in my countenance, in my tears, and
also in my trembling under the apprehension of the
Judgment that did hang over our heads; but all was
not sufficient to prevail with them to come with me. Christian's
fears of
perishing
might be
read in
his very
counte-
nance

CHAR. But what could they say for themselves,
why they came not?

CHR. Why, my Wife was afraid of losing this
World, and my Children were given to the foolish
Delights of youth: so what by one thing, and what
by another, they left me to wander in this manner
alone. The cause
why his
wife and
children
did not go
with him

CHAR. But did you not with your vain life, damp all that you by words used by way of persuasion to bring them away with you?

Christian's good conversation before his wife and children

CHR. Indeed I cannot commend my life; for I am conscious to myself of many failings therein: I know also, that a man by his conversation may soon overthrow, what by argument or persuasion he doth labour to fasten upon others for their good. Yet, this I can say, I was very wary of giving them occasion, by any unseemly action, to make them averse to going on Pilgrimage. Yea, for this very thing they would tell me I was too precise, and that I denied myself of things (for their sakes) in which they saw no evil. Nay, I think I may say, that if what they saw in me did hinder them, it was my great tenderness in sinning against God, or of doing any wrong to my Neighbor.

Christian clear of their blood if they perish

CHAR. Indeed *Cain* hated his Brother, because his own works were evil, and his Brother's righteous; and if thy Wife and Children have been offended with thee for this, they thereby shew themselves to be implacable to good, and thou hast delivered thy soul from their blood.

What Christian had to his supper

Now I saw in my Dream, that thus they sat talking together until supper was ready. So when they had made ready, they sat down to meat. Now the Table was furnished with fat things, and with Wine

Their talk at supper-time

that was well refined: and all their talk at the Table was about the LORD of the Hill; as namely, about what HE had done, and wherefore HE did what He did, and why HE had builded that House: and by what they said, I perceived that he had been a *great Warriour*, and had fought with and slain him that had the power of Death, but not without great danger to himself, which made me love him the more.

For, as they said, and as I believe (said *Christian*) he did it with the loss of much blood; but that which put Glory of Grace into all he did, was, that he did it out of pure love to his Country. And besides, there were some of them of the household that said they had seen and spoke with him since he did die on the Cross; and they have attested that they had it from his own lips, that he is such a lover of poor Pilgrims, that the like is not to be found from the East to the West.

They moreover gave an instance of what they affirmed, and that was, He had stript himself of his glory, that he might do this for the Poor; and that they heard him say and affirm, *That he would not dwell in the Mountain of Zion alone.* They said moreover, that he had made many Pilgrims Princes, though by nature they were Beggars born, and their original had been the dunghill. *[Christ makes princes of beggars]*

Thus they discoursed together till late at night; and after they had committed themselves to their Lord for protection, they betook themselves to rest: the Pilgrim they laid in a large upper chamber, whose window opened towards the Sun rising: the name of the chamber was *Peace,* where he slept till break of day, and then he awoke and sang, *[Christian's bed-chamber]*

> Where am I now? Is this the love and care
> Of Jesus for the men that Pilgrims are
> Thus to provide! That I should be forgiven
> And dwell already the next door to Heaven!

So in the morning they all got up, and after some more discourse, they told him that he should not depart till they had shewed him the *Rarities* of that place. And first they had him into the Study, where they shewed him Records of the greatest antiquity; in which, as I remember my Dream, they shewed him first the *Pedigree* of the Lord of the Hill, that he was the Son of the Antient of Days, and came by an Eternal Generation. Here also was more fully recorded the Acts that he had done, and the names of many hundreds that he had taken into his service; and how he had placed them in such Habitations that could neither by length of Days, nor decays of Nature, be dissolved. *[Christian had into the study, and what he saw there]*

Then they read to him some of the worthy Acts
that some of his servants had done: as, how they
had subdued Kingdoms, wrought Righteousness, obtained Promises, stopped the mouths of Lions,
quenched the violence of Fire, escaped the edge of
the Sword; out of weakness were made strong,
waxed valiant in fight, and turned to flight the
Armies of the *Aliens*.

Then they read again in another part of the
Records of the house, where it was shewed how
willing their Lord was to receive into his favour
any, even any, though they in time past had offered
great affronts to his Person and proceedings. Here
also were several other Histories of many other
famous things, of all which *Christian* had a view; as
of things both Antient and Modern: together with
Prophecies and Predictions of things that have
their certain accomplishment, both to the dread and
amazement of Enemies, and the comfort and solace
of Pilgrims.

Christian
had into
the
armoury

The next day they took him and had him into the
Armory, where they shewed him all manner of
Furniture, which their Lord had provided for Pilgrims, as Sword, Shield, Helmet, Breastplate, *All-
prayer*, and Shoes that would not wear out. And
there was here enough of this to harness out as
many men for the service of their Lord as there
be Stars in the Heaven for multitude.

Christian
is made
to see
ancient
things

They also shewed him some of the Engines with
which some of his Servants had done wonderful
things. They shewed him *Moses'* Rod; the Hammer
and Nail with which *Jael* slew *Sisera;* the Pitchers,
Trumpets and Lamps too, with which *Gideon* put
to flight the Armies of *Midian:* Then they shewed
him the Ox's goad wherewith *Shamgar* slew six
hundred men: They shewed him also the Jaw-bone
with which *Samson* did such mighty feats: They
shewed him moreover the Sling and Stone with
which *David* slew *Goliah* of *Gath;* and the Sword
also with which their Lord will kill the Man of

Sin, in the day that he shall rise up to the prey. They shewed him besides many excellent things, with which *Christian* was much delighted. This done, they went to their rest again.

Then I saw in my Dream, that on the morrow he got up to go forwards, but they desired him to stay till the next day also; and then, said they, we will (if the day be clear) shew you the Delectable Mountains, which, they said, would yet further add to his comfort, because they were nearer the desired Haven than the place where at present he was: so he consented and stayed. When the morning was up, they had him to the top of the House, and bid him look South; so he did: and behold at a great distance he saw a most pleasant Mountainous Country, beautified with Woods, Vineyards, Fruits of all sorts, Flowers also, with Springs and Fountains, very delectable to behold. Then he asked the name of the Country: *Christian showed the Delectable Mountains*

They said it was *Immanuel's Land;* and it is as common, they said, as this *Hill* is, to and for all the Pilgrims. And when thou comest there, from thence, said they, thou mayest see to the gate of the Cœlestial City, as the Shepherds that live there will make appear.

Now he bethought himself of setting forward, and they were willing he should: but first, said they, let us go again into the Armory: So they did; and when they came there, they harnessed him from head to foot with what was of proof, lest perhaps he should meet with assaults in the way. He being therefore thus accoutred, walketh out with his friends to the Gate, and there he asked the Porter if he saw any Pilgrims pass by: Then the Porter answered, Yes. *Christian sets forward* *Christian sent away armed*

CHR. Pray, did you know him? said he.

POR. I asked his name, and he told me it was *Faithful*.

CHR. O, said *Christian*, I know him; he is my Townsman, my near Neighbor, he comes from the

place where I was born: How far do you think he
may be before?

POR. He is got by this time below the Hill.

How
Christian
and the
Porter
greet at
parting

CHR. Well, said *Christian,* good Porter, the Lord
be with thee, and add to all thy blessings much increase, for the kindness that thou hast shewed to
me.

> Whilst *Christian* is among his godly friends,
> Their golden mouths make him sufficient mends
> For all his griefs, and when they let him go,
> He's clad with northern Steel from top to toe.

Then he began to go forward; but *Discretion,
Piety, Charity,* and *Prudence,* would accompany him
down to the foot of the Hill. So they went on together, reiterating their former discourses, till they
came to go down the Hill. Then said *Christian,*
As it was *difficult* coming up, so (so far as I can
see) it is *dangerous* going down. Yes, said *Prudence,* so it is, for it is a hard matter for a man to
go down into the Valley of *Humiliation,* as thou art
now, and to catch no slip by the way; therefore,
said they, are we come out to accompany thee down
the Hill. So he began to go down, but very warily;
yet he caught a slip or two.

Then I saw in my Dream that these good Companions, when *Christian* was gone down to the
bottom of the Hill, gave him a loaf of Bread, a
bottle of Wine, and a cluster of Raisins; and then
he went on his way.

But now, in this Valley of *Humiliation,* poor
Christian was hard put to it; for he had gone but
a little way, before he espied a foul *Fiend* coming
over the field to meet him; his name is *Apollyon.*
Then did *Christian* begin to be afraid, and to cast
in his mind whether to go back or to stand his
ground: But he considered again that he had no
Armor for his back, and therefore thought that to
turn the back to him might give him the greater
advantage with ease to pierce him with his Darts.

Therefore he resolved to venture and stand his Christian's ground; For, thought he, had I no more in mine resolution eye than the saving of my life, 'twould be the best at the approach of way to stand. Apollyon

So he went on, and *Apollyon* met him. Now the Monster was hideous to behold; he was cloathed with scales like a Fish (and they are his pride); he had wings like a Dragon, feet like a Bear, and out of his belly came Fire and Smoke; and his mouth was as the mouth of a Lion. When he was come up to *Christian,* he beheld him with a disdainful countenance, and thus began to question with him.

APOL. Whence come you? and whither are you bound?

CHR. I am come from the City of *Destruction,* which is the place of all evil, and am going to the City of *Zion.*

APOL. By this I perceive thou art one of my Sub- Discourse jects, for all that Country is mine, and I am the betwixt Christian Prince and God of it. How is it then that thou and hast run away from thy King? Were it not that Apollyon I hope thou mayest do me more service, I would strike thee now at one blow to the ground.

CHR. I was born indeed in your dominions, but your service was hard, and your wages such as a man could not live on, *for the wages of sin is death;* therefore when I was come to years, I did as other considerate persons do, look out, if perhaps I might mend myself.

APOL. There is no Prince that will thus lightly Apollyon's lose his Subjects, neither will I as yet lose thee: but flattery since thou complainest of thy service and wages, be content to go back; what our Country will afford, I do here promise to give thee.

CHR. But I have let myself to another, even to the King of Princes, and how can I with fairness go back with thee?

APOL. Thou hast done in this, according to the Proverb, changed a bad for a worse; but it is ordi-

Apollyon
under-
values
Christ's
service

nary for those that have professed themselves his Servants, after a while to give him the slip, and return again to me: Do thou so too, and all shall be well.

CHR. I have given him my faith, and sworn my allegiance to him; how then can I go back from this, and not be hanged as a Traitor?

Apollyon
pretends
to be
merciful

APOL. Thou didst the same to me, and yet I am willing to pass by all, if now thou wilt yet turn again and go back.

CHR. What I promised thee was in my nonage; and besides, I count that the Prince under whose Banner now I stand is able to absolve me; yea, and to pardon also what I did as to my compliance with thee; and besides, O thou destroying *Apollyon*, to speak truth, I like his Service, his Wages, his Servants, his Government, his Company and Country, better than thine; and therefore leave off to persuade me further; I am his Servant, and I will follow him.

Apollyon
pleads the
grievous
ends of
Christians,
to dissuade
Christian
from per-
sisting in
his way

APOL. Consider again when thou art in cool blood, what thou art like to meet with in the way that thou goest. Thou knowest that for the most part, his Servants come to an ill end, because they are transgressors against me and my ways: How many of them have been put to shameful deaths; and besides, thou countest his service better than mine, whereas he never came yet from the place where he is to deliver any that served him out of our hands; but as for me, how many times, as all the World very well knows, have I delivered, either by power or fraud, those that have faithfully served me, from him and his, though taken by them; and so I will deliver thee.

CHR. His forbearing at present to deliver them is on purpose to try their love, whether they will cleave to him to the end; and as for the ill end thou sayest they come to, that is most glorious in their account; for for present deliverance, they do not much expect it, for they stay for their Glory, and then they shall have it, when their Prince comes in his and the Glory of the Angels.

APOL. Thou hast already been unfaithful in thy service to him, and how dost thou think to receive wages of him?

CHR. Wherein, O *Apollyon,* have I been unfaithful to him?

APOL. Thou didst faint at first setting out, when thou wast almost choked in the Gulf of *Dispond;* thou didst attempt wrong ways to be rid of thy Burden, whereas thou shouldest have stayed till thy Prince had taken it off; thou didst sinfully sleep and lose thy choice thing; thou wast also almost persuaded to go back, at the sight of the Lions; and when thou talkest of thy Journey, and of what thou hast heard and seen, thou art inwardly desirous of vain-glory in all that thou sayest or doest. *Apollyon pleads Christian's infirmities against him*

CHR. All this is true, and much more which thou hast left out; but the Prince whom I serve and honor is merciful, and ready to forgive; but besides, these infirmities possessed me in thy Country, for there I sucked them in, and I have groaned under them, been sorry for them, and have obtained Pardon of my Prince.

APOL. Then *Apollyon* broke out into a grievous rage, saying, I am an enemy to this Prince; I hate his Person, his Laws, and People; I am come out on purpose to withstand thee. *Apollyon in a rage falls upon Christian*

CHR. *Apollyon,* beware what you do, for I am in the King's High-way, the way of Holiness, therefore take heed to yourself.

APOL. Then *Apollyon* straddled quite over the whole breadth of the way, and said, I am void of fear in this matter, prepare thyself to die; for I swear by my infernal Den, that thou shalt go no further; here will I spill thy soul.

And with that he threw a flaming Dart at his breast, but *Christian* had a Shield in his hand, with which he caught it, and so prevented the danger of that.

Christian
wounded
in his
under-
standing,
faith, and
conversa-
tion

Then did *Christian* draw, for he saw 'twas time to bestir him: and *Apollyon* as fast made at him, throwing Darts as thick as Hail; by the which, notwithstanding all that *Christian* could do to avoid it, *Apollyon* wounded him in his *head,* his *hand,* and *foot:* This made *Christian* give a little back; *Apollyon* therefore followed his work amain, and *Christian* again took courage, and resisted as manfully as he could. This sore Combat lasted for above half a day, even till *Christian* was almost quite spent; for you must know that *Christian,* by reason of his wounds, must needs grow weaker and weaker.

Apollyon
casteth
down to
the ground
Christian

Then *Apollyon* espying his opportunity, began to gather up close to *Christian,* and wrestling with him, gave him a dreadful fall; and with that *Christian's* Sword flew out of his hand. Then said *Apollyon, I am sure of thee now:* and with that he had almost pressed him to death, so that *Christian* began to despair of life: but as God would have it, while *Apollyon* was fetching of his last blow, thereby to make a full end of this good man, *Christian* nimbly stretched out his hand for his Sword, and caught it, saying, *Rejoice not against me, O mine Enemy! when I fall I shall arise;* and with that gave him a deadly thrust, which made him give back,

Christian's
victory
over
Apollyon

as one that had received his mortal wound: *Christian,* perceiving that, made at him again, saying, *Nay, in all these things we are more than Conquerors through him that loved us.* And with that *Apollyon* spread forth his Dragon's wings, and sped him away, that *Christian* for a season saw him no more.

A brief
relation of
the combat
by the
spectator

In this Combat no man can imagine, unless he had seen and heard as I did, what yelling and hideous roaring *Apollyon* made all the time of the fight, he spake like a Dragon; and on the other side, what sighs and groans burst from *Christian's* heart. I never saw him all the while give so much as one pleasant look, till he perceived he had wounded

Apollyon with his two-edged Sword; then indeed
he did smile, and look upward; but 'twas the dread-
fullest sight that ever I saw.

> A more unequal match can hardly be:
> *Christian* must fight an Angel; but you see
> The Valiant Man by handling Sword and Shield,
> Doth make him, tho' a Dragon, quit the field.

So when the Battle was over, *Christian* said, I
will here give thanks to him that hath delivered me
out of the mouth of the Lion, to him that did help
me against *Apollyon*. And so he did, saying, *Christian gives God thanks for deliverance*

> Great *Beelzebub*, the Captain of this Fiend,
> Design'd my ruin; therefore to this end
> He sent him harness'd out: and he with rage
> That hellish was, did fiercely me engage:
> But blessed *Michael* helped me, and I
> By dint of Sword did quickly make him fly.
> Therefore to him let me give lasting praise,
> And thank and bless his holy name always.

Then there came to him a hand, with some of the
leaves of the Tree of Life, the which *Christian* took,
and applied to the wounds that he had received in
the Battle, and was healed immediately. He also
sat down in that place to eat Bread, and to drink
of the Bottle that was given him a little before;
so being refreshed, he addressed himself to his
Journey, with his Sword drawn in his hand; for he
said, I know not but some other Enemy may be at
hand. But he met with no other affront from
Apollyon quite through this Valley. *Christian goes on his journey with his sword drawn in his hand*

Now at the end of this Valley was another, called
the Valley of the *Shadow of Death,* and *Christian*
must needs go through it, because the way to the
Cœlestial City lay through the midst of it. Now,
this Valley is a very solitary place. The Prophet
Jeremiah thus describes it: *A wilderness, a land of
desarts and of pits, a land of drought, and of the
shadow of death, a land that no man* (but a Chris-
tian) *passeth through, and where no man dwelt.* *The Valley of the Shadow of Death*

Now here *Christian* was worse put to it than in his fight with *Apollyon,* as by the sequel you shall see.

The children of the spies go back

I saw then in my Dream, that when *Christian* was got to the borders of the *Shadow of Death,* there met him two men, Children of them that brought up an evil report of the good land, making haste to go back; to whom *Christian* spake as follows,

CHR. Whither are you going?

MEN. They said, Back, back; and we would have you to do so too, if either life or peace is prized by you.

CHR. Why, what's the matter? said *Christian.*

MEN. Matter! said they; we were going that way as you are going, and went as far as we durst; and indeed we were almost past coming back; for had we gone a little further, we had not been here to bring the news to thee.

CHR. But what have you met with? said *Christian.*

MEN. Why we were almost in the Valley of the *Shadow of Death;* but that by good hap we looked before us, and saw the danger before we came to it.

CHR. But what have you seen? said *Christian.*

MEN. Seen! Why, the Valley itself, which is as dark as pitch; we also saw there the Hobgoblins, Satyrs, and Dragons of the Pit; we heard also in that Valley a continual howling and yelling, as of a people under unutterable misery, who there sat bound in affliction and irons; and over that Valley hangs the discouraging clouds of Confusion; Death also doth always spread his wings over it. In a word, it is every whit dreadful, being utterly without Order.

CHR. Then said *Christian,* I perceive not yet, by what you have said, but that this is my way to the desired Haven.

MEN. Be it thy way; we will not chuse it for ours. So they parted, and *Christian* went on his way, but still with his Sword drawn in his hand, for fear lest he should be assaulted.

I saw then in my Dream, so far as this Valley reached, there was on the right hand a very deep Ditch; that Ditch is it into which the blind have led the blind in all ages, and have both there miserably perished. Again, behold on the left hand, there was a very dangerous Quag, into which, if even a good man falls, he can find no bottom for his foot to stand on. Into that Quag King *David* once did fall, and had no doubt therein been smothered, had not he that is able pluckt him out.

The path-way was here also exceeding narrow, and therefore good *Christian* was the more put to it; for when he sought in the dark to shun the ditch on the one hand, he was ready to tip over into the mire on the other; also when he sought to escape the mire, without great carefulness he would be ready to fall into the ditch. Thus he went on, and I heard him here sigh bitterly; for, besides the dangers mentioned above, the path-way was here so dark, that ofttimes, when he lift up his foot to set forward, he knew not where, or upon what he should set it next.

> Poor man! where art thou now? Thy Day is Night.
> Good man be not cast down, thou yet art right:
> Thy way to Heaven lies by the gates of Hell;
> Chear up, hold out, with thee it shall go well.

About the midst of this Valley, I perceived the mouth of Hell to be, and it stood also hard by the wayside. Now thought *Christian*, what shall I do? And ever and anon the flame and smoke would come out in such abundance, with sparks and hideous noises (things that cared not for *Christian's* Sword, as did *Apollyon* before) that he was forced to put up his Sword, and betake himself to another weapon, called *All-prayer*. So he cried in my hearing, *O Lord I beseech thee deliver my Soul*. Thus he went on a great while, yet still the flames would

Christian put to a stand, but for a while

be reaching towards him: Also he heard doleful
voices, and rushings to and fro, so that sometimes
he thought he should be torn in pieces, or trodden
down like mire in the Streets. This frightful sight
was seen, and these dreadful noises were heard by
him for several miles together; and coming to a
place where he thought he heard a company of
Fiends coming forward to meet him, he stopt, and
began to muse what he had best to do. Sometimes
he had half a thought to go back; then again he
thought he might be half way through the Valley;
he remembered also how he had already vanquished
many a danger, and that the danger of going back
might be much more than for to go forward; so he
resolved to go on. Yet the *Fiends* seemed to come
nearer and nearer; but when they were come even
almost at him, he cried out with a most vehement
voice, *I will walk in the strength of the Lord God;*
so they gave back, and came no further.

Christian
made be-
lieve that
he spake
blasphe-
mies, when
it was
Satan that
suggested
them into
his mind

One thing I would not let slip; I took notice that
now poor *Christian* was so confounded, that he did
not know his own voice; and thus I perceived it;
Just when he was come over against the mouth of
the burning Pit, one of the wicked ones got behind
him, and stept up softly to him, and whisperingly
suggested many grievous blasphemies to him, which
he verily thought had proceeded from his own mind.
This put *Christian* more to it than anything that he
met with before, even to think that he should now
blaspheme him that he loved so much before; yet, if
he could have helped it, he would not have done it;
but he had not the discretion neither to stop his
ears, nor to know from whence those blasphemies
came.

When *Christian* had travelled in this disconsolate
condition some considerable time, he thought he
heard the voice of a man, as going before him,
saying, *Though I walk through the Valley of the
Shadow of Death, I will fear none ill, for thou art
with me.*

Then was he glad, and that for these reasons:

First, Because he gathered from thence, that some who feared God were in this Valley as well as himself.

Secondly, For that he perceived God was with them, though in that dark and dismal state; and why not, thought he, with me? though by reason of the impediment that attends this place, I cannot perceive it.

Thirdly, For that he hoped, could he overtake them, to have company by and by. So he went on, and called to him that was before; but he knew not what to answer, for that he also thought himself to be alone. And by and by the day broke; then said *Christian, He hath turned the Shadow of Death into the morning.*

Now morning being come, he looked back, not out of desire to return, but to see, by the light of the day, what hazards he had gone through in the dark. So he saw more perfectly the Ditch that was on the one hand, and the Quag that was on the other; also how narrow the way was which led betwixt them both; also now he saw the Hobgoblins, and Satyrs, and Dragons of the Pit, but all afar off; for after break of day, they came not nigh; yet they were discovered to him, according to that which is written, *He discovered deep things out of darkness, and bringeth out to light the Shadow of Death.*

Now was *Christian* much affected with his deliverance from all the dangers of his solitary way; which dangers, though he feared them more before, yet he saw them more clearly now, because the light of the day made them conspicuous to him. And about this time the Sun was rising, and this was another mercy to *Christian;* for you must note, that though the first part of the Valley of the *Shadow of Death* was dangerous, yet this second part which he was yet to go, was, if possible, far more dangerous: for from the place where he now stood, even to the end of the Valley, the way was all along set

Christian glad at break of day

The second part of this valley very dangerous

so full of Snares, Traps, Gins, and Nets here, and so full of Pits, Pitfalls, deep Holes, and Shelvings down there, that had it now been dark, as it was when he came the first part of the way, had he had a thousand souls, they had in reason been cast away; but as I said, just now the Sun was rising. Then said he, *His candle shineth on my head, and by his light I go through darkness.*

In this light therefore he came to the end of the Valley. Now I saw in my Dream, that at the end of this Valley lay blood, bones, ashes, and mangled bodies of men, even of Pilgrims that had gone this way formerly; and while I was musing what should be the reason, I espied a little before me a Cave, where two Giants, *Pope* and *Pagan,* dwelt in old time; by whose power and tyranny the men whose bones, blood, ashes, *&c.* lay there, were cruelly put to death. But by this place *Christian* went without much danger, whereat I somewhat wondered; but I have learnt since, that *Pagan* has been dead many a day; and as for the other, though he be yet alive, he is by reason of age, and also of the many shrewd brushes that he met with in his younger days, grown so crazy, and stiff in his joints, that he can now do little more than sit in his Cave's mouth, grinning at Pilgrims as they go by, and biting his nails, because he cannot come to them.

So I saw that *Christian* went on his way; yet at the sight of the *Old Man* that sat in the mouth of the Cave, he could not tell what to think, specially because he spake to him, though he could not go after him, saying, *You will never mend till more of you be burned:* But he held his peace, and set a good face on't, and so went by and catcht no hurt. Then sang *Christian,*

> O world of wonders! (I can say no less)
> That I should be preserv'd in that distress
> That I have met with here! O blessed be
> That hand that from it hath delivered me!
> Dangers in darkness, Devils, Hell, and Sin,

Did compass me, while I this Vale was in:
Yea, Snares, and Pits, and Traps, and Nets did lie
My path about, that worthless silly I
Might have been catch'd, intangled, and cast down;
But since I live, let JESUS wear the Crown.

Now as *Christian* went on his way, he came to a
little ascent, which was cast up on purpose that
Pilgrims might see before them. Up there therefore
Christian went, and looking forward, he saw *Faithful* before him, upon his Journey. Then said
Christian aloud, Ho, ho, So-ho; stay, and I will be
your Companion. At that *Faithful* looked behind
him; to whom *Christian* cried again, Stay, stay, till
I come up to you: But *Faithful* answered, No, I am
upon my life, and the Avenger of Blood is behind me.

At this *Christian* was somewhat moved, and *Christian*
putting to all his strength, he quickly got up with *overtakes*
Faithful, and did also overrun him, so the *last was* *Faithful*
first. Then did *Christian* vain-gloriously smile, because he had gotten the start of his Brother; but
not taking good heed to his feet, he suddenly
stumbled and fell, and could not rise again, until
Faithful came up to help him.

Then I saw in my Dream they went very lovingly *Christian's*
on together, and had sweet discourse of all things *fall makes*
that had happened to them in their Pilgrimage; and *Faithful*
thus *Christian* began: *and he go*
lovingly
CHR. My honoured and well beloved Brother *together*
Faithful, I am glad that I have overtaken you; and
that God has so tempered our spirits, that we can
walk as Companions in this so pleasant a path.

FAITH. I had thought, dear Friend, to have had
your company quite from our Town; but you did
get the start of me, wherefore I was forced to come
thus much of the way alone.

CHR. How long did you stay in the City of
Destruction, before you set out after me on your
Pilgrimage?

FAITH. Till I could stay no longer; for there was

Their talk
about the
country
from
whence
they came

great talk presently after you were gone out, that
our City would in short time with Fire from Heaven
be burned down to the ground.

CHR. What, did your Neighbors talk so?

FAITH. Yes, 'twas for a while in everybody's
mouth.

CHR. What, and did no more of them but you
come out to escape the danger?

FAITH. Though there was, as I said, a great talk
thereabout, yet I do not think they did firmly believe it. For in the heat of the discourse, I heard
some of them deridingly speak of you and of your
desperate Journey, (for so they called this your
Pilgrimage) but I did believe, and do still, that
the end of our City will be with Fire and Brimstone from above; and therefore I have made mine
escape.

CHR. Did you hear no talk of Neighbor *Pliable?*

FAITH. Yes *Christian,* I heard that he followed
you till he came at the Slough of *Dispond,* where,
as some said, he fell in; but he would not be known
to have so done; but I am sure he was soundly
bedabbled with that kind of dirt.

CHR. And what said the Neighbors to him?

How Pli-
able was
accounted
of, when
he got
home

FAITH. He hath since his going back been had
greatly in derision, and that among all sorts of people; some do mock and despise him; and scarce will
any set him on work. He is now seven times worse
than if he had never gone out of the City.

CHR. But why should they be so set against
him, since they also despise the way that he forsook?

FAITH. Oh, they say, Hang him, he is a Turn-
coat, he was not true to his profession: I think God
has stirred up even his Enemies to hiss at him, and
make him a Proverb, because he hath forsaken the
way.

CHR. Had you no talk with him before you came
out?

FAITH. I met him once in the Streets, but he

leered away on the other side, as one ashamed of what he had done; so I spake not to him.

CHR. Well, at my first setting out, I had hopes of that man; but now I fear he will perish in the overthrow of the City, for it is happened to him according to the true Proverb, *The Dog is turned to his Vomit again, and the Sow that was washed to her wallowing in the Mire.* The dog and the sow

FAITH. They are my fears of him too; but who can hinder that which will be?

CHR. Well Neighbor *Faithful,* said *Christian,* let us leave him, and talk of things that more immediately concern ourselves. Tell me now, what you have met with in the way as you came; for I know you have met with some things, or else it may be writ for a wonder.

FAITH. I escaped the Slough that I perceive you fell into, and got up to the Gate without that danger; only I met with one whose name was *Wanton,* that had like to have done me a mischief. Faithful assaulted by Wanton

CHR. 'Twas well you escaped her Net; *Joseph* was hard put to it by her, and he escaped her as you did; but it had like to have cost him his life. But what did she do to you?

FAITH. You cannot think (but that you know something) what a flattering tongue she had; she lay at me hard to turn aside with her, promising me all manner of content.

CHR. Nay, she did not promise you the content of a good conscience.

FAITH. You know what I mean, all carnal and fleshly content.

CHR. Thank God you have escaped her: The abhorred of the Lord shall fall into her Ditch.

FAITH. Nay, I know not whether I did wholly escape her or no.

CHR. Why, I tro you did not consent to her desires.

FAITH. No, not to defile myself; for I remembered an old writing that I had seen, which saith, *Her steps take hold of Hell.* So I shut mine eyes, because I would not be bewitched with her looks: then she railed on me, and I went my way.

CHR. Did you meet with no other assault as you came?

He is assaulted by Adam the First

FAITH. When I came to the foot of the Hill called *Difficulty,* I met with a very aged Man, who asked me, *What I was, and whither bound?* I told him, That I was a Pilgrim, going to the Cœlestial City. Then said the old man, Thou lookest like an honest fellow; wilt thou be content to dwell with me for the wages that I shall give thee? Then I asked him his name, and where he dwelt? He said his name was *Adam the First, and I dwell in the Town of* Deceit. I asked him then, What was his work? and what the wages that he would give? He told me, That his work was *many delights;* and his wages, *that I should be his Heir at last.* I further asked him, What House he kept, and what other Servants he had? So he told me, That his House was maintained with all the dainties in the world; and that his Servants were those of his own begetting. Then I asked how many Children he had? He said that he had but three Daughters: *The Lust of the Flesh, The Lust of the Eyes,* and *The Pride of Life,* and that I should marry them all if I would. Then I asked him how long time he would have me live with him? And he told me, As long as he lived himself.

CHR. Well, and what conclusion came the old man and you to at last?

FAITH. Why, at first, I felt myself somewhat inclinable to go with the man, for I thought he spake very fair; but looking in his forehead, as I talked with him, I saw there written, *Put off the old man with his deeds.*

CHR. And how then?

FAITH. Then it came burning hot into my mind, whatever he said, and however he flattered, when he got me home to his House, he would sell me for a slave. So I bid him forbear to talk, for I would not come near the door of his House. Then he reviled me, and told me that he would send such a one after me, that should make my way bitter to my Soul. So I turned to go away from him; but just as I turned myself to go thence, I felt him take hold of my flesh and give me such a deadly twitch back, that I thought he had pulled part of me after himself. This made me cry, *O wretched Man!* So I went on my way up the Hill.

Now when I had got about halfway up, I looked behind me, and saw one coming after me, swift as the wind; so he overtook me just about the place where the Settle stands.

CHR. Just there, said *Christian,* did I sit down to rest me; but being overcome with sleep, I there lost this Roll out of my bosom.

FAITH. But good Brother hear me out. So soon as the man overtook me, he was but a word and a blow, for down he knocked me, and laid me for dead. But when I was a little come to myself again, I asked him wherefore he served me so? He said, Because of my secret inclining to *Adam the First:* and with that he struck me another deadly blow on the breast, and beat me down backward, so I lay at his foot as dead as before. So when I came to myself again I cried him mercy; but he said, I know not how to shew mercy; and with that knocked me down again. He had doubtless made an end of me, but that one came by, and bid him forbear.

CHR. Who was that that bid him forbear?

FAITH. I did not know him at first, but as he went by, I perceived the holes in his hands and in his side; then I concluded that he was our Lord. So I went up the Hill.

CHR. That man that overtook you was *Moses:* The temper of Moses He spareth none, neither knoweth he how to shew mercy to those that transgress his Law.

FAITH. I know it very well; it was not the first time that he has met with me. 'Twas he that came to me when I dwelt securely at home, and that told me, He would burn my house over my head if I staid there.

CHR. But did you not see the house that stood there on the top of that Hill, on the side of which *Moses* met you?

FAITH. Yes, and the Lions too, before I came at it: but for the Lions, I think they were asleep, for it was about Noon; and because I had so much of the day before me, I passed by the Porter, and came down the Hill.

CHR. He told me indeed that he saw you go by, but I wish you had called at the house, for they would have shewed you so many Rarities, that you would scarce have forgot them to the day of your death. But pray tell me, Did you meet nobody in the Valley of *Humility?*

Faithful assaulted by Discontent

FAITH. Yes, I met with one *Discontent,* who would willingly have persuaded me to go back again with him; his reason was, for that the Valley was altogether without *honour.* He told me moreover, that there to go was the way to disobey all my friends, as *Pride, Arrogancy, Self-conceit, Worldly-glory,* with others, who he knew, as he said, would be very much offended, if I made such a Fool of myself as to wade through this Valley.

CHR. Well, and how did you answer him?

Faithful's answer to Discontent

FAITH. I told him, That although all these that he had named might claim kindred of me, and that rightly, (for indeed they were my Relations *according to the flesh*) yet since I became a Pilgrim they have disowned me, as I also have rejected them; and therefore they were to me now no more than if they had never been of my lineage. I told him moreover, that as to this Valley, he had quite misrepresented the thing; *for before Honour is Humility, and a haughty spirit before a fall.* Therefore said I, I had rather go through this Valley to the honour that was so accounted by the wisest, than chuse the way which he esteemed most worthy our affections.

CHR. Met you with nothing else in that Valley?

FAITH. Yes, I met with *Shame;* but of all the men that I met with in my Pilgrimage, he I think bears the wrong name. The other would be said nay, after a little argumentation, (and somewhat else) but this boldfaced *Shame* would never have done.

CHR. Why, what did he say to you?

FAITH. What! why he objected against Religion itself; he said it was a pitiful low sneaking business for a man to mind Religion; he said that a tender conscience was an unmanly thing; and that for a man to watch over his words and ways, so as to tie up himself from that hectoring liberty that the brave spirits of the times accustom themselves unto, would make him the ridicule of the times. He objected also, that but few of the Mighty, Rich, or Wise, were ever of my opinion; nor any of them neither, before they were persuaded to be Fools, and to be of a voluntary fondness to venture the loss of all, *for nobody else knows what.* He moreover objected the base and low estate and condition of those that were chiefly the Pilgrims of the times in which they lived: also their ignorance, and want of understanding in all Natural Science. Yea, he did hold me to it at that rate also, about a great many more things than here I relate; as, that it was a *shame* to sit whining and mourning under a Sermon, and a *shame* to come sighing and groaning home; that it was a *shame* to ask my Neighbour forgiveness for petty faults, or to make restitution where I had taken from any. He said also that Religion made a man grow strange to the great, because of a few vices (which he called by finer names) and made him own and respect the base, because of the same Religious Fraternity. And is not this, said he, a *shame?*

CHR. And what did you say to him?

FAITH. Say! I could not tell what to say at first. Yea, he put me so to it, that my blood came

He is assaulted with Shame

up in my face; even this *Shame* fetched it up, and had almost beat me quite off. But at last I began to consider, *That that which is highly esteemed among Men, is had in abomination with God.* And I thought again, this *Shame* tells me what *men* are; but it tells me nothing what *God* or the *Word of God* is. And I thought moreover, that at the day of doom, we shall not be doomed to death or life according to the hectoring spirits of the world, but according to the Wisdom and Law of the Highest. Therefore thought I, what God says is best, is best, though all the men in the world are against it. Seeing then that God prefers his Religion, seeing God prefers a tender Conscience, seeing they that make themselves Fools for the Kingdom of Heaven are wisest; and that the poor man that loveth Christ is richer than the greatest man in the world that hates him; *Shame* depart, thou art an enemy to my Salvation: shall I entertain thee against my Sovereign Lord? How then shall I look him in the face at his coming? Should I now be ashamed of his ways and Servants, how can I expect the blessing? But indeed this *Shame* was a bold villain; I could scarce shake him out of my company; yea, he would be haunting of me, and continually whispering me in the ear, with some one or other of the infirmities that attend Religion; but at last I told him, 'Twas but in vain to attempt further in this business; for those things that he disdained, in those did I see most glory; and so at last I got past this importunate one. And when I had shaken him off, then I began to sing:

> The tryals that those men do meet withal,
> That are obedient to the Heavenly call,
> Are manifold, and suited to the flesh,
> And come, and come, and come again afresh;
> That now, or some time else, we by them may
> Be taken, overcome, and cast away.
> Oh, let the Pilgrims, let the Pilgrims then,
> Be vigilant, and quit themselves like men.

CHR. I am glad, my Brother, that thou didst withstand this Villain so bravely; for of all, as thou sayest, I think he has the wrong name; for he is so bold as to follow us in the Streets, and to attempt to put us to shame before all men; that is, to make us ashamed of that which is good: but if he was not himself audacious, he would never attempt to do as he does; but let us still resist him; for notwithstanding all his bravadoes, he promoteth the Fool and none else. *The Wise shall inherit glory,* said *Solomon, but shame shall be the promotion of Fools.*

FAITH. I think we must cry to Him for help against *Shame,* that would have us to be valiant for *Truth* upon the Earth.

CHR. You say true; but did you meet nobody else in that Valley?

FAITH. No not I; for I had Sun-shine all the rest of the way through that, and also through the Valley of the Shadow of Death.

CHR. 'Twas well for you; I am sure it fared far otherwise with me; I had for a long season, as soon almost as I entred into that Valley, a dreadful Combat with that foul Fiend *Apollyon;* yea, I thought verily he would have killed me, especially when he got me down and crushed me under him, as if he would have crushed me to pieces; for as he threw he, my Sword flew out of my hand; nay, he told me, *He was sure of me:* but *I cried to God, and he heard me, and delivered me out of all my troubles.* Then I entred into the Valley of the Shadow of Death, and had no light for almost half the way through it. I thought I should have been killed there, over and over; but at last day brake, and the Sun rose, and I went through that which was behind with far more ease and quiet.

Moreover, I saw in my Dream, that as they went on, *Faithful,* as he chanced to look on one side, saw a man whose name is *Talkative,* walking at a distance besides them; (for in this place there was

Talkative described

room enough for them all to walk). He was a tall
man, and something more comely at a distance than
at hand. To this man *Faithful* addressed himself
in this manner.

FAITH. Friend, Whither away? Are you going
to the Heavenly Country?

TALK. I am going to the same place.

FAITH. That is well; then I hope we may have
your good company.

TALK. With a very good will will I be your Companion.

Faithful
and Talka-
tive enter
discourse

FAITH. Come on then, and let us go together, and
let us spend our time in discoursing of things that
are profitable.

TALK. To talk of things that are good, to me is
very acceptable, with you or with any other; and I
am glad that I have met with those that incline to so

Talkative's
dislike
of bad
discourse

good a work; for to speak the truth, there are but
few that care thus to spend their time (as they are
in their travels), but chuse much rather to be speaking of things to no profit; and this hath been a trouble
to me.

FAITH. That is indeed a thing to be lamented;
for what things so worthy of the use of the tongue
and mouth of men on Earth as are the things of the
God of Heaven?

TALK. I like you wonderful well, for your saying
is full of conviction; and I will add, What thing
so pleasant, and what so profitable, as to talk of the
things of God? What things so pleasant? (that is,
if a man hath any delight in things that are wonderful) for instance, if a man doth delight to talk of
the History or the Mystery of things; or if a man
doth love to talk of Miracles, Wonders, or Signs,
where shall he find things recorded so delightful,
and so sweetly penned, as in the Holy Scripture?

FAITH. That's true; but to be profited by such
things in our talk' should be that which we
design.

TALK. That's it that I said; for to *talk* of such

things is most profitable; for by so doing, a man may get knowledge of many things; as of the vanity of earthly things, and the benefit of things above: (Thus in general) but more particularly. By this a man may learn the necessity of the New-birth, the insufficiency of our works, the need of Christ's righteousness, &c. Besides, by this a man may learn by *talk,* what it is to repent, to believe, to pray, to suffer, or the like; by this also a man may learn what are the great promises and consolations of the Gospel, to his own comfort. Further, by this a man may learn to refute false opinions, to vindicate the truth, and also to instruct the ignorant. *Talkative's fine discourse*

FAITH. All this is true, and am I glad to hear these things from you.

TALK. Alas! the want of this is the cause that so few understand the need of faith, and the necessity of a work of Grace in their Soul, in order to eternal life; but ignorantly live in the works of the Law, by which a man can by no means obtain the Kingdom of Heaven.

FAITH. But by your leave, Heavenly knowledge of these is the gift of God; no man attaineth to them by human industry, or only by the talk of them.

TALK. All this I know very well; for a man can receive nothing, except it be given him from Heaven: all is of Grace, not of Works: I could give you a hundred Scriptures for the confirmation of this. *O brave Talkative*

FAITH. Well then, said *Faithful,* what is that one thing that we shall at this time found our discourse upon?

TALK. What you will. I will talk of things Heavenly, or things Earthly; things Moral, or things Evangelical; things Sacred or things Prophane; things past or things to come; things foreign or things at home; things more Essential, or things Circumstantial; provided that all be done to our profit. *O brave Talkative*

FAITH. Now did *Faithful* begin to wonder; and

Faithful
beguiled
by Talka-
tive

Christian
makes a
discovery
of Talka-
tive, telling
Faithful
who he
was

stepping to *Christian* (for he walked all this while by himself) he said to him, (but softly) What a brave Companion have we got! Surely this man will make a very excellent Pilgrim.

CHR. At this *Christian* modestly smiled, and said, This man with whom you are so taken, will beguile with this tongue of his, twenty of them that know him not.

FAITH. Do you know him then?

CHR. Know him! Yes, better than he knows himself.

FAITH. Pray what is he?

CHR. His name is *Talkative;* he dwelleth in our Town: I wonder that you should be a stranger to him, only I consider that our Town is large.

FAITH. Whose Son is he? And whereabout doth he dwell?

CHR. He is the son of one *Say-well;* he dwelt in *Prating Row;* and is known of all that are acquainted with him, by the name of *Talkative* in *Prating Row;* and notwithstanding his fine tongue, he is but a sorry fellow.

FAITH. Well, he seems to be a very pretty man.

CHR. That is, to them who have thorough acquaintance with him, for he is best abroad, near home he is ugly enough: Your saying that he is a *pretty man,* brings to my mind what I have observed in the work of the Painter, whose Pictures shew best at a distance, but very near, more unpleasing.

FAITH. But I am ready to think you do but jest, because you smiled.

CHR. God forbid that I should jest (though I smiled) in this matter, or that I should accuse any falsely: I will give you a further discovery of him: This man is for any company, and for any talk; as he talketh now with you, so he will talk when he is on the Ale-bench; and the more drink he hath in his crown, the more of these things he hath in his mouth; Religion hath no place in his heart, or house, or conversation; all he hath lieth in his tongue, and his Religion is to make a noise therewith.

FAITH. Say you so! Then am I in this man greatly deceived.

CHR. Deceived! you may be sure of it; remember the Proverb, *They say and do not: but the Kingdom of God is not in word, but in power.* *He talketh* of Prayer, of Repentance, of Faith, and of the New-birth; but he knows but only to *talk* of them. I have been in his Family, and have observed him both at home and abroad; and I know what I say of him is the truth. His house is as empty of Religion as the white of an Egg is of savour. There is there neither Prayer, nor sign of Repentance for sin; yea, the brute in his kind serves God better than he. He is the very stain, reproach, and shame of Religion, to all that know him; it can hardly have a good word in all that end of the Town where he dwells through him. Thus say the common people that know him, *A Saint abroad, and a Devil at home*. His poor Family finds it so; he is such a churl, such a railer at, and so unreasonable with his Servants, that they neither know how to do for, or speak to him. Men that have any dealings with him, say 'tis better to deal with a *Turk* than with him; for fairer dealing they shall have at their hands. This *Talkative* (if it be possible) will go beyond them, defraud, beguile, and over-reach them. Besides he brings up his Sons to follow his steps; and if he findeth in any of them *a foolish timorousness,* (for so he calls the first appearance of a tender conscience) he calls them fools and blockheads and by no means will imploy them in much, or speak to their commendations before others. For my part I am of opinion that he has by his wicked life caused many to stumble and fall; and will be, if God prevent not, the ruine of many more.

FAITH. Well, my Brother, I am bound to be-

Talkative talks, but does not

His house is empty of religion

He is a stain to religion

The proverb that goes of him

Men shun to deal with him

lieve you; not only because you say you know him, but also because like a Christian, you make your reports of men, For I cannot think that you speak these things of ill will, but because it is even so as you say.

CHR. Had I known him no more than you, I might perhaps have thought of him as at the first you did; yea, had he received this report at their hands only that are enemies to Religion, I should have thought it had been a slander: (a lot that often falls from bad men's mouths upon good men's names and professions;) but all these things, yea and a great many more as bad, of my own knowledge I can prove him guilty of. Besides, good men are ashamed of him; they can neither call him *Brother,* nor *Friend;* the very naming of him among them, makes them blush, if they know him.

FAITH. Well, I see that *saying* and *doing* are two things, and hereafter I shall better observe this distinction.

The carcass of religion

CHR. They are two things indeed, and are as diverse as are the Soul and the Body; for as the Body without the Soul is but a dead Carcass, so *Saying,* if it be alone, is but a dead Carcass also. The Soul of Religion is the practick part: *Pure Religion and undefiled, before God and the Father, is this, To visit the fatherless and widows in their affliction, and to keep himself unspotted from the world.* This *Talkative* is not aware of; he thinks that *hearing* and *saying* will make a good Christian, and thus he deceiveth his own soul. *Hearing* is but as the sowing of the Seed; *talking* is not sufficient to prove that fruit is indeed in the heart and life; and let us assure ourselves, that at the day of Doom men shall be judged according to their fruits. It will not be said then, *Did you believe?* but Were you *Doers,* or *Talkers* only? and accordingly shall they be judged. The end of the world is compared to our Harvest, and you know men at Harvest regard nothing but fruit. Not that anything can be accepted that is not of *Faith;* but I speak this to shew you how insignificant the profession of *Talkative* will be at that day.

FAITH. This brings to my mind that of *Moses,* by which he describeth the beast that is clean. He is such an one that parteth the Hoof and cheweth the Cud: not that parteth the Hoof only, or that cheweth the Cud only. The Hare cheweth the Cud, but yet is unclean, because he parteth not the Hoof. And this truly resembleth *Talkative;* he cheweth the Cud, he seeketh knowledge, he cheweth upon the Word; but he divideth not the Hoof, he parteth not with the way of sinners; but as the Hare, he retaineth the foot of a Dog or Bear, and therefore is unclean. *Faithful convinced of the badness of Talkative*

CHR. You have spoken, for ought I know, the true Gospel sense of those Texts: And I will add another thing; *Paul* calleth some men, yea and those great Talkers too, *sounding Brass and tinkling Cymbals;* that is, as he expounds them in another place, *Things without life, giving sound.* Things without life, that is, without the true Faith and Grace of the Gospel; and consequently things that shall never be placed in the Kingdom of Heaven among those that are the Children of life; though their *sound,* by their *talk,* be as if it were the tongue or voice of an Angel. *Talkative like to things that sound without life*

FAITH. Well, I was not so fond of his company at first, but I am as sick of it now. What shall we do to be rid of him?

CHR. Take my advice, and do as I bid you, and you shall find that he will soon be sick of your company too, except God shall touch his heart, and turn it.

FAITH. What would you have me to do?

CHR. Why, *go* to him, and enter into some serious discourse about *the power of Religion;* and ask him plainly (when he has approved of it, for that he will) whether this thing be set up in his Heart, House, or Conversation.

FAITH. Then *Faithful* stepped forward again,

and said to *Talkative, Come, what chear? How
is it now?*

TALK. Thank you, well. I thought we should have
had a great deal of talk by this time.

FAITH. Well, if you will, we will fall to it now;
and since you left it with me to state the question,
let it be this; How doth the saving Grace of God
discover itself, when it is in the heart of man?

Talkative's
false dis-
covery of
a work of
grace

TALK. I perceive then that our talk must be *about
the power of things:* Well, 'tis a very good question,
and I shall be willing to answer you. And take my
answer in brief thus: *First,* Where the Grace of
God is in the heart, it causeth there a great out-cry
against sin. *Secondly—*

FAITH. Nay hold, let us consider of one at once:
I think you should rather say, It shews itself by
inclining the Soul to abhor its sin.

TALK. Why, what difference is there between crying out against, and abhorring of sin?

To cry out
against sin

FAITH. Oh! a great deal; a man may cry out
against sin, or policy; but he cannot abhor it, but
by vertue of a godly antipathy against it: I have
heard many cry out against sin in the Pulpit, who
yet can abide it well enough in the heart, house, and
conversation. *Joseph's* Mistress cried out with a
loud voice, as if she had been very holy; but she
would willingly, notwithstanding that, have committed uncleanness with him. Some cry out against
sin, even as the Mother cries out against her Child
in her lap, when she calleth it slut and naughty girl,
and then falls to hugging and kissing it.

TALK. You lie at the catch, I perceive.

FAITH. No, not I; I am only for setting things
right. But what is the second thing whereby you
would prove a discovery of a work of Grace in the
heart?

TALK. Great knowledge of *Gospel Mysteries.*

Great
knowledge
no sign of
grace

FAITH. This sign should have been first; but first
or last, it is also false; for knowledge, great knowledge may be obtained in the mysteries of the Gospel,

and yet no work of Grace in the Soul. Yea, if a
man have all knowledge, he may yet be nothing;
and so consequently be no child of God. When
Christ said, *Do you know all these things?* and the   Knowledge
Disciples had answered, Yes; he addeth *Blessed are*   and
ye if ye do them. He doth not lay the blessing in   knowledge
the knowing of them, but in the doing of them.
For there is a knowledge that is not attended with
doing; *He that knoweth his Master's will, and doth*
it not. A man may know like an Angel, and yet
be no Christian, therefore your sign of it is not true.
Indeed to *know* is a thing that pleaseth Talkers
and Boasters; but to *do* is that which pleaseth God.
Not that the heart can be good without knowledge;
for without that the heart is naught. There is therefore knowledge and knowledge. Knowledge that
resteth in the bare speculation of things, and knowledge that is accompanied with the Grace of faith
and love, which puts a man upon doing even the
will of God from the heart; the first of these will   True
serve the Talker; but without the other the true   knowledge
Christian is not content. *Give me understanding,*   attended
and I shall keep thy Law; yea I shall observe it with   with
my whole heart.   endeavours

TALK. You lie at the catch again, this is not for
edification.

FAITH. Well, if you please propound another sign
how this work of Grace discovereth itself where
it is.

TALK. Not I, for I see we shall not agree.

FAITH. Well, if you will not, will you give me
leave to do it?

TALK. You may use your liberty.

FAITH. A work of Grace in the soul discovereth   One good
itself, either to him that hath it, or to standers-by.   sign of
  grace

To him that hath it thus: It gives him conviction
of sin, especially of the defilement of his nature and
the sin of unbelief (for the sake of which he is sure
to be damned, if he findeth not mercy at God's hand
by faith in Jesus Christ). This sight and sense of

things worketh in him sorrow and shame for sin;
he findeth moreover revealed in him the Saviour of
the world, and the absolute necessity of closing with
him for life, at the which he findeth hungrings and
thirstings after him, to which hungrings, &c. the
promise is made. Now according to the strength
or weakness of his Faith in his Saviour, so is his
joy and peace, so is his love to holiness, so are his
desires to know him more, and also to serve him in
this World. But though I say it discovereth itself
thus unto him, yet it is but seldom that he is able
to conclude that this is a work of Grace; because his
corruptions now, and his abused reason, make his
mind to misjudge in this matter; therefore in him
that hath this work, there is required a very sound
Judgment before he can with steadiness conclude
that this is a work of Grace.

To others it is thus discovered:

1. By an experimental confession of his Faith in
Christ.

2. By a life answerable to that confession, to wit,
a life of holiness, heart-holiness, family-holiness,
(if he hath a Family) and by conversation-holiness
in the World; which in the general teacheth him,
inwardly to abhor his sin, and himself for that in
secret, to suppress it in his Family, and to promote
holiness in the World; not by talk only, as an Hypocrite or Talkative person may do, but by a practical
subjection, in Faith and Love, to the power of the
Word: And now Sir, as to this brief description
of the work of Grace, and also the discovery of it,
if you have ought to object, object; if not, then give
me leave to propound to you a second question.

TALK. Nay my part is not now to object, but to
hear, let me therefore have your second question.

FAITH. It is this. Do you experience the first
part of this description of it? and doth your life
and conversation testify the same? or standeth your
Religion in *Word* or in *Tongue,* and not in *Deed*
and *Truth?* Pray, if you incline to answer me in

*Another
good sign
of grace*

this, say no more than you know the God above will say *Amen* to; and also nothing but what your conscience can justify you in; for, *not he that commendeth himself is approved, but whom the Lord commendeth*. Besides, to say I am thus and thus, when my Conversation and all my Neighbors tell me I lye, is great wickedness.

TALK. Then *Talkative* at first began to blush, but recovering himself, thus he replied, You come now to Experience, to Conscience, and God; and to appeal to him for justification of what is spoken: This kind of discourse I did not expect; nor am I disposed to give an answer to such questions, because I count not myself bound thereto, unless you take upon you to be a *Catechizer,* and, though you should so do, yet I may refuse to make you my Judge. But I pray will you tell me why you ask me such questions? *(margin: Talkative not pleased with Faithful's question)*

FAITH. Because I saw you forward to talk, and because I knew not that you had ought else but notion. Besides, to tell you all the truth, I have heard of you that you are a man whose Religion lies in talk, and that your conversation gives this your Mouth-profession the lye. They say you are a spot among Christians, and that religion fareth the worse for your ungodly Conversation, that some have already stumbled at your wicked ways, and that more are in danger of being destroyed thereby; your Religion, and an Ale-house, and Covetousness, and Uncleanness, and Swearing and Lying, and vain Company-keeping, &c. will stand together. The Proverb is true of you which is said of a Whore, to wit, That she is a shame to all Women; so you are a shame to all Professors. *(margin: The reasons why Faithful put to him that question)* *(margin: Faithful's plain dealing with Talkative)*

TALK. Since you are ready to take up reports, and to judge so rashly as you do, I cannot but conclude you are some peevish or melancholy man, not fit to be discoursed with; and so adieu. *(margin: Talkative flings away from Faithful)*

CHR. Then came up *Christian,* and said to his Brother, I told you how it would happen; your *(margin: A good riddance)*

words and his lusts could not agree; he had rather
leave your company than reform his life. But he
is gone, as I said; let him go, the loss is no man's
but his own, he has saved us the trouble of going
from him; for he continuing (as I suppose he will
do) as he is, he would have been but a blot in our
company: besides, the Apostle says, *From such
withdraw thyself*.

FAITH. But I am glad we had this little discourse with him, it may happen that he will think
of it again; however, I have dealt plainly with him,
and so am clear of his blood, if he perisheth.

CHR. You did well to talk so plainly to him as
you did. There is but little of this faithful dealing
with men now a days, and that makes Religion to
stink so in the nostrils of many, as it doth; for
they are these Talkative Fools whose Religion is
only in word, and are debauched and vain in their
Conversation, that (being so much admitted into
the fellowship of the godly) do puzzle the World,
blemish Christianity, and grieve the sincere. I
wish that all men would deal with such as you
have done: then should they either be made more
conformable to Religion, or the company of Saints
would be too hot for them. Then did *Faithful* say,

> How *Talkative* at first lifts up his Plumes!
> How bravely doth he speak! How he presumes
> To drive all before him! But so soon
> As *Faithful* talks of *Heart-work*, like the Moon
> That's past the full, into the wane he goes.
> And so will all, but he that *Heart-work* knows.

Thus they went on talking of what they had seen
by the way, and so made that way easy, which
would otherwise, no doubt, have been tedious to
them; for now they went through a Wilderness.
Evangelist overtakes them again Now when they were got almost quite out of this
Wilderness, *Faithful* chanced to cast his eye back,
and espied one coming after them, and he knew
him. Oh! said *Faithful* to his Brother, Who comes
yonder? Then *Christian* looked, and said, It is my

good friend *Evangelist*. Ay, and my good friend too, said *Faithful*, for 'twas he that set me the way to the Gate. Now was *Evangelist* come up unto them, and thus saluted them:

EVAN. Peace be with you, dearly beloved, and peace be to your helpers.

CHR. Welcome, welcome, my good *Evangelist*, the sight of thy countenance brings to my remembrance thy antient kindness and unwearied laboring for my eternal good.

They are glad at the sight of him

FAITH. And a thousand times welcome, said good *Faithful:* Thy company, O sweet *Evangelist*, how desirable is it to us poor Pilgrims!

EVAN. Then said *Evangelist*, How hath it fared with you my friends, since the time of our last parting? What have you met with, and how have you behaved yourselves?

Then *Christian* and *Faithful* told him of all things that had happened to them in the way; and how, and with what difficulty, they had arrived to that place.

EVAN. Right glad am I, said *Evangelist*, not that you have met with trials, but that you have been victors; and that you have (notwithstanding many weaknesses) continued in the way to this very day.

His exhortation to them

I say, right glad am I of this thing, and that for mine own sake and yours: I have sowed, and you have reaped; and the day is coming, when both he that sowed and they that reaped shall rejoice together; that is, if you hold out: for in due time ye shall reap, if you faint not. The Crown is before you, and it is an incorruptible one; so run that you may obtain it. Some there be that set out for this Crown, and after they have gone far for it, another comes in, and takes it from them; hold fast therefore that you have, let no man take your Crown. You are not yet out of the gun-shot of the Devil; you have not resisted unto blood, striving against sin; let the Kingdom be always before you, and believe stedfastly concerning things that are invisible. Let nothing that is on this side the other world get within you; and above all, look well to your own hearts, and to the lusts thereof, for they are deceitful above all things, and desperately wicked; set your faces like a flint; you have all power in Heaven and Earth on your side.

They do thank him for his exhortation

CHR. Then *Christian* thanked him for his exhortation, but told him withal, that they would have him speak farther to them for their help the rest of the way, and the rather, for that they well knew that he was a Prophet, and could tell them of things that might happen unto them, and also how they might resist and overcome them. To which request *Faithful* also consented. So *Evangelist* began as followeth:

He predicteth what troubles they shall meet with in Vanity Fair, and encourageth them to steadfastness

EVAN. My Sons, you have heard, in the words of the truth of the Gospel, that you must through many tribulations enter into the Kingdom of Heaven. And again, that in every City bonds and afflictions abide in you; and therefore you cannot expect that you should go long on your Pilgrimage without them, in some sort or other. You have found something of the truth of these testimonies upon you already, and more will immediately follow; for now, as you see, you are almost out of this Wilderness, and therefore you will soon come into a Town that you will by and by see before you; and in that Town you will be hardly beset with enemies, who will strain hard but they will kill you; and be ye sure that one or both of you must seal the testimony which you hold, with blood; but be you faithful unto death, and the King will give you a Crown of life. He that shall die there, although his death

He whose lot it will be there to suffer, will have the better of his brother

will be unnatural, and his pain perhaps great, he will yet have the better of his fellow; not only because he will be arrived at the Cœlestial City soonest, but because he will escape many miseries that the other will meet with in the rest of his Journey. But when you are come to the Town, and shall find fulfilled what I have here related, then remember your

friend, and quit yourselves like men, and commit the
keeping of your souls to your God in well-doing, as
unto a faithful Creator.

Then I saw in my Dream, that when they were
got out of the Wilderness, they presently saw a
Town before them, and the name of that Town is
Vanity; and at the Town there is a Fair kept, called
Vanity Fair: it is kept all the year long; it beareth
the name of *Vanity Fair,* because the Town where
'tis kept *is lighter than Vanity;* and also because all
that is there sold, or that cometh thither, is *Vanity.*
As is the saying of the wise, *All that cometh is
Vanity.*

This Fair is no new-erected business, but a thing
of antient standing; I will shew you the original
of it.

Almost five thousand years agone, there were The an-
Pilgrims walking to the Cœlestial City, as these two tiquity of
honest persons are; and *Beelzebub, Apollyon,* and this fair
Legion, with their Companions, perceiving by the
path that the Pilgrims made, that their way to the
City lay through this Town of *Vanity,* they con-
trived here to set up a Fair; a Fair wherein should
be sold *all sorts of Vanity,* and that it should last all
the year long: therefore at this Fair are all such
Merchandize sold, as Houses, Lands, Trades, Places,
Honours, Preferments, Titles, Countries, Kingdoms,
Lusts, Pleasures, and Delights of all sorts, as The mer-
Whores, Bawds, Wives, Husbands, Children, Mas- chandise of
ters, Servants, Lives, Blood, Bodies, Souls, Silver, this fair
Gold, Pearls, Precious Stones, and what not?

And moreover, at this Fair there is at all times to
be seen Jugglings, Cheats, Games, Plays, Fools,
Apes, Knaves, and Rogues, and that of every kind.

Here are to be seen too, and that for nothing,
Thefts, Murders, Adulteries, false-swearers, and
that of a blood-red colour.

And as in other Fairs of less moment, there The streets
are the several Rows and Streets under their proper of this fair
names, where such and such Wares are vended; so

here likewise you have the proper places, Rows, Streets, (*viz.* Countries and Kingdoms) where the Wares of this Fair are soonest to be found: Here is the *Britain* Row, the *French* Row, the *Italian* Row, the *Spanish* Row, the *German* Row, where several sorts of Vanities are to be sold. But as in other Fairs, some one commodity is as the chief of all the Fair, so the ware of *Rome* and her Merchandize is greatly promoted in this Fair; only our *English* nation, with some others, have taken a dislike thereat.

Christ went through this fair

Now, as I said, the way to the Cœlestial City lies just through this Town where this lusty Fair is kept; and he that will go to the City, and yet not go through this Town, must needs *go out of the world.* The Prince of Princes himself, when here, went through this Town to his own Country, and that upon a *Fair-day* too; yea, and as I think, it was *Beelzebub,* the chief Lord of this Fair, that invited him to buy of his Vanities: yea, would have made him Lord of the Fair, would he but have done him reverence as he went through the Town. Yea, because he was such a person of honour, *Beelzebub* had him from Street to Street, and shewed him all the Kingdoms of the World in a little time, that he might, (if possible) allure that Blessed One to cheapen and buy some of his Vanities; but he had no mind to the Merchandize, and therefore left the

Christ bought nothing in this fair

Town, without laying out so much as one Farthing upon these Vanities. This Fair therefore is an antient thing, of long standing, and a very great Fair.

The Pilgrims enter the fair

Now these Pilgrims, as I said, must needs go through this Fair. Well, so they did; but behold, even as they entered into the Fair, all the people

The fair in a hubbub about them

in the Fair were moved, and the Town itself as it were in a hubbub about them; and that for several reasons: for

First, The Pilgrims were cloathed with such kind of Raiment as was diverse from the Raiment of any that traded in that Fair. The people there- *The first* fore of the Fair made a great gazing upon them: *cause of* some said they were Fools, some they were Bed- *the hubbub* lams, and some they are Outlandishmen.

Secondly, And as they wondered at their Apparel, *Second* so they did likewise at their Speech; for few could *cause of* understand what they said: they naturally spoke the *the hubbub* language of *Canaan,* but they that kept the Fair were the men of this World; so that, from one end of the Fair to the other, they seemed Barbarians each to the other.

Thirdly, But that which did not a little amuse *Third* the Merchandizers was, that these Pilgrims set very *cause of* light by all their Wares, they cared not so much as *the hubbub* to look upon them; and if they called upon them to buy, they would put their fingers in their ears, and cry, *Turn away mine eyes from beholding Vanity,* and look upwards, signifying that their trade and traffick was in Heaven.

One chanced mockingly, beholding the carriages *Fourth* of the men, to say unto them, What will ye buy? *cause of* But they, looking gravely upon him, answered, *We* *the hubbub* *buy the Truth.* At that there was an occasion taken to despise the men the more; some mocking, some *They are* taunting, some speaking reproachfully, and some *mocked* calling upon others to smite them. At last things came to a hubbub and great stir in the Fair, inso- *The fair in* much that all order was confounded. Now was *a hubbub* word presently brought to the Great One of the Fair, who quickly came down and deputed some of his most trusty friends to take those men into examination, about whom the Fair was almost over- turned. So the men were brought to examination; *They are* and they that sat upon them, asked them whence *examined* they came, whither they went, and what they did there in such an unusual Garb? The men told them that they were Pilgrims and Strangers in the World, *They tell* and that they were going to their own Country, *who they* which was the Heavenly *Jerusalem;* and that they *are, and* had given no occasion to the men of the Town, nor *whence* *they came*

yet to the Merchandizers, thus to abuse them, and
to let them in their Journey, except it was for that,
when one asked them what they would buy, they
said they would *buy the Truth*. But they that were
They are
not
believed
appointed to examine them did not believe them to
be any other than Bedlams and Mad, or else such
as came to put all things into a confusion in the
Fair. Therefore they took them and beat them, and
They are
put in
the cage
besmeared them with dirt, and then put them into
the Cage, that they might be made a spectacle to
all the men of the Fair.

> Behold Vanity Fair, the Pilgrims there
> Are chained and stand beside:
> Even so it was our Lord passed here,
> And on Mount Calvary died.

There therefore they lay for some time, and
were made the objects of any man's sport, or
malice, or revenge, the Great One of the Fair
laughing still at all that befell them. But the
men being patient, and not rendring railing for
Their be-
haviour in
the cage
railing, but contrariwise blessing, and giving good
words for bad, and kindness for injuries done, some
men in the Fair that were more observing, and less
prejudiced than the rest, began to check and blame
the baser sort for their continual abuses done by
The men
of the fair
do fall out
among
themselves
about these
two men
them to the men; they therefore in angry manner
let fly at them again, counting them as bad as the
men in the Cage, and telling them that they seemed
confederates, and should be made partakers of their
misfortunes. The other replied, that for ought they
could see, the men were quiet, and sober, and intended nobody any harm; and that there were many
that traded in their Fair that were more worthy to
be put into the Cage yea, and Pillory too, than were
the men that they had abused. Thus, after divers
words had passed on both sides, (the men behaving
themselves all the while very wisely and soberly
before them) they fell to some blows among themselves, and did harm to one another. Then were

these two poor men brought before their examiners
again, and there charged as being guilty of the late
hubbub that had been in the Fair. So they beat
them pitifully and hanged irons upon them, and led
them in chains up and down the Fair, for an example and a terror to others, lest any should speak
in their behalf, or join themselves unto them. But
Christian and *Faithful* behaved themselves yet more
wisely, and received the ignominy and shame that
was cast upon them, with so much meekness and
patience, that it won to their side (though but few
in comparison of the rest) several of the men in the
Fair. This put the other party yet into a greater
rage, insomuch that they concluded the death of
these two men. Wherefore they threatened, that the
Cage, nor irons should serve their turn, but that they
should die, for the abuse they had done, and for de-
luding the men of the Fair.

They are made the authors of this disturbance

They are led up and down the fair in chains, for a terror to others

Some of the men of the fair won to them

Their adversaries resolve to kill them

Then were they re-manded to the Cage again,
until further order should be taken with them. So
they put them in, and made their feet fast in the
Stocks.

Here also they called again to mind what they
had heard from their faithful friend *Evangelist*, and
were the more confirmed in their way and sufferings, by what he told them would happen to them.
They also now comforted each other, that whose lot
it was to suffer, even he should have the best on't;
therefore each man secretly wished that he might
have that preferment: but committing themselves to
the All-wise dispose of Him that ruleth all things,
with much content they abode in the condition in
which they were, until they should be otherwise disposed of.

Then a convenient time being appointed, they
brought them forth to their Tryal, in order to their
condemnation. When the time was come, they were
brought before their enemies, and arraigned. The
Judge's name was Lord *Hategood*. Their Indictment was one and the same in substance, though

They are again put into the cage, and after brought to trial

somewhat varying in form, the contents whereof
was this:

Their
indictment

*That they were enemies to and disturbers of their
Trade; that they had made Commotions and Divisions
in the Town, and had won a party to their own most
dangerous Opinions in contempt of the Law of their
Prince.*

> Now *Faithful* play the Man, speak for thy God:
> Fear not the wicked's malice, nor their rod:
> Speak boldly man, the Truth is on thy side;
> Die for it, and to Life in triumph ride.

Faithful's
answer for
himself

Then *Faithful* began to answer, that he had only
set himself against that which had set itself against
Him that is higher than the highest. And said he,
as for Disturbance, I make none, being myself a
man of Peace; the parties that were won to us,
were won by beholding our Truth and Innocence,
and they are only turned from the worse to the
better. And as to the King you talk of, since he
is *Beelzebub,* the enemy of Our Lord, I defy him
and all his Angels.

Then Proclamation was made, that they that had
ought to say for their Lord the King against the
Prisoner at the Bar, should forthwith appear and
give in their evidence. So there came in three wit-
nesses, to wit, *Envy, Superstition,* and *Pickthank.*
They were then asked if they knew the Prisoner at
the Bar; and what they had to say for their Lord
the King against him.

Envy
begins

Then stood forth *Envy,* and said to this effect:
My lord, I have known this man a long time, and
will attest upon my Oath before this honourable
Bench, that he is—

JUDGE. Hold! Give him his Oath.

So they sware him. Then he said, My Lord, this
man, notwithstanding his plausible name, is one of
the vilest men in our Country. He neither re-
gardeth Prince nor People, Law nor Custom; but
doth all that he can to possess all men with certain

of his disloyal notions, which he in the general calls Principles of Faith and Holiness. And in particular, I heard him once myself affirm *That Christianity and the Customs of our Town of* Vanity *were diametrically opposite, and could not be reconciled.* By which saying, my Lord, he doth at once not only condemn all our laudable doings, but us in the doing of them.

JUDGE. Then did the Judge say to him, Hast thou any more to say?

ENVY. My Lord, I could say much more, only I would not be tedious to the Court. Yet if need be, when the other Gentlemen have given in their Evidence, rather than anything shall be wanting that will dispatch him, I will enlarge my Testimony against him. So he was bid stand by.

Then they called *Superstition,* and bid him look upon the Prisoner. They also asked, what he could say for their Lord the King against him? Then they sware him; so he began:

SUPER. My Lord, I have no great acquaintance with this man, nor do I desire to have further knowledge of him; however, this I know, that he is a very pestilent fellow, from some discourse that the other day I had with him in this Town; for then talking with him, I heard him say, That our Religion was naught, and such by which a man could by no means please God. Which sayings of his, my Lord, your Lordship very well knows, what necessarily thence will follow, to wit, That we still do worship in vain, are yet in our sins, and finally shall be damned; and this is that which I have to say. *Superstition follows*

Then was *Pickthank* sworn, and bid say what he knew, in behalf of their Lord the King, against the Prisoner at the Bar.

PICK. My Lord, and you Gentlemen all, This fellow I have known of a long time, and have heard him speak things that ought not to be spoke; for he hath railed on our noble Prince *Beelzebub,* and hath spoken contemptibly of his honourable *Pickthank's testimony*

Friends, whose names are the Lord *Old Man*, the Lord *Carnal Delight*, the Lord *Luxurious*, the Lord *Desire of Vain Glory*, my old Lord *Lechery*, Sir *Having Greedy*, with all the rest of our Nobility; and he hath said moreover, That if all men were of his mind, if possible, there is not one of these Noble men should have any longer a being in this Town; besides, he hath not been afraid to rail on you, my Lord, who are now appointed to be his Judge, calling you an ungodly villain, with many other suchlike vilifying terms, with which he hath bespattered most of the Gentry of our Town.

When this *Pickthank* had told his tale, the Judge directed his speech to the Prisoner at the Bar, saying, Thou Runagate, Heretick, and Traitor, hast thou heard what these honest Gentlemen have witnessed against thee?

FAITH. May I speak a few words in my own defence?

JUDGE. Sirrah, sirrah, thou deservedst to live no longer, but to be slain immediately upon the place; yet that all men may see our gentleness towards thee, let us see what thou hast to say.

FAITH. 1. I say then, in answer to what Mr. *Envy* hath spoken, I never said ought but this, *That what Rule, or Laws, or Custom, or People, were flat against the Word of God, are diametrically opposite to Christianity.* If I have said amiss in this, convince me of my error, and I am ready here before you to make my recantation.

2. As to the second, to wit, Mr. *Superstition*, and his charge against me, I said only this, *That in the worship of God there is required a Divine Faith; but there can be no Divine Faith without a Divine Revelation of the will of God: therefore whatever is thrust into the Worship of God that is not agreeable to Divine Revelation, cannot be done but by a human faith, which faith will not be profit to Eternal Life.*

3. As to what Mr. *Pickthank* hath said, I say,

(avoiding terms, as that I am said to rail, and the like) that the Prince of this Town, with all the rabblement his attendants, by this Gentleman named, are more fit for a being in Hell, than in this Town and Country: *and so, the Lord have mercy upon me.*

Then the Judge called to the Jury (who all this while stood by, to hear and observe) Gentlemen of the Jury, you see this man about whom so great an uproar hath been made in this Town: you have also heard what these worthy Gentlemen have witnessed against him: also you have heard his reply and confession: It lieth now in your breasts to hang him, or save his life; but yet I think meet to instruct you into our Law. *The Judge's speech to the jury*

There was an Act made in the days of *Pharaoh* the Great, Servant to our Prince, that lest those of a contrary Religion should multiply and grow too strong for him, their Males should be thrown into the river. There was also an Act made in the days of *Nebuchadnezzar* the Great, another of his Servants, that whoever would not fall down and worship his Golden Image, should be thrown into a Fiery Furnace. There was also an Act made in the days of *Darius,* that whoso, for some time, called upon any God but him, should be cast into the Lions' Den. Now the substance of these Laws this Rebel has broken, not only in thought (which is not to be borne) but also in word and deed; which must therefore needs be intolerable.

For that of *Pharaoh,* his Law was made upon a supposition, to prevent mischief, no Crime being yet apparent; but here is a Crime apparent. For the second and third, you see he disputeth against our Religion; and for the Treason he hath confessed, he deserveth to die the death.

Then went the Jury out, whose names were, Mr *Blind-man,* Mr *No-good,* Mr *Malice,* Mr *Love-lust,* Mr *Live-loose,* Mr *Heady,* Mr *High-mind,* Mr *Enmity,* Mr *Lyar,* Mr *Cruelty,* Mr *Hate-light,* and *The jury, and their names*

Mr *Implacable;* who every one gave in his private
Verdict against him among themselves, and afterwards unanimously concluded to bring him in guilty
before the Judge. And first among themselves, Mr
Blind-man the Foreman, said, *I see clearly that this
man is an Heretick.* Then said Mr *No-good, Away
with such a fellow from the earth. Ay,* said Mr
Malice, for I hate the very looks of him. Then said
Mr *Love-lust, I could never endure him. Nor I,*
said Mr *Live-loose, for he would always be con-
demning my way. Hang him, hang him,* said Mr
Heady. A sorry Scrub, said Mr *High-mind. My
heart riseth against him,* said Mr *Enmity. He is a
Rogue,* said Mr *Lyar. Hanging is too good for
him,* said Mr *Cruelty. Let us dispatch him out of
the way,* said Mr *Hate-light.* Then said Mr *Implacable, Might I have all the world given me, I
could not be reconciled to him; therefore let us
forthwith bring him in guilty of death.* And so they
did; therefore he was presently condemned to be
had from the place where he was, to the place from
whence he came, and there to be put to the most
cruel death that could be invented.

They therefore brought him out, to do with him
according to their Law; and first they Scourged
him, then they Buffeted him, then they Lanced his
flesh with Knives; after that they Stoned him with
stones, then pricked him with their Swords; and
last of all they burned him to ashes at the Stake.
Thus came *Faithful* to his end.

Now I saw that there stood behind the multitude
a Chariot and a couple of Horses, waiting for *Faithful,* who (so soon as his adversaries had dispatched
him) was taken up into it, and straitway was carried
up through the Clouds, with sound of Trumpet, the
nearest way to the Cœlestial Gate.

> Brave *Faithful,* bravely done in word and deed;
> Judge, Witnesses, and Jury have, instead
> Of overcoming thee, but shewn their rage:
> When they are Dead, thou'lt Live from age to age.

Marginal notes:

Every one's private verdict

They conclude to bring him in guilty of death

The cruel death of Faithful

A chariot and horses wait to take away Faithful

But as for *Christian,* he had some respite, and Christian is still alive was remanded back to prison; so he there remained for a space: But he that over-rules all things, having the power of their rage in his own hand, so wrought it about, that *Christian* for that time escaped them, and went his way. And as he went he sang, saying,

The Song that Christian made of Faithful after his death

Well *Faithful,* thou hast faithfully profest
Unto thy Lord; with whom thou shalt be blest,
When *faithless* ones, with all their vain delights,
Are crying out under their hellish plights:
Sing, *Faithful,* sing, and let thy name survive;
For though they kill'd thee, thou art yet alive.

Now I saw in my Dream, that *Christian* went not Christian has another companion forth alone, for there was one whose name was *Hopeful,* (being made so by the beholding of *Christian* and *Faithful* in their words and behaviour, in their sufferings at the Fair) who joined himself unto him, and entring into a brotherly covenant, told him that he would be his Companion. Thus one died to make Testimony to the Truth, and another rises out of his ashes to be a Companion with There are more of the men of the Fair will follow *Christian* in his Pilgrimage. This *Hopeful* also told *Christian,* that there were many more of the men in the Fair that would take their time and follow after.

So I saw that quickly after they were got out of They overtake By-ends the Fair, they overtook one that was going before them, whose name was *By-ends:* so they said to him, What Country-man, Sir? and how far go you this way? He told them that he came from the Town of *Fair-speech,* and he was going to the Cœlestial City, (but told them not his name.)

From *Fair-speech,* said *Christian.* Is there any good that lives there?

BY-ENDS. Yes, said *By-ends,* I hope.

CHR. Pray Sir, what may I call you?

BY-ENDS. I am a Stranger to you, and you to me: By-ends loath to tell his name if you be going this way, I shall be glad of your company; if not, I must be content.

CHR. This Town of *Fair-speech,* said *Christian,*

I have heard of it, and, as I remember, they say it's a wealthy place.

BY-ENDS. Yes, I will assure you that it is; and I have very many rich Kindred there.

CHR. Pray, who are your Kindred there? if a man may be so bold.

BY-ENDS. Almost the whole Town; and in particular, my Lord *Turn-about,* my Lord *Time-server,* my Lord *Fair-speech,* (from whose ancestors that Town first took its name) also Mr *Smooth-man,* Mr *Facing-both-ways,* Mr *Anything;* and the Parson of our Parish, Mr *Two-tongues,* was my Mother's own Brother by Father's side; and to tell you the truth, I am become a Gentleman of good Quality, yet my Great Grandfather was but a waterman, looking one way and rowing another; and I got most of my estate by the same occupation.

CHR. Are you a married man?

BY-ENDS. Yes, and my Wife is a very vertuous woman, the Daughter of a vertuous woman; she was my Lady *Feigning's* Daughter, therefore she came of a very honourable Family, and is arrived to such a pitch of breeding, that she knows how to carry it to all, even to Prince and Peasant. 'Tis true we somewhat differ in Religion from those of the stricter sort, yet but in two small points: First, we never strive against Wind and Tide: Secondly, we are always most zealous when Religion goes in his Silver Slippers; we love much to walk with him in the Street, if the Sun shines, and the people applaud him.

Then *Christian* stepped a little aside to his fellow *Hopeful,* saying, It runs in my mind that this is one *By-ends* of *Fair-speech,* and if it be he, we have as very a Knave in our company as dwelleth in all these parts. Then said *Hopeful,* Ask him; methinks he should not be ashamed of his name. *So Christian* came up with him again, and said, Sir, you talk as if you knew something more than all the world doth; and if I take not my mark amiss, I deem I

The wife and kindred of By-ends

Where By-ends differs from others in religion

have half a guess of you: Is not your name Mr *By-ends* of *Fair-speech?*

BY-ENDS. This is not my name, but indeed it is a nick-name that is given me by some that cannot abide me; and I must be content to bear it as a reproach, as other good men have borne theirs before me.

CHR. But did you never give an occasion to men to call you by this name?

BY-ENDS. Never, never! The worst that ever I did to give them an occasion to give me this name, was, that I had always the luck to jump in my Judgment with the present way of the times whatever it was, and my chance was to get thereby; but if things are thus cast upon me, let me count them a blessing, but let not the malicious load me therefore with reproach. *How By-ends got his name*

CHR. I thought indeed that you were the man that I heard of, and to tell you what I think, I fear this name belongs to you more properly than you are willing we should think it doth.

BY-ENDS. Well, if you will thus imagine, I cannot help it; you shall find me a fair company-keeper, if you will still admit me your associate. *He desires to keep company with Christian*

CHR. If you will go with us, you must go against Wind and Tide, the which, I perceive, is against your opinion; you must also own Religion in his Rags, as well as when in his Silver Slippers, and stand by him too, when bound in Irons, as well as when he walketh the Streets with applause.

BY-ENDS. You must not impose, nor lord it over my Faith; leave me to my liberty, and let me go with you.

CHR. Not a step further, unless you will do in what I propound, as we.

Then said *By-ends,* I shall never desert my old Principles, since they are harmless and profitable. If I may not go with you, I must do as I did before you overtook me, even go by myself, until some overtake me that will be glad of my company.

By-ends
and Chris-
tian part

Now I saw in my Dream that *Christian* and *Hopeful* forsook him, and kept their distance before him; but one of them looking back, saw three men following Mr *By-ends,* and behold, as they came up with him, he made them a very low congee, and they also gave him a compliment.

He has
new com-
panions

The men's names were Mr *Hold-the-world,* Mr *Money-love,* and Mr *Save-all;* men that Mr *By-ends* had formerly been acquainted with; for in their minority they were School-fellows, and were taught by one Mr *Gripeman,* a School-master in *Love-gain,* which is a Market-town in the County of *Coveting,* in the North. This School-master taught them the Art of Getting, either by violence, cousenage, flattery, lying, or by putting on a guise of Religion; and these four Gentlemen had attained much of the Art of their Master, so that they could each of them have kept such a School themselves.

Well when they had, as I said, thus saluted each other, Mr *Money-love* said to Mr *By-ends,* Who are they upon the Road before us? For *Christian* and *Hopeful* were yet within view.

By-ends'
character
of the
pilgrims

BY-ENDS. They are a couple of far country-men, that *after their mode* are going on Pilgrimage.

MONEY-LOVE. Alas! Why did they not stay, that we might have had their good company? for they, and we, and you Sir, I hope are all going on a Pilgrimage.

BY-ENDS. We are so indeed; but the men before us are so rigid, and love so much their own notions, and do also so lightly esteem the opinions of others, that let a man be never so godly, yet if he jumps not with them in all things, they thrust him quite out of their company.

SAVE-ALL. That's bad; but we read of some that are *righteous overmuch;* and such men's rigidness prevails with them to judge and condemn all but themselves. But I pray *what,* and *how many,* were the things wherein you differed?

BY-ENDS. Why they after their head-strong man-

ner, conclude that it is duty to rush on their Journey
all weathers, and I am for waiting for Wind and
Tide. They are for hazarding all for God at a clap,
and I am for taking all advantages to secure my
Life and Estate. They are for holding their notions, though all other men are against them; but
I am for Religion in what, and so far as the times
and my safety will bear it. They are for Religion
when in Rags and Contempt; but I am for him
when he walks in his Golden Slippers in the Sun-
shine, and with applause.

HOLD-THE-WORLD. Ay, and hold you there still,
good Mr *By-ends;* for for my part I can count him
but a Fool, that having the liberty to keep what he
has, shall be so unwise as to lose it. Let us be wise
as Serpents; 'tis best to make hay when the Sun
shines; you see how the Bee lieth still all winter,
and bestirs her only when she can have Profit with
Pleasure. God sends sometimes Rain, and sometimes Sun-shine; if they be such fools to go through
the first, yet let us be content to take fair weather
along with us. For my part I like that Religion
best that will stand with the security of God's good
blessings unto us; for who can imagine that is
ruled by his Reason, since God has bestowed upon
us the good things of this Life, but that he would
have us keep them for his sake? *Abraham* and
Solomon grew rich in Religion. And *Job* says, that
a good man *shall lay up Gold as Dust.* But he must
not be such as the men before us, if they be as you
have described them.

SAVE-ALL. I think that we are all agreed in this
matter, and therefore there needs no more words
about it.

MONEY-LOVE. No, there needs no more words
about this matter indeed; for he that believes neither
Scripture nor Reason (and you see we have both
on our side) neither knows his own liberty, nor
seeks his own safety.

BY-ENDS. My Brethren, we are, as you see, go-

ing all on Pilgrimage; and for our better diversion
from things that are bad, give me leave to propound unto you this question:

Suppose a man, a Minister, or a Tradesman, &c.
should have an advantage lie before him to get the
good blessings of this life, yet so as that he can by
no means come by them, except in appearance at
least, he becomes extraordinary zealous in some
points of Religion that he meddled not with before;
may he not use this means to attain his end, and
yet be a right honest man?

MONEY-LOVE. I see the bottom of your question,
and, with these Gentlemen's good leave, I will endeavour to shape you an answer. And first, to
speak to your question as it concerns a *Minister*
himself: Suppose a Minister, a worthy man, possess'd but of a very small benefice, and has in his
eye a greater, more fat and plump by far; he has
also now an opportunity of getting of it, yet so as
by being more studious, by preaching more frequently and zealously, and because the temper of the
people requires it, by altering of some of his principles; for my part I see no reason but a man may
do this, (provided he has a Call) ay, and more a
great deal besides, and yet be an honest man. For
why?

1. His desire of greater benefice is lawful
(this cannot be contradicted since 'tis set before
him by Providence); so then he may get it
if he can, making no question for Conscience
sake.

2. Besides, his desire after that benefice makes
him more studious, a more zealous Preacher, &c.
and so makes him a better man; yea makes him
better improve his parts, which is according to the
Mind of God.

3. Now as for his complying with the temper of
his people, by dissenting, to serve them, some of
his Principles, this argueth, 1. That he is of a self-
denying temper; 2. Of a sweet and winning deport-

ment; 3. And so more fit for the Ministerial function.

4. I conclude then, that a Minister that changes a *small* for a *great*, should not for so doing be judged as covetous; but rather, since he has improved in his parts and industry thereby, be counted as one that pursues his Call, and the opportunity put into his hand to do Good.

And now to the second part of the question, which concerns the *Tradesman* you mentioned. Suppose such an one to have but a poor imploy in the world, but by becoming Religious, he may mend his Market, perhaps get a rich Wife, or more and far better Customers to his shop; for my part I see no reason but this may be lawfully done. For why?

1. To become *Religious* is a Virtue, by what means soever a man becomes so.

2. Nor is it unlawful to get a rich Wife, or more Custom to my Shop.

3. Besides, the man that gets these by becoming religious, gets that which is good of them that are good, by becoming good himself; so then here is a good Wife, and good Customers, and good Gain, and all these by becoming religious, which is good; therefore to become religious to get all these, is a good and profitable design.

This answer thus made by this Mr *Money-love* to Mr *By-ends'* question was highly applauded by them all; wherefore they concluded upon the whole that it was most wholesome and advantageous. And because, as they thought, no man was able to contradict it, and because *Christian* and *Hopeful* were yet within call, they jointly agreed to assault them with the question as soon as they overtook them, and the rather because they had opposed Mr *By-ends* before. So they called after them, and they stopt, and stood still till they came up to them; but they concluded as they went that not Mr *By-ends*, but old Mr *Hold-the-world*, should propound the question to them, because, as they supposed, their

answer to him would be without the remainder of
that heat that was kindled betwixt Mr *By-ends*
and them, at their parting a little before.

So they came up to each other, and after a short
salutation, Mr *Hold-the-world* propounded the question
to *Christian* and his fellow, and bid them to
answer it if they could.

CHR. Then said *Christian,* Even a babe in Religion
may answer ten thousand such questions.
For if it be unlawful to follow Christ for loaves,
as it is *John* 6. how much more abominable is it
to make of him and Religion a Stalking-horse, to
get and enjoy the world. Nor do we find any other
than Heathens, Hypocrites, Devils, and Witches,
that are of this opinion.

1. *Heathens;* for when *Hamor* and *Shechem* had
a mind to the Daughter and Cattle of *Jacob,* and
saw that there was no ways for them to come
at them, but by becoming circumcised; they
said to their companions, If every male of us
be circumcised, as they are circumcised, shall not
their Cattle, and their substance, and every beast of
theirs, be ours? Their Daughter and their Cattle
were that which they sought to obtain, and their
Religion the Stalking-horse they made use of to
come at them. Read the whole story, *Gen.* 34. 20,
21, 22, 23.

2. The Hypocritical *Pharisees* were also of this
Religion; Long Prayers were their Pretence, but
to get widows' houses was their Intent; and greater
damnation was from God their Judgment, *Luke* 20.
46, 47.

3. *Judas* the Devil was also of this Religion; he
was religious for the Bag, that he might be possessed
of what was therein; but he was lost, cast
away, and the very son of Perdition.

4. *Simon* the *Witch* was of this Religion too; for
he would have had the Holy Ghost, that he might
have got Money therewith, and his sentence from
Peter's mouth was according, *Acts* 8, 19, 20, 21, 22.

5. Neither will it out of my mind, but that that man that takes up Religion for the World, will throw away Religion for the World; for so surely as *Judas* designed the World in becoming religious, so surely did he also sell Religion and his Master for the same. To answer the question therefore affirmatively, as I perceive you have done, and to accept of as authentick such answer, is both Heathenish, Hypocritical, and Devilish, and your Reward will be according to your Works. Then they stood staring one upon another, but had not wherewith to answer *Christian*. *Hopeful* also approved of the soundness of *Christian's* answer; so there was a great Silence among them. Mr *By-ends* and his company also staggered and kept behind, that *Christian* and *Hopeful* might outgo them. Then said *Christian* to his fellow, If these men cannot stand before the sentence of men, what will they do with the sentence of God? And if they are mute when dealt with by vessels of Clay, what will they do when they shall be rebuked by the flames of a devouring Fire?

Then *Christian* and *Hopeful* out-went them again, and went till they came to a delicate Plain called *Ease*, where they went with much content; but that Plain was but narrow, so they were quickly got over it. Now at the further side of that Plain was a little Hill called *Lucre*, and in that Hill a Silver-Mine, which some of them that had formerly gone that way, because of the rarity of it, had turned aside to see; but going too near the brink of the pit, the ground being deceitful under them, broke, and they were slain; some also had been maimed there, and could not to their dying day be their own men again. *The ease that pilgrims have is but little in this life*

Lucre Hill a dangerous hill

Then I saw in my Dream, that a little off the road, over against the *Silver-Mine*, stood *Demas* (gentlemanlike) to call to Passengers to come and see; who said to *Christian* and his fellow, Ho, turn aside hither, and I will shew you a thing. *Demas at the Hill Lucre. He calls to Christian and Hopeful to come to him*

CHR. What thing so deserving as to turn us out of the way?

DEMAS. Here is a *Silver-Mine,* and some digging in it for Treasure. If you will come, with a little pains you may richly provide for yourselves.

HOPE. Then said *Hopeful,* Let us go see.

Hopeful tempted to go, but Christian holds him back

CHR. Not I, said *Christian;* I have heard of this place before now, and how many have there been slain; and besides that Treasure is a snare to those that seek it, for it hindereth them in their Pilgrimage. Then *Christian* called to *Demas,* saying, Is not the place dangerous? Hath it not hindred many in their Pilgrimage?

DEMAS. Not very dangerous, except to those that are careless: but withal, he blushed as he spake.

CHR. Then said *Christian* to *Hopeful,* Let us not stir a step, but still keep on our way.

HOPE. I will warrant you, when *By-ends* comes up, if he hath the same invitation as we, he will turn in thither to see.

CHR. No doubt thereof, for his Principles lead him that way, and a hundred to one but he dies there.

DEMAS. Then *Demas* called again, saying, But will you not come over and see?

Christian roundeth up Demas

CHR. Then *Christian* roundly answered, saying, *Demas,* thou art an Enemy to the right ways of the Lord of this way, and hast been already condemned for thine own turning aside, by one of his Majesties Judges; and why seekest thou to bring us into the like condemnation? Besides, if we at all turn aside, our Lord the King will certainly hear thereof, and will there put us to shame, where we would stand with boldness before him.

Demas cried again, that he also was one of their fraternity; and that if they would tarry a little, he also himself would walk with them.

CHR. Then said *Christian,* What is thy name? Is it not the same by the which I have called thee?

DEMAS. Yes, my name is *Demas,* I am the Son of *Abraham.*

CHR. I know you, *Gehazi* was *your* Great Grand-father, and *Judas* your Father, and you have trod in their steps. It is but a devilish prank that thou usest; thy Father was hanged for a Traitor, and thou deservest no better reward. Assure thyself, that when we come to the King, we will do him word of this thy behaviour. Thus they went their way.

By this time *By-ends* and his Companions were come again within sight, and they at the first beck went over to *Demas.* Now whether they fell into the Pit by looking over the brink thereof, or whether they went down to dig, or whether they were smothered in the bottom by the damps that commonly arise, of these things I am not certain; but this I observed, that they never were seen again in the way. Then sang *Christian,*

By-ends goes over to Demas

> *By-ends* and Silver *Demas* both Agree ;
> One calls, the other runs, that he may be
> A Sharer in his Lucre ; so these do
> Take up in this World, and no further go.

Now I saw, that just on the other side of this Plain, the Pilgrims came to a place where stood an old *Monument,* hard by the High-way-side, at the sight of which they were both concerned, because of the strangeness of the form thereof; for it seemed to them as if it had been a *Woman* transformed into the shape of a Pillar; here therefore they stood looking and looking upon it, but could not for a time tell what they should make thereof. At last *Hopeful* espied written above upon the head thereof, a writing in an unusual hand; but he being no Scholar, called to *Christian* (for he was learned) to see if he could pick out the meaning; so he came, and after a little laying of letters together, he found the same to be this, *Remember Lot's Wife.* So he read it to his fellow; after which they both concluded that that was the Pillar of Salt into which *Lot's* Wife was turned, for her looking back with a *covetous heart,* when she was going from

They see a strange monument

Sodom for safety. Which sudden and amazing sight gave them occasion of this discourse.

CHR. Ah my Brother, this is a seasonable sight; it came opportunely to us after the invitation which *Demas* gave us to come over to view the Hill *Lucre;* and had we gone over as he desired us, and as thou wast inclining to do, my Brother, we had, for ought I know, been made ourselves like this Woman, a spectacle for those that shall come after to behold.

HOPE. I am sorry that I was so foolish, and am made to wonder that I am not now as *Lot's* Wife; for wherein was the difference 'twixt her sin and mine? she only looked back, and I had a desire to go see: let Grace be adored, and let me be ashamed that ever such a thing should be in mine heart.

CHR. Let us take notice of what we see here, for our help for time to come: This woman escaped one Judgment, for she fell not by the destruction of *Sodom;* yet she was destroyed by another, as we see she is turned into a Pillar of Salt.

HOPE. True, and she may be to us both *Caution* and *Example; caution,* that we should shun her sin, or a sign of what Judgment will overtake such as shall not be prevented by this caution: so *Korah, Dathan,* and *Abiram,* with the two hundred and fifty men that perished in their sin, did also become a sign or *example* to others to beware. But above all, I muse at one thing, to wit, how *Demas* and his fellows can stand so confidently yonder to look for that treasure, which this Woman, but for looking behind her after (for we read not that she stept one foot out of the way) was turned into a pillar of salt; especially since the Judgment which overtook her did make her an example, within sight of where they are: for they cannot chuse but see her, did they but lift up their eyes.

CHR. It is a thing to be wondered at, and it argueth that their hearts are grown desperate in the case; and I cannot tell who to compare them to so fitly, as to them that pick pockets in the presence of the Judge, or that will cut purses under the Gallows. It is said of the men of *Sodom, That they were sinners exceedingly*, because they were sinners *before the Lord;* that is, in his eye-sight, and notwithstanding the kindnesses that he had shewed them; for the land of *Sodom* was now, like the Garden of *Eden* heretofore. This therefore provoked him the more to jealousy, and made their plague as hot as the fire of the Lord out of Heaven could make it. And it is most rationally to be concluded, that such, even such as these are, that shall sin in the sight, yea, and that too in despite of such examples that are set continually before them, to caution them to the contrary, must be partakers of severest Judgments.

HOPE. Doubtless thou hast said the truth; but what a mercy is it, that neither thou, but especially I, am not made myself this example: this ministreth occasion to us to thank God, to fear before him, and always to remember *Lot's* Wife.

I saw then that they went on their way to a pleasant River, which *David* the King called the *River of God*, but *John*, the *River of the Water of Life*. Now their way lay just upon the bank of the River; here therefore *Christian* and his Companion walked with great delight; they drank also of the water of the River, which was pleasant and enlivening to their weary spirits: besides, on the banks of this River on either side were *green Trees*, that bore all manner of Fruit; and the Leaves of the Trees were good for Medicine; with the Fruit of these Trees they were also much delighted; and the Leaves they ate to prevent Surfeits, and other Diseases that are incident to those that heat their blood by Travels. On either side of the River was also a Meadow, curiously beautiful with Lilies; and it was green all the year long. In this Meadow they lay down and slept, for here they might *lie down safely*. When they awoke, they gathered again of the Fruit of the Trees, and drank again of the water of the

A river

Trees by the river. The fruit and leaves of the trees

A meadow in which they lie down to sleep

River, and then lay down again to sleep. Thus they did several days and nights. Then they sang,

> Behold ye how these Cristal streams do glide,
> (To comfort Pilgrims) by the High-way side;
> The Meadows green, beside their fragrant smell,
> Yield dainties for them: And he that can tell
> What pleasant fruit; yea Leaves, these Trees do yield,
> Will soon sell all, that he may buy this field.

So when they were disposed to go on (for they were not as yet at their Journey's end) they eat and drank, and departed.

By-path Meadow

Now I beheld in my Dream, that they had not journeyed far, but the River and the way for a time parted; at which they were not a little sorry, yet they durst not go out of the way. Now the way from the River was rough, and their feet tender by reason of their Travels; *so the soul of the Pilgrims was much discouraged because of the way.* Wherefore still as they went on, they wished for better way. Now a little before them, there was on the left hand of the road a *Meadow,* and a Stile to

One temptation does make way for another

go over into it, and that Meadow is called *By-path Meadow.* Then said *Christian* to his fellow, If this Meadow lieth along by our way-side, let's go over into it. Then he went to the Stile to see, and behold a Path lay along by the way on the other side of the fence. 'Tis according to my wish, said *Christian,* here is the easiest going; come good *Hopeful,* and let us go over.

HOPE. But how if this Path should lead us out of the way?

Strong Christians may lead weak ones out of the way

CHR. That's not like, said the other; look, doth it not go along by the way-side? So *Hopeful,* being persuaded by his fellow, went after him over the Stile. When they were gone over, and were got into the Path, they found it very easy for their feet: and withal, they looking before them, espied a man walking as they did, (and his name was *Vainconfidence*) so they called after him, and asked him whither that way led? He said, To the Cœlestial

Gate. Look, said *Christian,* did I not tell you so? by this you may see we are right. So they followed, and he went before them. But behold the night came on, and it grew very dark, so that they that were behind lost the sight of him that went before. *See what it is too suddenly to fall in with strangers*

He therefore that went before (*Vain-confidence* by name) not seeing the way before him, fell into a deep Pit, which was on purpose there made by the Prince of those grounds, to catch *vain-glorious* fools withal, and was dashed in pieces with his fall. *A pit to catch the vainglorious in*

Now *Christian* and his fellow heard him fall. So they called to know the matter, but there was none to answer, only they heard a groaning. Then said *Hopeful,* Where are we now? Then was his fellow silent, as mistrusting that he had led him out of the way; and now it began to rain, and thunder, and lighten in a very dreadful manner, and the water rose amain. *Reasoning between Christian and Hopeful*

Then *Hopeful* groaned in himself, saying, *Oh that I had kept on my way!*

CHR. Who could have thought that this Path should have led us out of the way?

HOPE. I was afraid on't at the very first, and therefore gave you that gentle caution. I would have spoken plainer, but that you are older than I.

CHR. Good Brother be not offended; I am sorry I have brought thee out of the way, and that I have put thee into such imminent danger; pray my Brother forgive me, I did not do it of an evil intent. *Christian's repentance for leading of his brother out of the way*

HOPE. Be comforted my brother, for I forgive thee; and believe too that this shall be for our good.

CHR. I am glad I have with me a merciful Brother; but we must not stand thus, let's try to go back again.

HOPE. But good Brother let me go before.

CHR. No, if you please let me go first, that if there be any danger, I may be first therein, because by my means we are both gone out of the way.

HOPE. No, said *Hopeful,* you shall not go first; for your mind being troubled may lead you out of

They are
in danger
of drown-
ing as they
go back
the way again. Then for their encouragement, they
heard the voice of one saying *Let thine heart be
towards the High-way, even the way that thou went-
est, turn again.* But by this time the waters were
greatly risen; by reason of which they way of going
back was very dangerous. (Then I thought that
it is easier going out of the way when we are in,
than going in when we are out.) Yet they ad-
ventured to go back; but it was so dark, and the
flood was so high, that in their going back they had
like to have been drowned nine or ten times.

They sleep
in the
grounds
of Giant
Despair
Neither could they, with all the skill they had,
get again to the Stile that night. Wherefore at
last, lighting under a little shelter, they sat down
there till the day brake; but being weary, they
fell asleep. Now there was not far from the place
where they lay, a Castle called *Doubting* Castle, the
owner whereof was Giant *Despair,* and it was in
his grounds they were now sleeping: wherefore he,
getting up in the morning early, and walking up and
down in his fields, caught *Christian* and *Hopeful*
He finds
them in his
grounds,
and carries
them to
Doubting
Castle
asleep in his grounds. Then with a *grim* and
surly voice he bid them awake, and asked them
whence they were? and what they did in his
grounds? They told him they were Pilgrims, and
that they had lost their way. Then said the Giant,
You have this night trespassed on me, by trampling
in and lying on my grounds, and therefore you
must go along with me. So they were forced to go,
because he was stronger than they. They also had
but little to say, for they knew themselves in a
fault. The Giant therefore drove them before him,
The griev-
ousness of
their im-
prisonment
and put them into his Castle, into a very dark Dungeon, nasty and stinking to the spirits of these two
men. Here then they lay from *Wednesday* morning
till *Saturday* night, without one bit of bread, or
drop of drink, or light, or any to ask how they did;
they were therefore here in evil case, and were far
from friends and acquaintance. Now in this place
Christian had double sorrow, because 'twas through

his unadvised haste that they were brought into
this distress.

> The Pilgrims now, to gratify the Flesh,
> Will seek its Ease ; but oh ! how they afresh
> Do thereby plunge themselves new Griefs into !
> Who seek to please the flesh themselves undo.

Now Giant *Despair* had a Wife, and her name
was *Diffidence*. So when he was gone to bed, he
told his Wife what he had done, to wit, that he had
taken a couple of Prisoners and cast them into his
Dungeon, for trespassing on his grounds. Then he
asked her also what he had best do further to them.
So she asked him what they were, whence they came,
and whither they were bound; and he told her.
Then she counselled him that when he arose in the
morning he should beat them without any mercy. So
when he arose, he getteth him a grievous Crab-tree
Cudgel, and goes down into the Dungeon to them,
and there first falls to rating of them, as if they
were dogs, although they gave him never a word
of distaste. Then he falls upon them, and beats
them fearfully, in such sort, that they were not able
to help themselves, or to turn them upon the floor.
This done, he withdraws and leaves them, there to
condole their misery, and to mourn under their
distress : so all that day they spent the time in nothing but sighs and bitter lamentations. The next
night she talking with her Husband about them further, and understanding that they were yet alive,
did advise him to counsel them to make away themselves. So when morning was come, he goes to
them in a surly manner as before, and perceiving
them to be very sore with the stripes that he had
given them the day before, he told them, that since
they were never like to come out of that place, their
only way would be forthwith to make an end of
themselves, either with Knife, Halter, or Poison;
For why, said he, should you chuse life, seeing it is
attended with so much bitterness ? But they desired

On Thursday, Giant Despair beats his prisoners

On Friday, Giant Despair counsels them to kill themselves

him to let them go. With that he looked ugly upon
them, and rushing to them had doubtless made
an end of them himself, but that he fell into one of
his Fits, (for he sometimes in Sun-shine weather
fell into Fits) and lost for a time the use of his
hand; wherefore he withdrew, and left them as
before, to consider what to do. Then did the
Prisoners consult between themselves, whether 'twas
best to take his counsel or no; and thus they began
to discourse:

CHR. Brother, said *Christian,* what shall we do?
The life that we now live is miserable: for my part
I know not whether is best, to live thus, or to die out
of hand. *My soul chuseth strangling rather than
life,* and the Grave is more easy for me than this
Dungeon. Shall we be ruled by the Giant?

HOPE. Indeed our present condition is dreadful,
and death would be far more welcome to me than
thus for ever to abide; but yet let us consider, the
Lord of the Country to which we are going hath
said, Thou shalt do no murder, no not to another
man's person; much more then are we forbidden to
take his counsel to kill ourselves. Besides, he that
kills another can but commit murder upon his body;
but for one to kill himself is to kill body and soul
at once. And moreover, my Brother, thou talkest of
ease in the Grave; but hast thou forgotten the Hell,
whither for certain the murderers go? For no
murderer hath eternal life, *&c.* And let us consider again, that all the Law is not in the hand of
Giant *Despair.* Others, so far as I can understand,
have been taken by him as well as we, and yet have
escaped out of his hand. Who knows but that God
that made the world may cause that Giant *Despair*
may die? or that at some time or other he may forget to lock us in? or but he may in short time have
another of his Fits before us, and may lose the use of
his limbs? and if ever that should come to pass
again, for my part I am resolved to pluck up the
heart of a man, and to try my utmost to get from

under his hand. I was a fool that I did not try to do it before; but however, my Brother, let's be patient, and endure a while; the time may come that may give us a happy release; but let us not be our own murderers. With these words *Hopeful* at present did moderate the mind of his Brother; so they continued together (in the dark) that day, in their sad and doleful condition.

Well, towards evening the Giant goes down into the Dungeon again, to see if his prisoners had taken his counsel; but when he came there he found them alive, and truly, alive was all; for now, what for want of Bread and Water, and by reason of the Wounds they received when he beat them, they could do little but breathe: But, I say, he found them alive; at which he fell into a grievous rage, and told them that seeing they disobeyed his counsel, it should be worse with them than if they had never been born.

At this they trembled greatly, and I think that *Christian* fell into a Swoon; but coming a little to himself again, they renewed their discourse about the Giant's counsel, and whether yet they had best to take it or no. Now *Christian* again seemed to be for doing it, but *Hopeful* made his second reply as followeth: _{Christian still dejected}

HOPE. My Brother, said he, rememberest thou not how valiant thou hast been heretofore? *Apollyon* could not crush thee, nor could all that thou didst hear, or see, or feel in the Valley of the *Shadow of Death*. What hardship, terror, and amazement hast thou already gone through, and art thou now nothing but fear? Thou seest that I am in the Dungeon with thee, a far weaker man by nature than thou art; also this Giant has wounded me as well as thee, and hath also cut off the Bread and Water from my mouth; and with thee I mourn without the light. But let's exercise a little more patience, remember how thou playedst the man at *Vanity Fair*, and wast neither afraid of the Chain, _{Hopeful comforts him again, by calling former things to remembrance}

nor Cage, nor yet of bloody Death: wherefore let us (at least to avoid the shame, that becomes not a Christian to be found in) bear up with patience as well as we can.

Now night being come again, and the Giant and his Wife being in bed, she asked him concerning the Prisoners, and if they had taken his counsel: To which he replied, They are sturdy Rogues, they chuse rather to bear all hardship, than to make away themselves. Then said she, Take them into the Castle-yard to-morrow, and shew them the Bones and Skulls of those that thou hast already dispatch'd, and make them believe, e'er a week comes to an end, thou also wilt tear them in pieces, as thou hast done their fellows before them.

On Saturday, the Giant threatened that shortly he would pull them in pieces

So when the morning was come, the Giant goes to them again, and takes them into the Castle-yard and shews them as his Wife had bidden him. These, said he, were Pilgrims as you are, once, and they trespassed in my grounds, as you have done; and when I thought fit, I tore them in pieces, and so within ten days I will do you. Go get you down to your Den again; and with that he beat them all the way thither. They lay therefore all day on *Saturday* in a lamentable case, as before. Now when night was come, and when Mrs Diffidence and her Husband the Giant were got to bed, they began to renew their discourse of their Prisoners; and withal the old Giant wondered, that he could neither by his blows nor counsel bring them to an end. And with that his Wife replied, I fear, said she, that they live in hope that some will come to relieve them, or that they have pick-locks about them, by the means of which they hope to escape. And sayest thou so, my dear? said the Giant, I will therefore search them in the morning.

Well on *Saturday* about midnight they began to *pray,* and continued in Prayer till almost break of day.

Now a little before it was day, good *Christian,* as

one half amazed, brake out in passionate speech: A key in
What a fool, quoth he, *am I, thus to lie in a stinking* bosom,
Dungeon, when I may as well walk at liberty. I called
have a Key in my bosom called Promise, that will, Promise,
I am persuaded, open any Lock in *Doubting* Castle. lock in
Then said *Hopeful*, That's good news; good Brother Doubting
pluck it out of thy bosom and try. Castle

Then *Christian* pulled it out of his bosom, and
began to try at the Dungeon door, whose bolt (as
he turned the Key) gave back, and the door flew open
with ease, and *Christian* and *Hopeful* both came
out. Then he went to the outward door that
leads into the Castle-yard, and with his Key opened
that door also. After he went to the iron Gate, for
that must be opened too, but that Lock went dam-
nable hard, yet the Key did open it. Then they
thrust open the Gate to make their escape with
speed; but that Gate as it opened made such a creak-
ing, that it waked Giant *Despair*, who hastily rising
to pursue his Prisoners, felt his limbs to fail, for
his Fits took him again, so that he could by no
means go after them. Then they went on, and
came to the King's High-way again, and so were
safe, because they were out of his jurisdiction.

Now when they were gone over the Stile, they A pillar
began to contrive with themselves what they should erected by
do at that Stile, to prevent those that should come and his
after from falling into the hands of Giant *Despair*. fellow
So they consented to erect there a Pillar, and to
engrave upon the side thereof this sentence, *Over
this Stile is the way to* Doubting *Castle, which is
kept by Giant* Despair, *who despiseth the King of the
Cœlestial Country, and seeks to destroy his holy
Pilgrims.* Many therefore that followed after read
what was written, and escaped the danger. This
done, they sang as follows:

> Out of the way we went, and then we found
> What 'twas to tread upon forbidden ground;
> And let them that come after have a care,
> Lest heedlessness makes them, as we, to fare.

Lest they for trespassing his prisoners are,
Whose Castle's *Doubting*, and whose name's *Despair*.

The Delectable Mountains

They went then till they came to the *Delectable Mountains,* which Mountains belong to the Lord of that Hill of which we have spoken before; so they went up to the Mountains, to behold the Gardens and Orchards, the Vineyards and Fountains

They are refreshed in the mountains

of water; where also they drank, and washed themselves, and did freely eat of the Vineyards. Now there were on the tops of these Mountains *Shepherds* feeding their flocks, and they stood by the High-way side. The Pilgrims therefore went to them, and leaning upon their staves (as is common with weary Pilgrims, when they stand to talk with

Talk with the Shepherds

any by the way) they asked, *Whose Delectable Mountains are these? And whose be the sheep that feed upon them?*

> Mountains Delectable they now ascend,
> Where Shepherds be, which to them do commend
> Alluring things, and things that Cautious are,
> Pilgrims are steady kept by Faith and Fear.

SHEP. These mountains are *Immanuel's Land,* and they are within sight of his City; and the sheep also are his, and he laid down his life for them.

CHR. Is this the way to the Cœlestial City?

SHEP. You are just in your way.

CHR. How far is it thither?

SHEP. Too far for any but those that shall get thither indeed.

CHR. Is the way safe or dangerous?

SHEP. Safe for those for whom it is to be safe, *but transgressors shall fall therein.*

CHR. Is there in this place any relief for Pilgrims that are weary and faint in the way?

SHEP. The Lord of these Mountains hath given us a charge *not to be forgotten to entertain strangers;* therefore the good of the place is before you.

I saw also in my Dream, that when the Shepherds

perceived that they were way-faring men, they also put questions to them (to which they made answer as in other places) as, Whence came you? and, How got you into the way? and, By what means have you so persevered therein? For but few of them that begin to come hither do shew their face on these Mountains. But when the Shepherds heard their answers, being pleased therewith, they looked very lovingly upon them, and said, *Welcome to the Delectable Mountains.*

The Shepherds, I say, whose names were *Knowl-* *edge, Experience, Watchful,* and *Sincere,* took them by the hand, and had them to their Tents, and made them partake of that which was ready at present. They said moreover, We would that ye should stay here a while, to be acquainted with us; and yet more to solace yourselves with the good of these Delectable Mountains. They then told them, that they were content to stay; and so they went to their rest that night, because it was very late.

Then I saw in my Dream, that in the morning the Shepherds called up *Christian* and *Hopeful* to walk with them upon the Mountains; so they went forth with them, and walked a while, having a pleasant prospect on every side. Then said the Shepherds one to another, Shall we shew these Pilgrims some wonders? So when they had concluded to do it, they had them first to the top of a Hill called *Error,* which was very steep on the furthest side, and bid them look down to the bottom. So *Christian* and *Hopeful* looked down, and saw at the bottom several men dashed all to pieces by a fall, that they had from the top. Then said *Christian,* What meaneth this? The Shepherds answered, Have you not heard of them that were made to err, by hearkening to *Hymeneus* and *Philetus,* as concerning the Faith of the Resurrection of the Body? They answered, Yes. Then said the Shepherds, Those that you see lie dashed in pieces at the bottom of this Mountain are they; and they have continued to this day unburied (as you see) for an example to others to take heed how they clamber too high, or how they come too near the brink of this Mountain.

Mount Caution

Then I saw that they had them to the top of another Mountain, and the name of that is *Caution,* and bid them look afar off; which when they did, they perceived, as they thought, several men walking up and down among the Tombs that were there; and they perceived that the men were blind, because they stumbled sometimes upon the Tombs, and because they could not get out from among them. Then said *Christian, What means this?*

The Shepherds then answered, Did you not see a little below these Mountains a Stile, that led into a Meadow, on the left hand of this way? They answered, Yes. Then said the Shepherds, From that Stile there goes a path that leads directly to *Doubting* Castle, which is kept by Giant *Despair;* and these men (pointing to them among the Tombs) came once on Pilgrimage, as you do now, even till they came to that same Stile; and because the right way was rough in that place, they chose to go out of it into that Meadow, and there were taken by Giant *Despair,* and cast into *Doubting* Castle; where, after they had been awhile kept in the Dungeon, he at last did put out their eyes, and led them among those Tombs, where he has left them to wander to this very day, that the saying of the Wise Man might be fulfilled, *He that wandereth out of the way of understanding, shall remain in the congregation of the dead.* Then *Christian* and *Hopeful* looked upon one another, with tears gushing out, but yet said nothing to the Shepherds.

A by-way to hell

Then I saw in my Dream, that the Shepherds had them to another place, in a bottom, where was a door in the side of a Hill, and they opened the door, and bid them look in. They looked in therefore, and saw that within it was very dark and smoky; they also thought that they heard there a rumbling noise as of Fire, and a cry of some tormented, and that they smelt the scent of Brimstone. Then said *Christian, What means this?* The Shepherds told them, This is a by-way to Hell, a way that Hypocrites go in at; namely, such as sell their Birth-right, with *Esau;* such as sell their Master, as *Judas;* such as blaspheme the Gospel, with *Alexander;* and that lie and dissemble, with *Ananias* and *Sapphira* his Wife. Then said *Hopeful* to the Shepherds, I perceive that these had on them, even everyone, a shew of Pilgrimage, as we have now; had they not?

SHEP. Yes, and held it a long time too.

HOPE. How far might they go on in Pilgrimage in their day, since they notwithstanding were thus miserably cast away?

SHEP. Some further, and some not so far as these Mountains.

Then said the Pilgrims one to another, *We had need to cry to the Strong for strength*.

SHEP. Ay, and you will have need to use it when you have it too.

By this time the Pilgrims had a desire to go forwards, and the Shepherds a desire they should; so they walked together towards the end of the Mountains. Then said the Shepherds one to another, Let us here shew to the Pilgrims the Gates of the Coelestial City, if they have skill to look through our Perspective-Glass. The Pilgrims then lovingly accepted the motion; so they had them to the top of a high Hill, called *Clear,* and gave them their Glass to look. *The Shepherds' perspective glass* *The Hill Clear*

Then they assayed to look, but the remembrance of that last thing that the Shepherds had shewed them, made their hands shake, by means of which impediment they could not look steadily through the Glass; yet they thought they saw something like the Gate, and also some of the Glory of the place. *The fruits of servile fear*

Then they went away and sang this song,

Thus by the Shepherds Secrets are reveal'd:
Which from all other men are kept conceal'd
Come to the Shepherds then if you would see
Things deep, things hid, and that mysterious be.

A twofold caution — When they were about to depart, one of the Shepherds gave them a *Note of the way*. Another of them bid them *beware of the Flatterer*. The third bid them *take heed that they sleep not on the Inchanted Ground*. And the fourth bid them *Godspeed*. So I awoke from my Dream.

And I slept, and Dreamed again, and saw the same two Pilgrims going down the Mountains along the High-way towards the City. Now a little below these Mountains, on the left hand lieth the Country

The country of Conceit, out of which came Ignorance — of *Conceit;* from which Country there comes into the way in which the Pilgrims walked, a little crooked Lane. Here therefore they met with a very brisk Lad, that came out of that Country; and his name was *Ignorance*. So *Christian* asked him *From what parts he came, and whither he was going?*

Christian and Ignorance have some talk — IGNOR. Sir, I was born in the Country that lieth off there a little on the left hand, and I am going to the Cœlestial City.

CHR. But how do you think to get in at the Gate, for you may find some difficulty there?

IGNOR. As other good people do, said he.

CHR. But what have you to shew at that Gate, that may cause that the Gate should be opened to you?

The ground of Ignorance's hope — IGNOR. I know my Lord's will, and I have been a good liver; I pay every man his own; I Pray, Fast, pay Tithes, and give Alms, and have left my Country for whither I am going.

CHR. But thou camest not in at the Wicket-Gate that is at the head of this way; thou camest in hither through that same crooked Lane, and therefore I fear, however thou mayest think of thyself, when the reckoning day shall come, thou wilt have laid to thy charge that thou art a Thief and a Robber, instead of getting admittance into the City.

IGNOR. Gentlemen, ye be utter strangers to me, He saith I know you not; be content to follow the Religion to every of your Country, and I will follow the Religion one that he is a fool of mine. I hope all will be well. And as for the Gate that you talk of, all the world knows that that is a great way off of our Country. I cannot think that any man in all our parts doth so much as know the way to it, nor need they matter whether they do or no, since we have, as you see, a fine pleasant Green Lane, that comes down from our Country the next way into the way.

When *Christian* saw that the man was wise in How to his own conceit, he said to *Hopeful* whisperingly, carry it to a fool *There is more hopes of a fool than of him.* And said moreover, *When he that is a fool walketh by the way, his wisdom faileth him, and he saith to every one that he is a fool.* What, shall we talk further with him, or outgo him at present, and so leave him to think of what he hath heard already, and then stop again for him afterwards, and see if by degrees we can do any good of him? Then said *Hopeful*,

> Let *Ignorance* a little while now muse
> On what is said, and let him not refuse
> Good counsel to imbrace, lest he remain
> Still ignorant of what's the chiefest gain.
> God saith, Those that no understanding have,
> (Although he made them) them he will not save.

HOPE. He further added, It is not good, I think, to say all to him at once; let us pass him by, if you will, and talk to him anon, *even as he is able to bear it.*

So they both went on, and *Ignorance* he came The de- after. Now when they had passed him a little way, struction of one they entered into a very dark Lane, where they met Turnaway a man whom seven Devils had bound with seven strong cords, and were carrying of him back to the Door that they saw on the side of the Hill. Now good *Christian* began to tremble, and so did *Hopeful* his Companion; yet as the Devils led

away the man, *Christian* looked to see if he knew
him, and he thought it might be one *Turn-away* that
dwelt in the Town of *Apostacy*. But he did not
perfectly see his face, for he did hang his head like
a Thief that is found. But being gone past, *Hopeful*
looked after him, and espied on his back a paper
with this inscription, *Wanton Professor and damna-*

Christian
telleth his
companion
a story of
Little-faith
ble Apostate. Then said *Christian* to his fellow,
Now I call to remembrance that which was told me
of a thing that happened to a good man hereabout.
The name of the man was *Little-faith*, but a good
man, and he dwelt in the Town of *Sincere*. The
thing was this; At the entering in of this passage,

Broad-way
Gate
there comes down from *Broad-way Gate*, a Lane
called *Dead Man's Lane*; so called because of the

Dead
Man's
Lane
Murders that are commonly done there; and this
Little-faith going on Pilgrimage as we do now,
chanced to sit down there and slept. Now there
happened at that time, to come down the *Lane* from
Broad-way Gate, three sturdy Rogues, and their
names were *Faint-heart, Mistrust,* and *Guilt,* (three
Brothers) and they espying *Little-faith* where he
was, came galloping up with speed. Now the good
man was just awaked from his sleep, and was getting
up to go on his Journey. So they came up all to
him, and with threatning language bid him stand.

Little-faith
robbed by
Faint-
heart, Mis-
trust, and
Guilt
At this *Little-faith* looked as white as a Clout, and
had neither power to fight nor fly. Then said
Faint-heart, Deliver thy Purse. But he making no
haste to do it (for he was loth to lose his Money)
Mistrust ran up to him, and thrusting his hand into

They got
away his
silver, and
knocked
him down
his Pocket, pull'd out thence a bag of silver. Then
he cried out, Thieves, Thieves. With that *Guilt*
with a great Club that was in his hand, struck
Little-faith on the head, and with that blow fell'd
him flat to the ground, where he lay bleeding as
one that would bleed to death. All this while the
Thieves stood by. But at last, they hearing that
some were upon the road, and fearing lest it should
be one *Great-grace* that dwells in the City of *Good-*

confidence, they betook themselves to their heels, and left this good man to shift for himself. Now after a while *Little-faith* came to himself, and getting up made shift to scrabble on his way. This was the story.

HOPE. But did they take from him all that ever he had?

CHR. No; the place where his Jewels were they never ransacked, so those he kept still; but as I was told, the good man was much afflicted for his loss, for the Thieves got most of his spending Money. That which they got not (as I said) were Jewels, also he had a little odd Money left, but scarce enough to bring him to his Journey's end; nay, if I was not misinformed, he was forced to beg as he went, to keep himself alive, for his Jewels he might not sell. But beg, and do what he could, he went (as we say) *with many a hungry belly* the most part of the rest of the way. _{Little-faith lost not his best things}

(margin note: Little-faith lost not his best things)

(margin note: Little-faith forced to beg to his journey's end)

HOPE. But is it not a wonder that they got from him his Certificate, by which he was to receive his admittance at the Cœlestial Gate?

CHR. 'Tis a wonder but they got not that, though they missed it not through any good cunning of his; for he being dismayed with their coming upon him, had neither power nor skill to hide anything; so 'twas more by good Providence than by his endeavour, that they miss'd of that good thing.

(margin note: He kept not his best things by his own cunning (2 Tim. i. 14))

HOPE. But it must needs be a comfort to him that they got not this Jewel from him.

CHR. It might have been great comfort to him, had he used it as he should; but they that told me the story said that he made but little use of it all the rest of the way, and that because of the dismay that he had in their taking away his Money; indeed he forgot it a great part of the rest of his Journey; and besides, when at any time it came into his mind, and he began to be comforted therewith, then would fresh thoughts of his loss come again upon him, and those thoughts would swallow up all.

He is pitied by both

HOPE. Alas poor man! This could not but be a great grief to him.

CHR. Grief! ay, a grief indeed. Would it not have been so to any of us, had we been used as he, to be robbed, and wounded too, and that in a strange place, as he was? 'Tis a wonder he did not die with grief, poor heart! I was told that he scattered almost all the rest of the way with nothing but doleful and bitter complaints; telling also to all that over-took him, or that he over-took in the way as he went, where he was robbed, and how; who they were that did it, and what he lost; how he was wounded, and that he hardly escaped with his life.

HOPE. But 'tis a wonder that his necessity did not put him upon *selling* or *pawning* some of his Jewels, that he might have wherewith to relieve himself in his Journey.

Christian snubbeth his fellow for unadvised speaking

CHR. Thou talkest like one upon whose head is the Shell to this very day; for what should he pawn them, or to whom should he sell them? In all that Country where he was robbed, his Jewels were not accounted of; nor did he want that relief which could from thence be administered to him. Besides, had his Jewels been missing at the Gate of the Cœlestial City, he had (and that he knew well enough) been excluded from an Inheritance there; and that would have been worse to him than the appearance and villany of ten thousand Thieves.

HOPE. Why art thou so tart my Brother? *Esau* sold his Birth-right, and that for a mess of Pottage, and that Birth-right was his greatest Jewel; and if he, why might not *Little-faith* do so too?

A discourse about Esau and Little-faith

CHR. *Esau* did sell his Birth-right indeed, and so do many besides, and by so doing exclude themselves from the chief blessing, as also that caitiff did; but you must put a difference betwixt *Esau* and *Little-faith,* and also betwixt their Estates.

Esau was ruled by his lusts

Esau's Birth-right was typical, but *Little-faith's* Jewels were not so: *Esau's* belly was his god, but *Little-faith's* belly was not so: *Esau's* want lay in his fleshly appetite, *Little-faith's* did not so. Besides, *Esau* could see no further than to the fulfilling of his lusts: *For I am at the point to die,* said he, *and what good will this Birth-right do me?* But *Little-faith,* though it was his lot to have but a *little faith,* was by his *little faith* kept from such extravagancies, and made to see and prize his Jewels more than to sell them, as *Esau* did his Birth-right. You read not anywhere that *Esau* had *faith,* no not so much as a *little;* therefore no marvel if where the flesh only bears sway (as it will in that man where no faith is to resist) if he sells his Birth-right, and his Soul and all, and that to the Devil of Hell; for it is with such, as it is with the Ass, *who in her occasions cannot be turned away.* When their minds are set upon their lusts, they will have them whatever they cost. But *Little-faith* was of another temper, his mind was on things Divine; his livelihood was upon things that were Spiritual, and from above; therefore to what end should he that is of such a temper sell his Jewels (had there been any that would have bought them) to fill his mind with empty things? Will a man give a penny to fill his belly with Hay? or can you persuade the *Turtle-dove* to live upon Carrion like the *Crow?* Though *faithless* ones can, for carnal Lusts, pawn or mortgage, or sell what they have, and themselves outright to boot; yet they that have *faith, saving faith,* though but a little of it, cannot do so. Here therefore my Brother is thy mistake.

Esau never had faith

Little-faith could not live upon Esau's pottage

A comparison between the turtle-dove and the crow

HOPE. I acknowledge it; but yet your severe reflection had almost made me angry.

CHR. Why, I did but compare thee to some of the Birds that are of the brisker sort, who will run to and fro in trodden paths, with the Shell upon their heads; but pass by that, and consider the matter under debate, and all shall be well betwixt thee and me.

HOPE. But *Christian,* these three fellows, I am persuaded in my heart, are but a company of Cow-

Hopeful swaggers

ards; would they have run else, think you, as they did, at the noise of one that was coming on the road? Why did not *Little-faith* pluck up a greater heart? He might, methinks, have stood one brush with them, and have yielded when there had been no remedy.

No great heart for God, where there is but little faith

CHR. That they are Cowards, many have said, but few have found it so in the time of Trial. As for a great heart, *Little-faith* had none; and I perceive by thee, my Brother, hadst thou been the man concerned, thou art but for a brush, and then to yield. And verily since this is the height of thy stomach, now they are at a distance from us, should they appear to thee as they did to him, they might put thee to second thoughts.

We have more courage when out, than when in the conflict

Christian tells his own experience in this case

But consider again, they are but journeymen Thieves; they serve under the King of the bottomless Pit, who, if need be, will come in to their aid himself, and his voice is *as the roaring of a Lion*. I myself have been engaged as this *Little-faith* was, and I found it a terrible thing. These three Villains set upon me, and I beginning like a Christian to resist, they gave but a call, and in came their Master: I would, as the saying is, have given my life for a penny; but that, as God would have it, I was cloathed with Armor of proof. Ay, and yet though I was so harnessed, I found it hard work to quit myself like a man: no man can tell what in that Combat attends us, but he that hath been in the Battle himself.

HOPE. Well, but they ran, you see, when they did but suppose that one *Great-grace* was in the way.

The King's champion

CHR. True, they have often fled, both they and their Master, when *Great-grace* hath but appeared; and no marvel, for he is the *King's Champion*. But I tro you will put some difference between *Little-faith* and the *King's Champion*. All the King's Subjects are not his Champions, nor can they when tried do such feats of War as he. Is it meet to think that a little child should handle *Goliah* as *David* did? Or that there should be the strength of an *Ox* in a *Wren?* Some are strong, some are weak; some have great faith, some have little: this man was one of the weak, and therefore he went to the wall.

HOPE. I would it had been *Great-grace* for their sakes.

CHR. If it had been he, he might have had his hands full; for I must tell you, that though *Great-grace* is excellent good at his Weapons, and has, and can, so long as he keeps them at Sword's point, do well enough with them; yet if they get within him, even *Faint-heart, Mistrust,* or the other, it shall go hard but they will throw up his heels. And when a man is down, you know, what can he do?

Whoso looks well upon *Great-grace's* face, shall see those scars and cuts there, that shall easily give demonstration of what I say. Yea, once I heard he should say, (and that when he was in the Combat) *We despaired even of life.* How did these sturdy Rogues and their fellows make *David* groan, mourn, and roar? Yet, *Heman* and *Hezekiah* too, though Champions in their day, were forced to bestir them when by these assaulted; and yet notwithstanding they had their Coats soundly brushed by them. *Peter* upon a time would go try what he could do; but though some do say of him that he is the Prince of the Apostles, they handled him so, that they made him at last afraid of a sorry Girl.

Besides their King is at their whistle. He is never out of hearing; and if at any time they be put to the worst, he if possible comes in to help them; and of him it is said, *The Sword of him that layeth at him cannot hold, the Spear, the Dart, nor the Habergeon: he esteemeth Iron as Straw, and Brass as rotten Wood. The Arrow cannot make him fly; Sling-stones are turned with him into Stubble, Darts are counted as Stubble: he laugheth at the shaking of a Spear.* What can a man do in this case? 'Tis true, if a man could at every turn have *Job's* Horse, and had skill and courage to

[marginal note: Leviathan's sturdiness]

ride him, he might do notable things; *for his Neck is cloathed with Thunder, he will not be afraid as the Grasshopper, the glory of his Nostrils is terrible, he paweth in the Valley, rejoiceth in his strength, and goeth out to meet the armed men. He mocketh at fear, and is not affrighted, neither turneth back from the Sword. The Quiver rattleth against him, the glittering Spear, and the Shield. He swalloweth the ground with fierceness and rage, neither believeth he that it is the sound of the Trumpet. He saith among the Trumpets, Ha, ha; and he smelleth the Battle afar off, the thundering of the Captains, and the Shoutings.*

But for such footmen as thee and I are, let us never desire to meet with an enemy, nor vaunt as if we could do better, when we hear of others that they have been foiled, nor be tickled at the thoughts of our own manhood; for such commonly come by the worst when tried. Witness *Peter,* of whom I made mention before. He would swagger, ay he would; he would, as his vain mind prompted him to say, do better, and stand more for his Master than all men; but who so foiled and run down by these Villains as he?

When therefore we hear that such Robberies are done on the King's High-way, two things become us to do: First, To go out harnessed and to be sure to take a Shield with us; for it was for want of that, that he that laid so lustily at *Leviathan* could not make him yield; for indeed if that be wanting he fears us not at all. Therefore he that had skill hath said, *Above all take the Shield of Faith, wherewith ye shall be able to quench all the fiery darts of the wicked.*

'Tis good also that we desire of the King a Convoy, yea that he will go with us himself. This made *David* rejoice when in the Valley of the *Shadow of Death:* and *Moses* was rather for dying where he stood, than to go one step without his God. O my Brother, if he will but go along with us, what need we be afraid of ten thousands that shall set themselves against us? But without him, *the proud helpers fall under the slain*.

I for my part have been in the fray before now, and though (through the goodness of him that is best) I am, as you see, alive; yet I cannot boast of my manhood. Glad shall I be, if I meet with no more such brunts, though I fear we are not got beyond all danger. However, since the Lion and the Bear have not as yet devoured me, I hope God will also deliver us from the next uncircumcised *Philistine*. Then sang *Christian*,

> Poor *Little-faith!* Hast been among the Thieves?
> Wast robb'd? Remember this: Whoso believes
> And gets more Faith, shall then a victor be
> Over ten thousand, else scarce over three.

So they went on, and *Ignorance* followed. They went then till they came at a place where they saw a way put itself into their way, and seemed withal to lie as straight as the way which they should go: and here they knew not which of the two to take, for both seemed straight before them; therefore here they stood still to consider. And as they were thinking about the way, behold a man black of flesh, but covered with a very light Robe, came to them, and asked them why they stood there? They answered they were going to the Cœlestial City, but knew not which of these ways to take. Follow me, said the man, it is thither that I am going. So they followed him in the way that but now came into the road, which by degrees turned, and turned them so from the City that they desired to go to, that in little time their faces were turned away from it: yet they followed him. But by-and-by, before they were aware, he led them both within the compass of a Net, in which they were both so intangled, that they knew not what to do; and with that *the white Robe fell off the black man's back*: then they saw where they were. Wherefore there they lay

(margin notes) A way, and a way — The flatterer finds them — Christian and his fellow deluded — They are taken in a net

crying some time, for they could not get themselves out.

They bewail their condition

CHR. Then said *Christian* to his fellow, Now do I see myself in an error. Did not the Shepherds bid us beware of the flatterers? As is the saying of the Wise man, so we have found it this day, *A man that flattereth his Neighbour, spreadeth a Net for his feet.*

A Shining One comes to them with a whip in his hand

HOPE. They also gave us a Note of directions about the way, for our more sure finding thereof; but therein we have also forgotten to read, and have not kept ourselves from the paths of the destroyer. Here *David* was wiser than we; for saith he, *Concerning the works of men, by the word of thy lips I have kept me from the paths of the destroyer.* Thus they lay bewailing themselves in the Net. At last they espied a Shining One coming towards them with a Whip of small cord in his hand. When he was come to the place where they were, he asked them whence they came? and what they did there? They told him that they were poor Pilgrims going to *Sion,* but were led out of their way by a black man, cloathed in white, who bid us, said they, follow him, for he was going thither too. Then said he with the Whip, It is *Flatterer,* a false Apostle, that hath transformed himself into an Angel of Light. So he rent the Net, and let the men out. Then said he to them, Follow me, that I may set you in your way again: so he led them back to the way which they had left to follow the *Flatterer.* Then he asked them, saying, Where did you lie the last night?

They are examined, and convicted of forgetfulness

They said, With the Shepherds upon the Delectable Mountains. He asked them then, If they had not of those Shepherds *a Note of direction for the way?* They answered, Yes. But did you, said he, when you were at a stand pluck out and read your Note? They answered, No. He asked them, Why? They said they forgot. He asked moreover, If the Shepherds did not bid them beware of the *Flatterer?*

Deceivers fine spoken

They answered, Yes; but we did not imagine, said they, *that this fine-spoken man had been he.*

Then I saw in my Dream, that he commanded *They are* them to *lie down;* which when they did, he chastised *whipped,* *and sent* them sore, to teach them the good way wherein *on their* they should walk; and as he chastised them he said, *way* *As many as I love, I rebuke and chasten; be zealous therefore, and repent.* This done, he bid them go on their way, and take good heed to the other directions of the Shepherds. So they thanked him for all his kindness, and went softly along the right way, singing,

> Come hither, you that walk along the way,
> See how the Pilgrims fare that go astray ;
> They catched are in an intangling Net,
> 'Cause they good Counsel lightly did forget ;
> 'Tis true they rescu'd were, but yet you see
> They're scourg'd to boot : Let this your caution be.

Now after a while, they perceived afar off one coming softly and alone all along the High-way to meet them. Then said *Christian* to his fellow, Yonder is a man with his back toward *Sion,* and he is coming to meet us.

HOPE. I see him, let us take heed to ourselves *The Athe-* now, lest he should prove a *Flatterer* also. So he *ist meets* *them* drew nearer and nearer, and at last came up unto them. His name was *Atheist,* and he asked them whither they were going.

CHR. We are going to the Mount *Sion.*

Then *Atheist* fell into a very great Laughter.   *He laughs*

CHR. What is the meaning of your Laughter?   *at them*

ATHEIST. I laugh to see what ignorant persons you are, to take upon you so tedious a Journey, and you are like to have nothing but your travel for your pains.

CHR. Why man? Do you think we shall not be *They* received?   *reason* *together*

ATHEIST. Received! There is no such place as you dream of in all this World.

CHR. But there is in the World to come.

ATHEIST. When I was at home in mine own Country, I heard as you now affirm, and from that hearing went out to see, and have been seeking this City this twenty years; but find no more of it than I did the first day I set out.

CHR. We have both heard and believe that there is such a place to be found.

ATHEIST. Had not I when at home believed, I had not come thus far to seek; but finding none, (and yet I should, had there been such a place to be found, for I have gone to seek it further than you) I am going back again, and will seek to refresh myself with the things that I then cast away, for hopes of that which I now see is not.

Christian proveth his brother

CHR. Then said *Christian* to *Hopeful* his fellow, Is it true which this man hath said?

HOPE. Take heed, he is one of the Flatterers; remember what it hath cost us once already for our hearkening to such kind of fellows. What! no Mount *Sion?* Did we not see from the Delectable Mountains the Gate of the City? Also, are we not now to walk by Faith. Let us go on, said *Hopeful,* lest the man with the Whip overtake us again. You should have taught me that lesson, which I will round you in the ears withal: *Cease, my Son, to hear the instruction that causeth to err from the words of knowledge.* I say my Brother, cease to hear him, and let us believe to the saving of the Soul.

Hopeful's gracious answer

A remembrance of former chastisements is a help against present temptations

A fruit of an honest heart

CHR. My Brother, I did not put the question to thee for that I doubted of the Truth of our belief myself, but to prove thee, and to fetch from thee a fruit of the honesty of thy heart. As for this man, I know that he is blinded by the god of this World. Let thee and I go on, knowing that we have belief of the Truth, and no lie is of the Truth.

HOPE. Now do I rejoice in hope of the glory of God. So they turned away from the man; and he laughing at them went his way.

They are come to the Enchanted Ground

I saw then in my Dream, that they went till they come into a certain Country, whose air naturally tended to make one drowsy, if he came a stranger into it. And here *Hopeful* began to be very dull

and heavy of sleep; wherefore he said unto *Chris-* Hopeful begins to be drowsy
tian, I do now begin to grow so drowsy that I can
scarcely hold up mine eyes, let us lie down here and
take one nap.

CHR. By no means, said the other, lest sleeping Christian keeps him awake
we never awake more.

HOPE. Why my Brother? Sleep is sweet to the
labouring man; we may be refreshed if we take
a nap.

CHR. Do you not remember that one of the
Shepherds bid us beware of the Inchanted Ground?
He meant by that, that we should beware of sleeping; wherefore let us not sleep as do others, but
let us watch and be sober.

HOPE. I acknowledge myself in a fault, and had He is thankful
I been here alone I had by sleeping run the danger
of death. I see it is true that the Wise man saith,
Two are better than one. Hitherto hath thy company been my mercy, *and thou shalt have a good
reward for thy labour.*

Now then, said *Christian,* to prevent drowsiness To prevent drowsiness they fall to good discourse
in this place, let us fall into good discourse.

HOPE. With all my heart, said the other.

CHR. Where shall we begin?

HOPE. Where God began with us. But do you Good discourse prevents drowsiness
begin, if you please.

CHR. I will sing you first this song:

> When Saints do sleepy grow, let them come hither, The dream-er's note
> And hear how these two Pilgrims talk together:
> Yea, let them learn of them in any wise,
> Thus to keep ope their drowsy, slumbring eyes.
> Saints' fellowship, if it be managed well,
> Keeps them awake, and that in spite of Hell.

CHR. Then *Christian* began and said, I will ask They begin at the beginning of their conversion
you a question: How came you to think at first of
doing as you do now?

HOPE. Do you mean, how came I at first to look
after the good of my soul?

CHR. Yes, that is my meaning.

HOPE. I continued a great while in the delight

of those things which were seen and sold at our
Fair; things which I believe now would have (had
I continued in them still) drowned me in perdition
and destruction.

CHR. What things were they?

Hopeful's life before conversion

HOPE. All the Treasures and Riches of the World.
Also I delighted much in Rioting, Revelling, Drinking, Swearing, Lying, Uncleanness, Sabbath-break-
ing, and what not, that tended to destroy the Soul.
But I found at last, by hearing and considering of
things that are Divine, which indeed I heard of you,
as also of beloved *Faithful,* that was put to death
for his faith and good living in *Vanity Fair, That
the end of these things is death.* And that for
these things' sake the wrath of God cometh upon
the children of disobedience.

CHR. And did you presently fall under the power
of this conviction?

Hopeful at first shuts his eyes against the light

HOPE. No, I was not willing presently to know
the evil of sin, nor the damnation that follows upon
the commission of it; but endeavoured, when my
mind at first began to be shaken with the Word, to
shut mine eyes against the light thereof.

CHR. But what was the cause of your carrying
of it thus to the first workings of God's blessed
Spirit upon you?

Reasons of his re-sisting of the light

HOPE. The causes were, 1. I was ignorant that
this was the work of God upon me. I never thought
that by awakenings for sin God at first begins the
conversion of a sinner. 2. Sin was yet very sweet
to my flesh, and I was loth to leave it. 3. I could
not tell how to part with mine old Companions, their
presence and actions were so desirable unto me.
4. The hours in which convictions were upon me,
were such troublesome and such heart-affrighting
hours, that I could not bear, no not so much as the
remembrance of them upon my heart.

CHR. Then as it seems, sometimes you got rid
of your trouble.

HOPE. Yes verily, but it would come into my mind

again, and then I should be as bad, nay worse, than I was before.

CHR. Why, what was it that brought your sins to mind again?

HOPE. Many things; as

1. If I did but meet a good man in the Streets; or,

2. If I have heard any read in the Bible; or,

3. If mine Head did begin to ake; or,

4. If I were told that some of my Neighbors were sick; or,

5. If I heard the Bell toll for some that were dead; or,

6. If I thought of Dying myself; or,

7. If I heard that sudden Death happened to others;

8. But especially, when I thought of myself, that I must quickly come to Judgment.

CHR. And could you at any time with ease get off the guilt of sin, when by any of these ways it came upon you?

HOPE. No, not latterly, for then they got faster hold of my conscience; and then, if I did but think of going back to sin, (though my mind was turned against it) it would be double torment to me.

CHR. And how did you do then?

HOPE. I thought I must endeavour to mend my life; for else, thought I, I am sure to be damned.

CHR. And did you endeavour to mend?

HOPE. Yes, and fled from not only my sins, but sinful Company too; and betook me to religious duties, as Prayer, Reading, Weeping for Sin, speaking Truth to my Neighbors, &c. These things did I, with many others, too much here to relate.

CHR. And did you think yourself well then?

HOPE. Yes, for a while; but at the last my trouble came tumbling upon me again, and that over the neck of all my reformations.

CHR. How came that about, since you were now reformed?

HOPE. There were several things brought it upon

Marginal notes:

When he had lost his sense of sin, what brought this again

When he could no longer shake off his guilt by sinful courses, then he endeavours to mend

Then he thought himself well

Reformation at last could not help, and why

me, especially such sayings as these: *All our right-eousnesses are as filthy rags. By the works of the Law no man shall be justified. When you have done all things, say, We are unprofitable:* with many more such like. From whence I began to reason with myself thus: If *all* my righteousnesses are filthy rags, if by the deeds of the Law, *no* man can be justified; and if, when we have done *all,* we are yet unprofitable, then 'tis but a folly to think of Heaven by the Law. I further thought thus: If a man runs 100*l.* into the Shop-keeper's debt, and

His being a debtor by the law troubled him

after that shall pay for all that he shall fetch; yet his old debt stands still in the Book uncrossed, for the which the Shop-keeper may sue him, and cast him into Prison till he shall pay the debt.

CHR. Well, and how did you apply this to yourself?

HOPE. Why, I thought thus with myself: I have by my sins run a great way into God's Book, and that my now reforming will not pay off that score; therefore I should think still under all my present amendments, But how shall I be freed from that damnation that I have brought myself in danger of by my former transgressions?

CHR. A very good application: but pray go on.

HOPE. Another thing that hath troubled me, even since my late amendments, is, that if I look nar-

His espying bad things in his best duties troubled him

rowly into the best of what I do now, I still see sin, new sin, mixing itself with the best of that I do; so that now I am forced to conclude, that not-withstanding my former fond conceits of myself and duties, I have committed sin enough in one duty to send me to Hell, though my former life had been faultless.

CHR. And what did you do then?

This made him break his mind to Faithful, who told him the way to be saved

HOPE. Do! I could not tell what to do, till I brake my mind to *Faithful,* for he and I were well acquainted. And he told me, that unless I could obtain the righteousness of a man that never had sinned, neither mine own, nor all the righteousness of the world could save me.

CHR. And did you think he spake true?

HOPE. Had he told me so when I was pleased and satisfied with mine own amendments, I had called him Fool for his pains: but now, since I see mine own infirmity, and the sin that cleaves to my best performance, I have been forced to be of his opinion.

CHR. But did you think, when at first he suggested it to you, that there was such a man to be found, of whom it might justly be said, That he never committed sin?

HOPE. I must confess the words at first sounded strangely; but after a little more talk and company with him, I had full conviction about it. *At which he started at present*

CHR. And did you ask him what man this was, and how you must be justified by him?

HOPE. Yes, and he told me it was the Lord *Jesus*, that dwelleth on the right hand of the Most High. And thus, said he, you must be justified by him, even by trusting to what he hath done by himself in the days of his flesh, and suffered when he did hang on the Tree. I asked him further, How that man's righteousness could be of that efficacy to justify another before God? And he told me he was the mighty God, and did what he did, and died the death also, not for himself, but for me; to whom his doings, and the worthiness of them should be imputed, if I believed on him. *A more particular discovery of the way to be saved*

CHR. And what did you do then?

HOPE. I made my objections against my believing, for that I thought he was not willing to save me. *He doubts of acceptation*

CHR. And what said *Faithful* to you then?

HOPE. He bid me go to him and see: then I said it was presumption: but he said, No, for I was invited to come. Then he gave me a Book of *Jesus* his inditing, to encourage me the more freely to come; and he said concerning that Book, that every jot and tittle thereof stood firmer than Heaven and Earth. Then I asked him, What I must do when I came? and he told me, I must entreat upon my knees with all my heart and soul, the Father to *He is better instructed* reveal him to me. Then I asked him further, How I must make my supplication to him? And he said, Go, and thou shalt find him upon a mercy-seat, where he sits all the year long, to give pardon and forgiveness to them that come. I told him that I knew not what to say when I came. And he

He is bid to pray

bid me say to this effect: *God be merciful to me a sinner, and make me to know and believe in Jesus Christ; for I see that if his righteousness had not been, or I have not faith in that righteousness, I am utterly cast away: Lord, I have heard that thou art a merciful God, and hast ordained that thy Son Jesus Christ should be the Saviour of the world; and moreover, that thou art willing to bestow him upon such a poor sinner as I am, (and I am a sinner indeed) Lord, take therefore this opportunity, and magnify thy grace in the Salvation of my soul, through thy Son Jesus Christ.* Amen.

He prays

CHR. And did you do as you were bidden?

HOPE. Yes, over and over and over.

CHR. And did the Father reveal his Son to you?

HOPE. Not at the first, nor second, nor third, nor fourth, nor fifth, no nor at the sixth time neither.

CHR. What did you do then?

HOPE. What! why I could not tell what to do.

CHR. Had you not thought of leaving off praying?

He thought to leave off praying

HOPE. Yes, an hundred times twice told.

CHR. And what was the reason you did not?

HOPE. I believed that that was true which had been told me, to wit, that without the righteousness of this Christ all the world could not save me; and

He durst not leave off praying, and why

therefore thought I with myself, If I leave off, I die, and can but die at the Throne of Grace. And withal, this came into my mind, *If it tarry, wait for it, because it will surely come, it will not tarry*. So I continued praying until the Father shewed me his Son.

CHR. And how was he revealed unto you?

HOPE. I did not see him with my bodily eyes, but

with the eyes of mine understanding; and thus Christ is revealed to him, and how it was: One day I was very sad, I think sadder than at any one time in my life, and this sadness was through a fresh sight of the greatness and vileness of my sins: and as I was then looking for nothing but Hell, and the everlasting damnation of my Soul, suddenly, as I thought, I saw the Lord Jesus look down from Heaven upon me, and saying, *Believe on the Lord Jesus Christ, and thou shalt be saved.*

But I replied, Lord, I am a great, a very great sinner. And he answered *My grace is sufficient for thee.* Then I said, But Lord, what is believing? And then I saw from that saying, *He that cometh to me shall never hunger, and he that believeth on me shall never thirst,* that believing and coming was all one; and that he that came, that, is, ran out in his heart and affections after salvation by Christ, he indeed believed in Christ. Then the water stood in mine eyes, and I asked further, But Lord, may such a great sinner as I am be indeed accepted of thee, and be saved by thee? And I heard him say, *And him that cometh to me I will in no wise cast out.* Then I said, But how, Lord, must I consider of thee in my coming to thee, that my faith may be placed aright upon thee? Then he said, *Christ Jesus came into the World to save sinners. He is the end of the Law for righteousness to every one that believes. He died for our sins, and rose again for our justification. He loved us and washed us from our sins in his own blood. He is Mediator between God and us. He ever liveth to make intercession for us.* From all which I gathered, that I must look for Righteousness in his Person, and for Satisfaction for my Sins by his Blood; that what he did in obedience to his Father's Law, and in submitting to the penalty thereof, was not for himself, but for him that will accept it for his Salvation, and be thankful. And now was my heart full of joy, mine eyes full of tears, and mine affections running over with love to the Name, People, and Ways of Jesus Christ.

CHR. This was a revelation of Christ to your soul indeed; but tell me particulaly what effect this had upon your spirit.

HOPE. It made me see that all the World, notwithstanding all the righteousness thereof, is in a state of condemnation. It made me see that God the Father, though he be just, can justly justify the coming sinner. It made me greatly ashamed of the vileness of my former life, and confounded me with the sense of mine own ignorance; for there never came thought into my heart before now, that shewed me so the beauty of Jesus Christ. It made me love a holy life, and long to do something for the Honour and Glory of the Name of the Lord Jesus; yea, I thought that had I now a thousand gallons of blood in my body, I could spill it all for the sake of the Lord Jesus.

I saw then in my Dream that *Hopeful* looked back and saw *Ignorance,* whom they had left behind, coming after. Look, said he to *Christian,* how far yonder youngster loitereth behind.

CHR. Ay, ay, I see him; he careth not for our company.

HOPE. But I tro it would not have hurt him, had he kept pace with us hitherto.

CHR. That's true, but I warrant you he thinketh otherwise.

Young Ignorance comes up again; their talk

HOPE. That I think he doth, but however let us tarry for him. So they did.

Then *Christian* said to him, Come away man, why do you stay so behind?

IGNOR. I take my pleasure in walking alone, even more a great deal than in Company, unless I like it the better.

Then said *Christian* to *Hopeful* (but softly) Did I not tell you he cared not for our company? But however, said he, come up, and let us talk away the time in this solitary place. Then directing his speech to *Ignorance,* he said, Come, how do you? How stands it between God and your Soul now?

IGNOR. I hope well; for I am always full of good motions, that come into my mind to comfort me as I walk.

Ignorance's hope, and the ground of it

CHR. What good motions? pray tell us.

IGNOR. Why, I think of God and Heaven.

CHR. So do the Devils and damned Souls.

IGNOR. But I think of them and desire them.

CHR. So do many that are never like to come there. *The Soul of the Sluggard desires, and hath nothing.*

IGNOR. But I think of them, and leave all for them.

CHR. That I doubt, for leaving all is an hard matter, yea a harder matter than many are aware of. But why, or by what, art thou persuaded that thou hast left all for God and Heaven?

IGNOR. My heart tells me so.

CHR. The wise man says, *He that trusts his own heart is a fool.*

IGNOR. This is spoken of an evil heart, but mine is a good one.

CHR. But how dost thou prove that?

IGNOR. It comforts me in hopes of Heaven.

CHR. That may be through its deceitfulness, for a man's heart may minister comfort to him in the hopes of that thing for which he yet has no ground to hope.

IGNOR. But my heart and life agree together, and therefore my hope is well grounded.

CHR. Who told thee that thy heart and life agree together?

IGNOR. My heart tells me so.

CHR. Ask my fellow if I be a Thief! Thy heart tells thee so! Except the Word of God beareth witness in this matter, other testimony is of no value.

IGNOR. But is it not a good heart that has good thoughts? and is not that a good life that is according to God's Commandments?

CHR. Yes, that is a good heart that hath good thoughts, and that is a good life that is according to God's Commandments; but it is one thing indeed to have these, and another thing only to think so.

IGNOR. Pray, what count you good thoughts, and a life according to God's Commandments?

CHR. There are good thoughts of divers kinds, some respecting ourselves, some God, some Christ, some other things.

What are
good
thoughts

IGNOR. What be good thoughts respecting ourselves?

CHR. Such as agree with the Word of God.

IGNOR. When do our thoughts of ourselves agree with the Word of God?

CHR. When we pass the same Judgment upon ourselves which the Word passes. To explain myself, the Word of God saith of persons in a natural condition, *There is none righteous, there is none that doth good.* It saith also, *That every imagination of the heart of man is only evil, and that continually.* And again, *The imagination of man's heart is evil from his youth.* Now then, when we think thus of ourselves, having sense thereof, then are our thoughts good ones, because according to the Word of God.

IGNOR. I will never believe that my heart is thus bad.

CHR. Therefore thou never hadst one good thought concerning thyself in thy life. But let me go on: As the Word passeth a Judgment upon our *Heart,* so it passeth a Judgment upon our *Ways;* and when our thoughts of our *Hearts* and *Ways* agree with the Judgment which the Word giveth of both, then are both good, because agreeing thereto.

IGNOR. Make out your meaning.

CHR. Why, the Word of God saith that man's ways are crooked ways, not good, but perverse. It saith they are naturally out of the good way, that they have not known it. Now when a man thus thinketh of his ways, I say, when he doth sensibly,

and with heart-humiliation thus think, then hath
he good thoughts of his own ways, because his
thoughts now agree with the Judgment of the Word
of God.

IGNOR. What are good thoughts concerning God?

CHR. Even as I have said concerning ourselves,
when our thoughts of God do agree with what the
Word saith of him; and that is, when we think
of his Being and Attributes as the Word hath taught,
of which I cannot now discourse at large: but to
speak of him with reference to us, then we have right
thoughts of God, when we think that he knows us
better than we know ourselves, and can see sin in us
when and where we can see none in ourselves; when
we think he knows our inmost thoughts, and that
our heart with all its depths is always open unto his
eyes; also when we think that all our Righteousness
stinks in his nostrils, and that therefore he cannot
abide to see us stand before him in any confidence,
even in all our best performances.

IGNOR. Do you think that I am such a fool as
to think God can see no further than I? or that
I would come to God in the best of my performances?

CHR. Why, how dost thou think in this matter?

IGNOR. Why, to be short, I think I must believe
in Christ for Justification.

CHR. How! think thou must believe in Christ,
when thou seest not thy need of him! Thou neither
seest thy original or actual infirmities; but hast
such an opinion of thyself, and of what thou doest,
as plainly renders thee to be one that did never
see a necessity of Christ's personal righteousness
to justify thee before God. How then dost thou
say I believe in Christ?

IGNOR. I believe well enough for all that.

CHR. How dost thou believe?

IGNOR. I believe that Christ died for sinners, and The
that I shall be justified before God from the faith of
Ignorance
curse, through his gracious acceptance of my obedi-

ence to his Law. Or thus, Christ makes my Duties that are religious, acceptable to his Father by virtue of his Merits; and so shall I be justified.

CHR. Let me give an answer to this Confession of thy Faith.

1. Thou believest with a fantastical Faith, for this Faith is nowhere described in the Word.

2. Thou believest with a false Faith, because it taketh Justification from the personal righteousness of Christ, and applies it to thy own.

3. This Faith maketh not Christ a Justifier of thy person, but of thy actions; and of thy person for thy actions' sake, which is false.

4. Therefore this Faith is deceitful, even such as will leave thee under wrath in the day of God Almighty; for true Justifying Faith puts the soul (as sensible of its lost condition by the Law) upon flying for refuge unto Christ's righteousness, (which righteousness of his is not an act of grace, by which he maketh for Justification *thy* obedience accepted by God; but *his* personal obedience to the Law, in doing and suffering for us what that required at our hands.) This righteousness, I say, true Faith accepteth; under the skirt of which the soul being shrouded, and by it presented as spotless before God, it is accepted, and acquit from condemnation.

IGNOR. What! would you have us trust to what Christ in his own person has done without us? This conceit would loosen the reins of our lust, and tolerate us to live as we list. For what matter how we live, if we may be Justified by Christ's personal righteousness from all, when we believe it?

CHR. *Ignorance* is thy name, and as thy name is, so art thou; even this thy answer demonstrateth what I say. *Ignorant* thou art of what Justifying Righteousness is, and as ignorant how to secure thy Soul through the Faith of it from the heavy wrath of God. Yea, thou also art ignorant of the true effects of saving Faith in this Righteousness of

Christ, which is to bow and win over the heart to God in Christ, to love his Name, his Word, Ways, and People, and not as thou ignorantly imaginest.

HOPE. Ask him if ever he had Christ revealed to him from Heaven.

IGNOR. What! you are a man for revelations! I believe that what both you, and all the rest of you, say about that matter, is but the fruit of distracted brains. *Ignorance jangles with them*

HOPE. Why man! Christ is so hid in God from the natural apprehensions of all flesh, that he cannot by any man be savingly known, unless God the Father reveals him to them.

IGNOR. That is your Faith, but not mine; yet mine I doubt not is as good as yours, though I have not in my head so many whimsies as you. *He speaks reproachfully of what he knows not*

CHR. Give me leave to put in a word: You ought not so slightly to speak of this matter: for this I will boldly affirm (even as my good Companion hath done) that no man can know Jesus Christ but by the revelation of the Father; yea, and Faith too, by which the soul layeth hold upon Christ, (if it be right) must be wrought by the exceeding greatness of his mighty power; the working of which Faith, I perceive, poor *Ignorance,* thou art ignorant of.

Be awakened then, see thine own wretchedness, and fly to the Lord Jesus; and by his righteousness, which is the righteousness of God, (for he himself is God) thou shalt be delivered from condemnation.

IGNOR. You go so fast I cannot keep pace with you, do you go on before, I must stay a while behind. *The talk broke up*

Then they said,

> Well *Ignorance*, wilt thou yet foolish be,
> To slight good Counsel, ten times given thee?
> And if thou yet refuse it, thou shalt know
> E're long the evil of thy doing so:
> Remember, man, in time; stoop, do not fear,
> Good Counsel taken well, saves; therefore hear:
> But if thou yet shall slight it, thou wilt be
> The loser, *Ignorance*, I'll warrant thee.

Then *Christian* addressed thus himself to his fellow.

CHR. Well, come my good *Hopeful*, I perceive that thou and I must walk by ourselves again.

So I saw in my Dream that they went on apace before, and *Ignorance* he came hobbling after. Then said *Christian* to his Companion, It pities me much for this poor man, it will certainly go ill with him at last.

HOPE. Alas, there are abundance in our Town in his condition, whole families, yea, whole Streets, and that of Pilgrims too; and if there be so many in our parts, how many think you, must there be in the place where he was born?

CHR. Indeed the Word saith, *He hath blinded their eyes, lest they should see*, &c. But now we are by ourselves, what do you think of such men? Have they at no time, think you, convictions of sin, and so consequently fears that their state is dangerous?

HOPE. Nay, do you answer that question yourself, for you are the elder man.

The good use of fear CHR. Then I say, sometimes (as I think) they may, but they being naturally ignorant, understand not that such convictions tend to their good; and therefore they do desperately seek to stifle them, and presumptuously continue to flatter themselves in the way of their own hearts.

HOPE. I do believe, as you say, that fear tends much to men's good, and to make them right at their beginning to go on Pilgrimage.

CHR. Without all doubt it doth, if it be right; for so says the Word, *The fear of the Lord is the beginning of Wisdom*.

Right fear HOPE. How will you describe right fear?

CHR. True or right fear is discovered by three things:

I. By its rise; it is caused by saving convictions for sin.

2. It driveth the soul to lay fast hold of Christ for salvation.

3. It begetteth and continueth in the soul a great reverence of God, his Word, and Ways, keeping it tender, and making it afraid to turn from them, to the right hand or to the left, to anything that may dishonour God, break its peace, grieve the Spirit, or cause the Enemy to speak reproachfully.

HOPE. Well said; I believe you have said the truth. Are we now almost got past the Inchanted Ground?

CHR. Why, art thou weary of this discourse?

HOPE. No, verily, but that I would know where we are.

CHR. We have not now above two miles further to go thereon. But let us return to our matter. Now the Ignorant know not that such convictions as tend to put them in fear are for their good, and therefore they seek to stifle them.

HOPE. How do they seek to stifle them?

CHR. 1. They think that those fears are wrought by the Devil, (though indeed they are wrought of God) and thinking so, they resist them as things that directly tend to their overthrow. 2. They also think that these fears tend to the spoiling of their Faith, when alas for them, poor men that they are, they have none at all! and therefore they harden their hearts against them. 3. They presume they ought not to fear, and therefore in despite of them wax presumptuously confident. 4. They see that these fears tend to take away from them their pitiful old self-holiness, and therefore they resist them with all their might.

HOPE. I know something of this myself; for before I knew myself it was so with me.

CHR. Well, we will leave at this time our Neighbor *Ignorance* by himself, and fall upon another profitable question.

HOPE. With all my heart, but you shall still begin.

CHR. Well then, did you not know about ten years

Talk about
one
Temporary ago, one *Temporary* in your parts, who was a forward man in Religion then?

Where he
dwelt HOPE. Know him! yes, he dwelt in *Graceless,* a town about two miles off of *Honesty,* and he dwelt next door to one *Turn-back*.

He was
towardly
once CHR. Right, he dwelt under the same roof with him. Well, that man was much awakened once; I believe that then he had some sight of his sins, and of the wages that were due thereto.

HOPE. I am of your mind, for (my house not being above three miles from him) he would ofttimes come to me, and that with many tears. Truly I pitied the man, and was not altogether without hope of him; but one may see it is not every one that cries, *Lord, Lord*.

CHR. He told me once, That he was resolved to go on Pilgrimage, as we do now; but all of a sudden he grew acquainted with one *Saveself,* and then he became a stranger to me.

HOPE. Now since we are talking about him, let us a little enquire into the reason of the sudden backsliding of him and such others.

CHR. It may be very profitable, but do you begin.

HOPE. Well then, there are in my judgment four reasons for it.

Reasons
why
towardly
ones
go back 1. Though the consciences of such men are awakened, yet their minds are not changed; therefore when the power of guilt weareth away, that which provoked them to be religious ceaseth. Wherefore they naturally turn to their own course again, even as we see the Dog that is sick of what he has eaten, so long as his sickness prevails, he vomits and casts up all; not that he doth this of a free mind, (if we may say a Dog has a mind) but because it troubleth his Stomach; but now when his sickness is over, and so his Stomach eased, his desire being not at all alienate from his vomit, he turns him about and licks up all; and so it is true which is written, *The Dog is turned to his own vomit again.* This I say, being hot for Heaven by vertue only of

the sense and fear of the torments of Hell, as their
sense of Hell and the fears of damnation chills and
cools, so their desires for Heaven and Salvation cool
also. So then it comes to pass, that when their guilt
and fear is gone, their desires for Heaven and Happiness die, and they return to their course again.

2. Another reason is, they have slavish fears that
do over-master them; I speak now of the fears that
they have of men, *For the fear of men bringeth a
snare*. So then, though they seem to be hot for
Heaven, so long as the flames of Hell are about their
ears, yet when that terror is a little over, they betake themselves to second thoughts; namely, that
'tis good to be wise, and not to run (for they know
not what) the hazard of losing all; or at least, of
bringing themselves into unavoidable and unneces-
sary troubles, and so they fall in with the world
again.

3. The shame that attends Religion lies also as a
block in their way; they are proud and haughty, and
Religion in their eye is low and contemptible; therefore when they have lost their sense of Hell and
wrath to come, they return again to their former
course.

4. Guilt, and to meditate terror, are grievous to
them; they like not to see their misery before they
come into it. Though perhaps the sight of it first,
if they loved that sight, might make them fly whither
the righteous fly and are safe. But because they
do, as I hinted before, even shun the thoughts of
guilt and terror, therefore when once they are rid
of their awakenings about the terrors and wrath of
God, they harden their hearts gladly, and chuse such
ways as will harden them more and more.

CHR. You are pretty near the business, for the
bottom of all is, for want of a change in their mind
and will. And therefore they are but like the
Felon that standeth before the Judge, he quakes and
trembles, and seems to repent most heartily, but
the bottom of all is the fear of the Halter, not that

he hath any detestation of the offence; as is evident, because, let but this man have his liberty, and he will be a Thief, and so a Rogue still; whereas, if his mind was changed, he would be otherwise.

HOPE. Now I have shewed you the reasons of their going back, do you show me the manner thereof.

CHR. So I will willingly.

How the apostate goes back 1. They draw off their thoughts, all that they may, from the remembrance of God, Death and Judgment to come.

2. Then they cast off by degrees private Duties, as Closet-prayer, Curbing their Lusts, Watching, Sorrow for Sin, and the like.

3. Then they shun the company of lively and warm Christians.

4. After that they grow cold to public Duty, as Hearing, Reading, Godly Conference, and the like.

5. Then they begin to pick holes, as we say, in the Coats of some of the Godly; and that devilishly, that they may have a seeming colour to throw Religion (for the sake of some infirmity they have spied in them) behind their backs.

6. Then they begin to adhere to, and associate themselves with carnal, loose and wanton men.

7. Then they give way to carnal and wanton discourses in secret; and glad are they if they can see such things in any that are counted honest, that they may the more boldly do it through their example.

8. After this, they begin to play with little sins openly.

9. And then, being hardened, they shew themselves as they are. Thus being launched again into the gulf of misery, unless a Miracle of Grace prevent it, they everlastingly perish in their own deceivings.

Angels   Now I saw in my Dream, that by this time the Pilgrims were got over the Inchanted Ground, and entering into the Country of *Beulah,* whose air was very sweet and pleasant, the way lying directly through it, they solaced themselves there for a sea-

son. Yea, here they heard continually the singing
of Birds, and saw every day the Flowers appear in
the earth, and heard the voice of the Turtle in the
land. In this Country the Sun shineth night and
day; wherefore this was beyond the Valley of the
Shadow of Death, and also out of the reach of Giant
Despair, neither could they from this place so much
as see *Doubting* Castle. Here they were within
sight of the City they were going to, also here met
them some of the inhabitants thereof; for in this
land the Shining Ones commonly walked, because it
was upon the borders of Heaven. In this land also
the contract between the Bride and the Bridegroom
was renewed; yea here, *as the Bridegroom rejoiceth
over the Bride, so did their God rejoice over them.*
Here they had no want of Corn and Wine; for in
this place they met with abundance of what they
had sought for in all their Pilgrimage. Here they
heard voices from out of the City, loud voices, saying, *Say ye to the daughter of* Zion *Behold thy
salvation cometh, behold his reward is with him.*
Here all the inhabitants of the Country called them,
*The holy People, The redeemed of the Lord, Sought
out,* &c.

Now as they walked in this land, they had more
rejoicing than in parts more remote from the Kingdom to which they were bound; and drawing near
to the City, they had yet a more perfect view
thereof. It was builded of Pearls and Precious
Stones, also the Street thereof was paved with Gold;
so that by reason of the natural glory of the City,
and the reflections of the Sun-beams upon it, *Christian* with desire fell sick, *Hopeful* also had a fit or
two of the same disease. Wherefore here they,
lay by it a while, crying out because of their pangs,
*If you see my Beloved, tell him that I am sick of
love.*

But being a little strengthened, and better able
to bear their sickness, they walked on their way, and
came yet nearer and nearer, where were Orchards,

Vineyards, and Gardens, and their gates opened
into the High-way. Now as they came up to these
places, behold the Gardener stood in the way, to
whom the Pilgrims said, Whose goodly Vineyards
and Gardens are these? He answered, They are the
King's and are planted here for his own delights,
and also for the solace of Pilgrims. So the Gardener had them into the Vineyards, and bid them
refresh themselves with Dainties. He also shewed
them there the King's walks, and the Arbors where
he delighted to be; and here they tarried and slept.

Now I beheld in my Dream, that they talked
more in their sleep at this time than ever they did
in all their Journey; and being in a muse thereabout,
the Gardener said even to me, Wherefore musest
thou at the matter? It is the nature of the fruit
of the Grapes of these Vinyards to go down so
sweetly as to cause the lips of them that are asleep
to speak.

So I saw that when they awoke, they addressed
themselves to go up to the City. But, as I said,
the reflection of the Sun upon the City (for the
City was pure Gold) was so extremely glorious, that
they could not as yet with open face behold it,
but through an *Instrument* made for that purpose.
So I saw that as they went on, there met them two
men, in Raiment that shone like Gold, also their
faces shone as the light.

These men asked the Pilgrims whence they came?
and they told them. They also asked them where
they had lodged, what difficulties and dangers, what
comforts and pleasures they had met in the way?
and they told them. Then said the men that met
them, You have but two difficulties more to meet
with, and then you are in the City.

Christian then and his Companion asked the men
to go along with them, so they told them they would.
But, said they, you must obtain it by your own
Faith. So I saw in my Dream that they went on
together till they came in sight of the Gate.

Now I further saw that betwixt them and the Death
Gate was a River, but there was no Bridge to go
over, the River was very deep: at the sight therefore of this River the Pilgrims were much stunned;
but the men that went with them said, You must
go through, or you cannot come at the Gate.

The Pilgrims then began to enquire if there was Death is
no other way to the Gate; to which they answered, not welcome to
Yes, but there hath not any, save two, to wit, *Enoch* nature,
and *Elijah*, been permitted to tread that path, since though by
it we pass
the foundation of the World, nor shall, until the out of this
last Trumpet shall sound. The Pilgrims then, es- world in
to glory
pecially *Christian*, began to dispond in his mind,
and looked this way and that, but no way could be
found by them by which they might escape the Angels
River. Then they asked the men if the Waters help us
not com-
were all of a depth? They said, No; yet they could fortably
not help them in that case, for said they, *you shall* through
death
find it deeper or shallower, as you believe in the
King of the place.

They then addressed themselves to the Water;
and entring, *Christian* began to sink, and crying
out to his good friend *Hopeful,* he said, I sink in
deep Waters; the Billows go over my head, all his
Waves go over me, *Selah.*

Then said the other, Be of good cheer my Brother, Christian's
conflict at
I feel the bottom, and it is good. Then said *Chris-* the hour
tian, Ah my friend, the sorrows of death have com- of death
passed me about, I shall not see the land that flows
with milk and honey. And with that a great darkness and horror fell upon *Christian,* so that he could
not see before him. Also here he in great measure
lost his senses, so that he could neither remember,
nor orderly talk of any of those sweet refreshments
that he had met with in the way of his Pilgrimage.
But all the words that he spake still tended to
discover that he had horror of mind, and heart-
fears that he should die in that River, and never
obtain entrance in at the Gate. Here also, as they
that stood by perceived, he was much in the trouble-

some thoughts of the sins that he had committed, both since and before he began to be a Pilgrim. 'Twas also observed that he was troubled with apparitions of Hobgoblins and evil Spirits, for ever and anon he would intimate so much by words. *Hopeful* therefore here had much ado to keep his Brother's head above water; yea sometimes he would be quite gone down, and then ere a while he would rise up again half dead. *Hopeful* also would endeavour to comfort him, saying, Brother, I see the Gate, and men standing by to receive us. But *Christian* would answer, 'Tis you, 'tis you they wait for, you have been *hopeful* ever since I knew you. And so have you, said he to *Christian*. Ah Brother, said he, surely if I was right, he would now arise to help me; but for my sins he hath brought me into the snare, and hath left me. Then said *Hopeful*, My Brother, you have quite forgot the Text, where it is said of the wicked, *There is no band in their death, but their strength is firm, they are not troubled as other men, neither are they plagued like other men.* These troubles and distresses that you go through in these Waters are no sign that God hath forsaken you, but are sent to try you, whether you will call to mind that which heretofore you have received of his goodness, and live upon him in your distresses.

Christian delivered from his fears in death

Then I saw in my Dream, that *Christian* was as in a muse a while. To whom also *Hopeful* added this word, *Be of good cheer, Jesus Christ maketh thee whole;* and with that *Christian* brake out with a loud voice, Oh I see him again, and he tells me, *When thou passest through the Waters, I will be with thee; and through the Rivers, they shall not overflow thee.* Then they both took courage, and the Enemy was after that as still as a stone, until they were gone over. *Christian* therefore presently found ground to stand upon, and so it followed that the rest of the River was but shallow. Thus they got over. Now upon the bank of the River on **the**

other side, they saw the two shining men again, *The angels do wait for them, so soon as they are passed out of this world*
who there waited for them; wherefore being come
out of the River, they saluted them saying, *We are*
ministring Spirits, sent forth to minister for those
that shall be heirs of salvation. Thus they went
along towards the Gate.

Now, now, look how the holy Pilgrims ride,
Clouds are their Chariots, Angels are their Guide:
Who would not here for him all hazards run,
That thus provides for his when this World's done?

Now you must note that the City stood upon a *They have put off mortality*
mighty Hill, but the Pilgrims went up that Hill with
ease because they had these two men to lead them
up by the arms; also they had left their *mortal Gar-*
ments behind them in the River, for though they
went in with them, they came out without them.
They therefore went up here with much agility
and speed, though the foundation upon which the
City was framed was higher than the Clouds. They
therefore went up through the Regions of the Air,
sweetly talking as they went, being comforted, because they safely got over the River, and had such
glorious Companions to attend them.

The talk that they had with the Shining Ones
was about the glory of the place, who told them
that the beauty and glory of it was inexpressible.
There, said they, is the Mount *Sion,* the heavenly
Jerusalem, the innumerable company of Angels, and
the Spirits of just men made perfect. You are
going now, said they, to the Paradise of God, wherein you shall see the Tree of Life, and eat of the
never-fading fruits thereof; and when you come
there, you shall have white Robes given you, and
your walk and talk shall be every day with the
King, even all the days of Eternity. There you
shall not see again such things as you saw when
you were in the lower Region upon the earth, to
wit, sorrow, sickness, affliction, and death, *for the*
former things are passed away. You are now going

to *Abraham*, to *Isaac*, and *Jacob,* and to the Prophets, men that God hath taken away from the evil to come, and that are now resting upon their beds, each one walking in his righteousness. The men then asked, What must we do in the holy place? To whom it was answered, You must there receive the comfort of all your toil, and have joy for all your sorrow; you must reap what you have sown, even the fruit of all your Prayers and Tears, and sufferings for the King by the way. In that place you must wear Crowns of Gold, and enjoy the perpetual sight and vision of the Holy one, *for there you shall see him as he is.* There also you shall serve him continually with praise, with shouting, and thanksgiving, whom you desired to serve in the World, though with much difficulty, because of the infirmity of your flesh. There your eyes shall be delighted with seeing, and your ears with hearing the pleasant voice of the Mighty One. There you shall enjoy your friends again, that are gone thither before you; and there you shall with joy receive even every one that follows into the holy place after you. There also shall you be cloathed with Glory and Majesty, and put into an equipage fit to ride out with the King of Glory. When he shall come with sound of Trumpet in the Clouds, as upon the wings of the Wind, you shall come with him; and when he shall sit upon the Throne of Judgment, you shall sit by him; yea, and when: he shall pass sentence upon all the workers of iniquity, let them be Angels or Men, you also shall have a voice in that Judgment, because they were his and your Enemies. Also when he shall again return to the City, you shall go too, with sound of Trumpet, and be ever with him.

Now while they were thus drawing towards the Gate, behold a company of the Heavenly Host came out to meet them: to whom it was said by the other two Shining Ones. These are the men that have loved our Lord when they were in the World, and that have left all for his Holy Name, and he hath sent us to fetch them, and we have brought them thus far on their desired Journey, that they may go in and look their Redeemer in the face with joy. Then the Heavenly Host gave a great shout, saying, *Blessed are they that are called to the Marriage Supper of the Lamb.* There came out also at this time to meet them, several of the King's Trumpeters, cloathed in white and shining Raiment, who with melodious noises and loud, made even the Heavens to echo with their sound. These Trumpeters saluted *Christian* and his fellow with ten thousand welcomes from the World, and this they did with shouting and sound of Trumpet.

This done, they compassed them round on every side; some went before, some behind, and some on the right hand, some on the left, (as 'twere to guard them through the upper Regions) continually sounding as they went with melodious noise, in notes on high: so that the very sight was to them that could behold it, as if Heaven itself was come down to meet them. Thus therefore they walked on together; and as they walked, ever and anon these Trumpeters, even with joyful sound, would, by mixing their musick with looks and gestures, still signify to *Christian* and his Brother, how welcome they were into their company, and with what gladness they came to meet them; and now were these two men as 'twere in Heaven before they came at it, being swallowed up with the sight of Angels, and with hearing of their melodious notes. Here also they had the City itself in view, and they thought they heard all the Bells therein ring to welcome them thereto. But above all, the warm and joyful thoughts that they had about their own dwelling there, with such company, and that for ever and ever. Oh, by what tongue or pen can their glorious joy be expressed! And thus they came up to the Gate.

Now when they were come up to the Gate, there

was written over it in Letters of Gold, *Blessed are they that do his Commandments, that they may have right to the Tree of Life, and may enter in through the Gates into the City.*

Then I saw in my Dream, that the Shining Men bid them call at the Gate; the which when they did, some from above looked over the Gate, to wit, *Enoch, Moses,* and *Elijah, &c.,* to whom it was said, These Pilgrims are come from the City of *Destruction* for the love that they bear to the King of this place; and then the Pilgrims gave in unto them each man his Certificate, which they had received in the beginning; those therefore were carried in to the King, who when he had read them, said, Where are the men? To whom it was answered, They are standing without the Gate. The King then commanded to open the Gate, *That the righteous nation,* saith he, *that keepeth Truth may enter in.*

Now I saw in my Dream that these two men went in at the Gate: and lo, as they entered, they were transfigured, and they had Raiment put on that shone like Gold. There was also that met them with Harps and Crowns, and gave them to them, the Harps to praise withal, and the Crowns in token of honour. Then I heard in my Dream that all the Bells in the City rang again for joy, and that it was said unto them, *Enter ye into the joy of your Lord.* I also heard the men themselves, that they sang with a loud voice, saying, *Blessing, Honour, Glory, and Power, be to him that sitteth upon the Throne, and to the Lamb for ever and ever.*

Now just as the Gates were opened to let in the men, I looked in after them, and behold, the City shone like the Sun: the Streets also were paved with Gold, and in them walked many men, with Crowns on their heads, Palms in their hands, and golden Harps to sing praises withal.

There were also of them that had wings, and they answered one another without intermission, saying, *Holy, Holy, Holy, is the Lord.* And after that they shut up the Gates. Which when I had seen, I wished myself among them.

Now while I was gazing upon all these things, I turned my head to look back, and saw *Ignorance* come up to the River-side; but he soon got over, and that without half that difficulty which the other two men met with. For it happened that there was then in that place one *Vain-hope* a Ferry-man, that with his Boat helped him over; so he, as the other I saw, did ascend the Hill to come up to the Gate, only he came alone; neither did any man meet him with the least encouragement. When he was come up to the Gate, he looked up to the writing that was above, and then began to knock, supposing that entrance should have been quickly administered to him; but he was asked by the men that looked over the top of the Gate, Whence came you? and what would you have? He answered, I have eat and drank in the presence of the King, and he has taught in our Streets. Then they asked him for his Certificate, that they might go in and shew it to the King. So he fumbled in his bosom for one, and found none. Then said they, Have you none? But the man answered never a word. So they told the King, but he would not come down to see him, but commanded the two Shining Ones that conducted *Christian* and *Hopeful* to the City, to go out and take *Ignorance,* and bind him hand and foot, and have him away. Then they took him up, and carried him through the air to the door that I saw in the side of the Hill, and put him in there. Then I saw that there was a way to Hell even from the Gates of Heaven, as well as from the City of *Destruction.* So I awoke, and behold it was a Dream.

Ignorance comes up to the river

Vain-hope does ferry him over

THE CONCLUSION

Now Reader, *I have told my Dream to thee;*
See if thou can'st interpret it to me,
Or to thyself, or Neighbor; but take heed
Of mis-interpreting; for that, instead
Of doing good, will but thyself abuse:
By mis-*interpreting, evil insues.*

Take heed also, that thou be not extreme,
In playing with the out-side of my Dream:
Nor let my figure or similitude
Put thee into a laughter or a feud;
Leave this for Boys and Fools; but as for thee,
Do thou the substance of my matter see.

Put by the Curtains, look within my Vail:
Turn up my Metaphors, and do not fail
There, if thou seekest them, such things to find
As will be helpful to an honest mind.

What of my dross *thou findest there, be bold*
To throw away, but yet preserve the Gold;
What if my Gold be wrapped up in Ore?
None throws away the Apple for the Core.
But if thou shalt cast away all as vain,
I know not but 'twill make me Dream again.

THE

PILGRIM'S PROGRESS

FROM THIS WORLD

TO THAT WHICH IS TO COME

THE SECOND PART

DELIVERED UNDER THE SIMILITUDE OF A DREAM

Wherein is set forth
the manner of the setting out of Christian's
Wife and Children, their Dangerous Journey, and
Safe Arrival at the Desired Country

By JOHN BUNYAN

I have used Similitudes. Hos. 12. 10.

THE AUTHOR'S WAY OF SENDING
FORTH HIS
SECOND PART OF THE PILGRIM

Go now my little Book, to every place
Where my first Pilgrim *has but shewn his Face:*
Call at their door; If any say, Who's there?
Then answer thou, Christiana is here.
If they bid thee Come in, *then enter thou,*
With all thy Boys; and then, as thou know'st how,
Tell who they are, also from whence they came;
Perhaps they'll know them by their looks, or name.
But if they should not, ask them yet again
If formerly they did not entertain
One Christian *a Pilgrim? If they say*
They did, and was delighted in his Way;
Then let them know that those related were
Unto him, yea, his Wife and Children are.

   Tell them that they have left their House and Home,
Are turned Pilgrims, *seek a World to come;*
That they have met with Hardships in the way:
That they do meet with Troubles night and day;
That they have trod on Serpents, fought with Devils,
Have also overcame a many evils.
Yea, tell them also of the next, who have
Of love to Pilgrimage *been stout and brave*
Defenders of that Way, and how they still
Refuse this World, to do their Father's will.

   Go tell them also of those dainty things,
That Pilgrimage unto the Pilgrim *brings.*
Let them acquainted be too, how they are

171

Beloved of their King, under his care;
What goodly Mansions for them he provides,
Tho' they meet with rough Winds and swelling Tides,
How brave a Calm they will enjoy at last,
Who to their Lord, and by his ways hold fast.

Perhaps with heart and hand they will embrace
Thee, as they did my Firstling, and will grace
Thee, and thy fellows, with such cheer and fare,
As shew will they of Pilgrims *lovers are.*

1 OBJECTION

But how if they will not believe of me
That I am truly thine, 'cause some there be
That counterfeit the Pilgrim and his name,
Seek by disguise to seem the very same,
And by that means have wrought themselves into
The hands and houses of I know not who?

ANSWER

'Tis true, some have of late, to counterfeit
My Pilgrim, *to their own my Title set;*
Yea others half my Name and Title too
Have stitched to their Book, to make them do;
But yet they by their Features do declare
Themselves not mine to be, whose ere they are.

If such thou meetst with, then thine only way
Before them all is to say out thy say,
In thine own native language, which no man
Now useth, nor with ease dissemble can.
If after all they still of you shall doubt,
Thinking that you like Gipsies *go about*
In naughty wise the Country to defile,
Or that you seek good people to beguile
With things unwarrantable; send for me,
And I will testifie you Pilgrims *be;*
Yea, I will testifie that only you
My Pilgrims *are; and that alone will do.*

2 OBJECTION

But yet perhaps I may inquire for him,
Of those that wish him damned life and limb.
What shall I do, when I at such a door
For *Pilgrims* ask, and they shall rage the more?

ANSWER

*Fright not thyself my Book, for such Bugbears
Are nothing else but ground for groundless fears:*
My Pilgrim's *Book has travell'd sea and land,
Yet could I never come to understand
That it was slighted, or turn'd out of door
By any Kingdom, were they rich or poor.*

In France *and* Flanders, *where men kill each other,*
My Pilgrim *is esteem'd a Friend, a Brother.*

In Holland *too 'tis said, as I am told,*
My Pilgrim *is with some worth more than Gold.*

Highlanders *and* Wild Irish *can agree*
My Pilgrim *should familiar with them be.*

'Tis in New England *under such advance,
Receives there so much loving countenance,
As to be trimm'd, new cloth'd, and deck't with Gems,
That it may shew its features and its limbs,
Yet more, so comely doth my Pilgrim walk,
That of him thousands daily sing and talk.*

If you draw nearer home, it will appear
My Pilgrim *knows no ground of shame or fear;
City and Country will him entertain
With Welcome* Pilgrim; *yea, they can't refrain
From smiling, if my Pilgrim be but by,
Or shews his head in any Company.*

Brave Galants do my Pilgrim *hug and love,
Esteem it much, yea, value it above
Things of a greater bulk: yea, with delight,
Say my* Lark's *leg is better than a* Kite.

*Young Ladies, and young Gentle-women too,
Do no small kindness to my* Pilgrim *shew;
Their Cabinets, their Bosoms, and their Hearts*
My Pilgrim *has, 'cause he to them imparts*

His pretty riddles in such wholesome strains,
As yield them profit double to their pains
Of reading. Yea, I think I may be bold
To say some prize him far above their Gold.

The very Children that do walk the street,
If they do but my holy Pilgrim meet,
Salute him will, will wish him well, and say,
He is the only Stripling of the Day.

They that have never seen him, yet admire
What they have heard of him, and much desire
To have his company, and hear him tell
Those Pilgrim stories which he knows so well.

Yea, some who did not love him at the first,
But call'd him Fool and Noddy, say they must
Now they have seen and heard him, him commend;
And to those whom they love they do him send.

Wherefore my Second Part, thou need'st not be
Afraid to shew thy Head; none can hurt thee,
That wish but well to him that went before,
'Cause thou com'st after with a second store
Of things as good, as rich, as profitable,
For Young, for Old, for Stagg'ring, and for Stable.

3 Objection

But some there be that say he laughs too loud;
And some do say his Head is in a Cloud.
Some say his Words and Stories are so dark,
They know not how by them to find his mark.

Answer

One may (I think) say, Both his laughs and cries
May well be guess'd at by his watery eyes.
Some things are of that nature as to make
One's Fancie chuckle, while his Heart doth ake,
When Jacob saw his Rachel with the sheep,
He did at the same time both kiss and weep.

Whereas some say, A Cloud is in his Head,
That doth but shew how Wisdom's covered
With its own mantles, and to stir the mind

To a search after what it fain would find:
Things that seem to be hid in words obscure,
Do but the Godly mind the more allure;
To study what those sayings should contain
That speak to us in such a Cloudy strain.

I also know a dark Similitude
Will on the Fancie more itself intrude,
And will stick faster in the Heart and Head,
Than things from Similies not borrowed.

Wherefore my Book, let no discouragement
Hinder thy travels. Behold, thou art sent
To Friends, not foes: to Friends that will give place
To thee, thy Pilgrims *and thy words embrace.*

Besides, what my first Pilgrim *left conceal'd,*
Thou my brave Second Pilgrim *hast reveal'd;*
What Christian *left lock't up, and went his way,*
Sweet Christiana *opens with her Key.*

4 OBJECTION

But some love not the method of your first,
Romance they count it, throw't away as dust.
If I should meet with such, what should I say?
Must I slight them as they slight me, or nay?

ANSWER

My Christiana, *if with such thou meet,*
By all means in all loving wise them greet;
Render them not reviling for revile;
But if they frown, I prithee on them smile;
Perhaps 'tis Nature, or some ill report,
Has made them thus despise, or thus retort.

Some love no Cheese, some love no Fish, and some
Love not their Friends, nor their own House or Home;
Some start at Pig, slight Chicken, love not Fowl,
More than they love a Cuckow or an Owl;
Leave such, my Christiana, *to their choice,*
And seek those who to find thee will rejoice;
By no means strive, but in all humble wise
Present thee to them in thy Pilgrim's *guise.*

Go then my little Book, and shew to all
That entertain, and bid thee welcome shall,
What thou shalt keep close, shut up from the rest,
And wish what thou shalt shew them may be blest
To them for good, may make them chuse to be
Pilgrims better by far than thee or me.

Go then, I say, tell all men who thou art,
Say, I am Christiana, *and my part*
Is now, with my four Sons, to tell you what
It is for men to take a Pilgrim's *lot:*
Go also tell them who and what they be,
That now do go on Pilgrimage *with thee;*
Say, Here's my Neighbor Mercy, *she is one*
That has long time with me a Pilgrim *gone.*
Come see her in her Virgin Face, and learn
'Twixt Idle ones and Pilgrims *to discern.*
Yea, let young Damsels learn of her to prize
The World which is to come, in any wise.
When little tripping Maidens follow God,
And leave old doting Sinners to his Rod;
'Tis like those days wherein the young ones cried
Hosanah, *to whom old ones did deride.*

Next tell them of old Honest, *who you found*
With his white hairs treading the Pilgrim's *ground.*
Yea, tell them how plain-hearted this man was,
How after his good Lord he bare his Cross;
Perhaps with some grey Head this may prevail
With Christ to fall in Love, and Sin bewail.

Tell them also how Master Fearing *went*
On Pilgrimage, *and how the time he spent*
In Solitariness, with Fears and Cries,
And how at last he won the joyful Prize.
He was a good man, though much down in Spirit,
He is a good man, and doth Life inherit.

Tell them of Master Feeble-mind *also,*
Who not before, but still behind would go;
Shew them also how he had like been slain,
And how one Great-heart *did his life regain.*
This man was true of Heart, tho' weak in Grace,
One might true Godliness read in his Face.

Then tell them of Master Ready-to-halt,
A man with Crutches, but much without fault;
Tell them how Master Feeble-mind and he
Did love, and in opinions much agree.
And let all know, tho' weakness was their chance,
Yet sometimes one could sing, the other dance.
  Forget not Master Valiant-for-the-truth,
That Man of courage, though a very Youth.
Tell every one his Spirit was so stout,
No man could ever make him face about,
And how Great-heart and he could not forbear,
But put-down Doubting Castle, slay Despair.
  Overlook not Master Despondancie,
Nor Much-afraid, his daughter, tho' they lie
Under such Mantles as may make them look
(With some) as if their God had them forsook.
They softly went, but sure, and at the end
Found that the Lord of Pilgrims was their Friend.
When thou hast told the world of all these things,
Then turn about, my Book, and touch these strings,
Which if but touched, will such Musick make,
They'll make a Cripple dance, a Giant quake.
  These Riddles that lie couch't within thy breast,
Freely propound, expound; and for the rest
Of thy mysterious lines, let them remain
For those whose nimble Fancies shall them gain.

  Now may this little Book a blessing be
To those who love this little Book and me,
And may its Buyer have no cause to say,
His Money is but lost or thrown away;
Yea, may this Second Pilgrim yield that fruit,
As may with each good Pilgrim's Fancie suit;
And may it persuade some that go astray,
To turn their Feet and Heart to the right way:

               Is the Hearty Prayer
                         of the Author
                                 JOHN BUNYAN.

THE PILGRIM'S PROGRESS

IN THE SIMILITUDE OF A DREAM,

THE SECOND PART

COURTEOUS Companions, some time since,
to tell you my Dream that I had of *Christian*
the Pilgrim, and of his dangerous Journey
toward the Cœlestial Country, was pleasant to me,
and profitable to you. I told you then also what I
saw concerning his *Wife* and *Children*, and how
unwilling they were to go with him on Pilgrimage,
insomuch that he was forced to go on his Progress
without them; for he durst not run the danger of
that destruction which he feared would come by
staying with them in the City of *Destruction*.
Wherefore as I then shewed you, he left them
and departed.

Now it hath so happened, through the multiplicity
of Business, that I have been much hindred and
kept back from my wonted Travels into those parts
whence he went, and so could not till now obtain
an opportunity to make further enquiry after whom
he left behind, that I might give you an account
of them. But having had some concerns that way
of late, I went down again thitherward. Now having taken up my Lodgings in a Wood about a mile
off the place, as I slept I dreamed again.

And as I was in my Dream, behold an aged
Gentleman came by where I lay; and because he
was to go some part of the way that I was travelling,
methought I got up and went with him. So as we
walked, and as Travellers usually do, I was as if we

fell into discourse, and our talk happened to be about
Christian and his Travels; for thus I began with the
old man.

Sir, said I, what Town is that there below, that
lieth on the left hand of our way?

Then said Mr *Sagacity*, (for that was his name)
It is the City of *Destruction,* a populous place, but
possessed with a very ill-conditioned and idle sort
of People.

I thought that was the City, quoth I, I went once
myself through that Town, and therefore know that
this report you give of it is true.

SAG. Too true, I wish I could speak truth in
speaking better of them that dwell therein.

Well, Sir, quoth I, then I perceive you to be a
well-meaning man; and so one that takes pleasure
to hear and tell of that which is good: pray did
you never hear what happened to a man some time
ago in this Town (whose name was *Christian*) that
went of Pilgrimage up towards the higher Regions?

Christians
are well
spoken of
when gone,
though
called fools
while they
are here

SAG. Hear of him! Ay, and I also heard of the
Molestations, Troubles, Wars, Captivities, Cries,
Groans, Frights, and Fears that he met with and
had in his Journey. Besides, I must tell you, all
our Country rings of him; there are but few houses
that have heard of him and his doings but have
sought after and got the Records of his Pilgrimage;
yea, I think I may say that his hazardous Journey has got a many well-wishers to his ways; for
though when he was here, he was *Fool* in every
man's mouth, yet now he is gone, he is highly commended of all. For 'tis said he lives bravely where
he is; yea, many of them that are resolved never
to run his hazards, yet have their mouths water at
his gains.

They may, quoth I, well think, if they think anything that is true, that he liveth well where he is;
for he now lives at and in the Fountain of Life,
and has what he has without labour and sorrow,
for there is no grief mixed therewith.

SAG. Talk! the people talk strangely about him. Christian's
Some say that he now walks in White, that he has King
will take
a Chain of Gold about his neck, that he has a Crown Christian's
of Gold, beset with Pearls, upon his head. Others part
say that the Shining Ones that sometimes shewed
themselves to him in his Journey, are become his
Companions, and that he is as familiar with them
in the place where he is, as here one Neighbor is
with another. Besides, 'tis confidently affirmed
concerning him, that the King of the place where
he is has bestowed upon him already a very rich
and pleasant dwelling at Court; and that he every
day eateth and drinketh, and walketh, and talketh
with him; and receiveth of the smiles and favours
of him that is Judge of all there. Moreover, it is
expected of some, that his Prince, the Lord of that
Country, will shortly come into these parts, and will
know the reason, if they can give any, why his
Neighbors set so little by him, and had him so much
in derision when they perceived that he would be
a Pilgrim. For they say, that now he is so in the
affections of his Prince, and that his Sovereign is
so much concerned with the indignities that were
cast upon *Christian* when he became a Pilgrim, that
he will look upon all as if done unto himself; and
no marvel, for 'twas for the love that he had to his
Prince that he ventured as he did.

I dare say, quoth I, I am glad on't; I am glad
for the poor man's sake, for that he now has rest
from his labour, and for that he now reapeth the
benefit of his Tears with Joy; and for that he has
got beyond the Gun-shot of his Enemies, and is out
of the reach of them that hate him. I also am
glad for that a rumour of these things is noised
abroad in this Country; who can tell but that it may
work some good effect on some that are left behind?
But pray Sir, while it is fresh in my mind, do you
hear anything of his Wife and Children? Poor
hearts, I wonder in my mind what they do!

SAG. Who! *Christiana* and her sons? They are

Good
tidings of
Christian's
wife and
children
like to do as well as did *Christian* himself; for
though they all play'd the fool at the first, and would
by no means be persuaded by either the tears or
entreaties of *Christian,* yet second thoughts have
wrought wonderfully with them; so they have packt
up, and are also gone after him.

Better and better, quoth I. But what! Wife and
Children and all?

SAG. It is true; I can give you an account of the
matter, for I was upon the spot at the instant, and
was throughly acquainted with the whole affair.

Then, said I, a man it seems may report it for a
Truth?

SAG. You need not fear to affirm it, I mean that
they are all gone on Pilgrimage, both the good
Woman and her four Boys. And being we are, as
I perceive, going some considerable way together, I
will give you an account of the whole of the matter.

First Part,
p. 162
This *Christiana* (for that was her name from the
day that she with her Children betook themselves
to a Pilgrim's life) after her Husband was gone
over the River, and she could hear of him no more,
her thoughts began to work in her mind. First,
for that she had lost her Husband, and for that the
loving bond of that relation was utterly broken
betwixt them. For you know, said he to me, Nature
can do no less but entertain the living with many
a heavy cogitation in the remembrance of the loss
of loving Relations. This therefore of her Husband
did cost her many a tear. But this was not all, for
Christiana did also begin to consider with herself,
Mark this,
you that
are churls
to your
godly
relations
whether her unbecoming behaviour towards her
Husband was not one cause that she saw him no
more, and that in such sort he was taken away from
her. And upon this came into her mind by *swarms,*
all her unkind, unnatural, and ungodly carriages
to her dear Friend; which also clogged her Conscience, and did load her with guilt. She was moreover much broken with calling to remembrance the
restless groans, brinish tears, and self-bemoanings

of her Husband, and how she did harden her heart against all his entreaties and loving persuasions (of her and her Sons) to go with him; yea, there was not anything that *Christian* either said to her, or did before her all the while that his Burden did hang on his back, but it returned upon her like a flash of lightning, and rent the caul of her Heart in sunder. Specially that bitter outcry of his, *What shall I do to be saved?* did ring in her ears most dolefully.

First Part
p. 14

Then said she to her Children, Sons, we are all undone. I have sinned away your Father, and he is gone: he would have had us with him; but I would not go myself, I also have hindred you of Life. With that the Boys fell all into tears, and cried out to go after their Father. Oh! said *Christiana,* that it had been but our lot to go with him, then had it fared well with us, beyond what 'tis like to do now; for tho' I formerly foolishly imagin'd concerning the troubles of your Father, that they proceeded of a foolish Fancy that he had, or for that he was overrun with melancholy Humours; yet now 'twill not out of my mind but that they sprang from another cause, to wit, for that the Light of Light was given him, by the help of which, as I perceive, he has escaped the snares of Death. Then they all wept again, and cried out, O Wo worth the day.

The next night *Christiana* had a Dream; and behold she saw as if a broad Parchment was opened before her, in which were recorded the sum of her ways; and the times, as she thought, look'd very black upon her. Then she cried out aloud in her sleep, *Lord have Mercy upon me a Sinner;* and the little Children heard her.

Christiana's dream

After this she thought she saw two very ill-favoured ones standing by her Bedside, and saying, *What shall we do with this Woman? for she cries out for Mercy waking and sleeping; if she be suffered to go on as she begins, we shall lose her as*

Mark this, this is the quintessence of hell

we have lost her Husband. Wherefore we must by
one way or other, seek to take her off from the
thoughts of what shall be hereafter, else all the
World cannot help it but she will become a Pilgrim.

Help against discouragement

Now she awoke in a great sweat, also a trembling
was upon her, but after a while she fell to sleeping
again. And then she thought she saw *Christian* her
Husband in a place of Bliss among many *Immortals,*
with an *Harp* in his Hand, standing and playing
upon it before one that sat on a Throne with a
Rainbow about his Head. She saw also as if he
bowed his Head with his Face to the pav'd-work
that was under the Prince's feet, saying, *I heartily
thank my Lord and King for bringing of me into
this Place.* Then shouted a company of them that
stood round about, and harped with their Harps;
but no man living could tell what they said, but
Christian and his Companions.

Convictions seconded with fresh tidings of God's readiness to pardon

Next morning when she was up, had prayed to
God, and talked with her Children a while, one
knocked hard at the door, to whom she spake out,
saying, *If thou comest in God's name, come in.*
So he said *Amen,* and opened the Door, and saluted
her with *Peace be to this house.* The which when
he had done, he said, *Christiana,* knowest thou
wherefore I am come? Then she blushed and
trembled, also her Heart began to wax warm with
desires to know whence he came, and what was his
errand to her. So he said unto her, My name is
Secret, I dwell with those that are high. It is talked
of where I dwell, as if thou hadst a desire to go
thither; also there is a report that thou art aware
of the evil thou hast formerly done to thy Husband,
in hardening of thy Heart against his way, and in
keeping of these thy Babes in their Ignorance. *Christiana,* the Merciful One has sent me to tell thee that
he is a God ready to forgive, and that he taketh
delight to multiply to pardon offences. He would
also have thee know that he inviteth thee to come
into his presence, to his Table, and that he will

feed thee with the Fat of his house, and with the Heritage of *Jacob* thy Father.

There is *Christian* thy Husband *that was,* with Legions more his Companions, ever beholding that Face that doth minister Life to beholders; and they will all be glad when they shall hear the sound of thy feet step over thy Father's threshold.

Christiana at this was greatly abashed in herself, and bowing her head to the ground, this *Visitor* proceeded and said, *Christiana,* here is also a Letter for thee, which I have brought from thy Husband's King. So she took it and opened it, but it smelt after the manner of the best Perfume, also it was written in letters of Gold. The contents of the Letter was, *That the King would have her do as did* Christian *her Husband; for that was the way to come to his City, and to dwell in his Presence with Joy for ever.* At this the good Woman was quite overcome; so she cried out to her *Visitor, Sir, will you carry me and my Children with you, that we also may go and worship this King?* {.sidenote: Christiana quite overcome}

Then said the *Visitor, Christiana, the bitter is before the sweet:* thou must through troubles, as did he that went before thee, enter this Cœlestial City. Wherefore I advise thee to do as did *Christian* thy Husband: Go to the Wicket-gate yonder, over the Plain, for that stands in the head of the way up which thou must go, and I wish thee all good speed. Also I advise that thou put this Letter in thy bosom; that thou read therein to thyself and to thy Children, until you have got it by rote of heart, for it is one of the Songs that thou must sing while thou art in this House of thy Pilgrimage; also this thou must deliver in at the further Gate. {.sidenote: Further instruction to Christiana}

Now I saw in my Dream, that this old Gentleman, as he told me this story, did himself seem to be greatly affected therewith. He moreover proceeded and said, So *Christiana* called her Sons together, and began thus to address herself unto them: My Sons, I have as you may perceive, been of late under {.sidenote: Christiana prays well for her journey} much exercise in my Soul about the Death of your Father; not for that I doubt at all of his Happiness, for I am satisfied now that he is well. I have also been much affected with the thoughts of mine own state and yours, which I verily believe is by nature miserable. My carriages also to your Father in his distress, is a great load to my Conscience; for I hardened both my own heart and yours against him, and refused to go with him on Pilgrimage.

The thoughts of these things would now kill me outright, but that for a Dream which I had last night, and but for the encouragement that this stranger has given me this morning. Come my Children, let us pack up and be gone to the Gate that leads to the Cœlestial Country, that we may see your Father, and be with him and his Companions in peace, according to the Laws of that Land.

Then did her Children burst out into tears for joy that the heart of their Mother was so inclined. So their *Visitor* bid them farewell, and they began to prepare to set out for their Journey.

Chris-
tiana's
new
language
stuns
her old
neighbors

But while they were thus about to be gone, two of the women that were *Christiana's* Neighbors, came up to her house and knocked at her door. To whom she said as before, *If you come in God's name, come in.* At this the women were stunned, for this kind of language they used not to hear, or to perceive to drop from the lips of *Christiana.* Yet they came in: but behold they found the good woman a preparing to be gone from her house.

So they began and said, *Neighbor, pray what is your meaning by this?*

First Part,
p. 47

Christiana answered and said to the eldest of them, whose name was Mrs. *Timorous,* I am preparing for a Journey. (This *Timorous* was daughter to him that met *Christian* upon the Hill *Difficulty,* and would a had him gone back for fear of the Lions.)

TIM. For what Journey I pray you?

CHRIS. *Even to go after my good Husband.*
And with that she fell a weeping.

TIM. I hope not so, good Neighbor, pray for
your poor Children's sakes, do not so unwomanly
cast away yourself.

CHRIS. Nay, my Children shall go with me, not
one of them is willing to stay behind.

TIM. I wonder in my very heart, what or who
has brought you into this mind.

CHRIS. Oh, Neighbor, knew you but as much as
I do, I doubt not but that you would go with me.

TIM. Prithee what new knowledge hast thou got,
that so worketh off thy mind from thy Friends,
and that tempteth thee to go nobody knows where?

CHRIS. Then *Christiana* replied, I have been
sorely afflicted since my Husband's departure from
me, but specially since he went over the River.
But that which troubleth me most, is my churlish
carriages to him when he was under his distress.
Besides, I am *now* as he was *then;* nothing will
serve me but going on Pilgrimage. I was a dream-
ing last night that I saw him. O that my Soul
was with him. He dwelleth in the presence of
the King of the Country, he sits and eats with him
at his table, he is become a Companion of *Immortals,*
and has a House now given him to dwell in, to
which the best Palaces on Earth if compared, seem
to me to be but as a Dunghill. The Prince of the
place has also sent for me, with promise of entertainment if I shall come to him; his messenger was
here even now, and has brought me a Letter, which
invites me to come. And with that she pluck'd out
her Letter, and read it, and said to them, What now
will you say to this?

TIM. Oh the madness that has possessed thee and
thy Husband, to run yourselves upon such difficulties! You have heard, I am sure, what your Husband did meet with, even in a manner at the first
step that he took on his way, as our Neighbor
Obstinate can yet testify, for he went along with

[margin notes:] Timorous comes to visit Christiana, with Mercy, one of her neighbors

Death

First Part, pp. 15-20

him; yea and *Pliable* too, until they like wise men, were afraid to go any further. We also heard over and above, how he met with the Lions, *Apollyon*, the Shadow of Death, and many other things. Nor

The reasonings of the flesh

is the danger that he met with at *Vanity Fair* to be forgotten by thee; for if he, tho' a Man, was so hard put to it, what canst thou, being but a poor Woman, do? Consider also that these four sweet Babes are thy Children, thy Flesh and thy Bones. Wherefore though thou shouldest be so rash as to cast away thyself, yet for the sake of the Fruit of thy Body keep thou at home.

A pertinent reply to fleshly reasonings

But *Christiana* said unto her, tempt me not, my Neighbor. I have now a price put into mine hand to get gain, and I should be a Fool of the greatest size if I should have no heart to strike in with the opportunity. And for that you tell me of all these Troubles that I am like to meet with in the way, they are so far off from being to me a discouragement, that they shew I am in the right. *The bitter must come before the sweet,* and that also will make the sweet the sweeter. Wherefore since you came not to my house *in God's name,* as I said, I pray you to be gone, and not to disquiet me farther.

Mercy's bowels yearn over Christiana

Then *Timorous* also revil'd her, and said to her fellow, Come Neighbor *Mercy,* let us leave her in her own hands, since she scorns our Counsel and Company. But *Mercy* was at a stand, and could not so readily comply with her Neighbor, and that for a twofold reason. First, her bowels yearned over *Christiana:* so she said within herself, If my Neighbor will needs be gone, I will go a little way with her and help her. Secondly, her bowels yearned over her own Soul, (for what *Christiana* had said had taken some hold upon her mind.) Wherefore she said within herself again, I will yet have more talk with this *Christiana,* and if I find Truth and Life in what she shall say, myself with my heart shall also go with her. Wherefore *Mercy* began thus to reply to her Neighbor *Timorous.*

MERCY. Neighbor, I did indeed come with you to see *Christiana* this morning; and since she is, as you see, a taking of her last farewell of her Country, I think to walk this Sun-shine morning a little way with her to help her on the way. But she told her not of her second reason, but kept that to herself.

Timorous forsakes her, but Mercy cleaves to her

TIM. Well, I see you have a mind to go a fooling too, but take heed in time, and be wise: while we are out of danger, we are out; but when we are in, we are in. So Mrs *Timorous* returned to her house, and *Christiana* betook herself to her Journey. But when *Timorous* was got home to her house, she sends for some of her Neighbors, to wit, Mrs *Bat's-eyes,* Mrs *Inconsiderate,* Mrs *Light-mind,* and Mrs *Know-nothing.* So when they came to her house, she falls to telling of the story of *Christiana* and of her intented Journey. And thus she began her tale.

Timorous acquaints her friends what the good Christiana intends to do

TIM. Neighbors, having had little to do this morning, I went to give *Christiana* a visit; and when I came at the door, I knocked, as you know 'tis our custom. And she answered, *If you come in God's name, come in.* So in I went, thinking all was well. But when I came in, I found her preparing herself to depart the Town, she and also her Children. So I asked her what was her meaning by that? And she told me in short, that she was now of a mind to go on Pilgrimage, as did her Husband. She told me also a Dream that she had, and how the King of the Country where her Husband was had sent her an inviting Letter to come thither.

Then said Mrs *Know-nothing,* And what do you think she will go?

Mrs Know-nothing

TIM. Ay, go she will, whatever come on't; and methinks I know it by this, for that which was my great argument to persuade her to stay at home (to wit, the Troubles she was like to meet with in the way) is one great argument with her to put her

forward on her Journey. For she told me in so
many words, *The bitter goes before the sweet.* Yea,
and for as much as it so doth, it makes the sweet
the sweeter.

Mrs Bat's-
eyes

Mrs *Bat's-eyes.* Oh this blind and foolish woman, said she, will she not take warning by her
Husband's afflictions? For my part I see if he was
here again, he would rest him content in a whole
skin, and never run so many hazards for nothing.

Mrs In-
considerate

Mrs *Inconsiderate* also replied, saying, Away
with such Fantastical Fools from the Town! A
good riddance for my part I say of her. Should
she stay where she dwells, and retain this her mind,
who could live quietly by her? for she will either be
dumpish or unneighborly, or talk of such matters
as no wise body can abide; wherefore for my part
I shall never be sorry for her departure; let her go,
and let better come in her room: 'twas never a
good World since these whimsical Fools dwelt in it.

Mrs
Light-mind
Madame
Wanton,
she that
had like
to have
been too
hard for
Faithful
in time
past

First Part,
p. 73

Then Mrs *Light-mind* added as followeth: Come
put this kind of talk away. I was yesterday at
Madam *Wanton's,* where we were as merry as the
maids. For who do you think should be there, but
I and Mrs *Love-the-flesh,* and three or four more,
with Mr *Lechery,* Mrs *Filth,* and some others. So
there we had musick and dancing, and what else was
meet to fill up the pleasure. And I dare say my
Lady herself is an admirably well-bred Gentle-wom-
an, and Mr *Lechery* is as pretty a fellow.

Discourse
betwixt
Mercy
and good
Christiana

By this time *Christiana* was got on her way, and
Mercy went along with her. So as they went, her
Children being there also, *Christiana* began to discourse. And *Mercy,* said *Christiana,* I take this as
an unexpected favour, that thou shouldst set foot
out of doors with me, to accompany me a little in
my way.

Mercy
inclines
to go

MERCY. Then said young *Mercy* (for she was
but young) If I thought it would be to purpose to go
with you, I would never go near the Town any
more.

CHRIS. Well *Mercy,* said *Christiana,* cast in thy lot with me: I well know what will be the end of our Pilgrimage; my Husband is where he would not but be for all the Gold in the *Spanish* Mines. Nor shalt thou be rejected, though thou goest but upon *my Invitation.* The King who hath sent for me and my Children is one that delighteth in *Mercy.* Besides, if thou wilt, I will hire thee, and thou shalt go along with me as my servant; yet we will have all things in common betwixt thee and me, only go along with me. *(Christiana would have her neighbour with her)*

MERCY. But how shall I be ascertained that I also shall be entertained? Had I this hope but from one that can tell, I would make no stick at all, but would go, being helped by him that can help, tho' the way was never so tedious. *(Mercy doubts of acceptance)*

CHRIS. Well loving *Mercy,* I will tell thee what thou shalt do. Go with me to the *Wicket-gate,* and there I will further enquire for thee; and if there thou shalt not meet with encouragement, I will be content that thou shalt return to thy place. I also will pay thee for thy kindness which thou shewest to me and my Children, in thy accompanying us in our way as thou doest. *(Christiana allures her to the gate, which is Christ, and promiseth there to inquire for her)*

MERCY. Then I will go thither, and will take what shall follow, and the Lord grant that my lot may there fall even as the King of Heaven shall have his heart upon me. *(Mercy prays)*

Christiana then was glad at her heart, not only that she had a Companion, but also for that she had prevailed with this poor Maid to fall in love with her own Salvation. So they went on together, and *Mercy* began to weep. Then said *Christiana,* Wherefore weepeth my Sister so? *(Christiana glad of Mercy's company)*

MERCY. Alas! said she, who can but lament, that shall but rightly consider what a state and condition my poor Relations are in that yet remain in our sinful Town: and that which makes my grief the more heavy is, because they have no Instructor, nor any to tell them what is to come. *(Mercy grieves for her carnal relations)*

Christian's prayers were answered for his relations after he was dead

CHRIS. Bowels becometh Pilgrims; and thou dost for thy Friends as my good *Christian* did for me when he left me; he mourned for that I would not heed nor regard him, but his Lord and ours did gather up his Tears, and put them into his Bottle; and now both I and thou and these my sweet Babes, are reaping the fruit and benefit of them. I hope, *Mercy*, these Tears of thine will not be lost; for the truth hath said, *That they that sow in Tears shall reap in Joy, in singing. And he that goeth forth and weepeth, bearing precious seed, shall doubtless come again with rejoicing, bringing his Sheaves with him.*

Then said *Mercy*,

> Let the Most Blessed be my guide,
> If 't be his blessed will,
> Unto his Gate, unto his Fold,
> Up to his Holy Hill.
>
> And let him never suffer me
> To swerve or turn aside
> From his free grace and holy ways,
> Whate'er shall me betide.
>
> And let him gather them of mine,
> That I have left behind;
> Lord make them pray they may be thine,
> With all their heart and mind.

First Part, p. 19

Now my old Friend proceeded and said: But when *Christiana* came up to the Slough of *Dispond*, she began to be at a stand; for said she, This is the place in which my dear Husband had like to have

Their own carnal conclusions, instead of the Word of life

been smothered with mud. She perceived also, that notwithstanding the command of the King to make this place for Pilgrims good, yet it was rather worse than formerly. So I asked if that was true. Yes, said the Old Gentleman, too true, for that many there be that pretend to be the King's Labourers, and that say they are for mending the King's Highway, that bring *dirt* and *dung* instead of *stones,* and so mar instead of mending. Here *Christiana* therefore with her Boys, did make a stand; but said

Mercy, Come let us venture, only let us be wary. Mercy the boldest at the Slough of Dispond
Then they looked well to the *steps,* and made a
shift to get staggeringly over.

Yet *Christiana* had like to a been in, and that
not once nor twice. Now they had no sooner got
over, but they thought they heard words that said
unto them, *Blessed is she that believeth, for there
shall be a performance of the things that have been
told her from the Lord.*

Then they went on again; and said *Mercy* to
Christiana, Had I as good ground to hope for a loving reception at the *Wicket-gate* as you, I think
no Slough of *Dispond* would discourage me.

Well, said the other, you know your sore, and I
know mine; and good friend, we shall all have
enough evil before we come at our Journey's end.

For can it be imagined, that the people that design
to attain such excellent Glories *as we do,* and that
are so envied that Happiness *as we are;* but that we
shall meet with what Fears and Scares, with what
Troubles and Afflictions, they can possibly assault
us with that hate us?

And now Mr. *Sagacity* left me to dream out my Prayer should be made with considera-tion and fear, as well as in faith and hope
Dream by myself. Wherefore me-thought I saw
Christiana and *Mercy* and the Boys go all of them
up to the Gate; to which when they were come,
they betook themselves to a short debate about *how*
they must manage their calling at the Gate, and what
should be said to him that did open to them. So it
was concluded, since *Christiana* was the eldest, that
she should knock for entrance, and that she should
speak to him that did open for the rest. So *Chris-* First Part, p. 29
tiana began to knock, and as her poor Husband did,
she *knocked* and *knocked* again. But instead of any
that answered, they all thought that they heard The dog, the devil, an enemy to prayer
as if a Dog came barking upon them; a Dog, and
a great one too, and this made the Women and
Children afraid: nor durst they for a while to knock
any more, for fear the Mastiff should fly upon them.
Now therefore they were greatly tumbled up and

Christiana
and her
compan-
ions per-
plexed
about
prayer

down in their minds, and knew not what to do. Knock they durst not, for fear of the Dog; go back they durst not, for fear that the Keeper of that Gate should espy them as they so went, and should be offended with them. At last they thought of knocking again, and knocked more vehemently than they did at the first. Then said the Keeper of the Gate, Who is there? So the Dog left off to bark, and he opened unto them.

Then *Christiana* made low obeisance and said, Let not our Lord be offended with his Hand-maidens, for that we have knocked at this princely Gate. Then said the Keeper, Whence come ye, and what is that you would have?

Christiana answered, We are come from whence *Christian* did come, and upon the same Errand as he; to wit, to be if it shall please you, graciously admitted by this Gate into the way that leads to the Cœlestial City. And I answer, my Lord, in the next place, that I am *Christiana,* once the Wife of *Christian* that now is gotten above.

With that the Keeper of the Gate did marvel, saying, *What is she become now a Pilgrim, that but a while ago abhorred that life?* Then she bowed her head, and said, Yes, and so are these my sweet Babes also.

How
Christiana
is enter-
tained at
the gate

Then he took her by the hand, and let her in, and said also, *Suffer the little Children to come unto me;* and with that he shut up the Gate. This done, he called to a Trumpeter that was above over the Gate, to entertain *Christiana* with shouting and sound of Trumpet for joy. So he obeyed and sounded, and filled the air with his melodious notes.

Now all this while poor *Mercy* did stand without, trembling and crying for fear that she was rejected. But when *Christiana* had gotten admittance for herself and her Boys, then she began to make intercession for *Mercy.*

CHRIS. And she said, My Lord, I have a Com-

panion of mine that stands yet without, that is come Chris-
hither upon the same account as myself; one that tiana's
is much dejected in her mind, for that she comes, prayer
as she thinks, without sending for, whereas I was for her friend
sent to by my Husband's King to come. Mercy

Now *Mercy* began to be very impatient, for each The delays
minute was as long to her as an hour, wherefore she make the
prevented *Christiana* from a fuller interceding for hungering soul the
her, by knocking at the Gate herself. And she ferventer
knocked *then* so loud, that she made *Christiana* to
start. Then said the Keeper of the Gate, Who is
there? and said *Christiana,* It is my Friend.

So he opened the Gate, and looked out; but *Mercy* Mercy
was fallen down without in a swoon, for she fainted, faints
and was afraid that no Gate would be opened to her.

Then he took her by the hand, and said, Damsel,
I bid thee arise.

Oh Sir, said she, I am faint; there is scarce life
left in me. But he answered, That one once said,
*When my soul fainted within me; I remembred the
Lord, and my prayer came in unto thee, into thy
Holy Temple.* Fear not, but stand upon thy feet,
and tell me wherefore thou art come.

MERCY. I am come for that unto which I was The cause
never invited as my Friend *Christiana* was. Hers of her
was from the King, and mine was but from her: fainting
wherefore I fear I presume.

Did she desire thee to come with her to this
Place?

MERCY. Yes; and as my Lord sees I am come.
And if there is any grace or forgiveness of sins to
spare, I beseech that I thy poor Handmaid may
be partaker thereof.

Then he took her again by the hand, and led her Mark this
gently in, and said, I pray for all them that believe
on me, by what means soever they come unto me.
Then said he to those that stood by, Fetch something, and give it to *Mercy* to smell on, thereby
to stay her fainting. So they fetch'd her a bundle
of *Myrrh,* and a while after she was revived.

And now was *Christiana* and her Boys and *Mercy*, received of the Lord, at the head of the way, and spoke kindly unto by him.

Then said they yet further unto him, We are sorry for our sins, and beg of our Lord his Pardon, and further information what we must do.

I grant Pardon, said he, by word and deed; by word, in the promise of forgiveness; by deed, in the way I obtained it. Take the first from my lips with a kiss, and the other as it shall be revealed.

Christ crucified seen afar off

Now I saw in my Dream that he spake many good words unto them, whereby they were greatly gladded. He also had them up to the top of the Gate, and shewed them by what *deed* they were saved; and told them withal that that sight they would have again as they went along in the way, to their comfort.

Talk between the Christians

So he left them a while in a Summer Parlor below, where they entred into talk by themselves; and thus *Christiana* began: O Lord! how glad am I that we are got in hither.

MERCY. So you well may; but I of all have cause to leap for joy.

CHRIS. I thought one time, as I stood at the Gate (because I had knocked and none did answer) that all our labour had been lost, specially when that ugly Cur made such a heavy barking against us.

MERCY. But my worst fears was after I saw that you was taken into his favour and that I was left behind. Now thought I 'tis fulfilled which is written, *Two women shall be grinding together, the one shall be taken and the other left.* I had much ado to forbear crying out, Undone, undone.

First Part, p. 29

And afraid I was to knock any more; but when I looked up to what was written over the Gate, I took courage. I also thought that I must either knock again, or die; so I knocked, but I cannot tell how, for my spirit now struggled betwixt life and death.

CHRIS. Can you not tell how you knocked? I am

sure your knocks were so earnest, that the very sound of them made me start; I thought I never heard such knocking in all my life; I thought you would a come in by violent hands, or a took the Kingdom by storm. Christiana thinks her companion prays better than she

MERCY. Alas, to be in my case, who that so was could but a done so? You saw that the Door was shut upon me, and that there was a most cruel Dog thereabout. Who, I say, that was so faint-hearted as I, that would not have knocked with all their might? But pray what said my Lord to my rudeness? was he not angry with me?

CHRIS. When he heard your lumbering noise, he gave a wonderful innocent smile; I believe what you did pleased him well enough, for he shewed no sign to the contrary. But I marvel in my heart why he keeps such a Dog; had I known that afore, I fear I should not have had heart enough to a ventured myself in this manner. But now we are in, we are in, and I am glad with all my heart. Christ pleased with loud and restless praises If the soul at first did know all it should meet with in its journey to heaven, it would hardly even set out

MERCY. I will ask if you please next time he comes down, why he keeps such a filthy Cur in his yard; I hope he will not take it amiss.

Ay do, said the Children, and persuade him to hang him, for we are afraid he will bite us when we go hence. The children are afraid of the dog

So at last he came down to them again, and *Mercy* fell to the ground on her face before him and worshipped, and said, Let my Lord accept of the sacrifice of Praise which I now offer unto him with the calves of my lips.

So he said unto her, *Peace be to thee, stand up.* But she continued upon her face and said, *Righteous art thou O Lord when I plead with thee, yet let me talk with thee of thy Judgments.* Wherefore dost thou keep so cruel a Dog in thy yard, at the sight of which such Women and Children as we are ready to fly from thy Gate for fear? Mercy expostulates about the dog

He answered and said, That Dog has another owner; he also is kept close in another man's ground Devil

only my Pilgrims hear his barking; he belongs
to the Castle which you see there at a distance, but
can come up to the walls of this place. He has

*First Part,
p. 30*
frighted many an honest Pilgrim from worse to
better, by the great voice of his roaring. Indeed
he that owneth him doth not keep him of any good
will to me or mine, but with intent to keep the
Pilgrims from coming to me, and that they may be
afraid to knock at this Gate for entrance. Sometimes also he has broken out, and has *worried* some
that I love; but I take all at present patiently. I

*A check
to the car-
nal fear
of the
pilgrims*
also give my Pilgrims timely help, so they are not
delivered up to his power, to do to them what his
doggish nature would prompt him to. But what! my
purchased one, I tro, hadst thou known never so
much beforehand, thou wouldest not have been
afraid of a Dog.

The Beggars that go from Door to Door, will,
rather than they will lose a supposed Alms, run the
hazard of the bawling barking and biting too of a
Dog; and shall a Dog, a Dog in another man's yard,
a Dog whose barking I turn to the profit of Pilgrims,
keep any from coming to me? I deliver them from
the Lions, their Darling from the power of the
Dog.

*Christians,
when wise
enough,
acquiesce
in the
wisdom of
their Lord*
MERCY. Then said *Mercy,* I confess my ignorance;
I spake what I understood not; I acknowledge that
thou doest all things well.

CHRIS. Then *Christiana* began to talk of their
Journey, and to enquire after the way. So he fed
them, and washed their feet, and set them in the

*First Part,
p. 32*
way of his steps, according as he had dealt with
her Husband before. So I saw in my Dream that
they walk'd on their way, and had the weather
very comfortable to them.

Then *Christiana* began to sing, saying,

> Bless'd be the Day that I began
> A Pilgrim for to be;
> And blessed also be that man
> That thereto moved me.

'Tis true, 'twas long ere I began
To seek to live *for ever*:
But now I run fast as I can;
'Tis better late than never.

Our Tears to Joy, our Fears to Faith,
Are turned, as we see,
Thus our beginning (as one saith,)
Shews what our end will be.

Now there was, on the other side of the Wall that The devil's
fenced in the way up which *Christiana* and her garden
Companions were to go, a Garden, and that Garden
belonged to him whose was that *barking Dog* of
whom mention was made before. And some of the
Fruit-Trees that grew in that Garden shot their
branches over the Wall; and being mellow, they
that found them did gather them up, and oft eat of
them to their hurt. So *Christiana's* Boys, as Boys The chil-
are apt to do, being pleas'd with the trees, and with dren eat
the Fruit that did hang thereon, did plash[1] them, and enemy's
began to eat. Their mother did also chide them fruit
for so doing, but still the Boys went on.

Well, said she, my Sons, you transgress, for that Two ill-
Fruit is none of ours; but she did not know that favoured
they did belong to the Enemy; I'll warrant you if
she had, she would a been ready to die for fear.
But that passed, and they went on their way.
Now by that they were gone about two bow-shots
from the place that let them into the way, they
espied two very *ill-favoured ones* coming down
apace to meet them. With that *Christiana* and
Mercy her Friend covered themselves with their
Vails, and so kept on their Journey; the Children
also went on before, so that at last they met together. Then they that came down to meet them, They
came just up to the Women as if they would em- Christiana
brace them; but *Christiana* said, Stand back, or go
peaceably by as you should. Yet these two, as men The
that are deaf, regarded not *Christiana's* words, but pilgrims
began to lay hands upon them. At that *Christiana* with them

[1] Bend them down with sticks.

waxing very wroth, spurned at them with her feet. *Mercy* also as well as she could, did what she could to shift them. *Christiana* again said to them, Stand back, and be gone, for we have no money to lose, being Pilgrims as ye see, and such too as live upon the Charity of our Friends.

ILL-FAV. Then said one of the two of the men, We make no assault upon you for your Money, but are come out to tell you, that if you will grant one small request which we shall ask, we will make Women of you for ever.

CHRIS. Now *Christiana* imagining what they should mean, made answer again, We will neither hear, nor regard, nor yield to what you shall ask. We are in haste, cannot stay, our business is a business of Life and Death. So again she and her Companions made a fresh assay to go past them, but they letted them in their way.

ILL-FAV. And they said, We intend no hurt to your lives, 'tis another thing we would have.

She cries out

CHRIS. Ah, quoth *Christiana,* you would have us Body and Soul, for I know 'tis for that you are come; but we will die rather upon the spot, than suffer ourselves to be brought into such snares as shall hazard our well-being hereafter. And with that they both shrieked out, and cried, Murder, murder: and so put themselves under those Laws that are provided for the Protection of Women. But the men still made their approach upon them, with design to prevail against them: they therefore cried out again.

It is good to cry out when we are assaulted

Now they being, as I said, not far from the Gate in at which they came, their voice was heard from where they was, thither. Wherefore some of the House came out, and knowing that it was *Christiana's* tongue they made haste to her relief. But by that they was got within sight of them, the Women was in a very great scuffle, the children also stood crying by. Then did he that came in for their relief call out to the Ruffians, saying, What is that thing that you

The Reliever comes

do? Would you make my Lord's people to transgress? He also attempted to take them, but they did make their escape over the Wall into the Garden of the man to whom the great Dog belonged; so the Dog became their Protector. This *Reliever* then came up to the Women, and asked them how they did. So they answered, We thank thy Prince, pretty well, only we have been somewhat affrighted; we thank thee also for that thou camest in to our help, for otherwise we had been overcome. *The ill ones fly to the devil for relief*

RELIEVER. So after a few more words, this *Reliever* said as followeth; I marvelled much when you were entertained at the Gate above, being ye know that ye were but weak Women, that you petitioned not the Lord there for a Conductor; then might you have avoided these troubles and dangers, for he would have granted you one. *The Reliever talks to the women*

CHRIS. Alas! said *Christiana*, we were so taken with our present blessing, that dangers to come were forgotten by us; besides, who could have thought that so near the King's Palace there should have lurked such naughty ones? Indeed it had been well for us, had we asked our Lord for one; but since our Lord knew 'twould be for our profit, I wonder he sent not one along with us! *Mark this*

REL. It is not always necessary to grant things not asked for, lest by so doing they become of little esteem; but when the want of a thing is felt, it then comes under, in the eyes of him that feels it, that estimate that properly is its due, and so consequently will be thereafter used. Had my Lord granted you a Conductor, you would not neither so have bewailed that oversight of yours in not asking for one as now you have occasion to do. So all things work for good, and tend to make you more wary. *We lose for want of asking for*

CHRIS. Shall we go back again to my Lord, and confess our folly, and ask one?

REL. Your confession of your folly I will present him with. To go back again you need not; for in all places where you shall come, you will find no

want at all, for in every of my Lord's Lodgings
which he has prepared for the reception of his
Pilgrims, there is sufficient to furnish them against
all attempts whatsoever. But as I said, he will be
enquired of by them to do it for them: and 'tis
a poor thing that is not worth asking for. When he
had thus said, he went back to his place, and the
Pilgrims went on their way.

The mistake of Mercy

MERCY. Then said *Mercy,* What a sudden blank
is here! I made account we had now been past all
danger, and that we should never see sorrow more.

Christiana's guilt

CHRIS. Thy *innocency,* My Sister, said *Christiana*
to *Mercy,* may excuse thee much; but as for me, my
fault is so much the greater, for that I saw this
danger before I came out of the Doors, and yet did
not provide for it where provision might a been had.
I am therefore much to be blamed.

MERCY. Then said *Mercy,* How knew you this before you came from home? Pray open to me this
riddle.

Christiana's dream repeated

CHRIS. Why, I will tell you. Before I set foot out
of doors, one night as I lay in my bed, I had a
Dream about this; for methought I saw two men
as like these as ever the world they could look,
stand at my bed's feet, plotting how they might
prevent my Salvation. I will tell you their very
words. They said ('twas when I was in my
Troubles (*What shall we do with this Woman? for
she cries out waking and sleeping, for forgiveness:
if she be suffered to go on as she begins, we shall
lose her as we have lost her Husband.* This you
know might a made me take heed, and have provided when provision might a been had.

Mercy makes good use of their neglect of duty

MERCY. Well, said Mercy, as by this neglect we
have an occasion ministred unto us to behold our own
imperfections, so our Lord has taken occasion thereby to make manifest the riches of his Grace. For
he, as we see, has followed us with unasked kindness, and has delivered us from their hands that
were stronger than we, of his mere good pleasure.

Thus now when they had talked away a little Talk in the Interpreter's house about Christiana's going on pilgrimage more time, they drew nigh to an House which stood in the way, which House was built for the relief of Pilgrims; as you will find more fully related in the First Part of these Records of the *Pilgrim's Progress*. So they drew on towards the House (the House of the *Interpreter*); and when they came to the door, they heard a great talk in the House. They then gave ear, and heard, as they thought, *Christiana* mentioned by name. For you must know that there went along, even before her, a talk of her and her Children's going on Pilgrimage. And this thing was the more pleasing to them, because they had heard that she was *Christian's Wife*, that Woman who was some time ago so unwilling to hear She knocks at the door of going on Pilgrimage. Thus therefore they stood still and heard the good people within commending her, who they little thought stood at the door. At The door is opened to them by Innocent last *Christiana* knocked as she had done at the Gate before. Now when she had knocked, there came to the door a young Damsel, and opened the door and looked, and behold two Women was there.

DAMSEL. Then said the Damsel to them, With whom would you speak in this place?

CHRIS. *Christiana* answered, We understand that this is a privileged place for those that are become Pilgrims, and we now at this door are such; wherefore we pray that we may be partakers of that for which we at this time are come; for the day, as thou seest, is very far spent, and we are loth to-night to go any further.

DAMSEL. Pray what may I call your name, that I may tell it to my Lord within?

CHRIS. My name is *Christiana;* I was the Wife of that Pilgrim that some years ago did travel this way, and these be his four Children. This Maiden also is my Companion, and is going on Pilgrimage too.

INNOCENT. Then ran *Innocent* in (for that was her name) and said to those within, Can you think who is at the door? There is *Christiana* and her

Children and her Companion, all waiting for entertainment here. Then they leaped for joy, and went
and told their Master. So he came to the door, and
looking upon her, he said, Art thou that *Christiana*
whom *Christian* the Good-man left behind him, when
he betook himself to a Pilgrim's life?

CHRIS. I am that Woman that was so hard-hearted
as to slight my Husband's Troubles, and that left
him to go on in his Journey alone, and these are
his four Children; but now I also am come, for
I am convinced that no way is right but this.

INTER. Then is fulfilled that which is written of
the man that said to his Son, Go work to-day in
my Vine-yard; and he said to his Father, I will not;
but afterwards repented and went.

CHRIS. Then said *Christiana,* So be it, *Amen.*
God make it a true saying upon me, and grant that
I may be found at the last of him in peace without
spot and blameless.

INTER. But why standest thou thus at the door?
Come in, thou Daughter of *Abraham.* We was
talking of thee but now, for tidings have come to us
before how thou art become a Pilgrim. Come Children, come in; come Maiden, come in. So he had
them all into the House.

So when they were within, they were bidden sit
down and rest them; the which when they had done,
those that attended upon the Pilgrims in the House,
came into the Room to see them. And one smiled,
and another smiled, and they all smiled for joy that
Christiana was become a Pilgrim. They also looked
upon the Boys: they stroked them over the faces
with the hand, in token of their kind reception of
them. They also carried it lovingly to *Mercy,* and
bid them all welcome into their Master's House.

After a while, because Supper was not ready, the
Interpreter took them into his *significant* Rooms, and
shewed them what *Christian, Christiana's* Husband,
had seen some time before. Here therefore they
saw the Man in the Cage, the Man and his Dream,

the Man that cut his way through his Enemies, and First Part, pp. 32-41 the Picture of the biggest of them all, together with the rest of those things that were then so profitable to *Christian*.

This done, and after these things had been some- The man with the muck-rake expounded what digested by *Christiana* and her company, the *Interpreter* takes them apart again, and has them first into a Room where was a Man that could look no way but downwards, with a Muck-rake in his hand. There stood also one over his head with a Cœlestial Crown in his hand, and proffered him that Crown for his Muck-rake; but the man did neither look up, nor regard, but raked to himself the straws, the small sticks and dust of the floor.

Then said *Christiana*, I persuade myself that I know something of the meaning of this; for this is a figure of a Man of this World, is it not, good Sir?

INTER. Thou hast said the right said he, and his Muck-rake doth shew his carnal mind. And where- as thou seest him rather give heed to rake up straws and sticks and the dust of the floor, than to what he says that calls to him from above with the Cœlestial Crown in his hand, it is to shew that Heaven is but as a fable to some, and that things here are counted the only things substantial. Now whereas it was also shewed thee that the man could look no way but downwards, it is to let thee know that earthly things when they are with power upon men's minds, quite carry their hearts away from God.

CHRIS. Then said *Christiana*, O deliver me from Christiana's prayer against the muck-rake this Muck-rake.

INTER. That prayer, said the *Interpreter*, has lain by till 'tis almost rusty. *Give me not Riches*, is scarcely the prayer of one of ten thousand. Straws and sticks and dust with most are the great things now looked after.

With that *Mercy* and *Christiana* wept, and said, It is alas! too true.

When the *Interpreter* had shewed them this, he

had them into the very best Room in the House (a
very brave Room it was) so he bid them look round
about, and see if they could find anything profitable
there. Then they looked round and round, for there
was nothing there to be seen but a very great *Spider*
on the wall, and that they overlook'd.

MER. Then said *Mercy*, Sir, I see nothing; but
Christiana held her peace.

Of the
spider

INTER. But said the *Interpreter*, Look again; she
therefore look'd again and said, Here is not anything but an ugly *Spider*, who hangs by her hands
upon the wall. Then said he, Is there but one
Spider in all this spacious Room? Then the water
stood in *Christiana's* eyes, for she was a woman
quick of apprehension; and she said, Yes, Lord,

Talk about
the spider

there is here more than one. Yea, and *Spiders*
whose Venom is far more destructive than that
which is in her. The *Interpreter* then looked pleas-
antly upon her, and said, Thou hast said the truth.
This made *Mercy* blush, and the Boys to cover
their faces, for they all began now to understand the
Riddle.

The inter-
pretation

Then said the *Interpreter again, The Spider taketh hold with her hands as you see, and is in King's
Palaces*. And wherefore is this recorded, but to
shew you, that how full of the Venom of sin soever
you be, yet you may by the hand of faith lay hold
of and dwell in the best Room that belongs to the
King's House above?

CHRIS. I thought, said *Christiana*, of some
thing of this, but I could not imagine it all. I
thought that we were like *Spiders*, and that we
looked like ugly creatures, in what fine Room soever
we were; but that by this *Spider*, this venomous and
ill-favoured creature, we were to learn *how to act
Faith*, came not into my mind. And yet she has
taken hold with her hands, as I see, and dwells in
the best Room in the House. God has made nothing in vain.

Then they seemed all to be glad, but the water

stood in their eyes; yet they looked one upon another, and also bowed before the *Interpreter.*

He had them then into another Room where was a Hen and Chickens, and bid them observe a while. So one of the Chickens went to the trough to drink, and every time she drank she lift up her head and her eyes towards Heaven. See, said he, what this little Chick doth, and learn of her to acknowledge whence your mercies come, by receiving them with looking up. Yet again, said he, observe and look; so they gave heed and perceived that the Hen did walk in a four-fold method towards her Chickens. 1. She had a *common call.* and that she hath all day long. 2. She had a *special call,* and that she had but sometimes. 3. She had a *brooding note.* And 4. She had an *out-cry.* Of the hen and chickens

Now said he, compare this Hen to your King, and these Chickens to his obedient ones. For answerable to her, himself has his methods which he walketh in towards his People; by his *common call* he gives nothing; by his *special call* he always has something to give; he has also *a brooding voice* for them that are under his wing; and he has an *out-cry* to give the alarm when he seeth the Enemy come. I chose, my Darlings, to lead you into the Room where such things are, because you are Women, and they are easy for you.

CHRIS. And Sir, said *Christiana,* pray let us see some more. So he had them into the Slaughter-house, where was a Butcher a killing of a Sheep; and behold the Sheep was quiet, and took her death patiently. Then said the *Interpreter,* You must learn of this Sheep to suffer, and to put up wrongs without murmurings and complaints. Behold how quietly she taketh her death, and without objecting she suffereth her skin to be pulled over her ears. Your King doth call you his Sheep. Of the - butcher and the sheep

After this he led them into his Garden, where was great variety of Flowers, and he said, Do you Of the garden

see all these? So *Christiana* said, Yes. Then said
he again, Behold the Flowers are diverse in *stature*,
in *quality* and *colour* and *smell* and *vertue*, and some
are better than some; also where the Gardener has
set them there they stand, and quarrel not with one
another.

Of the
field

Again, he had them into his Field, which he
had sowed with Wheat and Corn; but when they
beheld, the tops of all was cut off, only the straw
remained. He said again, This ground was dunged
and plowed and sowed, but what shall we do with
the Crop? Then said *Christiana*, Burn some, and
make muck of the rest. Then said the *Interpreter*
again, Fruit you see is that thing you look for,
and for want of that you condemn it to the fire, and
to be trodden under foot of men; beware that in this
you condemn not yourselves.

Of the
robin and
the spider

Then as they were coming in from abroad, they
espied a little *Robin* with a great *Spider* in his
mouth. So the *Interpreter* said, Look here. So
they looked, and *Mercy* wondered; but *Christiana*
said, What a disparagement is it to such a little
pretty bird as the *Robin-red-breast* is, he being also
a bird above many that loveth to maintain a kind
of sociableness with man; I had thought they had
lived upon crums of bread, or upon other such harmless matter. I like him worse than I did.

The *Interpreter* then replied, This *Robin* is an
emblem very apt to set forth some Professors by; for
to sight they are as this *Robin*, pretty of *note colour*
and *carriage*. They seem also to have a very great
love for Professors that are sincere; and above all
other to desire to associate with, and to be in their
company, as if they could live upon the good man's
crums. They pretend also that therefore it is
that they frequent the house of the godly, and the
appointments of the Lord: but when they are by
themselves, as the *Robin*, they can catch and gobble
up *Spiders*, they can change their diet, drink
Iniquity, and swallow down Sin like water.

So when they were come again into the house, because Supper as yet was not ready, *Christiana* again desired that the *Interpreter* would either shew or tell of some other things that are profitable.

Then the *Interpreter* began and said, *The fatter the Sow is, the more she desires the Mire; the fatter the Ox is, the more gamesomely he goes to the slaughter; and the more healthy the lusty man is, the more prone he is unto evil.*

There is a desire in Woman to go neat and fine and it is a comely thing to be adorned with that that in God's sight is of great price.

'Tis easier watching a night or two, than to sit up a whole year together; so 'tis easier for one to begin to profess well, than to hold out as he should to the end.

Every Ship-master when in a Storm, will willingly cast that overboard that is of the smallest value in the vessel; but who will throw the best out first? None but he that feareth not God.

One Leak will sink a ship, and one sin will destroy a *Sinner.*

He that forgets his Friend is ungrateful unto him, but he that forgets his Saviour is unmerciful to himself.

He that lives in Sin, and looks for Happiness hereafter, is like him that soweth Cockle, and thinks to fill his Barn with Wheat or Barley.

If a man would live well, let him fetch his last day to him, and make it always his Company-keeper.

Whispering and change of thoughts proves that Sin is in the World.

If the World which God sets light by, is counted a thing of that worth with men, what is Heaven which God commendeth?

If the Life that is attended with so many Troubles, is so loth to be let go by us, what is the Life above?

Everybody will cry up the Goodness of Men; but who is there that is, as he should, affected with the goodness of God?

*We seldom sit down to meat, but we eat and.
leave; so there is in Jesus Christ more Merit and
Righteousness than the whole World has need of.*

**Of the
tree that
is rotten
at heart**

When the *Interpreter* had done, he takes them
out into his Garden again, and had them to a Tree
whose *inside* was all rotten and gone, and yet it
grew and had Leaves. Then said *Mercy,* What
means this? This Tree, said he, whose *outside* is
fair, and whose *inside* is rotten, it is to which
many may be compared that are in the Garden of
God; who with their mouths speak high in behalf
of God, but indeed will do nothing for him; whose
Leaves are fair, but their heart good for nothing
but to be *tinder* for the Devil's *tinder-box.*

**They are
at supper**

Now Supper was ready, the Table spread, and
all things set on the board; so they sate down and
did eat when one had given thanks. And the
Interpreter did usually entertain those that lodged
with him with Musick at Meals, so the Minstrels
played. There was also one that did sing, and a
very fine voice he had. His Song was this:

> The Lord is only my support,
> And he that doth me feed;
> How can I then want anything
> Whereof I stand in need?

**Talk at
supper**

When the Song and Musick was ended, the
Interpreter asked *Christiana,* What it was that at
first did move her to betake herself to a Pilgrim's
life?

**A repeti-
tion of
Chris-
tiana's
experience**

Christiana answered, First, the loss of my Husband came into my mind, at which I was heartily
grieved; but all that was but natural affection. Then
after that came the Troubles and Pilgrimage of
my Husband's into my mind, and also how like
a churl I had carried it to him as to that. So guilt
took hold of my mind, and would have drawn me
into the Pond; but that opportunely I had a Dream
of the well-being of my Husband, and a Letter
sent me by the King of that Country where my

Husband dwells, to come to him. The Dream and the Letter together so wrought upon my mind, that they forced me to this way.

INTER. But met you with no opposition afore you set out of doors?

CHRIS. Yes, a Neighbor of mine, one Mrs. *Timorous* (she was akin to him that would have persuaded my Husband to go back for fear of the Lions). She all to-befooled[1] me for as she called it my intended desperate adventure; she also urged what she could to dishearten me to it, the hardship and Troubles that my Husband met with in the way: but all this I got over pretty well. But a Dream that I had of two ill-looked ones, that I thought did plot how to make me miscarry in my Journey, that hath troubled me much; yea, it still runs in my mind, and makes me afraid of every one that I meet, lest they should meet me to do me a mischief, and to turn me out of the way. Yea, I may tell my Lord, tho' I would not have everybody know it, that between this and the Gate by which we got into the way, we were both so sorely assaulted, that we were made to cry out Murder, and the two that made this assault upon us were like the two that I saw in my Dream.

Then said the *Interpreter*, Thy beginning is good, thy latter end shall greatly increase. So he addressed himself to *Mercy*, and said unto her, And what moved thee to come hither sweet heart? *A question put to Mercy*

Then *Mercy* blushed and trembled, and for a while continued silent.

INTER. Then said he, Be not afraid, only believe, and speak thy mind.

MERCY. So she began and said, Truly Sir, my want of Experience is that that makes me covet to be in silence, and that also that fills me with fears of coming short at last. I cannot tell of Visions and Dreams as my friend *Christiana* can, nor know *Mercy's answer*

---

[1] The force of the "to" is intensive.

I what it is to mourn for my refusing of the counsel of those that were good Relations.

INTER. What was it then, dear heart, that hath prevailed with thee to do as thou hast done?

MERCY. Why, when our friend here was packing up to be gone from our Town, I and another went accidently to see her. So we knocked at the door and went in. When we were within and seeing what she was doing, we asked what was her meaning. She said she was sent for to go to her Husband; and then she up and told us how she had seen him in a Dream, dwelling in a curious place among *Immortals*, wearing a Crown, playing upon a Harp, eating and drinking at his Prince's Table, and singing Praises to him for bringing him hither, *&c.* Now methought while she was telling these things unto us, my heart burned within me; and I said in my heart, If this be true, I will leave my Father and my Mother and the Land of my Nativity, and will, if I may, go along with *Christiana.*

So I asked her further of the truth of these things, and if she would let me go with her; for I saw now that there was no dwelling, but with the danger of ruine, any longer in our Town. But yet I came away with a heavy heart, not for that I was unwilling to come away, but for that so many of my Relations were left behind. And I am come with all the desire of my heart, and will go, if I may, with *Christiana,* unto her Husband and his King.

INTER. Thy setting out is good, for thou hast given credit to the truth. Thou art a *Ruth,* who did for the love she bore to *Naomi* and to the Lord her God, leave Father and Mother and the Land of her Nativity, to come out, and go with a people that she knew not heretofore. *The Lord recompense thy work, and a full reward be given thee of the Lord God of* Israel, *under whose Wings thou art come to trust.*

Now Supper was ended, and Preparation was made for Bed; the Women were laid singly alone, and the Boys by themselves. Now when *Mercy* was in Bed, she could not sleep for joy, for that now her doubts of missing at last were removed further from her than ever they were before. So she lay blessing and praising God who had had such favour for her. They address themselves for bed Mercy's good night's rest

In the morning they arose with the Sun, and prepared themselves for their departure; but the *Interpreter* would have them tarry awhile, for said he, you must orderly go from hence. Then said he to the Damsel that at first opened unto them, Take them and have them into the Garden to the Bath, and there wash them, and make them clean from the soil which they gathered by travelling. Then *Innocent* the Damsel took them, and had them into the Garden, and brought them to the Bath; so she told them that there they must wash and be clean, for so her Master would have the Women to do that called at his house, as they were going on Pilgrimage. They then went in and washed, yea they and the Boys and all; and they came out of that Bath, not only sweet and clean, but also much enlivened and strengthened in their joints. So when they came in, they looked fairer a deal than when they went out to the washing. The bath Sanctification They wash in it

When they were returned out of the Garden from the Bath, the *Interpreter* took them and looked upon them and said unto them, *Fair as the Moon.* Then he called for the *Seal* wherewith they used to be *sealed* that were washed in his Bath. So the *Seal* was brought, and he set his Mark upon them, that they might be known in the places whither they were yet to go. Now the *Seal* was the contents and sum of the Passover which the Children of *Israel* did eat when they came out from the land of *Egypt,* and the Mark was set between their eyes. This *Seal* greatly added to their beauty, for it was an ornament to their faces. It also added to their They are sealed gravity, and made their countenances more like them of Angels.

Then said the *Interpreter* again to the Damsel that waited upon these Women, Go into the Vestry and fetch out Garments for these people; so she went and fetched out white Raiment, and laid it down before him; so he commanded them to put it on. *It was fine linen, white and clean.* When the Women were thus adorned, they seemed to be a terror one to the other, for that they could not see that glory each one on herself which they could see in each other. Now therefore they began to esteem each other better than themselves. For you are fairer than I am, said one; and you are more comely than I am, said another. The Children also stood amazed to see into what fashion they were brought.

The *Interpreter* then called for a Man-servant of his, one *Great-heart,* and bid him take *sword* and *helmet* and *shield;* and take these my Daughters, said he, and conduct them to the house called *Beautiful,* at which place they will rest next. So he took his Weapons and went before them, and the *Interpreter* said, God speed. Those also that belonged to the Family sent them away with many a good wish. So they went on their way and sung,

This place has been our second stage,
Here we have heard and seen
Those good things that from age to age,
To others hid have been.
  The Dunghill-raker, the Spider, Hen,
The Chicken too to me
Hath taught a lesson; let me then
Conformed to it be.
  The Butcher, Garden, and the Field,
The Robin and his bait,
Also the Rotten Tree doth yield
Me argument of weight,
  To move me for to watch and pray,
To strive to be sincere,
To take my Cross up day by day,
And serve the Lord with fear.

Now I saw in my Dream that they went on, and *Great-heart* went before them; so they went and came to the place where *Christian's* Burden fell off his back and tumbled into a Sepulchre. Here then they made a pause, and here also they blessed God. Now said *Christiana,* it comes to my mind what was said to us at the Gate, to wit, that we should have pardon by *word* and *deed:* by *word,* that is, by the promise; by *deed,* to wit, in the way it was obtained. What the promise is, of that I know something; but what it is to have pardon by deed, or in the way that it was obtained, Mr *Great-heart,* I suppose you know; wherefore if you please let us hear your discourse thereof.

GREAT-HEART. Pardon by the deed done, is pardon obtained by some one for another that hath need thereof, not by the person pardoned, but in the way, *saith another,* in which I have obtained it. So then to speak to the question more large, the pardon that you and *Mercy* and these Boys have attained, was obtained by another, to wit, by him that let you in at the Gate; and he hath obtain'd it in this double way, he has performed Righteousness to cover you, and spilt Blood to wash you in.

A comment upon what was said at the gate, or a discourse of our being justified by Christ

CHRIS. But if he parts with his Righteousness to us, what will he have for himself?

GREAT-HEART. He has more Righteousness than you have need of, or than he needeth himself.

CHRIS. Pray make that appear.

GREAT-HEART. With all my heart; but first I must premise that he of whom we are now about to speak is one that has not his fellow. He has two Natures in one Person, plain to be *distinguished,* impossible to be *divided.* Unto each of these Natures a Righteousness belongeth, and each Righteousness is essential to that Nature; so that one may as easily cause the Nature to be extinct, as to separate its Justice or Righteousness from it. Of these Righteousnesses therefore we are not made partakers, so as that they, or any of them, should be put upon us that we might be made just, and live thereby. Besides these there is a Righteousness which this Person has, as these two Natures are joined in one. And this is not the Righteousness of the *Godhead,* as distinguished from the *Manhood;* nor the Righteousness of the *Manhood,* as distinguished from the *Godhead;* but a Righteousness which standeth in the union of both Natures, and may properly be called, the Righteousness that is essential to his being prepared of God to the capacity of the Mediatory Office which he was to be intrusted with. If he parts with his first Righteousness, he parts with his *Godhead;* if he parts with his second Righteousness, he parts with the purity of his *Manhood;* if he parts with this third, he parts with that perfection that capacitates him to the Office of Mediation. He has therefore another Righteousness, which standeth in performance, or obedience to a revealed will; and that is that he puts upon Sinners, and that by which their sins are covered. Wherefore he saith, *as by one man's disobedience many were made Sinners, so by the obedience of one shall many be made Righteous.*

CHRIS. But are the other Righteousnesses of no use to us?

GREAT-HEART. Yes, for though they are essential to his Natures and Office, and so cannot be communicated unto another, yet it is by vertue of them that the Righteousness that justifies is for that purpose efficacious. The Righteousness of his *Godhead* gives virtue to his Obedience; the Righteousness of his *Manhood* giveth capability to his obedience to justify; and the Righteousness that standeth in the union of these two Natures to his Office, giveth authority to that Righteousness to do the work for which it is ordained.

So then here is a Righteousness that Christ as God has no need of, for he is God without it; here is a Righteousness that Christ as Man has no need of to make him so, for he is perfect Man without

it; again, here is a Righteousness that Christ as
God-man has no need of, for he is perfectly so without it. Here then is a Righteousness that Christ,
as God, as Man, as God-man, has no need of, with
reference to himself, and therefore he can spare it;
a justifying Righteousness that he for himself
wanteth not, and therefore he giveth it away; hence
'tis called *the gift of Righteousness*. This Righteousness, since Christ Jesus the Lord has made himself under the Law, *must* be given away: for the
Law doth not only bind him that is under it *to
do justly*, but to use Charity. Wherefore he *must*,
he *ought* by the Law, if he hath two Coats, to give
one to him that hath none. Now our Lord indeed
hath two Coats, one for himself, and one to spare;
wherefore he freely bestows one upon those that
have none. And thus *Christiana*, and *Mercy*, and
the rest of you that are here, doth your pardon
come by *deed*, or by the work of another man.
Your Lord Christ is he that has worked, and has
given away what he wrought for to the next poor
beggar he meets.

But again, in order to pardon by *deed*, there must
something be paid to God as a price, as well as
something prepared to cover us withal. Sin has
delivered us up to the just curse of a righteous Law;
now from this curse we must be justified by way
of redemption, a price being paid for the harms
we have done; and this is by the Blood of your
Lord, who came and stood in your place and stead,
and died your death for your transgressions. Thus
has he ransomed you from your transgressions by
Blood, and covered your polluted and deformed
souls with Righteousness. For the sake of which
God passeth by you, and will not hurt you when
he comes to judge the World.

CHRIS. This is brave. Now I see that there Christiana
was something to be learned by our being pardoned affected
by *word* and *deed*. Good *Mercy*, let us labour to with this
way of re-
keep this in mind, and my Children, do you remem- demption

ber it also. But Sir, was not this it that made my good *Christian's* Burden fall from off his shoulder, and that made him give three leaps for joy?

GREAT-HEART. Yes, 'twas the belief of this that cut those strings that could not be cut by other means, and 'twas to give him a proof of the vertue of this, that he was suffered to carry his Burden to the Cross.

CHRIS. I thought so, for tho' my heart was lightful and joyous before, yet it is ten times more lightsome and joyous now. And I am persuaded by what I have felt, tho' I have felt but little as yet, that if the most burdened man in the world was here, and did see and believe as I now do, 'twould make his heart the more merry and blithe.

GREAT-HEART. There is not only comfort, and the ease of a Burden brought to us, by the sight and consideration of these, but an indeared affection begot in us by it; for who can, if he doth but once think that pardon comes, not only by promise but thus, but be affected by the way and means of his redemption, and so with the man that hath wrought it for him?

CHRIS. True, methinks it makes my heart bleed to think that he should bleed for me. Oh! thou loving One. Oh! thou blessed One. Thou deservest to have me, thou hast bought me: thou deservest to have me all; thou hast paid for me ten thousand times more than I am worth. No marvel that this made the water stand in my Husband's eyes, and that it made him trudge so nimbly on; I am persuaded he wished me with him; but vile wretch that I was, I let him come all alone. O *Mercy*, that thy Father and Mother were here; yea, and Mrs *Timorous* also; nay, I wish now with all my heart, that here was Madam *Wanton* too. Surely, surely, their hearts would be affected; nor could the fear of the one, nor the powerful lusts of the other, prevail with them to go home again, and to refuse to become good Pilgrims.

How the strings that bound Christian's burden to him were cut

How affection to Christ is begot in the soul

First Part, p. 41.

Cause of admiration

GREAT-HEART. You speak now in the warmth of your affections: will it, think you, be always thus with you? Besides, this is not communicated to every one, nor to every one that did see your Jesus bleed. There was that stood by, and that saw the Blood run from his heart to the ground, and yet were so far off this, that instead of lamenting, they laughed at him; and instead of becoming his Disciples, did harden their hearts against him. So that all that you have, my Daughters, you have by a peculiar impression made by a divine contemplating upon what I have spoken to you. Remember that 'twas told you, that the *Hen* by her common call gives no meat to the *Chickens*. This you have therefore by a special Grace. *To be affected with Christ and with what he has done, is a thing special*

Now I saw still in my Dream, that they went on until they were come to the place that *Simple* and *Sloth* and *Presumption* lay and slept in, when *Christian* went by on Pilgrimage. And behold they were hanged up in irons, a little way off on the other side. *Simple, and Sloth, and Presumption hanged, and why*

MERCY. Then said *Mercy* to him that was their Guide and Conductor, What are those three men? and for what are they hanged there?

GREAT-HEART. These three men were men of very bad qualities, they had no mind to be Pilgrims themselves, and whosoever they could they hindered. They were for sloth and folly themselves, and whoever they could persuade with, they made so too, and withal taught them to presume that they should do well at last. They were asleep when *Christian* went by, and now you go by they are hanged.

Behold here how the slothful are a sign,
Hung up 'cause holy ways they did decline.
See here too how the child doth play the man,
And weak grow strong when *Great-heart* leads the van.

MERCY. But could they persuade any to be of their opinion?

GREAT-HEART. Yes, they turned several out of the

Their
crimes

way. There was *Slow-pace* that they persuaded
to do as they. They also prevailed with one *Short-
wind,* with one *No-heart,* with one *Linger-after-lust,*

Who they
; revailed
upon to
turn out
of the way

and with one *Sleepy-head,* and with a young woman
her name was *Dull,* to turn out of the way and
become as they. Besides they brought up an ill
report of your Lord, persuading others that he was
a Task-master. They also brought up an evil report
of the good Land, saying 'twas not half so good
as some pretend it was. They also began to vilify
his Servants, and to count the very best of them
meddlesome troublesome busy-bodies. Further, they
would call the Bread of God *Husks,* the Comforts
of his Children *Fancies,* the Travel and Labour of
Pilgrims things to no purpose.

CHRIS. Nay, said *Christiana,* if they were such,
they shall never be bewailed by me. They have
but what they deserve, and I think it is well that
they hang so near the High-way that others may
see and take warning. But had it not been well
if their crimes had been ingraven in some plate of
iron or brass, and left here, even where they did
their mischiefs, for a caution to other bad men?

GREAT-HEART. So it is, as you well may perceive
if you will go a little to the Wall.

MERCY. No, no, let them hang, and their names
rot, and their crimes live for ever against them.
I think it a high favour that they were hanged
afore we came hither, who knows else what they
might a done to such poor women as we are? Then
she turned it into a Song, saying,

> Now then you three, hang there and be a sign
> To all that shall against the truth combine.
> And let him that comes after fear this end,
> If unto Pilgrims he is not a Friend.
> And thou, my soul, of all such men beware,
> That unto holiness opposers are.

First Part,
p. 46

Thus they went on, till they came at the foot of
the Hill *Difficulty,* where again their good Friend
Mr *Great-heart,* took an occasion to tell them of

what happened there when *Christian* himself went
by. So he had them first to the Spring. Lo, saith It is
he, this is the Spring that *Christian* drank of before difficult
he went up this Hill, and then 'twas clear and good, of good
but now 'tis dirty with the feet of some that are doctrine in
not desirous that Pilgrims here should quench their times
thirst. Thereat *Mercy* said, And why so envious,
tro? But said the Guide, It will do, if taken up,
and put into a vessel that is sweet and good; for
then the dirt will sink to the bottom, and the water
will come out by itself more clear. Thus therefore
Christiana and her Companions were compelled to
do. They took it up, and put it into an earthen pot,
and so let it stand till the dirt was gone to the
bottom, and then they drank thereof.

Next he shewed them the two *by-ways* that were By-paths,
at the foot of the Hill, where *Formality* and *Hypoc-* though
risy lost themselves. And said he, these are dan- barred up,
gerous Paths. Two were here cast away when keep all
Christian came by; and although, as you see, these from going
ways are since stopped up with *chains posts* and a in them
ditch, yet there are that will chuse to adventure
here, rather than take the pains to go up this Hill.

CHRIS. The way of transgressors is hard. 'Tis
a wonder that they can get into those ways without
danger of breaking their necks.

GREAT-HEART. They will venture; yea, if at any
time any of the King's servants doth happen to
see them, and doth call unto them, and tell them
that they are in the wrong ways, and do bid them
beware the danger, then they will railingly return
them answer and say, *As for the word that thou
hast spoken unto us in the name of the King, we
will not hearken unto thee; but we will certainly
do whatsoever thing goeth out of our own mouths,*
&c. Nay if you look a little farther, you shall see
that these ways are made cautionary enough, not
only by these *posts* and *ditch* and *chain,* but also by
being hedged up; yet they will chuse to go there.

CHRIS. They are idle, they love not to take pains,

The reason why some do choose to go in by-ways up-hill way is unpleasant to them. So it is fulfilled unto them as it is written, The way of the slothful man is a Hedge of Thorns. Yea, they will rather chuse to walk upon a Snare, than to go up this Hill, and the rest of this way to the City.

The hill puts the pilgrims to it Then they set forward, and began to go up the Hill, and up the Hill they went; but before they got to the top, *Christiana* began to pant, and said, I dare say this is a breathing Hill. No marvel if they that love their ease more than their souls, chuse to themselves a smoother way. Then said *Mercy*, I must sit down; also the least of the Children began to cry. Come, come, said *Great-heart*, sit not down here, for a little above is the Prince's *Arbor*. Then took he the little Boy by the hand, and led him up thereto.

They sit in the arbor When they were come to the *Arbor*, they were very willing to sit down, for they were all in a pelting heat. Then said *Mercy*, How sweet is rest to them that labour. And how good is the Prince of Pilgrims to provide such resting-places for them.

First Part, pp. 47, 48 Of this *Arbor* I have heard much, but I never saw it before. But here let us beware of sleeping; for as I have heard, for that it cost poor *Christian* dear.

The little boy's answer to the guide, and also to Mercy Then said Mr *Great-heart* to the little ones, Come my pretty Boys, how do you do? What think you now of going on Pilgrimage? Sir, said the least, I was almost beat out of heart, but I thank you for lending me a hand at my need. And I remember now what my Mother has told me, namely, That the way to Heaven is as up a Ladder, and the way to Hell is as down a Hill. But I had rather go up the Ladder to Life, than down the Hill to Death.

Which is hardest, up hill or down hill? Then said *Mercy*, But the Proverb is, *To go down the Hill is easy*. But *James* said (for that was his name) The day is coming when in my opinion *going down Hill will be the hardest of all*. 'Tis a good Boy, said his Master, thou hast given her a right answer. Then *Mercy* smiled, but the little Boy did blush.

CHRIS. Come, said *Christiana,* will you eat a bit, They
a little to sweeten your mouths, while you sit here refresh
to rest your legs? For I have here a piece of Pom- themselves
granate, which Mr *Interpreter* put in my hand, just
when I came out of his doors. He gave me also
a piece of an Hony-comb, and a little Bottle of
Spirits. I thought he gave you something, said
Mercy, because he called you a to-side. Yes, so he
did, said the other; but *Mercy,* it shall still be, as
I said it should, when at first we came from home,
thou shalt be a sharer in all the good that I have,
because thou so willingly didst become my Companion. Then she gave to them, and they did eat,
both *Mercy* and the Boys. And said *Christiana* to
Mr *Great-heart,* Sir, will you do as we? But he
answered, You are going on Pilgrimage, and presently I shall return: much good may what you have
do to you, at home I eat the same every day. Now
when they had eaten and drank, and had chatted
a little longer, their Guide said to them, The day
wears away, if you think good, let us prepare to be
going. So they got up to go, and the little Boys
went before. But *Christiana* forgat to take her Christiana
Bottle of Spirits with her, so she sent her little forgets
Boy back to fetch it. Then said *Mercy,* I think this of spirits
is a losing place. Here *Christian* lost his *Roll,*
and here *Christiana* left her Bottle behind her. Sir,
what is the cause of this? So their Guide made
answer and said, The cause is *sleep* or *forgetfulness:*
some *sleep* when they should keep *awake,* and some
forget when they should *remember;* and this is the
very cause, why often at the resting-places, some
Pilgrims in some things come off losers. Pilgrims Mark this
should watch, and remember what they have already
received under their greatest enjoyment; but for
want of doing so, oft-times their Rejoicing ends in First Part.
Tears, and their Sun-shine in a Cloud: witness the pp. 47, 48
story of *Christian* at this place.

    When they were come to the place where *Mistrust*
and *Timorous* met *Christian* to persuade him to go

back for fear of the Lions, they perceived as it were a Stage, and before it towards the Road a broad plate with a Copy of Verses written thereon, and underneath, the reason of raising up of that Stage in that place rendered. The Verses were these:

> Let him that sees this Stage take heed
> Unto his Heart and Tongue;
> Lest if he do not, here he speed
> As some have long agone.

The words underneath the Verses were, *This Stage was built to punish such upon, who through* timorousness *or* mistrust, *shall be afraid to go further on Pilgrimage. Also on this Stage both* Mistrust *and* Timorous *were burned through the Tongue with an hot Iron, for endeavouring to hinder* Christian *in his Journey.*

Then said *Mercy,* This is much like to the saying of the Beloved, *What shall be given unto thee? or what shall be done unto thee, thou false Tongue? Sharp Arrows of the mighty, with coals of Juniper.*

First Part. p. 49

An emblem of those that go on bravely when there is no danger, but shrink when troubles come

So they went on, till they came within sight of the Lions. Now Mr *Great-heart* was a strong man, so he was not afraid of a Lion; but yet when they were come up to the place where the Lions were, the Boys that went before were glad to cringe behind, for they were afraid of the Lions; so they stept back, and went behind. At this their Guide smiled, and said, How now, my Boys, do you love to go before when no danger doth approach, and love to come behind so soon as the Lions appear?

Of Grim the Giant, and of his backing the lions

Now as they went up, Mr *Great-heart* drew his Sword, with intent to make a way for the Pilgrims in spite of the Lions. Then there appeared one, that it seems, had taken upon him to back the Lions; and he said to the Pilgrims' Guide, What is the cause of your coming hither? Now the name of that man was *Grim,* or *Bloody-man,* because of his slaying of Pilgrims, and he was of the race of the Giants.

GREAT-HEART. Then said the Pilgrims' Guide, These Women and Children are going on Pilgrimage, and this is the way they must go, and go it they shall in spite of thee and the Lions.

GRIM. This is not their way, neither shall they go therein. I am come forth to withstand them, and to that end will back the Lions.

Now to say truth, by reason of the fierceness of the Lions, and of the *grim* carriage of him that did back them, this way had of late lain much un-occupied, and was almost all grown over with Grass.

CHRIS. Then said *Christiana,* Tho' the High-ways have been un-occupied heretofore, and tho' the Travellers have been made in time past to walk through by-paths, it must not be so now I am risen, *now I am risen a Mother in* Israel.

GRIM. Then he swore *by the Lions,* but it should, and therefore bid them turn aside, for they should not have passage there.

GREAT-HEART. But their Guide made first his approach unto *Grim,* and laid so heavily at him with his Sword, that he forced him to a retreat.

GRIM. Then said he (that attempted to back the Lions) Will you slay me upon mine own ground?

GREAT-HEART. 'Tis the King's High-way that we are in, and in his way it is that thou hast placed thy Lions; but these Women and these Children, tho' weak, shall hold on their way in spite of thy Lions. And with that he gave him again a downright blow, and brought him upon his knees. With this blow he also broke his Helmet, and with the next he cut off an arm. Then did the Giant roar so hideously, that his voice frighted the Women, and yet they were glad to see him lie sprawling upon the ground. Now the Lions were chained, and so of themselves could do nothing. Wherefore when old *Grim* that intended to back them was dead, Mr *Great-heart* said to the Pilgrims, Come now and follow me, and no hurt shall happen to you from

A fight betwixt Grim and Great-heart

The victory

They pass by the lions the Lions. They therefore went on, but the Women trembled as they passed by them; the Boys also looked as if they would die, but they all got by without further hurt.

They come to the porter's lodge Now then they were within sight of the Porter's Lodge, and they soon came up unto it; but they made the more haste after this to go thither, because 'tis dangerous travelling there in the Night. So when they were come to the Gate, the Guide knocked, and the Porter cried, *Who is there?* But as soon as the Guide had said, *It is I,* he knew his voice, and came down (for the Guide had oft before that come thither as a Conductor of Pilgrims). When he was come down, he opened the Gate, and seeing the Guide standing just before it (for he saw not the Women, for they were behind him) he said unto him, How now, Mr *Great-heart,* what is your business here so late to-night? I have brought, said he, some Pilgrims hither, where by my Lord's commandment they must lodge. I had been here some time ago, had I not been opposed by the Giant that did use to back the Lions; but I after a long and tedious combat with him, have cut him off, and have brought the Pilgrims hither in safety.

Great-heart attempts to go back PORTER. Will you not go in, and stay till morning?

GREAT-HEART. No, I will return to my Lord to-night.

The pilgrims implore his company still CHRIS. Oh Sir, I know not how to be willing you should leave us in our Pilgrimage, you have been so faithful and so loving to us, you have fought so stoutly for us, you have been so hearty in counselling of us, that I shall never forget your favour towards us.

MERCY. Then said *Mercy,* O that we might have thy company to our Journey's end. How can such poor Women as we hold out in a way so full of troubles as this way is, without a Friend and Defender?

JAMES. Then said *James,* the youngest of the

Boys, Pray Sir, be persuaded to go with us, and help us, because we are so weak, and the way so dangerous as it is.

GREAT-HEART. I am at my Lord's commandment. If he shall allot me to be your Guide quite through, I will willingly wait upon you. But here you failed at first; for when he bid me come thus far with you, then you should have begged me of him to have gone quite through with you, and he would have granted your request. However at present I must withdraw, and so, good *Christiana, Mercy,* and my brave Children, Adieu. *Help lost for want of asking for*

Then the Porter, Mr *Watchful,* asked *Christiana* of her Country, and of her Kindred. And she said, I came from the City of Destruction, I am a Widow woman, and my Husband is dead, his name was *Christian* the Pilgrim. How, said the Porter, was he your Husband? Yes, said she, and these are his Children; and this, pointing to *Mercy,* is one of my Towns-women. Then the Porter rang his bell, as at such times he is wont, and there came to the door one of the Damsels, whose name was *Humble-mind.* And to her the Porter said, Go tell it within that *Christiana* the Wife of *Christian,* and her Children, are come hither on Pilgrimage. She went in therefore and told it. But O what a noise for gladness was there within, when the Damsel did but drop that word out of her mouth. *First Part, p. 50* *Christiana makes her-self known to the porter; he tells it to a damsel* *Joy at the noise of the pilgrims coming*

So they came with haste to the Porter, for *Chris-tiana* stood still at the door. Then some of the most grave said unto her, *Come in* Christiana, *come in thou Wife of that good man, come in thou blessed woman, come in with all that are with thee.* So she went in, and they followed her that were her Children and her Companions. Now when they were gone in, they were had into a very large room, where they were bidden to sit down; so they sat down, and the Chief of the house was called to see and welcome the Guests. Then they came in, and understanding who they were, did salute each other *Christians' love is kindled at the sight of one another*

with a kiss, and said, Welcome ye Vessels of the
Grace of God, welcome to us your Friends.

Now because it was somewhat late, and because
the Pilgrims were weary with their Journey, and
also made faint with the sight of the Fight and of
the terrible Lions, therefore they desired as soon as
might be, to prepare to go to rest. Nay, said those
of the Family, refresh yourselves first with a morsel
of Meat. For they had prepared for them a Lamb,
with the accustomed Sauce belonging thereto; for
the Porter had heard before of their coming, and
had told it to them within. So when they had
supped, and ended their Prayer with a Psalm, they
desired they might go to rest. But let us, said
Christiana, if we may be so bold as to chuse, be in
that Chamber that was my Husband's when he was
here. So they had them up thither, and they lay
all in a room. When they were at rest, Christiana
and Mercy entred into discourse about things that
were convenient.

First Part,
p. 57

Christ's
bosom
is for all
pilgrims

CHRIS. Little did I think once, that when my
Husband went on Pilgrimage, I should ever a followed.

MERCY. And you as little thought of lying in his
Bed and in his Chamber to rest, as you do now.

CHRIS. And much less did I ever think of seeing
his face with comfort, and of worshipping the Lord
the King with him, and yet now I believe I shall.

MERCY. Hark, don't you hear a noise?

Music

CHRIS. Yes, 'tis as I believe, a noise of Musick
for joy that we are here.

MERCY. Wonderful! Musick in the House, Musick in the Heart, and Musick also in Heaven, for
joy that we are here.

Thus they talked awhile, and then betook themselves to sleep. So in the morning, when they were
awake, Christiana said to Mercy:

Mercy did
laugh in
her sleep

CHRIS. What was the matter that you did laugh
in your sleep to-night. I suppose you was in a
Dream.

MERCY. So I was, and a sweet Dream it was, but are you sure I laughed?

CHRIS. Yes, you laughed heartily; but prithee *Mercy*, tell me thy dream.

MERCY. I was a dreamed that I sat all alone in a solitary place, and was bemoaning of the hardness of my Heart. *Mercy's dream*

Now I had not sat there long, but methought many were gathered about me, to see me, and to hear what it was that I said. So they hearkened, and I went on bemoaning the hardness of my Heart. At this some of them laughed at me, some called me Fool, and some began to thrust me about. With that, methought I looked up, and saw one coming with Wings towards me. So he came directly to me, and said, *Mercy*, what aileth thee? Now when he had heard me make my complaint, he said, *Peace be to thee*. He also wiped mine eyes with his Handkerchief, and clad me in Silver and Gold: he put a Chain about my Neck, and Ear-rings in mine Ears, and a beautiful Crown upon my Head. Then he took me by the Hand, and said *Mercy*, come after me. So he went up, and I followed, till we came at a Golden Gate. Then he knocked; and when they within had opened, the man went in, and I followed him up to a Throne, upon which one sat, and he said to me, *Welcome Daughter*. The place looked bright and twinkling like the Stars, or rather like the Sun, and I thought that I saw your Husband there. So I awoke from my Dream. But did I laugh? *What her dream was*

CHRIS. Laugh: ay, and well you might, to see yourself so well. For you must give me leave to tell you, that I believe it was a good Dream, and that as you have begun to find the first part true, so you shall find the second at last. *God speaks once, yea twice, yet man perceiveth it not. In a Dream, in a Vision of the night, when deep sleep falleth upon men, in slumbring upon the bed.* We need not, when a-bed, lie awake to talk with God.

He can visit us while we sleep, and cause us then to hear his voice. Our heart oft-times wakes when we sleep; and God can speak to that, either by words, by Proverbs, by Signs and Similitudes, as well as if one was awake.

Mercy glad of her dream

MERCY. Well, I am glad of my Dream, for I hope ere long to see it fulfilled, to the making of me laugh again.

CHRIS. I think it is now high time to rise, and to know what we must do.

MERCY. Pray, if they invite us to stay a while, let us willingly accept of the proffer. I am the willinger to stay a while here, to grow better acquainted with these Maids. Methinks *Prudence Piety* and *Charity* have very comely and sober countenances.

CHRIS. We shall see what they will do. So when they were up and ready, they came down. And they asked one another of their rest, and if it was comfortable or not.

MERCY. Very good, said *Mercy;* it was one of the best night's Lodging that ever I had in my life.

They stay here some time

Then said *Prudence* and *Piety,* If you will be persuaded to stay here a while, you shall have what the house will afford.

Prudence desires to catechise Christiana's children

CHAR. Ay, and that with a very good will, said *Charity.* So they consented, and stayed there about a month or above, and became very profitable one to another. And because *Prudence* would see how *Christiana* had brought up her Children, she asked leave of her to catechise them. So she gave her free consent. Then she began at the youngest, whose name was *James.*

James catechised

PRUDENCE. And she said, Come *James,* canst thou tell who made thee?

JAMES. God the Father, God the Son, and God the Holy Ghost.

PRUD. Good Boy. And canst thou tell me who saves thee?

JAMES. God the Father, God the Son, and God the Holy Ghost.

PRUD. Good Boy still. But how doth God the Father save thee?

JAMES. By his Grace.

PRUD. How doth God the Son save thee?

JAMES. By his Righteousness, Death, and Blood, and Life.

PRUD. And how doth God the Holy Ghost save thee?

JAMES. By his Illumination, by his Renovation, and by his Preservation.

Then said *Prudence* to *Christiana,* You are to be commended for thus bringing up your Children. I suppose I need not ask the rest these questions, since the youngest of them can answer them so well. I will therefore now apply myself to the youngest next.

PRUD. Then she said, Come *Joseph* (for his name was *Joseph*) will you let me catechise you?   Joseph catechised

JOSEPH. With all my heart.

PRUD. What is Man?

JOSEPH. A Reasonable Creature, so made by God, as my Brother said.

PRUD. What is supposed by this word *saved?*

JOSEPH. That Man by Sin has brought himself into a state of Captivity and Misery.

PRUD. What is supposed by his being saved by the Trinity?

JOSEPH. That Sin is so great and mighty a Tyrant, that none can pull us out of its clutches but God; and that God is so good and loving to man, as to pull him indeed out of this miserable state.

PRUD. What is God's design in saving of poor Men?

JOSEPH. The glorifying of his Name, of his Grace and Justice, &c. and the everlasting Happiness of his Creature.

PRUD. Who are they that must be saved.

JOSEPH. Those that accept of his Salvation.

PRUD. Good Boy, *Joseph,* thy Mother has taught
thee well, and thou hast hearkened to what she hath
said unto thee.

Then said *Prudence* to *Samuel,* who was the
eldest but one.

Samuel catechised

PRUD. Come *Samuel,* are you willing that I should
catechise you also?

SAMUEL. Yes, forsooth, if you please.

PRUD. What is Heaven?

SAM. A place and state most blessed, because
God dwelleth there.

PRUD. What is Hell?

SAM. A place and state most woful, because it is
the dwelling place of Sin, the Devil, and Death.

PRUD. Why wouldst thou go to Heaven?

SAM. That I may see God, and serve him without
weariness; that I may see Christ, and love him
everlastingly; that I may have that fulness of the
Holy Spirit in me that I can by no means here
enjoy.

PRUD. A very good Boy also, and one that has
learned well.

Matthew catechised

Then she addressed herself to the eldest, whose
name was *Matthew;* and she said to him, Come
Matthew, shall I also catechise you?

MATTHEW. With a very good will.

PRUD. I ask then, if there was ever anything that
had a being antecedent to or before God,

MATT. No, for God is eternal, nor is there anything excepting himself that had a being until the
beginning of the first day. *For in six days the
Lord made Heaven and Earth, the Sea and all that
in them is.*

PRUD. What do you think of the Bible?

MATT. It is the Holy Word of God.

PRUD. Is there nothing written therein but what
you understand?

MATT. Yes a great deal.

PRUD. What do you do when you meet with such
places therein that you do not understand?

MATT. I think God is wiser than I. I pray also that he will please to let me know all therein that he knows will be for my good.

PRUD. How believe you as touching the Resurrection of the Dead?

MATT. I believe they shall rise, the same that was buried, the same in *nature,* tho' not in *corruption.* And I believe this upon a double account. First, because God has promised it. Secondly, because he is able to perform it.

Then said *Prudence* to the Boys, You must still hearken to your Mother, for she can learn you more. You must also diligently give ear to what good talk you shall hear from others, for for your sakes do they speak good things. Observe also and that with carefulness, what the Heavens and the Earth do teach you; but especially be much in the meditation of that Book that was the cause of your Father's becoming a Pilgrim. I for my part, my Children, will teach you what I can while you are here, and shall be glad if you will ask me Questions that tend to godly edifying. *(margin: Prudence's conclusion upon the catechising of the boys)*

Now by that these Pilgrims had been at this place a week, *Mercy* had a visitor that pretended some good will unto her, and his name was Mr *Brisk.* A man of some breeding, and that pretended to Religion, but a man that stuck very close to the World. So he came once or twice or more to *Mercy,* and offered love unto her. Now *Mercy* was of fair countenance, and therefore the more alluring. *(margin: Mercy has a sweetheart)*

Her mind also was, to be always busying of herself in doing, for when she had nothing to do for herself, she would be making of Hose and Garments for others, and would bestow them upon them that had need. And Mr *Brisk* not knowing where or how she disposed of what she made, seemed to be greatly taken for that he found her never idle. I will warrant her a good housewife, quoth he to himself. *(margin: Mercy's temper)*

Mercy
inquires of
the maids
concerning
Mr Brisk
Mercy then revealed the business to the Maidens that were of the house, and enquired of them concerning him, for they did know him better than she. So they told her that he was a very busy young man, and one that pretended to Religion, but was as they feared, a stranger to the Power of that which was good.

Nay then, said *Mercy,* I will look no more on him, for I purpose never to have a clog to my soul.

Prudence then replied, That there needed no great matter of discouragement to be given to him, her continuing so as she had began to do for the poor, would quickly cool his courage.

Talk
betwixt
Mercy and
Mr Brisk
So the next time he comes, he finds her at her old work, a making of things for the poor. Then said he, What, always at it? Yes, said she, either for myself or for others. And what canst thou earn a day? quoth he. I do these things, said she, *that I may be rich in Good Works, laying up in store a good Foundation against the time to come, that I may lay hold on Eternal Life.* Why prithee what dost thou with them? said he. Cloath the naked, said she. With that his countenance fell. So he forbore to come at her again. And when he was asked the reason why, he said *that Mercy was a pretty lass, but troubled with ill conditions.*

He for-
sakes her,
and why

Mercy
in the
practice
of mercy
rejected;
while
Mercy in
the name
of mercy
is liked
When he had left her, *Prudence* said, Did I not tell thee, that Mr *Brisk* would soon forsake thee? yea, he will raise up an ill report of thee; for notwithstanding his pretence to Religion, and his seeming love to *Mercy,* yet *Mercy* and he are of tempers so different, that I believe they will never come together.

MERCY. I might a had Husbands afore now, tho' I spake not of it to any; but they were such as did not like my Conditions, though never did any of them find fault with my Person. So they and I could not agree.

PRUD. *Mercy* in our days is little set by any

further than as to its Name; the Practice, which
is set forth by thy Conditions, there are but few
that can abide.

MERCY. Well, said *Mercy,* if nobody will have me, Mercy's
I will die a Maid, or my Conditions shall be to me resolution
as a Husband. For I cannot change my nature, and
to have one that lies cross to me in this, that I
purpose never to admit of as long as I live. I had
a Sister named *Bountiful,* that was married to one How
of these churls; but he and she could never agree; Mercy's
sister was
but because my Sister was resolved to do as she had served
began, that is, to shew kindness to the poor, there- by her
husband
fore her Husband first cried her down at the Cross,[1]
and then turned her out of his doors.

PRUD. And yet he was a Professor, I warrant
you.

MERCY. Yes, such a one as he was, and of such
as he the world is now full: but I am for none of
them at all.

Now *Matthew* the eldest Son of *Christiana* fell Matthew
sick, and his sickness was sore upon him, for he was falls sick
much pained in his Bowels, so that he was with it
at times, pulled as 'twere both ends together. There
dwelt also not far from thence, one Mr *Skill,* an
antient and well-approved Physician. So *Christiana*
desired it, and they sent for him, and he came.
When he was entred the room, and had a little observed the Boy, he concluded that he was sick of
the Gripes. Then he said to his Mother, What diet Gripes of
has *Matthew* of late fed upon? Diet, said *Chris-* conscience
tiana, nothing but that which is wholesome. The
Physician answered, This Boy has been tampering The
with something that lies in his maw undigested, and physician's
judgment
that will not away without means. And I tell
you he must be purged, or else he will die.

SAM. Then said *Samuel,* Mother, Mother, what
was that which my Brother did gather up and eat,
so soon as we were come from the Gate that is at

---

[1] Gave notice that he would not be responsible for debts contracted
by his wife.

Samuel
puts his
mother
in mind
of the
fruit his
brother
did eat

the head of this way, You know that there was an
Orchard on the left hand, on the other side of the
wall, some of the trees hung over the wall, and my
Brother did plash and did eat.

CHRIS. True my Child, said *Christiana,* he did
take thereof and did eat, naughty Boy as he was. I
did chide him, and yet he would eat thereof.

SKILL. I knew he had eaten something that was
not wholesome food, and that food, to wit, that
Fruit, is even the most hurtful of all. It is the
Fruit of *Beelzebub's* Orchard. I do marvel that
none did warn you of it; many have died thereof.

CHRIS. Then *Christiana* began to cry, and she
said, O naughty Boy, and O careless Mother, what
shall I do for my Son?

SKILL. Come, do not be too much dejected; the
Boy may do well again, but he must purge and vomit.

CHRIS. Pray Sir, try the utmost of your skill with
him whatever it costs.

Potion
prepared

SKILL. Nay, I hope I shall be reasonable. So
he made him a Purge, but it was too weak. 'Twas
said it was made of the Blood of a Goat, the Ashes
of a Heifer, and with some of the Juice of Hyssop,
&c. When Mr *Skill* had seen that that Purge was
too weak, he made him one to the purpose, 'twas

The Latin
I borrow

made *Ex Carne & Sanguine Christi.* (You know
Physicians give strange Medicines to their Patients.)
And it was made up into Pills, with a Promise or
two, and a proportionable quantity of Salt. Now
he was to take them three at a time fasting, in half
a quarter of a pint of the Tears of Repentance.

The boy
loath to
take the
physick

When this Potion was prepared and brought to the
Boy he was loth to take it, tho' torn with the
Gripes as if he should be pulled in pieces. Come,
come, said the Physician, you must take it. It goes
against my stomach, said the Boy. I must have
you take it, said his Mother. I shall vomit it up
again, said the Boy. Pray Sir, said *Christiana* to
Mr *Skill,* how does it taste? It has no ill taste,
said the Doctor, and with that she touched one of

the Pills with the tip of her tongue. Oh *Matthew,* The
said she, this Potion is sweeter than Hony. If mother tastes it,
thou lovest thy Mother, if thou lovest thy Brothers, and per-
if thou lovest *Mercy,* if thou lovest thy Life, take suades him
it. So with much ado, after a short prayer for
the blessing of God upon it, he took it, and it
wrought kindly with him. It caused him to purge,
it caused him to sleep and rest quietly, it put him
into a fine heat and breathing sweat, and did quite
rid him of his Gripes.

So in little time he got up and walked about with A word of
a staff, and would go from room to room, and talk God in the hand of
with *Prudence Piety* and *Charity* of his Distemper, his faith
and how he was healed.

So when the Boy was healed, *Christiana* asked Mr
Skill, saying Sir, what will content you for your
pains and care to and of my Child? And he
said, You must pay the Master of the College of
Physicians, according to rules made in that case
and provided.

CHRIS. But Sir, said she, what is this Pill good
for else?

SKILL. It is a universal Pill, it is good against all This pill an
the diseases that Pilgrims are incident to, and when universal remedy
it is well prepared, it will keep good time out of
mind.

CHRIS. Pray Sir, make me up twelve boxes of
them, for if I can get these, I will never take other
Physick.

SKILL. These Pills are good to prevent diseases, In a glass
as well as to cure when one is sick. Yea, I dare of the tears of
say it, and stand to it, that if a man will but use repentance
this Physick as he should, *it will make him live
for ever.* But good *Christiana,* thou must give
these Pills no other way but as I have prescribed,
for if you do, they will do no good. So he gave
unto *Christiana* Physick for herself and her Boys
and for *Mercy,* and bid *Matthew* take heed how he
eat any more green Plums, and kissed them and
went his way.

It was told you before that *Prudence* bid the
Boys, that if at any time they would, they should
ask her some Questions that might be profitable, and
she would say something to them.

Of physick   MATT. Then *Matthew* who had been sick, asked
her, *Why for the most part Physick should be bitter
to our palates?*

PRUD. To shew how unwelcome the Word of
God and the effects thereof are to a Carnal Heart.

Of the effects of physick   MATT. Why does Physick, if it does good, purge,
and cause that we vomit?

PRUD. To shew that the Word, when it works effectually, cleanseth the Heart and Mind. For look,
what the one doth to the Body the other doth to
the Soul.

Of fire and of the sun   MATT. What should we learn by seeing the Flame
of our Fire go upwards? and by seeing the Beams
and sweet Influences of the Sun strike downwards?

PRUD. By the going up of the Fire we are taught
to ascend to Heaven by fervent and hot desires; and
by the Sun his sending his Heat Beams and sweet
Influences downwards, we are taught that the Saviour of the world, tho' high, reaches down with his
Grace and Love to us below.

Of the clouds   MATT. Where have the Clouds their water?

PRUD. Out of the Sea.

MATT. What may we learn from that?

PRUD. That Ministers should fetch their Doctrine
from God.

MATT. Why do they empty themselves upon the
Earth?

PRUD. To shew that Ministers should give out
what they know of God to the World.

Of the rainbow   MATT. Why is the Rainbow caused by the Sun?

PRUD. To shew that the covenant of God's Grace
is confirmed to us in Christ.

MATT. Why do the Springs come from the Sea
to us through the Earth?

PRUD. To shew that the Grace of God comes to us
through the Body of Christ.

MATT. Why do some of the Springs rise out of the tops of high Hills? *Of the springs*

PRUD. To shew that the Spirit of Grace shall spring up in *some* that are Great and Mighty, as well as in *many* that are Poor and Low.

MATT. Why doth the Fire fasten upon the Candle-wick? *Of the candle*

PRUD. To shew that unless Grace doth kindle upon the Heart, there will be no true Light of Life in us.

MATT. Why is the Wick and Tallow and all, spent to maintain the light of the Candle?

PRUD. To shew that Body and Soul and all, should be at the service of, and spend themselves to maintain in good condition, that Grace of God that is in us.

MATT. Why doth the Pelican pierce her own Breast with her Bill? *Of the pelican*

PRUD. To nourish her young ones with her Blood, and thereby to shew that Christ the blessed so loved his young, his people, as to save them from Death by his Blood.

MATT. What may one learn by hearing the Cock to crow? *Of the cock*

PRUD. Learn to remember *Peter's* sin, and *Peter's* repentance. The Cock's crowing shews also that Day is coming on; let then the crowing of the Cock put thee in mind of that last and terrible Day of Judgment.

Now about this time their month was out, wherefore they signified to those of the house that 'twas convenient for them to up and be going. Then said *Joseph* to his Mother, It is convenient that you forget not to send to the house of Mr *Interpreter*, to pray him to grant that Mr *Great-heart* should be sent unto us, that he may be our Conductor the rest of our way. Good Boy, said she, I had almost forgot. So she drew up a Petition, and prayed Mr *Watchful* the Porter to send it by some fit man to her good Friend Mr *Interpreter;* who when it was *The weak may sometimes call the strong to prayers* come, and he had seen the contents of the Petition, said to the Messenger, Go tell them that I will send him.

They provide to be gone on their way

When the Family where *Christiana* was, saw that they had a purpose to go forward, they called the whole house together, to give thanks to their King for sending of them such profitable Guests as these. Which done, they said to *Christiana,* And shall we not shew thee something, according as our custom is to do to Pilgrims, on which thou mayest meditate when thou art upon the way? So they took *Christiana* her Children and *Mercy,* into the closet, and

Eve's apple

shewed them one of the Apples that *Eve* did eat of, and that she also did give to her Husband, and that for the eating of which they both were turned out of Paradise, and asked her what she thought that

A sight of sin is amazing

was? Then *Christiana* said, 'Tis Food or Poison, I know not which. So they opened the matter to her, and she held up her hands and wondered.

Jacob's ladder

Then they had her to a place, and shewed her *Jacob's* Ladder. Now at that time there were some Angels ascending upon it. So *Christiana* looked and looked, to see the Angels go up, and so did the rest of the Company. Then they were going in to another place to shew them something else, but

A sight of Christ is taking

James said to his Mother, Pray bid them stay here a little longer, for this is a curious sight. So they turned again, and stood feeding their eyes with this so pleasant a prospect. After this they had them

Golden anchor

into a place where did hang up a Golden Anchor, so they bid *Christiana* take it down, For, said they, you shall have it with you, for 'tis of absolute necessity that you should, that you may lay hold of that within the vail, and stand steadfast, in case you should meet with turbulent weather. So they were glad thereof. Then they took them, and had them to the

Of Abraham offering up Isaac

Mount upon which *Abraham* our Father had offered up *Isaac* his Son, and shewed them the Altar, the Wood, the Fire, and the Knife, for they remain to be seen to this very day. When they had seen it, they held up their hands and blest themselves, and said, Oh what a man for love to his Master, and for denial to himself was *Abraham*. After they had shewed them all these things, *Prudence* took them into the Dining-room, where stood a pair of excellent Virginals, so she played upon them, and turned what she had shewed them into this excellent song, saying, Pru-dence's virginals

> *Eve's* Apple we have shew'd you,
>   Of that be you aware;
> You have seen *Jacob's* Ladder too,
>   Upon which Angels are.
> An Anchor you received have,
>   But let not these suffice,
> Until with *Abr'am* you have gave
>   Your best a Sacrifice.

Now about this time, one knocked at the door; so the Porter opened, and behold Mr *Great-heart* was there; but when he was come in, what joy was there? For it came now fresh again into their minds, how but a while ago he had slain old *Grim Bloody-man* the Giant, and *delivered* them from the Lions. Mr Great-heart come again

Then said Mr *Great-heart* to *Christiana* and to *Mercy*, My Lord has sent each of you a Bottle of Wine, and also some parched Corn, together with a couple of Pomgranates. He has also sent the Boys some Figs and Raisins to refresh you on your way. He brings a token from his Lord with him

Then they addressed themselves to their Journey, and *Prudence* and *Piety* went along with them. When they came at the gate, *Christiana* asked the Porter if any of late went by? He said, No, only one some time since, who also told me that of late there had been a great robbery committed on the King's Highway, as you go; but he saith the thieves are taken, and will shortly be tried for their lives. Then *Christiana* and *Mercy* were afraid, but *Matthew* said, Mother fear nothing, as long as Mr *Great-heart* is to go with us and to be our Conductor. Robbery

Then said *Christiana* to the Porter, Sir, I am

Christiana
takes her
leave of
the Porter

The
Porter's
blessing

much obliged to you for all the kindnesses that you have shewed me since I came hither, and also for that you have been so loving and kind to my Children. I know not how to gratify your kindness. Wherefore pray as a token of my respects to you, accept of this small mite. So she put a gold Angel in his hand, and he made her a low obeisance, and said, Let thy Garments be always white, and let thy Head want no Ointment. Let *Mercy* live and not die, and let not her works be few. And to the Boys he said, Do you fly youthful lusts, and follow after Godliness with them that are grave and wise, so shall you put gladness into your Mother's heart, and obtain praise of all that are sober-minded. So they thanked the Porter and departed.

Now I saw in my Dream that they went forward until they were come to the brow of the Hill, where *Piety* bethinking herself, cried out, Alas! I have forgot what I intended to bestow upon *Christiana* and her Companions, I will go back and fetch it. So she ran and fetched it. While she was gone, *Christiana* thought she heard in a Grove a little way off on the right hand, a most curious, melodious note, with words much like these,

> Through all my Life thy Favour is
>   So frankly shew'd to me,
> That in thy House for evermore
>   My dwelling-place shall be.

And listening still she thought she heard another answer it, saying,

> For why? The Lord our God is good,
>   His Mercy is for ever sure;
> His Truth at all times firmly stood,
>   And shall from age to age endure.

So *Christiana* asked *Prudence* what 'twas that made those curious notes? They are, said she, our Country Birds; they sing these notes but seldom, except it be at the Spring, when the Flowers appear, and the Sun shines warm, and then you may hear them all day long. I often, said she, go out to hear them, we also oft-times keep them tame in our house. They are very fine company for us when we are melancholy, also they make the Woods and Groves and Solitary places, places desirous to be in.

By this time Piety was come again; so she said to *Christiana,* Look here, I have brought thee a scheme of all those things that thou hast seen at our house, upon which thou mayest look when thou findest thyself forgetful, and call those things again to remembrance for thy edification and comfort. Piety bestoweth something on them at parting

Now they began to go down the Hill into the Valley of *Humiliation.* It was a steep Hill, and the way was slippery; but they were very careful, so they got down pretty well. When they were down in the Valley, *Piety* said to *Christiana,* This is the place where *Christian* your Husband met with that foul Fiend *Apollyon,* and where they had that Fight that they had; I know you cannot but have heard thereof. But be of good courage; as long you have here Mr *Great-heart* to be your Guide and Conductor, we hope you will fare the better. So when these two had committed the Pilgrims unto the conduct of their Guide, he went forward and they went after. First Part, p. 60

GREAT-HEART. Then said Mr *Great-heart,* we need not to be so afraid of this Valley, for here is nothing to hurt us unless we procure it to ourselves. 'Tis true, *Christian* did here meet with *Apollyon,* with whom he also had a sore Combat; but that *fray* was the fruit of those slips that he got in his going down the Hill; for they that get *slips* there, must look for *combats* here. And hence it is that this Valley has got so hard a name; for the common people when they hear that some frightful thing has befallen such a one in such a place, are of an opinion that that place is haunted with some foul Fiend or evil Spirit; when alas it is for the fruit of their doing, that such things do befall them there. Mr Great-heart at the Valley of Humiliation First Part, p. 61

This Valley of *Humiliation* is of itself as fruitful

The rea-
son why
Christian
was so
beset here

a place as any the Crow flies over; and I am persuaded if we could hit upon it, we might find some-
where hereabouts, something that might give us an
account why *Christian* was so hardly beset in this
place.

A pillar
with an
inscription
on it

Then *James* said to his Mother, Lo, yonder stands
a Pillar, and it looks as if something was written
thereon, let us go and see what it is.   So they went,
and found there written, *Let* Christian's *slips before he came hither, and the Battles that he met with
in this place, be a warning to those that come after*.
Lo, said their Guide, did not I tell you that there
was something hereabouts that would give intima-
tion of the reason why *Christian* was so hard beset
in this place?   Then turning himself to *Christiana*,
he said, No disparagement to *Christian* more than
to many others whose hap and lot his was; for 'tis
easier going *up* than *down* this Hill, and that can
be said but of few Hills in all these parts of the
world.   But we will leave the good man, he is
at rest, he also had a brave Victory over his Enemy,
let him grant that dwelleth above, that we fare no
worse when we come to be tried than he.

This
valley a
brave
place

But we will come again to this Valley of *Humiliation*.   It is the best and most fruitful piece of
ground in all those parts.   It is fat ground, and as
you see, consisteth much in meadows; and if a man
was to come here in the Summer-time, as we do
now, if he knew not anything before thereof, and
if he also delighted himself in the sight of his eyes,
he might see that that would be delightful to him.
Behold how green this Valley is, also how beautified
with *Lillies*.   I have also known many labouring
men that have got good estates in this Valley of

Men thrive
in the Val-
ley of Hu-
miliation

Humiliation (for God resisteth the Proud, but gives
more Grace to the Humble) for indeed it is a
very fruitful soil, and doth bring forth by handfuls.
Some also have wished that the next way to their
Father's house were here, that they might be
troubled no more with either Hills or Mountains,

to go over; but the way is the way, and there's an end.

Now as they were going along and talking, they espied a Boy feeding his Father's Sheep. The Boy was in very mean cloaths, but of a very fresh and well-favoured countenance, and as he sate by himself, he sung. Hark, said Mr *Great-heart,* to what the Shepherd's Boy saith. So they hearkened, and he said,

> He that is down needs fear no fall,
>   He that is low no pride;
> He that is humble, ever shall
>   Have God to be his Guide.
> I am content with what I have,
>   Little be it, or much:
> And Lord, contentment still I crave,
>   Because thou savest such.
> Fulness to such a burden is
>   That go on Pilgrimage;
> Here little, and hereafter Bliss,
>   Is best from age to age.

Phil. iv. 12, 13

Heb. xiii. 5

Then said their Guide, Do you hear him? I will dare to say, that this Boy lives a merrier life, and wears more of that Herb called *Heart's-ease* in his bosom, than he that is clad in Silk and Velvet; but we will proceed in our discourse.

In this Valley our Lord formerly had his Countryhouse; he loved much to be here; he loved also to walk these Meadows, for he found the air was pleasant. Besides here a man shall be free from the noise, and from the hurryings of this life. All states are full of Noise and Confusion, only the Valley of *Humiliation* is that empty and solitary place. Here a man shall not be so let and hindred in his Contemplation, as in other places he is apt to be. This is a Valley that nobody walks in, but those that love a Pilgrim's life. And tho' *Christian* had the hard hap to meet here with *Apollyon,* and to enter with him a brisk encounter, yet I must tell you, that in former times men have met with Angels here, have found Pearls here, and have in this place found the words of Life.

Christ, when in the flesh, had his country-house in the Valley of Humiliation

Did I say our Lord had here in former days
his Country-house, and that he loved here to walk?
I will add, in this place, and to the people that live
and trace these Grounds, he has left a yearly rev-
enue to be faithfully payed them at certain seasons,
for their maintenance by the way, and for their
further encouragement to go on in their Pilgrimage.

SAMUEL. Now as they went on, *Samuel* said to
Mr. *Great-heart*, Sir, I perceive that in this Valley
my Father and *Apollyon* had their Battle, but whereabout was the Fight, for I perceive this Valley is
large?

Forgetful
Green

GREAT-HEART. Your Father had that Battle with
Apollyon at a place yonder before us, in a narrow
passage just beyond *Forgetful Green*. And indeed
that place is the most dangerous place in all these
parts. For if at any time the Pilgrims meet with
any brunt, it is when they forget what favours they
have received, and how unworthy they are of them.
This is the place also where others have been hard
put to it; but more of the place when we are come
to it; for I persuade myself that to this day there
remains either some sign of the Battle, or some
Monument to testify that such a Battle there was
fought.

Humility
a sweet
grace

MERCY. Then said *Mercy*, I think I am as well in
this Valley as I have been anywhere else in all our
Journey, the place methinks suits with my spirit.
I love to be in such places where there is no rattling
with Coaches, nor rumbling with Wheels. Methinks here one may without much molestation, be
thinking what he is, whence he came, what he has
done, and to what the King has called him. Here
one may think, and break at heart, and melt in one's
spirit, until one's eyes become like *the Fishpools of*
Heshbon. They that go rightly through this Valley
of Baca make it a Well, the Rain that God sends
down from Heaven upon them that are here also
filleth the Pools. This Valley is that from whence
also the King will give to their vineyards, and they

that go through it shall sing, as *Christian* did for all he met with *Apollyon*.

GREAT-HEART. 'Tis true, said their Guide, I have gone through this Valley many a time, and never was better than when here. An experiment of it

I have also been a Conduct to several Pilgrims, and they have confessed the same, *To this man will I look,* saith the King, *even to him that is Poor, and of a Contrite Spirit, and that trembles at my Word.*

Now they were come to the place where the afore mentioned Battle was fought. Then said the Guide to *Christiana* her Children and *Mercy,* This is the place, on this ground *Christian* stood, and up there came *Apollyon* against him. And look, did not I tell you? Here is some of your Husband's Blood upon these stones to this day; behold also how here and there are yet to be seen upon the place some of the shivers of *Apollyon's* broken Darts. See also how they did beat the ground with their feet as they fought, to make good their places against each other, how also with their by-blows they did split the very stones in pieces. Verily *Christian* did here play the man, and shewed himself as stout, as could, had he been there, even *Hercules* himself. When *Apollyon* was beat, he made his retreat to the next Valley, that is called the Valley of the *Shadow of Death,* unto which we shall come anon. The place where Christian and the fiend did fight. Some signs of the battle remain

Lo yonder also stands a Monument, on which is engraven this Battle, and *Christian's* Victory, to his fame throughout all ages. So because it stood just on the way-side before them, they stept to it and read the writing, which word for word was this. A monument of the battle

> Hard by here was a Battle fought,
>   Most strange, and yet most true;
> *Christian* and *Apollyon* sought
>   Each other to subdue.
> The Man so bravely play'd the Man,
>   He made the *Fiend* to fly;
> Of which a Monument I stand,
>   The same to testify.

A monument of Christian's victory

First Part,
p. 65
When they had passed by this place, they came
upon the borders of the *Shadow of Death;* and
this Valley was longer than the other; a place also
most strangely haunted with evil things, as many
are able to testify.   But these Women and Children
went the better through it because they had day-
light, and because Mr *Great-heart* was their Conductor.

Groanings
heard
When they were entred upon this Valley, they
thought that they heard a groaning as of dead men,
a very great groaning.   They thought also they did
hear words of Lamentation spoken, as of some
in extreme Torment.   These things made the Boys
to quake, the Women also looked pale and wan;
but their Guide bid them be of good comfort.

The
ground
shakes
So they went on a little further, and they thought
that they felt the ground begin to shake under
them, as if some hollow place was there; they heard
also a kind of hissing as of Serpents, but nothing
as yet appeared.   Then said the Boys, Are we not
yet at the end of this doleful place?   But the Guide
also bid them be of good courage, and look well to
their feet, lest haply, said he, you be taken in some
Snare.

James sick
with fear
Now *James* began to be sick, but I think the
cause thereof was fear; so his Mother gave him
some of that glass of Spirits that she had given her
at the *Interpreter's* house, and three of the Pills that
Mr *Skill* had prepared, and the Boy began to revive.
Thus they went on till they came to about the middle of the Valley, and then *Christiana* said, Methinks

The fiend
appears
I see something yonder upon the road before us, a
thing of such a shape such as I have not seen.
Then said *Joseph,* Mother, what is it?   An ugly
thing, Child, an ugly thing, said she.   But Mother,

The
Pilgrims
are afraid
what is it like? said he.   'Tis like I cannot tell what,
said she.   And now it was but a little way off.
Then said she, It is nigh.

Well, well, said Mr *Great-heart,* Let them that are
most afraid keep close to me.   So the Fiend came

on, and the Conductor met it; but when it was just come to him, it vanished to all their sights. Then remembred they what had been said some time ago, *Resist the Devil, and he will fly from you*.

Greatheart encourages them

They went therefore on, as being a little refreshed; but they had not gone far, before *Mercy* looking behind her, saw, as she thought, something most like a Lion, and it came a great padding pace after; and it had a hollow Voice of Roaring, and at every Roar that it gave it made all the Valley echo, and their hearts to ake, save the heart of him that was their Guide. So it came up, and Mr *Greatheart* went behind, and put the Pilgrims all before him. The Lion also came on apace, and Mr *Greatheart* addressed himself to give him Battle. But when he saw that it was determined that resistance should be made, he also drew back and came no further.

A lion

Then they went on again, and their Conductor did go before them, till they came at a place where was cast up a Pit the whole breadth of the way, and before they could be prepared to go over that, a great Mist and a Darkness fell upon them, so that they could not see. Then said the Pilgrims, Alas! now what shall we do? But their Guide made answer, Fear not, stand still and see what an end will be put to this also. So they stayed there because their path was marr'd. They then also thought that they did hear more apparently the noise and rushing of the Enemies, the fire also and the smoke of the Pit was much easier to be discerned. Then said *Christiana* to *Mercy*, Now I see what my poor Husband went through, I have heard much of this place, but I never was here afore now. Poor man, he went here all alone in the night; he had night almost quite through the way; also these Fiends were busy about him as if they would have torn him in pieces. Many have spoke of it, but none can tell what the Valley of the *Shadow of Death* should mean, until they come in it themselves. *The heart*

A pit and darkness

Christiana now knows what her husband felt

knows its own Bitterness, and a stranger intermeddleth not with its Joy. To be here is a fearful thing.

Great-heart's reply

GREAT-HEART. This is like doing business in great Waters, or like going down into the deep; this is like being in the heart of the Sea, and like going down to the bottoms of the Mountains; now it seems as if the Earth with its bars were about us for ever. *But let them that walk in Darkness and have no Light, trust in the name of the Lord, and stay upon their God.* For my part, as I have told you already, I have gone often through this Valley, and have been much harder put to it than now I am, and yet you see I am alive. I would not boast, for that I am not mine own saviour, but I trust we shall have a good Deliverance. Come let us pray for Light to him that can lighten our Darkness, and that can rebuke not only these, but all the Satans in Hell.

They pray

So they cried and prayed, and God sent Light and Deliverance, for there was now no let in their way, no not there where but now they were stopt with a Pit. Yet they were not got through the Valley; so they went on still, and behold great stinks and loathsome smells, to the great annoyance of them. Then said *Mercy* to *Christiana,* There is not such pleasant being here as at the Gate, or at the *Interpreter's,* or at the house where we lay last.

One of the boys' reply

Oh but, said one of the Boys, it is not so bad to go through here as it is to *abide* here always, and for ought I know, one reason why we must go this way to the house prepared for us, is, that our home might be made the sweeter to us.

Well said *Samuel,* quoth the Guide, thou hast now spoke like a man. Why, if ever I get out here again, said the Boy, I think I shall prize light and good way better than ever I did in all my life. Then said the Guide, We shall be out by and by.

Heedless is slain, and Take-heed preserved

So on they went, and *Joseph* said, Cannot we see to the end of this Valley as yet? Then said the Guide, Look to your feet, for you shall presently be among the Snares. So they looked to their feet and went on, but they were troubled much with the Snares. Now when they were come among the Snares, they espied a man cast into the Ditch on the left hand, with his flesh all rent and torn. Then said the Guide. That is one *Heedless,* that was a going this way, he has lain there a great while. There was one *Take-heed* with him when he was taken and slain, but he escaped their hands. You cannot imagine how many are killed hereabouts, and yet men are so foolishly venturous, as to set out lightly on Pilgrimage, and to come without a Guide. Poor *Christian,* it was a wonder that he here escaped; but he was beloved of his God, also he had a good heart of his own, or else he could never a done it. Now they drew towards the end of the way, and just there where *Christian* had seen the Cave when he went by, out thence came forth *Maul* a Giant. This *Maul* did use to spoil young Pilgrims with Sophistry; and he called *Great-heart* by his name, and said unto him, How many times have you been forbidden to do these things? Then said Mr *Great-heart,* What things? What things? quoth the Giant, you know what things, but I will put an end to your trade. But pray, said Mr *Great-heart,* before we fall to it, let us understand wherefore we must fight. Now the Women and Children stood trembling, and knew not what to do. Quoth the Giant, You rob the Country, and rob it with the worst of thefts. These are but generals, said Mr *Great-heart,* come to particulars, man.

Then said the Giant, Thou practisest the craft of a Kidnapper, thou gatherest up Women and Children, and carriest them into a strange Country, to the weakening of my master's Kingdom. But now *Great-heart* replied, I am a servant of the God of Heaven, my business is to persuade sinners to repentance, I am commanded to do my endeavour to turn Men Women and Children, from darkness to light, and from the power of Satan to God; and

First Part, p. 70

Maul, a giant

He quarrels with Great-heart

God's ministers counted as kidnappers

The giant
and Mr
Great-
heart
must fight
if this be indeed the ground of thy quarrel, let us fall to it as soon as thou wilt.

Then the Giant came up, and Mr *Great-heart* went to meet him; and as he went he drew his Sword, but the Giant had a Club. So without more ado they fell to it, and at the first blow the Giant stroke Mr *Great-heart* down upon one of his knees;
Weak
folks'
prayers do
sometimes
help strong
folks' cries
with that the Women and Children cried out; so Mr *Great-heart* recovering himself, laid about him in full lusty manner, and gave the Giant a wound in his arm; thus he fought for the space of an hour to that height of heat, that the breath came out of the Giant's nostrils, as the heat doth out of a boiling Caldron.

Then they sat down to rest them, but Mr *Great-heart* betook him to prayer; also the Women and Children did nothing but sigh and cry all the time that the Battle did last.
The giant
struck
down
When they had rested them, and taken breath, they both fell to it again, and Mr *Great-heart* with a full blow fetched the Giant down to the ground. Nay hold and let me recover, quoth he. So Mr *Great-heart* fairly let him get up. So to it they went again, and the Giant missed but little of all to breaking Mr *Great-heart's* skull with his Club.

Mr *Great-heart* seeing that, runs to him in the full heat of his spirit, and pierceth him under the fifth rib; with that the Giant began to faint, and could hold up his Club no longer. Then Mr *Great-heart* seconded his blow, and smit the head of the Giant from his shoulders. Then the Women and Children rejoiced, and Mr *Great-heart* also praised God for the deliverance he had wrought.
He is
slain, and
his head
disposed of
When this was done, they among them erected a Pillar, and fastned the Giant's head thereon, and wrote underneath in letters that Passengers might read,

> He that did wear this head, was one
> That Pilgrims did misuse;
> He stopt their way, he spared none,

But did them all abuse;
Until that I *Great-heart* arose,
The Pilgrim's Guide to be;
Until that I did him oppose
That was their Enemy.

Now I saw that they went to the Ascent that First Part was a little way off cast up to be a Prospect for P. 71 Pilgrims, (that was the place from whence *Christian* had the first sight of *Faithful* his Brother) wherefore here they sat down and rested, they also here did eat and drink and make merry, for that they had gotten deliverance from this so dangerous an Enemy. As they sat thus and did eat, *Christiana* asked the Guide if he had caught no hurt in the Battle. Then said Mr *Great-heart,* No, save a little on my flesh; yet that also shall be so far from being to my determent, that it is at present a proof of my love to my Master and you, and shall be a means by Grace to increase my reward at last.

CHRIS. But was you not afraid, good Sir, when Discourse you see him come out with his club? of the fight

GREAT-HEART. It is my duty, said he, to distrust mine own ability, that I may have reliance on him that is stronger than all.

CHRIS. But what did you think when he fetched you down to the ground at the first blow?

GREAT-HEART. Why I thought, quoth he, that so my Master himself was served, and yet he it was that conquered at the last.

MATT. When you all have thought what you Matthew please, I think God has been wonderful good unto here admires us, both in bringing us out of this Valley, and in goodness delivering us out of the hand of this Enemy; for my part I see no reason why we should distrust our God any more, since he has *now,* and in *such* a place as this, given us such testimony of his love as this.

Then they got up and went forward. Now a Old Honest asleep little before them stood an Oak, and under it when under they came to it, they found an old Pilgrim fast an oak asleep; they knew that he was a Pilgrim by his Cloaths and his Staff and his Girdle.

So the Guide Mr *Great-heart* awaked him, and the old Gentleman as he lift up his eyes, cried out, What's the matter? who are you? and what is your business here?

GREAT-HEART. Come man be not so hot, here is none but Friends: yet the old man gets up and stands upon his guard, and will know of them what they were. Then said the Guide, My name is *Great-heart,* I am the Guide of these Pilgrims which are going to the Cœlestial Country.

One saint sometimes takes another for his enemy

HONEST. Then said Mr *Honest,* I cry you mercy, I fear'd that you had been of the company of those that some time ago did rob *Little-faith* of his money; but now I look better about me, I perceive you are honester people.

Talk between Great-heart and he

GREAT-HEART. Why what would or could you a done to a helped yourself, if we indeed had been of that company?

HON. Done! why I would a fought as long as breath had been in me; and had I so done, I am sure you could never have given me the worst on't; for a Christian can never be overcome, unless he shall yield of himself.

GREAT-HEART. Well said, Father *Honest,* quoth the Guide, for by this I know thou art a cock of the right kind, for thou hast said the truth.

HON. And by this also I know that thou knowest what true Pilgrimage is, for all others do think that we are the soonest overcome of any.

Whence Mr Honest came

GREAT-HEART. Well now we are so happily met, pray let me crave your name, and the name of the place you came from.

HON. My name I cannot, but I came from the Town of *Stupidity,* it lieth about four degrees beyond the City of *Destruction.*

GREAT-HEART. Oh! are you that Countryman then? I deem I have half a guess of you, your name is Old *Honesty,* is it not, So the old Gentleman blushed, and said, Not *Honesty* in the abstract, but *Honest* is my name, and I wish that my *nature* shall agree to what I am called.

HON. But Sir, said the old Gentleman, how could you guess that I am such a man, since I came from such a place?

GREAT-HEART. I had heard of you before, by my Master, for he knows all things that are done on the Earth; but I have often wondered that any should come from your place, for your Town is worse than is the City of *Destruction* itself.

Stupefied ones are worse than those merely carnal

HON. Yes, we lie more off from the Sun, and so are more cold and senseless; but was a man in a Mountain of Ice, yet if the Sun of Righteousness will arise upon him, his frozen heart shall feel a thaw; and thus it hath been with me.

GREAT-HEART. I believe, it, Father *Honest*, I believe it, for I know the thing is true.

Then the old Gentleman saluted all the Pilgrims with a holy kiss of charity, and asked them of their names, and how they had fared since they set out on their Pilgrimage.

CHRIS. Then said *Christiana*, My name I suppose you have heard of, good *Christian* was my Husband, and these four were his Children. But can you think how the old Gentleman was taken, when she told them who she was! He skipped, he smiled, and blessed them with a thousand good wishes, saying,

Old Honest and Christiana talk

HON. I have heard much of your Husband, and of his travels and Wars which he underwent in his days. Be it spoken to your comfort, the name of your Husband rings over all these parts of the world: his Faith, his Courage, his Enduring, and his Sincerity under all, has made his name famous. Then he turned him to the Boys, and asked them of their names, which they told him. And then said he unto them, *Matthew,* be thou like *Matthew* the Publican, not in *vice* but in *vertue*. *Samuel,* said he, be thou like *Samuel* the Prophet, a man of

He also talks with the boys.

Old Mr Honest's blessing on them

faith and *prayer*. *Joseph,* said he, be thou like *Joseph* in *Potiphar's* house, *chaste,* and *one that flies from temptation*. And *James* be thou like *James the Just* and like *James* the Brother of our Lord.

He blesseth MercyThen they told him of *Mercy,* and how she had left her Town and her Kindred to come along with *Christiana* and with her Sons. At that the old *honest* man said, *Mercy* is thy name? by Mercy shalt thou be sustained, and carried through all those difficulties that shall assault thee in thy way, till thou shalt come thither where thou shalt look the Fountain of Mercy in the face with comfort.

All this while the Guide Mr *Great-heart* was very much pleased, and smiled upon his Companion.

Talk of one Mr FearingNow as they walked along together, the Guide asked the old Gentleman if he did not know one Mr *Fearing,* that came on Pilgrimage out of his parts?

HON. Yes, very well, said he. He was a man that had the root of the matter in him, but he was one of the most troublesome Pilgrims that ever I met with in all my days.

GREAT-HEART. I perceive you knew him, for you have given a very right character of him.

HON. Knew him! I was a great Companion of his; I was with him most an end; when he first began to think of what would come upon us hereafter, I was with him.

GREAT-HEART. I was his Guide from my Master's house to the gates of the Cœlestial City.

HON. Then you knew him to be a troublesome one.

GREAT-HEART. I did so, but I could very well bear it, for men of my calling are oftentimes intrusted with the conduct of such as he was.

HON. Well then, pray let us hear a little of him, and how he managed himself under your conduct.

GREAT-HEART. Why, he was always afraid that he should come short of whither he had a desire to go. Everything frightned him that he heard Mr Fearing's troublesome pilgrimage anybody speak of, that had but the least appearance of opposition in it. I hear that he lay roaring at the Slough of *Dispond* for above a month together, nor durst he, for all he saw several go over before His behaviour at the Slough of Dispond him, venture, tho' they, many of them, offered to lend him their hand. He would not go back again neither. The Cœlestial City, he said, he should die if he came not to it, and yet was dejected at every difficulty, and stumbled at every Straw that anybody cast in his way. Well, after he had lain at the Slough of *Dispond* a great while, as I have told you; one Sun-shine morning, I do not know how, he ventured, and so got over. But when he was over, he would scarce believe it. He had, I think, a Slough of *Dispond* in his mind, a Slough that he carried everywhere with him, or else he could never have been as he was. So he came up to the Gate, you know what I mean, that stands at the head of this way, and there also he stood a good while before he would adventure to knock. When the Gate was opened he would give back, and give place to others, and say that he was not worthy; for for all he gat before some to the Gate, yet many of them went in before him. There the poor man would stand shaking and shrinking, I dare say it would have pitied one's heart to have seen him, nor would he go back again. At last he took the Hammer that hanged on the Gate in his hand, and gave a small Rap or two; then one opened to him, but he shrank back as before. He that opened stept out after him, and said, Thou trembling one, what wantest thou? With that he fell down to the ground. He that spoke to him wondered to see him His behaviour at the gate so faint. So he said to him, Peace be to thee, up, for I have set open the door to thee, come in, for thou art blest. With that he gat up, and went in trembling, and when he was in, he was ashamed to shew his face. Well, after he had been entertained there a while, as you know how the manner is, he

His be-
haviour at
the Inter-
preter's
door

was bid go on his way, and also told the way he
should take. So he came till he came to our house.
But as he behaved himself at the Gate, so he did
at my Master the *Interpreter's* door. He lay thereabout in the cold a good while, before he would adventure to call, yet he would not go back, and the
nights were long and cold then. Nay he had a
Note of Necessity in his bosom to my Master, to
receive him and grant him the comfort of his house,
and also to allow him a stout and valiant Conduct
because he was himself so *chickin-hearted* a man;
and yet for all that he was afraid to call at the door.
So he lay up and down thereabouts till, poor man,
he was almost starved. Yea so great was his De-
jection, that tho' he saw several others for knocking
got in, yet he was afraid to venture. At last, I
think I looked out of the window, and perceiving
a man to be up and down about the door, I went
out to him, and asked what he was; but, poor man,
the water stood in his eyes; so I perceived what he
wanted. I went therefore in and told it in the

How he
was en-
tertained
there

house, and we shewed the thing to our Lord. So
he sent me out again, to entreat him to come in;
but I dare say I had hard work to do it. At last
he came in, and I will say that for my Lord, he
carried it wonderful lovingly to him. There were
but few good bits at the Table but some of it was
laid upon his trencher. Then he presented the Note,
and my Lord looked thereon, and said his desire

He is a
little en-
couraged
at the In-
terpreter's
house

should be granted. So when he had been there a
good while, he seemed to get some heart, and to
be a little more comfortable; for my Master, you
must know, is one of very tender bowels, specially
to them that are afraid; wherefore he carried it so
towards him as might tend most to his encouragement. Well, when he had had a sight of the things
of the place, and was ready to take his Journey
to go to the City, my Lord, as he did to *Christian*
before, gave him a Bottle of Spirits, and some comfortable things to eat. Thus we set forward, and

I went before him; but the man was but of few words, only he would sigh aloud.

When we were come to where the three fellows were hanged, he said that he doubted that that would be his end also. Only he seemed glad when he saw the Cross and the Sepulchre. There I confess he desired to stay a little to look, and he seemed for a while after to be a little cheery. When we came to the Hill *Difficulty,* he made no stick at that, nor did he much fear the Lions; for you must know that his trouble was not about such things as those, his fear was about his acceptance at last.

He was greatly afraid when he saw the gibbet; cheery when he saw the cross

I got him in at the House *Beautiful,* I think, before he was willing. Also when he was in, I brought him acquainted with the Damsels that were of the place, but he was ashamed to make himself much for company. He desired much to be alone, yet he always loved good talk, and often would get behind the Screen to hear it. He also loved much to see antient things, and to be pondering them in his mind. He told me afterwards that he loved to be in those two houses from which he came last, to wit, at the Gate, and that of the *Interpreter's,* but that he durst not be so bold to ask.

Dumpish at the House Beautiful

When we went also from the House *Beautiful,* down the Hill into the Valley of *Humiliation,* he went down as well as ever I saw man in my life; for he cared not how mean he was, so he might be happy at last. Yea, I think there was a kind of sympathy betwixt that Valley and him, for I never saw him better in all his Pilgrimage than when he was in that Valley.

He went down into, and was very pleasant in the Valley of Humiliation

Here he would lie down, embrace the ground and kiss the very Flowers that grew in this Valley. He would now be up every morning by break of day, tracing and walking to and fro in this Valley.

But when he was come to the entrance of the Valley of the *Shadow of Death,* I thought I should have lost my man; not for that he had any inclination to go back, that he always abhorred, but he

Much perplexed in the Valley of the Shadow of Death

was ready to die for fear. O, the *Hobgoblins* will
have me, the *Hobgoblins* will have me, cried he, and
I could not beat him out on't. He made such a
noise and such an outcry here, that, had they but
heard him, 'twas enough to encourage them to come
and fall upon us.

But this I took very great notice of, that this
Valley was as quiet while he went through it, as
ever I knew it before or since. I suppose these
Enemies here had now a special check from our
Lord, and a command not to meddle until Mr
Fearing was past over it.

His be-
haviour
at Vanity
Fair

It would be too tedious to tell you of all. We
will therefore only mention a passage or two more.
When he was come at *Vanity Fair,* I thought he
would have fought with all the men in the Fair.
I feared there we should both have been knock'd o'
the head, so hot was he against their fooleries.
Upon the Inchanted Ground he was also very wake-
ful. But when he was come at the River where
was no Bridge, there again he was in a heavy case.
Now, now, he said, he should be drowned for ever,
and so never see that face with comfort that he
had come so many miles to behold.

His
boldness
at last

And here also I took notice of what was very
remarkable, the Water of that River was lower
at this time than ever I saw it in all my life. So
he went over at last, not much above wet-shod.
When he was going up to the Gate, Mr *Great-heart*
began to take his leave of him, and to wish him
a good reception above. So he said, *I shall, I shall.*
Then parted we asunder, and I saw him no
more.

Hon. Then it seems he was well at last.

Great-heart. Yes, yes; I never had doubt about
him; he was a man of a choice spirit, only he was
always kept very low, and that made his life so
burdensome to himself, and so troublesome to others.
He was above many tender of sin. He was so
afraid of doing injuries to others, that he often

would deny himself of that which was lawful, because he would not offend.

Hon. But what should be the reason that such a good man should be all his days so much in the dark?

Great-heart. There are two sorts of reasons for it. One is, the wise God will have it so, some must *pipe* and some must *weep*. Now Mr *Fearing* was one that played upon this *Base;* he and his fellows sound the *sackbut,* whose notes are more doleful than the notes of other Musick are; though indeed some say the Base is the Ground of Musick. And for my part I care not at all for that profession that begins not in heaviness of mind. The first string that the Musician usually touches is the Base, when he intends to put all in tune. God also plays upon this string first, when he sets the soul in tune for himself. Only here was the imperfection of Mr *Fearing,* he could play upon no other Musick but this, till towards his latter end.

Reasons why good men are so in the dark

I make bold to talk thus metaphorically, for the ripening of the Wits of young Readers; and because in the Book of the Revelations, the saved are compared to a company of Musicians that play upon their Trumpets and Harps, and sing their Songs before the Throne.

Hon. He was a very zealous man, as one may see by what relation you have given of him. Difficulties, Lions or *Vanity Fair,* he feared not at all. 'Twas only Sin Death and Hell that was to him a terror, because he had some doubts about his interest in that Cœlestial Country.

Great-heart. You say right. *Those* were the things that were his troublers, and they, as you have well observed, arose from the weakness of his mind there-about, not from weakness of spirit as to the practical part of a Pilgrim's life. I dare believe that, as the Proverb is, *he could have bit a Fire-brand, had it stood in his way;* but the things with which he was oppressed, no man ever yet could shake off with ease.

A close about him

Chris-
tiana's
sentence

CHRIS. Then said *Christiana,* This relation of Mr *Fearing* has done me good. I thought nobody had been like me, but I see there was some semblance 'twixt this good man and I, only we differed in two things. His troubles were so great, they brake out, but mine I kept within. His also lay so hard upon him, they made him that he could not knock at the houses provided for Entertainment, but my trouble was always such as made me knock the louder.

Mercy's
sentence

MERCY. If I might also speak my heart, I must say that something of him has also dwelt in me; for I have ever been more afraid of the Lake and the loss of a place in *Paradise,* than I have been of the loss of other things. Oh, thought I, may I have the happiness to have a habitation *there,* 'tis enough, though I part with all the world to win it.

Matthew's
sentence

MATT. Then said *Matthew,* Fear was one thing that made me think that I was far from having that within me that accompanies Salvation, but if it was so with such a good man as he, why may it not also go well with me?

James's
sentence

JAMES. No fears, no Grace, said *James.* Tho' there is not always Grace where there is the fear of Hell, yet to be sure there is no Grace where there is no fear of God.

GREAT-HEART. Well said, *James,* thou hast hit the mark, for the fear of God is the beginning of Wisdom, and to be sure they that want the *beginning* have neither *middle* nor *end.* But we will here conclude our discourse of Mr *Fearing,* after we have sent after him this farewell.

Their
farewell
about him

Well, Master *Fearing,* thou didst fear
Thy God, and wast afraid
Of doing anything while here
That would have thee betray'd.

And didst thou fear the Lake and Pit?
Would others do so too.
For as for them that want thy wit,
They do themselves undo.

Now I saw that they still went on in their talk; Of Mr Self-will for after Mr *Great-heart* had made an end with Mr *Fearing,* Mr *Honest* began to tell them of another, but his name was Mr *Self-will.* He pretended himself to be a Pilgrim, said Mr *Honest,* but I persuade myself he never came in at the Gate that stands at the head of the way.

GREAT-HEART. Had you ever any talk with him about it?

HON. Yes, more than once or twice, but he would Old Honest had talked with him always be like himself, self-willed. He neither cared for man, nor argument, nor yet example; what his mind prompted him to do, that he would do, and nothing else could he be got to.

GREAT-HEART. Pray what principles did he hold? for I suppose you can tell.

HON. He held that a man might follow the Vices Self-will's opinions as well as the Vertues of the Pilgrims, and that if he did both he should be certainly saved.

GREAT-HEART. How? if he had said 'tis possible for the best to be guilty of the Vices, as well as to partake of the Vertues of Pilgrims, he could not much have been blamed. For indeed we are exempted from no Vice absolutely, but on condition that we watch and strive. But this I perceive is not the thing; but if I understand you right, your meaning is, that he was of that opinion, that it was allowable so to be?

HON. Ay, ay, so I mean, and so he believed and practised.

GREAT-HEART. But what Ground had he for his so saying?

HON. Why, he said he had the Scripture for his Warrant.

GREAT-HEART. Prithee, Mr *Honest,* present us with a few particulars.

HON. So I will. He said to have to do with other men's Wives had been practised by *David,* God's beloved, and therefore he could do it. He said to have more Women than one, was a thing that *Solomon* practised, and therefore he could do it. He said that *Sarah* and the godly Midwives of *Egypt* lied, and so did save *Rahab*, and therefore he could do it. He said that the Disciples went at the bidding of their Master, and took away the owner's Ass, and therefore he could do so too. He said that *Jacob* got the Inheritance of his Father in a way of Guile and Dissimulation, and therefore he could do so too.

GREAT-HEART. High base indeed, and you are sure he was of this opinion?

HON. I have heard him plead for it, bring Scripture for it, bring Argument for it, *&c.*

GREAT-HEART. An opinion that is not fit to be with any allowance in the world.

HON. You must understand me rightly. He did not say that any man might do this, but that those that had the Vertues of those that did such things, might also do the same.

GREAT-HEART. But what more false than such a conclusion? for this is as much as to say, that because good men heretofore have sinned of infirmity, therefore he had allowance to do it of a presumptuous mind. Or if because a Child by the Blast of the Wind, or for that it stumbled at a Stone, fell down and defiled itself in mire, therefore he might wilfully lie down and wallow like a Boar therein. Who could a thought that any one could so far a been blinded by the power of Lust? But what is written must be true, They stumble at the word being disobedient, whereunto also they were appointed.

His supposing that such may have the godly man's Vertues, who addict themselves to their Vices, is also a delusion as strong as the other. 'Tis just as if the Dog should say, I have or may have the qualities of the Child, because I lick up its stinking Excrements. To eat up the Sin of God's People, is no sign of one that is possessed with their Vertues. Nor can I believe that one that is of this opinion can at present have Faith or Love in him. But I know you have made strong objections against him, prithee what can he say for himself?

Hon. Why, he says, To do this by way of opinion, seems abundance more honest than to do it, and yet hold contrary to it in opinion.

Great-heart. A very wicked answer, for tho' to let loose the Bridle to Lusts while our opinions are against such things, is bad; yet to sin and plead a toleration so to do, is worse. The one stumbles Beholders accidentally, the other pleads them into the Snare.

Hon. There are many of this man's mind, that have not this man's mouth, and *that* makes going on Pilgrimage of so little esteem as it is.

Great-heart. You have said the truth, and it is to be lamented. But he that feareth the King of *Paradise* shall come out of them all.

Chris. There are strange opinions in the world, I know one that said, 'Twas time enough to repent when they come to die.

Great-heart. Such are not over wise. That man would a been loth, might he have had a Week to run twenty mile in for his life, to have deferred that Journey to the last hour of that Week.

Hon. You say right, and yet the generality of them that count themselves Pilgrims do indeed do thus. I am, as you see, an old man, and have been a traveller in this road many a day, and I have taken notice of many things.

I have seen some that have set out as if they would drive all the world afore them, who yet have in few days died as they in the Wilderness, and so never gat sight of the Promised Land.

I have seen some that have promised nothing at first setting out to be Pilgrims, and that one would a thought could not have lived a day, that have yet proved very good Pilgrims.

I have seen some who have spoke very well of

that again have after a little time run as fast just
back again.

I have seen some who have spoke very well of
a Pilgrim's life at first, that after a while have
spoken as much against it.

I have heard some when they first set out for
Paradise, say positively there is such a place, who
when they have been almost there, have come back
again and said there is none.

I have heard some vaunt what they would do in
case they should be opposed, that have even at a
false alarm fled Faith, the Pilgrim's way, and all.

Fresh news
of trouble
Now as they were thus in their way, there came
one running to meet them, and said, Gentlemen
and you of the weaker sort, if you love Life shift
for yourselves, for the Robbers are before you.

First Part,
p. 130
GREAT-HEART. Then said Mr *Great-heart,* They
be the three that set upon *Little-faith* heretofore.
Well, said he, we are ready for them. So they

Great-
heart's
resolution
went on their way. Now they looked at every
turning, when they should a met with the Villains;
but whether they heard of Mr *Great-heart,* or
whether they had some other game, they came not
up to the Pilgrims.

Christiana
wisheth
for an inn
Christiana then wished for an Inn for herself
and her Children, because they were weary. Then
said Mr *Honest,* There is one a little before us,

Gaius
where a very honorable Disciple, one *Gaius,* dwells.
So they all concluded to turn in thither, and the
rather because the old Gentleman gave him so good

They enter
into his
house
a report. So when they came to the door, they
went in, not knocking, for Folks use not to knock
at the door of an Inn. Then they called for the
Master of the house, and he came to them. So
they asked if they might lie there that night?

Gaius
entertains
them,
and how
GAIUS. Yes Gentlemen, if you be true men, for
my house is for none but Pilgrims. Then was
Christiana, Mercy and the Boys the more glad,
for that the Innkeeper was a lover of Pilgrims.
So they called for Rooms, and he shewed them

one for *Christiana* and her Children and *Mercy,* and another for Mr *Great-heart* and the old Gentleman.

GREAT-HEART. Then said Mr *Great-heart,* Good *Gaius,* what hast thou for Supper? for these Pilgrims have come far to-day, and are weary.

GAIUS. It is late, said *Gaius,* so we cannot conveniently go out to seek food, but such as we have you shall be welcome to, if that will content.

GREAT-HEART. We will be content with what thou hast in the house, forasmuch as I have proved thee, thou art never destitute of that which is convenient.

Then he went down and spake to the Cook, whose name was *Taste-that-which-is-good,* to get ready Supper for so many Pilgrims. This done, he comes up again, saying, Come my good Friends, you are welcome to me, and I am glad that I have a house to entertain you; and while Supper is making ready, if you please, let us entertain one another with some good discourse. So they all said, Content. Gaius's cook

GAIUS. Then said *Gaius,* Whose Wife is this aged Matron? and whose Daughter is this young Damsel? Talk between Gaius and his guests

GREAT-HEART. The Woman is the Wife of one *Christian* a Pilgrim of former times, and these are his four Children. The Maid is one of her Acquaintance, one that she hath persuaded to come with her on Pilgrimage. The Boys take all after their Father, and covet to tread in his steps; yea, if they do but see any place where the old Pilgrim hath lain, or any print of his foot, it ministreth joy to their hearts, and they covet to lie or tread in the same. Mark this

GAIUS. Then said *Gaius,* Is this *Christian's* Wife? and are these *Christian's* Children? I knew your Husband's Father, yea, also his Father's Father. Many have been good of this stock, their Ancestors dwelt first at *Antioch.* *Christian's* Progenitors (I suppose you have heard your Husband talk of them) were very worthy men. They have above any that I know, shewed themselves men of great Vertue Of Christian's ancestors

and Courage for the Lord of Pilgrims, his ways,
and them that loved him. I have heard of many
of your Husband's Relations that have stood all
trials for the sake of the Truth. *Stephen* that was
one of the first of the Family from whence your
Husband sprang, was knocked o' the head with
Stones. *James,* another of this Generation, was slain
with the edge of the Sword. To say nothing of
Paul and *Peter,* men antiently of the Family from
whence your Husband came, there was *Ignatius*
who was cast to the Lions, *Romanus* whose flesh
was cut by pieces from his bones, and *Polycarp* that
played the man in the Fire. There was he that was
hanged up in a Basket in the Sun for the Wasps
to eat, and he whom they put into a Sack and cast
him into the Sea to be drowned. 'Twould be impossible utterly to count up all of that Family that
have suffered Injuries and Death for the love of
a Pilgrim's life. Nor can I but be glad to see that
thy Husband has left behind him four such Boys
as these. I hope they will bear up their Father's
name, and tread in their Father's *steps,* and come
to their Father's *end.*

GREAT-HEART. Indeed Sir, they are likely Lads,
they seem to chuse heartily their Father's ways.

GAIUS. That is it that I said, wherefore *Christian's* Family is like still to spread abroad upon the
face of the ground, and yet to be numerous upon
the face of the earth. Wherefore let *Christiana*
look out some Damsels for her Sons, to whom they
may be betrothed, *&c.* that the name of their
Father and the house of his Progenitors may never
be forgotten in the world.

HON. 'Tis pity this Family should fall and be
extinct.

GAIUS. Fall it cannot, but be diminished it may;
but let *Christiana* take my advice, and that's the way
to uphold it.

And *Christiana,* said this Innkeeper, I am glad
to see thee and thy friend *Mercy* together here,

*Advice to
Christiana
about
her boys*

a lovely couple. And may I advise, take *Mercy* Mercy and into a nearer Relation to thee. If she will, let her Matthew marry be given to *Matthew* thy eldest Son, 'tis the way to preserve you a Posterity in the earth. So this match was concluded, and in process of time they were married. But more of that hereafter.

Gaius also proceeded and said, I will now speak Why women on the behalf of Women, to take away their Re- of old proach. For as Death and the Curse came into so much the world by a Woman, so also did Life and Health: desired children *God sent forth his Son, made of a Woman.* Yea, to shew how much those that came after did abhor the act of their Mother, this sex in the Old Testament coveted Children, if happily this or that Woman might be the Mother of the Saviour of the World.

I will say again, that when the Saviour was come, Women rejoiced in him before either Man or Angel. I read not, that ever any Man did give unto Christ so much as one Groat, but the Women followed him and ministered to him of their Substance. 'Twas a Woman that washed his Feet with Tears, and a Woman that anointed his Body to the Burial. They were Women that wept when he was going to the Cross, and Women that followed him from the Cross, and that sat by his Sepulchre when he was buried. They were Women that was first with him at his Resurrection-morn, and Women that brought tiding first to his Disciples that he was risen from the Dead. Women therefore are highly favoured, and shew by these things that they are sharers with us in the Grace of Life.

Now the Cook sent up to signify that Supper was Supper ready almost ready, and sent one to lay the Cloath, the Trenchers, and to set the Salt and Bread in order.

Then said *Matthew,* The sight of this Cloath and of this forerunner of the Supper, begetteth in me a greater Appetite to my food than I had before.

GAIUS. So let all ministring doctrines *to* thee in this life, beget *in* thee a greater desire to sit at the

What to be
gathered
from lay-
ing of the
board
with the
cloth and
trenchers

Supper of the great King in his Kingdom; for all Preaching Books and Ordinances here, are but as the laying of the Trenchers and as setting of Salt upon the Board, when compared with the Feast that our Lord will make for us when we come to his House.

So Supper came up, and first a Heave-shoulder and a Wave-breast was set on the Table before them, to shew that they must begin their meal with Prayer and Praise to God. The Heave-shoulder *David* lifted his Heart up to God with, and with the Wave-breast, where his Heart lay, with that he used to lean upon his Harp when he played. These two Dishes were very fresh and good, and they all eat heartily well thereof.

The next they brought up was a Bottle of Wine, red as Blood. So *Gaius* said to them, Drink freely, this is the Juice of the true Vine that makes glad the heart of God and Man. So they drank and were merry.

A dish
of milk

The next was a dish of Milk well crumbed. But *Gaius* said, Let the Boys have that, that they may grow thereby.

Of hony
and butter

Then they brought up in course a dish of Butter and Hony. Then said *Gaius*, Eat freely of this, for this is good to cheer up and strengthen your Judgments and Understandings. This was our Lord's dish when he was a Child, *Butter and Hony shall he eat, that he may know to refuse the Evil and chuse the Good.*

A dish
of apples

Then they brought them up a dish of Apples, and they were very good tasted Fruit. Then said *Matthew*, May we eat Apples, since they were such, by and with which the Serpent beguiled our first Mother?

Then said *Gaius*,

> *Apples* were they with which we were beguil'd,
> Yet *sin*, not Apples, hath our souls defil'd.
> Apples forbid, if eat, corrupts the Blood;
> To eat such when commanded, does us good.

> Drink of *his* Flagons, then, thou Church, his Dove,
> And eat *his* Apples, who are sick of Love.

Then said *Matthew,* I made the scruple because I a while since was sick with eating of Fruit.

GAIUS. Forbidden Fruit will make you sick, but not what our Lord has tolerated.

While they were thus talking, they were presented with another dish, and 'twas a dish of Nuts. Then said some at the Table, Nuts spoil tender Teeth, specially the Teeth of Children; which when *Gaius* heard, he said,

A dish of nuts

> Hard Texts are Nuts (I will not call them cheaters)
> Whose Shells do keep their Kernels from the Eaters.
> Ope then the Shells, and you shall have the Meat,
> They here are brought for you to crack and eat.

Then were they very merry, and sat at the Table a long time, talking of many things. Then said the old Gentleman, My good Landlord, while we are cracking your Nuts, if you please, do you open this Riddle:

> A man there was, tho' some did count him mad,
> The more he cast away the more he had.

A riddle put forth by Old Honest

Then they all gave good heed, wondring what good *Gaius* would say; so he sat still a while, and then thus replied:

> He that bestows his Goods upon the Poor,
> Shall have as much again, and ten times more.

Gaius opens it

Then said *Joseph,* I dare say Sir, I did not think you could a found it out.

Joseph wonders

Oh, said *Gaius,* I have been trained up in this way a great while, nothing teaches like experience. I have learned of my Lord to be kind, and have found by experience that I have gained thereby. *There is that scattereth, yet increaseth, and there is that withholdeth more than is meet, but it tendeth to Poverty. There is that maketh himself Rich, yet*

hath nothing, there is that maketh himself Poor,
yet hath great Riches.

Then *Samuel* whispered to *Christiana* his Mother,
and said, Mother, this is a very good man's house,
let us stay here a good while, and let my Brother
Matthew be married here to *Mercy* before we go
any further.

The which *Gaius* the Host overhearing said,
With a very good will, my Child.

Matthew
and Mercy
are
married

So they stayed there more than a month, and
Mercy was given to *Matthew* to Wife.

While they stayed here, *Mercy,* as her custom was,
would be making Coats and Garments to the Poor,
by which she brought up a very good report upon
the Pilgrims.

The boys
go to bed,
the rest
sit up

But to return again to our Story. After Supper
the Lads desired a Bed, for that they were weary
with travelling. Then *Gaius* called to shew them
their chamber, but said *Mercy,* I will have them to
Bed. So she had them to Bed, and they slept well.
But the rest sat up all night, for *Gaius* and they
were such suitable Company that they could not
tell how to part. Then after much talk of their
Lord, themselves, and their Journey, old Mr *Honest,*
he that put forth the Riddle to *Gaius,* began to

Old Hon-
est nods

nod. Then said *Great-heart,* What Sir, you begin to
be drowsy, come, rub up, now here's a Riddle for
you. Then said Mr *Honest,* Let's hear it.

Then said Mr *Great-heart:*

A riddle

He that will kill, must first be overcome;
Who live abroad would, first must die at home.

Hah, said Mr. *Honest,* it is a hard one, hard to
expound, and harder to practise. But come Landlord, said he, I will if you please, leave my part to
you, do you expound it, and I will hear what you
say.

No said *Gaius,* 'twas put to you, and 'tis expected that you should answer it.

Then said the old Gentleman,

He first by Grace must conquer'd be,   The riddle
That Sin would mortify;   opened
And who, that lives, would convince me,
Unto himself must die.

It is right, said *Gaius,* good Doctrine and Experience teaches this. For *First,* until Grace dis-
plays itself, and overcomes the soul with its Glory,
it is altogether without heart to oppose Sin. Besides, if Sin is Satan's Cords by which the soul
lies bound, how should it make resistance before it
is loosed from that infirmity?

Secondly, Nor will any that knows either Reason
or Grace, believe that such a man can be a living
Monument of Grace that is a Slave to his own
Corruptions.

And now it comes in my mind, I will tell you a   A question
Story worth the hearing. There were two men   worth the
that went on Pilgrimage, the one began when he   minding
was young, the other when he was old. The
young man had strong Corruptions to grapple
with, the old man's were decayed with the decays
of nature. The young man trod his steps as even
as did the old one, and was every way as light as
he. Who now, or which of them, had their Graces
shining clearest, since both seemed to be alike?

HON. The young man's, doubtless. For that   A com-
which heads it against the greatest opposition, parison
gives best demonstration that it is strongest. Specially when it also holdeth pace with that that meets
not with half so much, as to be sure old age
does not.

Besides, I have observed that old men have blessed A mistake
themselves with this mistake, namely, taking the
decays of Nature for a gracious Conquest over
Corruptions, and so have been apt to beguile themselves. Indeed old men that are gracious are best
able to give advice to them that are young, because
they have seen most of the emptiness of things.
But yet, for an old and a young to set out both
together, the young one has the advantage of the

fairest discovery of a work of Grace within him, tho the old man's Corruptions are naturally the weakest,

Another question

Thus they sat talking till break of day. Now when the Family was up, *Christiana* bid her Son *James* that he should read a Chapter, so he read the 53d of *Isaiah*. When he had done, Mr *Honest* asked, why it was said *that the Saviour is said to come out of a dry ground, and also that he had no form nor comeliness in him?*

GREAT-HEART. Then said Mr *Great-heart*, To the First I answer, Because the Church of the Jews, of which Christ came, had then lost almost all the Sap and Spirit of Religion. To the Second I say, the words are spoken in the person of the Unbelievers, who because they want that Eye that can see into our Prince's Heart, therefore they judge of him by the meanness of his Outside. Just like those that know not that Precious Stones are covered over with a homely Crust, who when they have found one, because they know not what they have found, cast it again away as men do a common Stone.

Giant Slay-good assaulted and slain

Well, said *Gaius*, now you are here, and since, as I know, Mr *Great-heart* is good at his Weapons, if you please, after we have refreshed ourselves, we will walk into the Fields to see if we can do any good. About a mile from hence there is one *Slay-good*, a Giant that doth much annoy the King's High-way in these parts; and I know whereabout his Haunt is. He is Master of a number of Thieves. 'Twould be well if we could clear these parts of him.

So they consented and went, Mr *Great-heart* with his Sword, Helmet and Shield, and the rest with Spears and Staves.

He is found with one Feeble-mind in his hands

When they came to the place where he was, they found him with one *Feeble-mind* in his hands, whom his Servants had brought unto him, having taken him in the way. Now the Giant was rifling of him, with a purpose after that to pick his Bones, for he was of the nature of Flesh-eaters.

Well, so soon as he saw Mr *Great-heart* and his Friends at the Mouth of his cave with their Weapons, he demanded what they wanted?

GREAT-HEART. We want thee, for we are come to revenge the quarrel of the many that thou hast slain of the Pilgrims, when thou hast dragged them out of the King's High-way, wherefore come out of thy Cave. So he armed himself and came out, and to a Battle they went, and fought for above an hour and then stood still to take wind.

SLAY. Then said the Giant, Why are you here on my ground?

GREAT-HEART. To revenge the Blood of Pilgrims, as I also told thee before. So they went to it again, and the Giant made Mr *Great-heart* give back; but he came up again, and in the greatness of his mind he let fly with such stoutness at the Giant's head and sides, that he made him let his Weapon fall out of his hand. So he smote him and slew him, and cut off his Head, and brought it away to the Inn. He also took *Feeble-mind* the Pilgrim, and brought him with him to his Lodgings. When they were come home, they shewed his head to the Family, and then set it up, as they had done others before, for a terror to those that should attempt to do as he hereafter. *One Feeble-mind rescued from the giant*

Then they asked Mr *Feeble-mind* how he fell into his hands?

FEEBLE-MIND. Then said the poor man, I am a sickly man as you see, and, because Death did usually once a day knock at my door, I thought I should never be well at home; so I betook myself to a Pilgrim's life, and have travelled hither from the Town of *Uncertain*, where I and my Father were born. I am a man of no strength at all of body, nor yet of mind; but would if I could, tho' I can but *crawl*, spend my life in the Pilgrim's way. When I came at the Gate that is at the head of the way, the Lord of that place did entertain me freely, neither objected he against my weekly looks, ncr against *How Feeble-mind came to be a pilgrim*

my feeble mind; but gave me such things that were
necessary for my Journey, and bid me hope to the
end.   When I came to the house of the *Interpreter*,
I received much kindness there, and because the
Hill *Difficulty* was judged too hard for me, I was
carried up that by one of his servants.   Indeed I
have found much relief from Pilgrims, tho' none
was willing to go so softly as I am forced to do;
yet still as they came on, they bid me be of good
cheer, and said that it was the will of their Lord
that comfort should be given to the *feeble-minded*,
and so went on their own pace.   When I was come
up to *Assault* Lane, then this Giant met with me,
and bid me prepare for an Encounter; but alas,
feeble one that I was, I had more need of a Cordial.

Mark this So he came up and took me.   I conceited he should
not kill me.   Also when he had got me into his
Den, since I went not with him willingly, I believed
I should come out alive again; for I have heard that
not only any Pilgrim that is taken captive by violent
hands, if he keeps heart-whole towards his Master,
is by the Laws of Providence to die by the hand
of the Enemy.   Robbed I looked to be, and robbed
to be sure I am; but I am, as you see, escaped with
Life, for the which I thank my King as Author,
and you as the Means.   Other brunts I also look for,

Mark this but this I have resolved on, to wit, to *run* when I
can, to *go* when I cannot *run*, and to *creep* when
I cannot *go*.   As to the main, I thank him that
loves me, I am fixed.   My way is before me, my
Mind is beyond the River that has no Bridge, tho'
I am, as you see, but of a *feeble* Mind.

HON. Then said old Mr *Honest*, Have you not
some time ago been acquainted with one Mr *Fearing* a Pilgrim?

Mr Fear-   FEEBLE. Acquainted with him, Yes.   He came
ing, Mr   from the Town of *Stupidity*, which lieth four de-
Feeble-   grees to the northward of the City of *Destruction*,
mind's
uncle   and as many off of where I was born; yet we were
well acquainted, for indeed he was mine Uncle, my

Father's Brother. He and I have been much of a temper. He was a little shorter than I, but yet we were much of a complexion.

HON. I perceive you know him, and I am apt to believe also that you were related one to another; for you have his whitely Look, a Cast like his with your eye, and your Speech is much alike. Feeble-mind has some of Mr Fearing's features

FEEBLE. Most have said so that have known us both, and besides, what I have read in him, I have for the most part found in myself.

GAIUS. Come Sir, said good *Gaius,* be of good cheer, you are welcome to me and to my house, and what thou hast a mind to, call for freely; and what thou would'st have my servants to do for thee, they will do it with a ready mind. Gaius comforts him

Then said Mr *Feeble-mind,* This is unexpected Favour, and as the Sun shining out of a very dark Cloud. Did Giant *Slay-good* intend me this favour when he stopped me, and resolved to let me go no further? Did he intend that after he had rifled my Pockets, I should go to *Gaius* mine Host? Yet so it is. Notice to be taken of Providence

Now just as Mr *Feeble-mind* and *Gaius* was thus in talk, there comes one running and called at the door, and told, That about a mile and a half off there was one Mr *Not-right* a Pilgrim struck dead upon the place where he was with a Thunderbolt. Tidings how one Not-right was slain with a thunder-bolt,

FEEBLE. Alas, said Mr *Feeble-mind,* is he slain? He overtook me some days before I came so far as hither, and would be my Company-keeper. He also was with me when *Slay-good* the Giant took me, but he was nimble of his heels and escaped. But it seems he escaped to die, and I was took to live. and Mr Feeble-mind's comments upon it

> What one would think doth seek to slay outright,
> Ofttimes delivers from the saddest plight.
> That very Providence whose face is Death,
> Doth ofttimes to the lowly Life bequeath.
> I taken was, he did escape and flee,
> Hands cross'd gives Death to him, and Life to me.

Now about this time *Matthew* and *Mercy* were married. Also *Gaius* gave his Daughter *Phebe* to

James, Matthew's Brother, to Wife; after which time they yet stayed above ten days at *Gaius's* house, spending their time and the seasons like as Pilgrims use to do.

The pilgrims prepare to go forward

When they were to depart, *Gaius* made them a Feast, and they did eat and drink and were merry. Now the hour was come that they must be gone, wherefore Mr *Great-heart* called for a Reckoning. But *Gaius* told him that at his house it was not the custom for Pilgrims to pay for their Entertainment.

How they greet one another at parting

He boarded them by the year, but looked for his pay from the good *Samaritan,* who had promised him at his return, whatsoever charge he was at with them faithfully to repay him. Then said Mr *Great-heart* to him,

GREAT-HEART. *Beloved, thou dost faithfully whatsoever thou dost to the Brethren and to Strangers, which have borne witness of thy Charity before the Church; whom if thou (yet) bring forward on their Journey after a Godly sort, thou shalt do well.*

Gaius, his last kindness to Feeblemind

Then *Gaius* took his leave of them all, and of his Children, and particularly of Mr *Feeble-mind.* He also gave him something to drink by the way.

Now Mr *Feeble-mind,* when they were going out of the door, made as if he intended to linger. The which when Mr *Great-heart* espied, he said, Come Mr *Feeble-mind,* pray do you go along with us, I will be your Conductor, and you shall fare as the rest.

Feeblemind for going behind

FEEBLE. Alas, I want a suitable Companion, you are all lusty and strong, but I, as you see, am weak. I chuse therefore rather to come behind, lest by reason of my many Infirmities I should be both a Burden to myself and to you. I am, as I said, a man of a weak and feeble mind, and shall be offended and made weak at that which others can bear. I shall like no Laughing, I shall like no gay Attire, I shall like no unprofitable Questions. Nay I am so weak a man, as to be offended with that which others have a liberty to do. I do not yet know all the Truth. I am a very ignorant *Christian man.* Sometimes if I hear some rejoice in the Lord, it troubles me because I cannot do so too. It is with me as it is with a weak man among the strong, or as with a sick man among the healthy, or as a Lamp despised, (*He that is ready to slip with his feet, is as a Lamp despised in the thought of him that is at ease.*) So that I know not what to do. His excuse for it

GREAT-HEART. But Brother, said Mr *Great-heart,* I have it in Commission to comfort the *feeble-minded,* and to support the weak. You must needs go along with us; we will wait for you, we will lend you our help, we will deny ourselves of some things both opinionative and practical for your sake, we will not enter into doubtful disputations before you, we will be made all things to you rather than you shall be left behind. Great-heart's commission A Christian spirit

Now all this while they were at *Gaius's* door; and behold as they were thus in the heat of their discourse Mr *Ready-to-halt* came by with his Crutches in his hand, and he also was going on Pilgrimage. Promises

FEEBLE. Then said Mr *Feeble-mind* to him, Man, how camest thou hither? I was but just now complaining that I had not a suitable Companion, but thou art according to my wish. Welcome, welcome, good Mr *Ready-to-halt,* I hope thee and I may be some help. Feeble-mind glad to see Ready-to-halt come by

READY-TO-HALT. I shall be glad of thy Company, said the other; and good Mr *Feeble-mind,* rather than we will part, since we are thus happily met, I will lend thee one of my Crutches.

FEEBLE. Nay, said he, tho' I thank thee for thy good will, I am not inclined to halt before I am lame. Howbeit, I think when occasion is, it may help me against a Dog.

READY. If either myself or my Crutches can do thee a pleasure, we are both at thy command, good Mr *Feeble-mind.*

Thus therefore they went on, Mr *Great-heart* and Mr *Honest* went before, *Christiana* and her Children went next, and Mr *Feeble-mind* and Mr *Ready-to-halt* came behind with his Crutches. Then said Mr *Honest*,

New talk

HON. Pray Sir, now we are upon the Road, tell us some profitable things of some that have gone on Pilgrimage before us.

First Part, pp. 59-69

GREAT-HEART. With a good will. I suppose you have heard how *Christian* of old did meet with *Apollyon* in the Valley of *Humiliation*, and also what hard work he had to go through the Valley of the *Shadow of Death*. Also I think you cannot but have heard how *Faithful* was put to it with Madam *Wanton*, with *Adam* the First, with one *Discontent*, and *Shame*, four as deceitful Villains as a man can meet with upon the road.

HON. Yes, I have heard of all this; but indeed good *Faithful* was hardest put to it with *Shame*, he was an unwearied one.

GREAT-HEART. Ay, for as the Pilgrim well said, he of all men had the wrong name.

First Part, p. 79

HON. But pray Sir, where was it that *Christian* and *Faithful* met *Talkative?* That same was also a notable one.

GREAT-HEART. He was a confident Fool, yet many follow his ways.

HON. He had like to a beguiled *Faithful*.

First Part p. 82

GREAT-HEART. Ay, but *Christian* put him into a way quickly to find him out. Thus they went on till they came at the place where *Evangelist* met with *Christian* and *Faithful*, and prophesied to them of what should befall them at *Vanity Fair.*

GREAT-HEART. Then said their Guide, Hereabouts did *Christian* and *Faithful* meet with *Evangelist*, who prophesied to them of what Troubles they should meet with at *Vanity Fair.*

HON. Say you so? I dare say it was a hard Chapter that then he did read unto them.

GREAT-HEART. 'Twas so; but he gave them en-

couragement withal. But what do we talk of them? First Part,
they were a couple of lion-like men, they had set p. 91
their faces like flint. Don't you remember how un-
daunted they were when they stood before the
Judge?

Hon. Well, *Faithful* bravely suffered.

Great-heart. So he did, and as brave things
came on't, for *Hopeful* and some others, as the
Story relates it, were converted by his Death.

Hon. Well, but pray go on, for you are well acquainted with things.

Great-heart. Above all that *Christian* met with First Part,
after he had passed through *Vanity Fair,* one *By-* p. 103
ends was the arch one.

Hon. *By-ends,* What was he?

Great-heart. A very arch Fellow, a downright
Hypocrite. One that would be religious which way
ever the World went, but so cunning that he would
be sure neither to lose nor suffer for it. He had
his mode of Religion for every fresh occasion, and
his Wife was as good at it as he. He would turn
and change from opinion to opinion, yea, and plead
for so doing too. But so far as I could learn, he
came to an ill end with his *by-ends,* nor did I ever
hear that any of his Children were ever of any
esteem with any that truly feared God.

Now by this time they were come within sight They are
of the Town of *Vanity* where *Vanity Fair* is kept. come within
So when they saw that they were so near the Town, sight of
they consulted with one another how they should Vanity
pass through the Town, and some said one thing
and some another. At last Mr *Great-heart* said,
I have, as you may understand, often been a Conductor of Pilgrims through this Town, now I am They
acquainted with one Mr *Mnason,* a *Cyprusian* by enter into
one Mr
Nation, an old Disciple, at whose house we may Mnason's
lodge. If you think good, said he, we will turn to lodge
in there.

Content, said old *Honest,* Content, said *Chris-*
tiana, Content said Mr *Feeble-mind,* and so they

said all. Now you must think it was eventide
by that they got to the outside of the Town, but
Mr *Great-heart* knew the way to the old man's
house. So thither they came; and he called at the
door, and the old man within knew his tongue so
soon as ever he heard it; so he opened, and they
all came in. Then said *Mnason* their Host, How
far have ye come to-day? so they said, From the
house of *Gaius* our Friend. I promise you, said he,
you have gone a good stitch, you may well be a
weary, sit down. So they sat down.

GREAT-HEART. Then said their Guide, Come, what
cheer Sirs? I dare say you are welcome to my
Friend.

They are glad of entertainment

MNASON. I also, said Mr *Mnason,* do bid you
welcome, and whatever you want, do but say, and
we will do what we can to get it for you.

HON. Our great want a while since was Harbour
and good Company, and now I hope we have both.

MNASON. For Harbour, you see what it is, but
for good Company, that will appear in the trial.

GREAT-HEART. Well, said Mr *Great-heart,* will
you have the Pilgrims up into their Lodging?

MNASON. I will, said Mr *Mnason.* So he had
them to their respective places; and also shewed
them a very fair Dining-room, where they might
be and sup together, until time was come to go
to Rest.

Now when they were set in their places, and were
a little cheery after their Journey, Mr *Honest* asked
his Landlord if there were any store of good people
in the Town?

MNASON. We have a few, for indeed they are but
a few when compared with them on the other side.

They desire to see some of the good people of the town

HON. But how shall we do to see some of them?
for the sight of good men to them that are going
on Pilgrimage, is like to the appearing of the Moon
and the Stars to them that are sailing upon the
Seas.

Then Mr *Mnason* stamped with his foot, and

his daughter *Grace* came up; so he said unto her, Some sent for *Grace*. go you tell my Friends, Mr *Contrite*, Mr *Holy-man*, Mr *Love-saint*, Mr *Dare-not-lye*, and Mr *Penitent*, that I have a Friend or two at my house that have a mind this evening to see them.

So *Grace* went to call them, and they came and after Salutation made, they sat down together at the Table.

Then said Mr *Mnason* their Landlord, My Neighbors, I have, as you see, a Company of Strangers come to my house, they are Pilgrims, they come from afar, and are going to Mount *Sion*. But who, quoth he, do you think this is, pointing with his finger to *Christiana*, it is *Christiana* the Wife of *Christian* that famous Pilgrim, who with *Faithful* his Brother were so shamefully handled in our Town. At that they stood amazed, saying, We little thought to see *Christiana*, when *Grace* came to call us, wherefore this is a very comfortable surprise. Then they asked her of her welfare, and if these young men were her Husband's Sons? And when she had told them they were, they said, The King whom you love and serve, make you as your Father, and bring you where he is in Peace.

HON. Then Mr *Honest* (when they were all sat Some talk betwixt Mr Honest and Contrite down) asked Mr *Contrite* and the rest in what posture their Town was at present?

CONTRITE. You may be sure we are full of hurry in Fair-time. 'Tis hard keeping our hearts and spirits in any good order, when we are in a cumbered condition. He that lives in such a place as The fruit of watchfulness this is, and that has to do with such as we have, has need of an Item, to caution him to take heed every moment of the day.

HON. But how are your Neighbors for quietness?

CONTRITE. They are much more moderate now Persecution not so hot at Vanity Fair as formerly than formerly. You know how *Christian* and *Faithful* were used at our Town; but of late, I say, they have been far more moderate. I think the blood of *Faithful* lieth with load upon them till now, for since they burned him they have been ashamed to burn any more. In *those* days we were afraid to walk the Streets, but *now* we can shew our heads. *Then* the name of a Professor was odious, *now,* specially in some parts of our Town (for you know our Town is large) Religion is counted honourable.

Then said Mr *Contrite* to them, Pray how fareth ·it with you in your Pilgrimage? How stands the Country affected towards you?

HON. It happens to us as it happeneth to Way-faring men; sometimes our way is clean, sometimes foul, sometimes up hill, sometimes down hill. We are seldom at a certainty, the Wind is not always on our backs, nor is every one a Friend that we meet with in the way. We have met with some notable Rubs already, and what are yet behind we know not, but for the most part we find it true that has been talked of of old, *A good man must suffer Trouble.*

CONTRITE. You talk of Rubs, what Rubs have you met withal?

HON. Nay, ask Mr *Great-heart* our Guide, for he can give the best account of that.

GREAT-HEART. We have been beset three or four times already. First *Christiana* and her Children were beset with two Ruffians, that they feared would a took away their lives. We was beset with Giant *Bloody-man,* Giant *Maul* and Giant *Slay-good.* Indeed we did rather beset the last, than were beset of him. And thus it was: After we had been some time at the house of *Gaius, mine Host and of the whole Church,* we were minded upon a time to take our Weapons with us, and so go see if we could light upon any of those that were Enemies to Pilgrims, (for we heard that there was a notable one thereabouts.) Now *Gaius* knew his Haunt better than I, because he dwelt thereabout, so we looked and looked till at last we discerned the Mouth of his Cave, then we were glad and plucked up our

Spirits. So we approached up to his Den, and lo when we came there, he had dragged by mere force into his Net this poor Man Mr *Feeble-mind,* and was about to bring him to his end. But when he saw us, supposing as we thought he had had another Prey, he left the poor man in his Hole, and came out. So we fell to it full sore, and he lustily laid about him; but in conclusion he was brought down to the ground, and his Head cut off, and set up by the Way-side for a terror to such as should after practise such Ungodliness. That I tell you the truth, here is the man himself to affirm it, who was as a Lamb taken out of the Mouth of the Lion.

FEEBLE-MIND. Then said Mr *Feeble-mind,* I found this true to my Cost and Comfort, to my Cost when he threatened to pick my Bones every moment, and to my Comfort when I saw Mr *Great-heart* and his Friends with their Weapons approach so near for my Deliverance.

HOLY-MAN. Then said Mr *Holy-man,* There are two things that they have need to be possessed with that go on Pilgrimage, *courage,* and an *unspotted life.* If they have not *courage,* they can never hold on their way, and if their Lives be *loose,* they will make the very name of a Pilgrim stink. *Mr Holy-man's speech*

LOVE-SAINT. Then said Mr *Love-saint,* I hope this caution is not needful amongst you. But truly there are many that go upon the road, that rather declare themselves Strangers to Pilgrimage than Strangers and Pilgrims in the Earth. *Mr Love-saint's speech*

DARE-NOT-LYE. Then said Mr *Dare-not-lye,* 'Tis true, they neither have the Pilgrim's Weed, nor the Pilgrim's Courage; they go not uprightly, but all awry with their feet; one Shoe goes *inward,* another *outward,* and their Hosen out behind; there a Rag, and there a Rent, to the Disparagement of their Lord. *Mr Dare-not-lye's speech*

PENITENT. These things, said Mr *Penitent,* they ought to be troubled for, nor are the Pilgrims like to have that Grace put upon them and their *Mr Penitent's speech*

Pilgrim's Progress as they desire, until the way is cleared of such Spots and Blemishes.

Thus they sat talking and spending the time, until Supper was set upon the Table; unto which they went and refreshed their weary bodies; so they went to Rest. Now they stayed in this Fair a great while at the house of this Mr *Mnason*, who in process of time gave his daughter *Grace* unto *Samuel Christiana's* Son to Wife, and his Daughter *Martha* to *Joseph*.

The time as I said, that they lay here was long, (for it was not now as in former times.) Wherefore the Pilgrims grew acquainted with many of the good people of the Town, and did them what service they could. *Mercy,* as she was wont, laboured much for the Poor, wherefore their Bellies and Backs blessed her, and she was there an Ornament to her Profession. And to say the truth for *Grace Phebe* and *Martha,* they were all of a very good Nature, and did much good in their place. They were also all of them very Fruitful, so that *Christian's* name, as was said before, was like to live in the World.

A monster   While they lay here, there came a Monster out of the Woods, and slew many of the people of the Town. It would also carry away their Children, and teach them to suck its Whelps. Now no man in the Town durst so much as face this Monster, but all men fled when they heard of the Noise of his coming.

His shape,   The Monster was like unto no one Beast upon
his nature   the earth; its Body was like the Dragon, and it had seven Heads and ten Horns. It made great havock of Children, and yet it was governed by a Woman. This Monster propounded Conditions to men, and such men as loved their Lives more than their Souls, accepted of those Conditions. So they came under.

Now this Mr *Great-heart,* together with these that came to visit the Pilgrims at Mr *Mnason's*

house, entered into a Covenant to go and engage
this Beast, if perhaps they might deliver the people
of this Town from the Paws and Mouth of this
so devouring a Serpent.

Then did Mr *Great-heart*, Mr *Contrite*, Mr
Holy-man, Mr *Dare-not-lye,* and Mr *Penitent,* with
their Weapons go forth to meet him. Now the
Monster at first was very rampant, and looked upon
these Enemies with great Disdain, but they so be-
laboured him, being sturdy men at Arms, that they
made him make a Retreat. So they came home to
Mr *Mnason's* house again.

The Monster, you must know, had his certain
Seasons to come out in, and to make his Attempts
upon the Children of the people of the Town; also
these Seasons did these valiant Worthies watch
him in, and did still continually assault him; insomuch that in process of time he became not only
wounded but lame, also he has not made that havock
of the Towns-men's Children as formerly he has
done. And it is verily believed by some, that this
Beast will die of his Wounds.

This therefore made Mr *Great-heart* and his
Fellows of great Fame in this Town, so that many
of the people that wanted their taste of things, yet
had a reverend Esteem and Respect for them. Upon
this account therefore it was that these Pilgrims
got not much hurt here. True there were some of
the baser sort, that could see no more than a Mole,
nor understand more than a Beast, these had no
reverence for these men, nor took they notice of
their Valour or Adventures.

Well the time grew on that the Pilgrims must go
on their way, wherefore they prepared for their
Journey. They sent for their Friends, they con-
ferred with them, they had some time set apart
therein to commit each other to the Protection of
their Prince. There was again that brought them
of such things as they had, that was fit for the
Weak and the Strong, for the Women and the

How he is
engaged

Men, and so laded them with such things as was necessary.

Then they set forwards on their way, and their Friends accompanying them so far as was convenient, they again committed each other to the Protection of their King, and parted.

They therefore that were of the Pilgrims' Company went on, and Mr *Great-heart* went before them. Now the Women and Children being weakly, they were forced to go as they could bear, by this means Mr *Ready-to-halt* and Mr *Feeble-mind* had more to sympathize with their Condition.

When they were gone from the Towns-men, and when their Friends had bid them farewell they quickly came to the place where *Faithful* was put to Death. There therefore they made a stand, and thanked Him that had enabled him to bear his Cross so well, and the rather because they now found that they had a benefit by such a manly Suffering as his was.

They went on therefore after this a good way further, talking of *Christian* and *Faithful*, and how *Hopeful* joined himself to *Christian* after that *Faithful* was dead.

First Part, p. 111 Now they were come up with the Hill *Lucre*, where the Silver-mine was, which took *Demas* off from his Pilgrimage, and into which, as some think, *By-ends* fell and perished; wherefore they considered that. But when they were come to the old Monument that stood over against the Hill *Lucre*, to wit, to the Pillar of Salt that stood also within view of *Sodom* and its stinking Lake, they marvelled, as did *Christian* before, that men of that Knowledge and ripeness of Wit as they was, should be so blinded as to turn aside here. Only they considered again that Nature is not affected with the Harms that others have met with, especially if that thing upon which they look has an attracting vertue upon the foolish eye.

I saw now that they went on till they came at

the River that was on this side of the Delectable First Part,
Mountains. To the River where the fine Trees p. 59
grow on both sides, and whose Leaves, if taken
inwardly, are good against Surfeits, where the Meadows are green all the year long, and where they
might lie down safely.

By this River side in the Meadow there were
Cotes and Folds for Sheep, an House built for the
nourishing and bringing up of those Lambs, the
Babes of those Women that go on Pilgrimage.
Also there was here one that was intrusted with
them who could have Compassion, and that could
gather these Lambs with his Arm and carry them
in his Bosom, and that could gently lead those that
were with young. Now to the care of *this Man,*
Christiana admonished her four Daughters to commit their little ones, that by these Waters they might
be housed, harboured, suckered, and nourished,
and that none of them might be lacking in time
to come. This Man, if any of them go astray or be
lost, he will bring them again: he will also bind up
that which was broken, and will strengthen them
that are sick. Here they will never want Meat
and Drink and Cloathing, here they will be kept
from Thieves and Robbers, for this Man will die
before one of those committed to his trust shall
be lost. Besides, here they shall be sure to have
good Nurture and Admonition, and shall be taught
to walk in right paths, and that you know is a
Favour of no small account. Also here, as you see,
are delicate Waters, pleasant Meadows, dainty Flowers, variety of Trees, and such as bear wholesome Fruit, Fruit not like that that *Matthew* eat
of, that fell over the Wall out of *Beelzebub's* Garden,
but Fruit that procureth Health where there is
none, and that continueth and increaseth it where
it is.

So they were content to commit their little ones
to him; and that which was also an encouragement
to them so to do, was, for that all this was to

be at the Charge of the King, and so was as an Hospital for young Children and Orphans.

First Part, p. 116

Now they went on; and when they were come to *By-path* Meadow, to the Stile over which *Christian* went with his Fellow *Hopeful,* when they were

They being come to By-path stile, have a mind to have a pluck with Giant Despair

taken by Giant *Despair* and put into *Doubting* Castle, they sat down and consulted what was best to be done; to wit, now they were so strong, and had got such a man as Mr *Great-heart* for their Conductor, whether they had not best make an attempt upon the Giant, demolish his Castle, and if there were any Pilgrims in it, to set them at liberty before they went any further. So one said one thing, and another said the contrary. One questioned if it was lawful to go upon *unconsecrated* ground, another said they might provided their end was good, but Mr *Great-heart* said, Though that Assertion offered last cannot be universally true, yet I have a Commandment to resist Sin, to overcome Evil, to fight the good Fight of Faith, and I pray, with whom should I fight this good Fight, if not with Giant *Despair?* I will therefore attempt the taking away of his Life, and the demolishing of *Doubting* Castle. Then said he, who will go with me? Then said old *Honest,* I will. And so will we too, said *Christiana's four Sons, Matthew Samuel James* and *Joseph,* for they were young men and strong. So they left the Women in the Road, and with them Mr *Feeble-mind* and Mr *Ready-to-halt* with his Crutches to be their Guard, until they came back; for in that place, tho' Giant *Despair* dwelt so near, they keeping in the Road, a little Child might lead them.

So Mr *Great-heart,* old *Honest* and the four young men went to go up to *Doubting* Castle to look for Giant *Despair.* When they came at the Castle-gate, they knocked for entrance with an unusual Noise. At that the old Giant comes to the Gate, and *Diffidence* his Wife follows. Then said he, Who and what is he that is so hardy as after this manner to molest the Giant *Despair?* Mr *Great-heart* replied, It is I, *Great-heart,* one of the King of the Cœlestial Country's Conductors of Pilgrims to their place, and I demand of thee that thou open thy Gates for my Entrance. Prepare thyself also to fight, for I am come to take away thy Head, and to demolish *Doubting* Castle.

Now Giant *Despair,* because he was a Giant, thought no man could overcome him; and again, thought he, since heretofore I have made a Conquest of Angels, shall *Great-heart* make me afraid? So he harnessed himself and went out. He had a Cap of Steel upon his Head, a Breast-plate of Fire girded to him, and he came out in Iron Shoes, with a great Club in his Hand. Then these six men made up to him, and beset him behind and before. Also when *Diffidence* the Giantess came up to help him, old Mr *Honest* cut her down at one Blow. Then they fought for their Lives, and Giant *Despair* was brought down to the Ground, but was very loth to die. He struggled hard, and had, as they say, as many Lives as a Cat, but *Great-heart* was his Death, for he left him not till he had severed his Head from his Shoulders.

Then they fell to demolishing *Doubting* Castle, and that you know might with ease be done since Giant *Despair* was dead. They were seven days in destroying of that; and in it of Pilgrims they found one Mr *Dispondency,* almost starved to Death, and one *Much-afraid* his Daughter; these two they saved alive. But it would a made you a wondered to have seen the dead Bodies that lay here and there in the Castle-yard, and how full of dead men's Bones the Dungeon was.

When Mr *Great-heart* and his Companions had performed this exploit, they took Mr *Dispondency* and his Daughter *Much-afraid* into their protection, for they were honest people tho' they were Prisoners in *Doubting* Castle to that Tyrant Giant *Despair.* They therefore I say, took with them the Head of

[marginal notes:] Despair has overcome angels

Despair is loath to die

Doubting Castle demolished

They have music and dancing for joy

the Giant (for his Body they had buried under a heap of Stones) and down to the Road and to their Companions they came, and shewed them what they had done. Now when *Feeble-mind* and *Ready-to-halt* saw that it was the Head of Giant *Despair* indeed, they were very jocund and merry. Now *Christiana,* if need was, could play upon the Vial, and her Daughter *Mercy* upon the Lute; so since they were so merry disposed, she played them a Lesson, and *Ready-to-halt* would dance. So he took *Dispondency's* Daughter named *Much-afraid* by the hand, and to dancing they went in the Road. True he could not dance without one Crutch in his hand, but I promise you he footed it well. Also the Girl was to be commended, for she answered the Musick handsomely.

As for Mr *Dispondency,* the Musick was not much to him, he was for feeding rather than dancing, for that he was almost starved. So *Christiana* gave him some of her Bottle of Spirits for present relief, and then prepared him something to eat; and in little time the old Gentleman came to himself, and began to be finely revived.

Now I saw in my Dream, when all these things were finished, Mr *Great-heart* took the Head of Giant *Despair,* and set it upon a Pole by the Highway side, right over against the Pillar that *Christian* erected for a Caution to Pilgrims that came after, to take heed of entering into his grounds.

> Though *Doubting* Castle be demolished,
> And the Giant *Despair* hath lost his Head,
> Sin can rebuild the Castle, make't remain,
> And make *Despair* the Giant live again.

Then he writ under it upon a Marble-stone these verses following:

A monument of deliverance

> This is the Head of him, whose Name only
> In former times did Pilgrims terrify.
> His Castle's down, and *Diffidence* his Wife
> Brave Master *Great-heart* has bereft of Life.
> *Dispondency,* his Daughter *Much-afraid,*

Great-heart for them also the Man has play'd.
Who hereof doubts, if he'll but cast his eye
Up hither, may his scruples satisfy:
This Head also, when doubting Cripples dance,
Doth shew from Fears they have Deliverance.

When these men had thus bravely shewed themselves against *Doubting* Castle, and had slain Giant *Despair,* they went forward, and went on till they came to the *Delectable* Mountains, where *Christian* and *Hopeful* refreshed themselves with the varieties of the place. They also acquainted themselves with the Shepherds there, who welcomed them, as they had done *Christian* before, unto the *Delectable* Mountains.

Now the Shepherds seeing so great a Train follow Mr *Great-heart,* (for with him they were well acquainted) they said unto him, Good Sir, you have got a goodly Company here, pray where did you find all these?

Then Mr *Great-heart* replied,

First here is *Christiana* and her Train,
Her Sons, and her Sons' Wives, who like the *Wain,*
Keep by the Pole, and do by Compass steer
From Sin to Grace, else they had not been here;
Next here's old *Honest* come on Pilgrimage,
Ready-to-halt too, who I dare engage
True-hearted is, and so is *Feeble-mind,*
Who willing was not to be left behind;
Dispondency, good man, is coming after,
And so also is *Much-afraid* his Daughter.
May we have entertainment here, or must
We further go? Let's know whereon to trust.

The Guide's speech to the Shepherds

Then said the Shepherds, This is a comfortable Company. You are welcome to us, for we have comfort for the *feeble* as for the *strong.* Our Prince has an eye to what is done to the least of these, therefore Infirmity must not be a block to our Entertainment. So they had them to the Palace door, and then said unto them, Come in Mr *Feeble-mind,* Come in Mr *Ready-to-halt,* Come in Mr

Their entertainment

A descrip-
tion of
false
shepherds *Dispondency*, and Mr *Much-afraid* his Daughter.
These, Mr *Great-heart*, said the Shepherds to the
Guide, we call in by name, for that they are most
subject to draw back, but as for you and the rest
that are *strong*, we leave you to your wonted Liberty. Then said Mr *Great-heart,* This day I see
that Grace doth shine in your Faces, and that you
are my Lord's Shepherds indeed; for that you have
not *pushed* these diseased neither with Side nor
Shoulder, but have rather strewed their way into
the Palace with Flowers, as you should.

So the feeble and weak went in, and Mr *Great-
heart* and the rest did follow. When they were
also set down, the Shepherds said to those of the
weakest sort, What is it that you would have? for,
said they, all things must be managed here to the
supporting of the weak, as well as the warning of
the unruly.

So they made them a Feast of things easy of
Digestion, and that were pleasant to the Palate, and
nourishing; the which when they had received, they
went to the Rest, each one respectively unto his
proper place. When Morning was come, because
the Mountains were high, and the day clear, and
because it was the custom of the Shepherds to shew
to the Pilgrims before their departure, some Rarities; therefore after they were ready, and had
refreshed themselves, the Shepherds took them out
into the Fields, and shewed them first what they
had shewed to *Christian* before.

Mount
Marvel Then they had them to some new places. The
first was to Mount *Marvel,* where they looked, and
beheld a man at a distance, *that tumbled the Hills
about with Words.* Then they asked the Shepherds
what that should mean? So they told them, that
that man was the Son of one *Greatgrace,* of whom
First Part,
p. 130 you read in the First Part of the Records of the
Pilgrim's Progress. And he is set there to teach
Pilgrims how to believe down or to tumble out of
their ways what Difficulties they shall meet with,

by Faith. Then said Mr *Great-heart,* I know him, he is a man above many.

Then they had them to another place called Mount *Innocent,* and there they saw a man cloathed all in White, and two men *Prejudice* and *Ill-will* continually casting Dirt upon him. Now behold the Dirt whatsoever they cast at him would in a little time fall off again, and his Garment would look as clear as if no Dirt had been cast thereat. Mount Innocent

Then said the Pilgrims, What means this? The Shepherds answered, This man is named *Godlyman,* and this Garment is to shew the Innocency of his life. Now those that throw Dirt at him, are such as hate his *well-doing,* but as you see the Dirt will not stick upon his Cloaths, so it shall be with him that liveth truly innocently in the World. Whoever they be that would make such men dirty, they labour all in vain; for God, by that a little time is spent, will cause that their Innocence shall break forth as the Light, and their Righteousness as the Noon-day.

Then they took them, and had them to Mount *Charity,* where they shewed them a man that had a bundle of cloth lying before him, out of which he cut Coats and Garments for the Poor that stood about him; yet his Bundle or Roll of Cloth was never the less. Mount Charity

Then said they, What should this be? This is, said the Shepherds, to shew you, that he that has a heart to give of his Labour to the Poor, shall never want where-withal. He that watereth shall be watered himself. And the Cake that the Widow gave to the Prophet did not cause that she had ever the less in her Barrel.

They had them also to a place where they saw one *Fool* and one *Want-wit* washing of an *Ethiopian* with intention to make him white, but the more they washed him the blacker he was. They then asked the Shepherds what that should mean. So they told them, saying, Thus shall it be with the The work of one Fool, and one Want-wit vile person. All means used to get such an one a good name shall in conclusion tend but to make him more abominable. Thus it was with the *Pharisees,* and so shall it be with all Hypocrites.

Mercy has a mind to see the hole in the hill

Then said *Mercy* the Wife of *Matthew* to *Christiana* her Mother, Mother, I would, if it might be, see the Hole in the Hill, or that commonly called the By-way to Hell. So her Mother brake her mind to the Shepherds. Then they went to the Door. It was in the side of a Hill, and they opened it, and Bid *Mercy* hearken awhile. So she hearkened, and heard one saying, *Cursed be my Father for holding of my feet back from the way of Peace and Life;* and another said, *O that I had been torn in pieces before I had, to save my Life, lost my Soul;* and another said, *If I were to live again, how would I deny myself, rather than come to this place.* Then there was as if the very Earth had groaned and quaked under the feet of this young Woman for fear. So she looked white, and came trembling away, saying, Blessed be he and she that is delivered from this place.

First Part, p. 126

Mercy longeth, and for what

Now when the Shepherds had shewed them all these things, then they had them back to the Palace, and entertained them with what the house would afford. But *Mercy* being a young and breeding Woman, longed for something that she saw there, but was ashamed to ask. Her Mother-in-law then asked her what she ailed, for she looked as one not well. Then said *Mercy,* There is a looking-glass hangs up in the Dining-room, off of which I can not take my mind, if therefore I have it not, I think I shall miscarry. Then said her Mother, I will mention thy wants to the Shepherds, and they will not deny it thee. But she said, I am ashamed that these men should know that I longed. Nay my Daughter, said she, it is no Shame, but a Vertue, to long for such a thing as that, So *Mercy* said, Then Mother, if you please, ask the Shepherds if they are willing to sell it.

Now the Glass was one of a thousand. It would It was the Word of God present a man, one way, with his own Feature exactly, and, turn it but another way, and it would shew one the very Face and Similitude of the Prince of Pilgrims himself. Yea I have talked with them that can tell, and they have said that they have seen the very Crown of Thorns upon his Head, by looking in that Glass, they have therein also seen the Holes in his Hands, in his Feet, and his Side. Yea such an excellency is there in that Glass, that it will shew him to one where they have a mind to see him, whether living or dead, whether in Earth or Heaven, whether in a state of Humiliation or in his Exaltation, whether coming to Suffer or coming to Reign.

Christiana therefore went to the Shepherds apart First Part, p. 125 (now the names of the Shepherds are *Knowledge, Experience, Watchful,* and *Sincere*) and said unto them, There is one of my Daughters, a breeding Woman, that I think doth long for something she hath seen in this house, and she thinks she shall miscarry if she should by you be denied.

EXPERIENCE. Call her, call her, she shall as- She doth not lose her longing suredly have what we can help her to. So they called her, and said to her, *Mercy,* what is that thing thou wouldest have? Then she blushed, and said, The great Glass that hangs up in the Diningroom. So *Sincere* ran and fetched it, and with a joyful consent it was given her. Then she bowed her head, and gave thanks, and said, By this I know that I have obtained favour in your eyes.

They also gave to the other young Women such things as they desired, and to their Husbands great Commendations for that they joined with Mr *Greatheart* to the slaying of Giant *Despair* and the demolishing of *Doubting* Castle.

About *Christiana's* Neck the Shepherds put a How the Shepherds adorn the pilgrims Bracelet, and so they did about the Necks of her four Daughters, also they put Ear-rings in their Ears, and Jewels on their Fore-heads.

First Part,
p. 127 When they were minded to go hence, they let
them go in peace, but gave not to them those certain
Cautions which before were given to *Christian* and
his Companion. The reason was for that these
had *Great-heart* to be their Guide, who was one that
was well acquainted with things, and so could
give them their Cautions more seasonably, to wit,
even then when the Danger was nigh the approach-
ing.

First Part,
p. 127 What Cautions *Christian* and his Companions had
received of the Shepherds, they had also lost by that
the time was come that they had need to put them
in practice. Wherefore here was the advantage that
this Company had over the other.

From hence they went on singing, and they said,

> Behold, how fitly are the stages set
> For their Relief that Pilgrims are become;
> And how they us receive without one let,
> That make the other life our mark and home!
> What Novelties they have to us they give,
> That we, tho' Pilgrims, joyful lives may live;
> They do upon us too such things bestow,
> That shew we Pilgrims are where'er we go.

First Part,
p. 129 When they were gone from the Shepherds, they
quickly came to the place where *Christian* met with
one *Turn-away*, that dwelt in the town of *Apostacy*.
Wherefore of him Mr *Great-heart* their Guide did
now put them in mind, saying, This is the place
How one
Turn-away where *Christian* met with one *Turn-away*, who car-
managed ried with him the character of his Rebellion at his
his back. And this I have to say concerning this man,
apostacy he would hearken to no counsel, but once a falling,
persuasion could not stop him.

When he came to the place where the Cross
and the Sepulchre was, he did meet with one that did
bid him look there; but he gnashed with his teeth,
and stamped, and said he was resolved to go back
to his own Town. Before he came to the Gate, he
met with *Evangelist*, who offered to lay hands on
him to turn him into the way again. But this

Turn-away resisted him, and having done much despite unto him, he got away over the Wall, and so escaped his hand.

Then they went on; and just at the place where Little-faith formerly was robbed, there stood a man with his Sword drawn, and his Face all bloody. Then said Mr *Great-heart,* What art thou? The man made answer, saying, I am one whose name is *Valiant-for-truth.* I am a Pilgrim, and am going to the Cœlestial City. Now as I was in my way, there were three men did beset me and propounded unto me these three things: 1. Whether I would become one of them? 2. Or go back from whence I came? 3. Or die upon the place? To the first I answered, I had been a true man a long season, and therefore it could not be expected that I now should cast in my Lot with Thieves. Then they demanded what I would say to the second. So I told them that the place from whence I came, had I not found Incommodity there, I had not forsaken it at all; but finding it altogether unsuitable to me, and very unprofitable for me, I forsook it for this way. Then they asked me what I said to the third. And I told them, My life cost more dear far than that I should lightly give it away. Besides, you have nothing to do thus to put things to my Choice, wherefore at your Peril be it if you meddle. Then these three, to wit *Wild-head, Inconsiderate* and *Pragmatick,* drew upon me, and I also drew upon them. *[One Valiant-for-truth beset with thieves]*

So we fell to it, one against three, for the space of above three hours. They have left upon me, as you see, some of the marks of their Valour, and have also carried away with them some of mine. They are but just now gone. I suppose they might, as the saying is, hear your Horse dash, and so they betook them to flight. *[How he behaved himself, and put them to flight]*

GREAT-HEART. But here was great odds, three against one. *[Great-heart wonders at his valour]*

VALIANT. 'Tis true, but little or more are nothing

to him that has the Truth on his side. *Tho' an Host encamp against me*, said one, *my heart shall not fear; tho' War should rise against me, in this will I be confident*, &c. Besides, saith he, I have read in some Records, that one man has fought an Army; and how many did *Samson* slay with the Jaw-bone of an Ass?

GREAT-HEART. Then said the Guide, Why did you not cry out, that some might a come in for your succour?

VALIANT. So I did, to my King, who I knew could hear, and afford invisible help, and that was sufficient for me.

GREAT-HEART. Then said *Great-heart* to Mr *Valiant-for-truth,* Thou hast worthily behaved thyself. Let me see thy Sword. So he shewed it him. When he had taken it in his hand, and looked thereon a while, he said, Ha, *it is a right* Jerusalem *Blade.*

VALIANT. It is so. Let a man have one of these Blades, with a Hand to wield it and Skill to use it, and he may venture upon an Angel with it. He need not fear its holding, if he can but tell how to lay on. Its edges will never blunt. It will cut *flesh* and *bones* and *soul* and *spirit* and all.

GREAT-HEART. But you fought a great while, I wonder you was not weary.

The Word
The Faith
Blood

VALIANT. I fought till my Sword did cleave to my Hand; and when they were joined together, as if a Sword grew out of my Arm, and when the Blood ran through my Fingers, then I fought with most courage.

GREAT-HEART. Thou hast done well. Thou hast resisted unto Blood, striving against Sin. Thou shalt abide by us, come in and go out with us, for we are thy Companions.

Then they took him and washed his Wounds, and gave him of what they had to refresh him, and so they went on together. Now as they went on, because Mr. *Great-heart* was delighted in him (for he loved one greatly that he found to be a man of his hands) and because there were with his Company them that was feeble and weak, therefore he questioned with him about many things, as first, what Country-man he was?

VALIANT. I am of *Dark-land,* for there I was born, and there my Father and Mother are still.

GREAT-HEART. *Dark-land,* said the Guide, doth not that lie upon the same Coast with the City of *Destruction?*

VALIANT. Yes it doth. Now that which caused me to come on Pilgrimage was this; we had one Mr *Tell-true* came into our parts, and he told it about what *Christian* had done, that went from the City of *Destruction,* namely, how he had forsaken his Wife and Children, and had betaken himself to a Pilgrim's life. It was also confidently reported how he had killed a Serpent that did come out to resist him in his Journey, and how he got through to whither he intended. It was also told what Welcome he had at all his Lord's Lodgings, especially when he came to the Gates of the Cœlestial City, for there, said the man, he was received with sound of Trumpet by a company of Shining Ones. He told it also, how all the Bells in the City did ring for joy at his reception, and what Golden Garments he was cloathed with, with many other things that now I shall forbear to relate. In a word, that man so told the story of *Christian* and his Travels, that my heart fell into a burning haste to be gone after him, nor could Father or Mother stay me: so I got from them, and am come thus far on my way. *[How Mr Valiant came to go on pilgrimage]*

GREAT-HEART. You came in at the Gate, did you not?

VALIANT. Yes, yes, for the same man also told us that all would be nothing, if we did not begin to enter this way at the Gate. *[He begins right]*

GREAT-HEART. Look you, said the Guide to *Christiana,* the Pilgrimage of your Husband, and what he has gotten thereby, is spread abroad far and near. *[Christian's name famous]*

VALIANT. Why, is this *Christian's* wife?

GREAT-HEART. Yes, that it is, and these are also her four Sons.

VALIANT. What, and going on Pilgrimage too?

GREAT-HEART. Yes verily they are following after.

He is much rejoiced to see Christian's wife

VALIANT. It glads me at heart. Good man, how joyful will he be when he shall see them that would not go with him, yet to enter after him in at the Gates into the City.

GREAT-HEART. Without doubt it will be a comfort to him; for next to the joy of seeing himself there, it will be a joy to meet there his Wife and his Children.

VALIANT. But now you are upon that, pray let me hear your opinion about it. Some make a question, Whether we shall know one another when we are there?

GREAT-HEART. Do they think they shall know themselves then, or that they shall rejoice to see themselves in that Bliss? and if they think they shall know and do these, why not know others, and rejoice in their Welfare also?

Again, since Relations are our second self, though that state will be dissolved there, yet why may it not be rationally concluded that we shall be more glad to see them there than to see they are wanting?

VALIANT. Well, I perceive whereabouts you are as to this. Have you any more things to ask me about my beginning to come on Pilgrimage?

GREAT-HEART. Yes. Was your Father and Mother willing that you should become a Pilgrim?

VALIANT. Oh no. They used all means imaginable to persuade me to stay at home.

GREAT-HEART. What could they against it?

The great stumbling-blocks that by his friends were laid in his way

VALIANT. They said it was an *idle* life, and if I myself were not inclined to Sloth and Laziness, I would never countenance a Pilgrim's condition.

GREAT-HEART. And what did they say else?

VALIANT. Why, they told me that it was a dangerous way; yea, the most dangerous way in the World, said they, is that which the Pilgrims go.

GREAT-HEART. Did they shew wherein this way is so dangerous?

VALIANT. Yes, and that in many particulars.

GREAT-HEART. Name some of them.

VALIANT. They told me of the Slough of *Dis-* pond, where *Christian* was well nigh smothered. They told me that there were Archers standing ready in *Beelzebub-castle* to shoot them that should knock at the Wicket-gate for entrance. They told me also of the Wood and dark Mountains, of the Hill *Difficulty*, of the Lions, and also of the three Giants, *Bloody-man, Maul* and *Slay-good*. They said moreover that there was a foul Fiend haunted the Valley of *Humiliation*, and that *Christian* was by him almost bereft of Life. Besides, say they, you must go over the Valley of the *Shadow of Death*, where the Hobgoblins are, where the Light is Darkness, where the way is full of Snares, Pits, Traps, and Gins. They told me also of Giant *Despair*, of *Doubting* Castle and of the ruin that the Pilgrims met with there. Further, they said I must go over the Inchanted Ground, which was dangerous. And that after all this, I should find a River, over which I should find no Bridge, and that that River did lie betwixt me and the Cœlestial Country. — The first stumbling-block

GREAT-HEART. And was this all?

VALIANT. No. They also told me that this way was full of Deceivers, and of persons that laid await there, to turn good men out of the Path. — The second

GREAT-HEART. But how did they make that out?

VALIANT. They told me that Mr *Worldly Wiseman* did there lie in wait to deceive. They also said that there was *Formality* and *Hypocrisy* continually on the road. They said also that *By-ends, Talkative* or *Demas* would go near to gather me up, that the *Flatterer* would catch me in his Net, or that with green-headed *Ignorance* I would presume to go on to the Gate, from whence he always was sent back to the Hole that was in the side of the Hill, and made to go the By-way to Hell.

GREAT-HEART. I promise you this was enough to discourage, but did they make an end here?

The third VALIANT. No, stay. They told me also of many that had tried that way of old, and that had gone a great way therein, to see if they could find something of the Glory there that so many had so much talked of from time to time; and how they came back again, and befooled themselves for setting a foot out of doors in that Path, to the satisfaction of all the Country. And they named several that did so, as *Obstinate* and *Pliable, Mistrust* and *Timorous, Turnaway* and old *Atheist,* with several more, who, they said, had some of them gone far to see if they could find, but not one of them found so much advantage by going as amounted to the weight of a Feather.

GREAT-HEART. Said they anything more to discourage you?

The fourth VALIANT. Yes. They told me of one Mr *Fearing* who was a Pilgrim, and how he found this way so solitary that he never had comfortable hour therein. Also that Mr *Dispondency* had like to have been starved therein; yea, and also, which I had almost forgot, that *Christian* himself, about whom there has been such a noise, after all his ventures for a Cœlestial Crown, was certainly drowned in the black River, and never went foot further, however it was smothered up.

GREAT-HEART. And did none of these things discourage you?

VALIANT. No, they seemed but as so many nothings to me.

GREAT-HEART. How came that about?

How he got over these stumbling-blocks VALIANT. Why I still believed what Mr *Tell-true* had said, and that carried me beyond them all.

GREAT-HEART. Then this was your Victory, even your Faith.

VALIANT. It was so; I believed, and therefore came out, got into the Way, fought all that set themselves against me, and by believing am come to this place.

> Who would True valour see,
> Let him come hither;
> One here will constant be,
> Come Wind, come Weather.
> There's no Discouragement
> Shall make him once relent
> His first avow'd intent
> To be a Pilgrim.
>
> Who so beset him round
> With dismal Stories,
> Do but themselves confound,
> His Strength the more is;
> No Lion can him fright,
> He'll with a Giant fight,
> But he will have a right
> To be a Pilgrim.
>
> Hobgoblin nor foul Fiend
> Can daunt his spirit;
> He knows he at the end
> Shall Life inherit.
> Then Fancies fly away,
> He'll fear not what men say,
> He'll labour night and day
> To be a Pilgrim.

By this time they were got to the Inchanted First Part, Ground, where the air naturally tended to make one p. 140 *drowsy,* and that place was all grown over with Briars and Thorns, excepting here and there where was an Inchanted Arbor, upon which if a man sits, or in which if a man sleeps, 'tis a question, say some, whether ever he shall rise or wake again in this world. Over this Forest therefore they went, both one with another, and Mr *Great-heart* went before for that he was the Guide, and Mr *Valiant-for-truth* he came behind, being there a Guard for fear lest peradventure some Fiend or Dragon or Giant or Thief should fall upon their Rear, and so do mischief. They went on here each man with his Sword drawn in his hand, for they knew it was a dangerous place. Also they cheered up one another as well as they could; *Feeble-mind*, Mr *Great-heart* commanded should come up after him, and Mr *Dispondency* was under the eye of Mr *Valiant*.

Now they had not gone far, but a great Mist and a Darkness fell upon them all, so that they could scarce for a great while see the one the other. Wherefore they were forced for some time to feel for one another by Words, for they walked not by Sight.

But any one must think that here was but sorry going for the best of them all, but how much worse for the Women and Children, who both of *feet* and *heart* were but tender. Yet so it was, that through the encouraging words of him that led in the front, and of him that brought them up behind, they made a pretty good shift to wag along.

The way also was here very wearisome through Dirt and Slabbiness. Nor was there on all this ground so much as one Inn or Victualling-house, therein to refresh the feebler sort. Here therefore was grunting and puffing and sighing. While one tumbleth over a Bush, another sticks fast in the Dirt; and the Children, some of them, lost their Shoes in the Mire. While one cries out, I am down; and another, Ho, where are you? and a third, The Bushes have got such fast hold on me, I think I cannot get away from them.

An arbor on the Inchanted Ground

Then they come at an Arbor, warm, and promising much refreshing to the Pilgrims; for it was finely wrought above head, beautified with Greens, furnished with Benches and Settles. It also had in it a soft Couch whereon the weary might lean. This you must think, all things considered, was tempting, for the Pilgrims already began to be foiled with the badness of the way, but there was not one of them that made so much as a motion to stop there. Yea, for ought I could perceive, they continually gave so good heed to the advice of their Guide, and he did so faithfully tell them of Dangers, and of the nature of Dangers, when they were at them, that usually when they were nearest to them they did most pluck up their Spirits, and hearten one another to deny the Flesh. This Arbor was called the *Slothful's Friend*, on purpose to allure, if it might be, some of the Pilgrims there to take up their Rest when weary. *The name of the arbor*

I saw then in my Dream, that they went on in this their solitary ground, till they came to a place at which a man is apt to lose his way. Now tho' when it was *light*, their Guide could well enough tell how to miss those ways that led wrong, yet in the *dark* he was put to a stand; but he had in his Pocket a Map of all ways leading to or from the Cœlestial City; wherefore he struck a Light (for he never goes also without his Tinder-box) and takes a view of his Book or Map, which bids him be careful in that place to turn to the right-hand way. And had he not here been careful to look in his Map, they had all in probability been smothered in the Mud, for just a little before them, and that at the end of the cleanest way too, was a Pit, none knows how deep, full of nothing but Mud, there made on purpose to destroy the Pilgrims in. *The way difficult to find* *The guide has a map of all ways leading to or from the city*

Then thought I with myself, who that goeth on Pilgrimage but would have one of these Maps about him, that he may look when he is at a stand, which is the way he must take? *God's Book*

They went on then in this Inchanted Ground till they came to where there was another Arbor, and it was built by the High-way side. And in that Arbor there lay two men whose names were *Heed-less* and *Too-bold*. These two went thus far on Pilgrimage, but here being wearied with their Journey, they sat down to rest themselves, and so fell asleep. When the Pilgrims saw them, they stood still, and shook their heads, for they knew that the sleepers were in a pitiful case. Then they consulted what to do, whether to go on and leave them in their *An arbor and two asleep therein* sleep, or to step to them and try to awake them. So they concluded to go to them and awake them, that is, if they could; but with this caution, namely, to take heed that themselves did not sit down nor imbrace the offered benefit of that Arbor.

The pilgrims try to wake them

So they went in and spake to the men, and called each by his name, (for the Guide it seems did know them) but there was no voice nor answer. Then the Guide did shake them, and do what he could to disturb them. Then said one of them, *I will pay you when I take my Mony.* At which the Guide shook his Head. *I will fight so long as I can hold my Sword in my hand,* said the other. At that one of the Children laughed.

Their endeavor is fruitless

Then said *Christiana,* What is the meaning of this? The Guide said, *They talk in their Sleep.* If you strike them, beat them, or whatever else you do to them, they will answer you after this fashion; or as one of them said in old time, when the Waves of the Sea did beat upon him, and he slept as one upon the Mast of a Ship, *When I awake I will seek it again.* You know when men talk in their Sleeps they say anything, but their words are not governed either by Faith or Reason. There is an incoherency in their words now, as there was before betwixt their going on Pilgrimage and sitting down here. This then is the mischief on't, when *heedless* ones go on Pilgrimage 'tis twenty to one but they are served thus. For this Inchanted Ground is one of the last Refuges that the Enemy to Pilgrims has; wherefore it is, as you see, placed almost at the end of the Way, and so it standeth against us with the more advantage. For when, thinks the Enemy, will these Fools be so desirous to sit down, as when they are weary? and when so like to be weary, as when almost at their Journey's end? therefore it is I say, that the Inchanted Ground is placed so nigh to the Land *Beulah,* and so near the end of their Race. Wherefore let Pilgrims look to themselves, lest it happen to them as it has done

to these, that, as you see, are fallen asleep, and none
can wake them.

Then the Pilgrims desired with trembling to go The light of the Word
forward; only they prayed their Guide to strike a
Light, that they might go the rest of their way
by the help of the Light of a Lanthorn. So he
struck a Light, and they went by the help of that
through the rest of this way, tho' the Darkness was
very great.

But the Children began to be sorely weary, and The children cry for weariness
they cried out unto him that loveth Pilgrims to make
their way more comfortable. So by that they had
gone a little further, a Wind arose that drove away
the Fog, so the Air became more clear.

Yet they were not off (by much) of the Inchanted
Ground, only now they could see one another better,
and the way wherein they should walk.

Now when they were almost at the end of this Stand-fast upon his knees in the En-chanted ground
ground, they perceived that a little before them
was a solemn Noise, as of one that was much concerned. So they went on and looked before them;
and behold they saw, as they thought, a man upon
his Knees, with Hands and Eyes lift up, and speaking, as they thought, earnestly to one that was above.
They drew nigh, but could not tell what he said;
so they went softly till he had done. When he had
done, he got up and began to run towards the Cœlestial City. Then Mr *Great-heart* called after him,
saying, Soho Friend, let us have your Company, if
you go, as I suppose you do, to the Cœlestial City.
So the man stopped, and they came up to him. But
so soon as Mr *Honest* saw him, he said. I know this
man. Then said Mr *Valiant-for-truth*, Prithee,
who is it? 'Tis one, said he, who comes from The story of Stand-fast
whereabouts I dwelt, his name is *Stand-fast*, he is
certainly a right good Pilgrim.

So they came up one to another; and presently Talk be-tween him and Mr Honest
Stand-fast said to old *Honest*, Ho Father *Honest*,
are you there? Ay, said he, that I am, as sure as
you are there. Right glad am I, said Mr *Stand-*

fast, that I have found you on this Road. And as glad am I, said the other, that I espied you upon your Knees. Then Mr *Stand-fast* blushed, and said, But why, did you see me? Yes, that I did, quoth the other, and with my heart was glad at the sight. Why, what did you think? said *Stand-fast*. Think, said old *Honest*, what should I think? I thought we had an honest man upon the Road. and therefore should have his Company by and by. If you thought not amiss [said *Stand-fast*] how happy am I, but if I be not as I should, I alone must bear it. That is true, said the other, but your fear doth further confirm me that things are right betwixt the Prince of Pilgrims and your Soul, for he saith, *Blessed is the man that feareth always.*

They found him at prayer

VALIANT. Well but Brother, I pray thee tell us what was it that was the cause of thy being upon thy Knees even now? Was it for that some special mercy laid obligations upon thee, or how?

What it was that fetched him upon his knees

STAND-FAST. Why we are, as you see, upon the Inchanted Ground, and as I was coming along, I was musing with myself of what a dangerous Road the Road in this place was, and how many that had come even thus far on Pilgrimage had here been stopt and been destroyed. I thought also of the manner of the Death with which this place destroyeth men. Those that die here, die of no violent Distemper. The Death which such die is not grievous to them, for he that goeth away in a *sleep* begins that Journey with Desire and Pleasure; yea, such acquiesce in the will of that Disease.

HON. Then Mr *Honest* interrupting of him said, Did you see the two men asleep in the Arbor?

Madam Bubble, or this vain world

STAND-FAST. Ay, ay, I saw *Heedless* and *Too-bold* there, and for ought I know, there they will lie till they rot. But let me go on in my Tale. As I was thus musing, as I said, there was one in very pleasant attire, but old, who presented herself unto me, and offered me three things, to wit, her Body her Purse and her Bed. Now the truth is, I was

both a-weary and sleepy, I am also as poor as a
Howlet, and that perhaps the Witch knew. Well
I repulsed her once and twice, but she put by my
repulses, and smiled. Then I began to be angry,
but she mattered that nothing at all. Then she
made offers again, and said, If I would be ruled
by her, she would make me great and happy, for
said she, I am the Mistress of the World, and men
are made happy by me. Then I asked her name,
and she told me it was Madam *Bubble.* This set
me further from her, but she still followed me with
Inticements. Then I betook me, as you see, to
my Knees, and with hands lift up and cries, I pray'd
to him that had said he would help. So just as you
came up, the Gentlewoman went her way. Then
I continued to give thanks for this my great Deliverance, for I verily believe she intended no good,
but rather sought to make stop of me in my
Journey.

HON. Without doubt her Designs were bad. But
stay, now you talk of her, methinks I either have
seen her, or have read some story of her.

STAND-FAST. Perhaps you have done both.

HON. Madam *Bubble,* is she not a tall comely
Dame, something of a swarthy Complexion?

STAND-FAST. Right, you hit it, she is just such
an one.

HON. Doth she not speak very smoothly, and
give you a Smile at the end of a Sentence?

STAND-FAST. You fall right upon it again, for
these are her very Actions.

HON. Doth she not wear a great Purse by her
side, and is not her Hand often in it fingering her
Mony, as if that was her heart's delight?

STAND-FAST. 'Tis just so; had she stood by all
this while, you could not more amply have set her
forth before me, nor have better described her
Features.

HON. Then he that drew her picture was a good
Limner, and he that wrote of her said true.

The World   GREAT-HEART. This woman is a Witch, and it is
by vertue of her Sorceries that this ground is inchanted. Whoever doth lay their Head down in
her Lap, had as good lay it down upon that Block
over which the Ax doth hang; and whoever lay
their Eyes upon her Beauty, are counted the Enemies
of God. This is she that maintaineth in their
splendor all those that are the Enemies of Pilgrims.
Yea, this is she that hath bought off many a man
from a Pilgrim's Life. She is a great Gossiper,
she is always, both she and her Daughters, at one
Pilgrim's heels or another, now commending and
then preferring the excellencies of this Life. She
is a bold and impudent Slut, she will talk with
any man. She always laugheth *poor* Pilgrims to
scorn, but highly commends the *rich*. If there be
one cunning to get Mony in a place, she will speak
well of him from house to house. She loveth Ban-
queting and Feasting mainly well, she is always
at one full Table or another. She has given it out
in some places that she is a Goddess, and therefore
some do worship her. She has her times and open
places of Cheating, and she will say and avow it
that none can shew a good comparable to hers.
She promiseth to dwell with Children's Children,
if they will but love and make much of her. She
will cast out of her Purse Gold like Dust, in some
places, and to some persons. She loves to be sought
after, spoken well of, and to lie in the Bosoms of
Men. She is never weary of commending her
Commodities, and she loves them most that think
best of her. She will promise to some Crowns
and Kingdoms if they will but take her advice, yet
many has she brought to the Halter, and ten thousand times more to Hell.

STAND-FAST. Oh, said *Stand-fast*, what a mercy
is it that I did resist her, for whither might she
a drawn me?

GREAT-HEART. Whither, nay, none but God knows
whither. But in general to be sure, she would a

drawn thee *into many foolish and hurtful Lusts,
which drown men in Destruction and Perdition.*

'Twas she that set *Absalom* against his Father,
and *Jeroboam* against his Master. 'Twas she that
persuaded *Judas* to sell his Lord, and that prevailed
with *Demas* to forsake the godly Pilgrim's Life.
None can tell of the Mischief that she doth. She
makes variance betwixt Rulers and Subjects, betwixt
Parents and Children, 'twixt Neighbor and Neighbor, 'twixt a Man and his Wife, 'twixt a Man and
Himself, 'twixt the Flesh and the Heart.

Wherefore good Master *Stand-fast,* be as your
name is, and when you have done all, *stand.*

At this Discourse there was among the Pilgrims
a mixture of Joy and Trembling, but at length they
brake out, and sang,

> What danger is the Pilgrim in,
> How many are his Foes,
> How many ways there are to sin,
> No living mortal knows.
>
> Some of the Ditch shy are, yet can
> Lie tumbling on the Mire;
> Some tho' they shun the Frying-pan,
> Do leap into the Fire.

After this I beheld until they were come unto First Part,
the Land of *Beulah,* where the Sun shineth Night p. 158
and Day. Here, because they was weary, they
betook themselves a while to rest. And because
this Country was common for Pilgrims, and because
the Orchards and Vineyards that were here belonged
to the King of the Cœlestial Country, therefore
they were licensed to make bold with any of his
things. But a little while soon refreshed them here;
for the Bells did so ring, and the Trumpets continually sound so melodiously, that they could not
sleep; and yet they received as much refreshing as
if they had slept their sleep never so soundly. Here
also all the noise of them that walked the Streets,
was, *More Pilgrims are come to Town.* And

another would answer, saying, And so many went
over the Water, and were let in at the Golden Gates
to-day. They would cry again, There is now a
Legion of Shining Ones just come to Town, by
which we know that there are more Pilgrims upon
the road, for here they come to wait for them, and
to comfort them after all their Sorrow. Then the
Pilgrims got up and walked to and fro; but how
were their Ears now filled with Heavenly Noises,
and their eyes delighted with Cœlestial Visions!
In this Land they heard nothing, saw nothing,
felt nothing, smelt nothing, tasted nothing, that
was offensive to their Stomach or Mind; only
when they tasted of the Water of the River over
which they were to go, they thought that tasted a
little *bitterish* to the Palate, but it proved sweeter
when 'twas down.

In this place there was a Record kept of the
names of them that had been Pilgrims of old, and
a History of all the famous Acts that they had done.
It was here also much discoursed how the River
to some had had its *flowings,* and what *ebbings* it
has had while others have gone over. It has been
in a manner dry for some, while it has overflowed
its banks for others.

In this place the Children of the Town would go
into the King's Gardens and gather Nosegays for
the Pilgrims, and bring them to them with much
affection. Here also grew *Camphire* with *Spike-
nard* and *Saffron Calamus* and *Cinnamon,* with all
its Trees of *Frankincense Myrrh* and *Aloes,* with
all chief Spices. With these the Pilgrim's Cham-
bers were perfumed while they stayed here, and with
these were their Bodies anointed, to prepare them
to go over the River when the time appointed was
come.

Now while they lay here and waited for the good
hour, there was a noise in the Town that there was
a Post come from the Cœlestial City, with matter
of great importance to one *Christiana* the Wife

Marginal notes:

Death
bitter to
the flesh,
but sweet
to the soul

Death has
its ebbings
and flow-
ings like
the tide

A mes-
senger of
death
sent to
Christiana

of *Christian* the Pilgrim. So enquiry was made for
her, and the house was found out where she was.
So the Post presented her with a Letter, the contents whereof was, *Hail, good Woman, I bring thee* His
Tidings that the Master calleth for thee, and ex- message
*pecteth that thou shouldest stand in his presence in
Cloaths of Immortality, within this ten days.*

When he had read this Letter to her, he gave her How wel-
therewith a sure token that he was a true Messenger, come is
and was come to bid her make haste to be gone. them that
The token was an *Arrow* with a point sharpened have noth-
with Love, let easily into her heart, which by de- but to die
grees wrought so effectually with her, that at the
time appointed she must be gone.

When *Christiana* saw that her time was come, Her speech
and that she was the first of this Company that to her
was to go over, she called for Mr *Great-heart* her guide
Guide, and told him how matters were. So he told
her he was heartily glad of the News, and could
have been glad had the Post come for him. Then
she bid that he should give advice how all things
should be prepared for her Journey. So he told
her, saying, Thus and thus it must be, and we that
survive will accompany you to the River-side.

Then she called for her Children, and gave them To her
her Blessing, and told them that she yet read with children
comfort the Mark that was set in their Foreheads,
and was glad to see them with her there, and that
they had kept their Garments so white. Lastly, she
bequeathed to the Poor that little she had, and commanded her Sons and her Daughters to be ready
against the Messenger should come for them.

When she had spoken these words to her Guide To Mr
and to her Children, she called for Mr *Valiant-for-* Valiant
truth, and said unto him, Sir, you have in all places
shewed yourself true-hearted, be faithful unto Death,
and my King will give you a Crown of Life. I
would also entreat you to have an eye to my Children, and if at any time you see them faint, speak
comfortably to them. For my Daughters, my Sons'

To Mr
Stand-fast
Wives, they have been faithful, and a fulfilling of
the Promise upon them will be their end. But she
gave Mr *Stand-fast* a Ring.

To old
Honest
Then she called for old Mr *Honest,* and said of
him, Behold an *Israelite* indeed, in whom is no
Guile. Then said he, I wish you a fair day when
you set out for Mount *Sion,* and shall be glad to
see that you go over the River dry-shod. But she
answered, Come wet, come dry, I long to be gone,
for however the Weather is in my Journey, I shall
have time enough when I come there to sit down
and rest me and dry me.

To Mr
Ready-
to-halt
Then came in that good man Mr *Ready-to-halt*
to see her. So she said to him, Thy Travel hither
has been with difficulty, but that will make thy
Rest the sweeter. But watch and be ready, for at an
hour when you think not, the Messenger may come.

To Dis-
pondency
and his
daughter
After him came in Mr *Dispondency* and his
Daughter *Much-afraid,* to whom she said, You
ought with thankfulness for ever to remember
your Deliverance from the hands of Giant *Despair* and out of *Doubting* Castle. The effect
of that Mercy is, that you are brought with
safety hither. Be ye watchful and cast away Fear,
be sober and hope to the end.

To Feeble-
mind
Then she said to Mr *Feeble-mind,* Thou wast delivered from the mouth of Giant *Slay-good,* that
thou mightest live in the Light of the Living for
ever, and see thy King with comfort. Only I advise
thee to repent thee of thine aptness to fear and
doubt of his goodness before he sends for thee,
lest thou shouldest when he comes, be forced to
stand before him for that fault with blushing.

Her last
day, and
manner of
departure
Now the day drew on that *Christiana* must be
gone. So the Road was full of People to see her
take her Journey. But behold all the Banks beyond
the River were full of Horses and Chariots, which
were come down from above to accompany her to
the City Gate. So she came forth and entered the
River, with a beckon of Farewell to those that fol-

lowed her to the River-side. The last word she was
heard to say here was, *I come Lord, to be with thee
and bless thee.*

So her Children and Friends returned to their
place, for that those that waited for *Christiana* had
carried her out of their sight. So she went and
called, and entered in at the Gate with all the
Ceremonies of Joy that her Husband *Christian* had
done before her.

At her departure her Children wept, but Mr
Great-heart and Mr *Valiant* played upon the well-
tuned Cymbal and Harp for Joy. So all departed
to their respective places.

In process of time there came a Post to the Town
again, and his business was with Mr *Ready-to-halt.*
So he enquired him out, and said to him, I am
come to thee in the name of him whom thou hast
loved and followed, tho' upon Crutches; and my
Message is to tell thee that he expects thee at his
Table to sup with him in his Kingdom the next
day after *Easter,* wherefore prepare thyself for
this Journey.

Then he also gave him a Token that he was a true
Messenger, saying, *I have broken thy golden bowl,
and loosed thy silver cord.*

After this Mr *Ready-to-halt* called for his fellow
Pilgrims, and told them, saying, I am sent for, and
God shall surely visit you also. So he desired Mr
Valiant to make his Will. And because he had
nothing to bequeath to them that should survive him
but his Crutches and his good Wishes, therefore
thus he said, *These Crutches I bequeath to my
Son that shall tread in my steps, with a hundred
warm wishes that he may prove better than I have
done.*

Then he thanked Mr *Great-heart* for his Conduct
and Kindness, and so addressed himself to his Journey. When he came at the Brink of the River he
said, *Now I shall have no more need of these*

Ready-
to-halt
summoned

Promises

His will

His last
words

Crutches, since yonder are Chariots and Horses
for me to ride on. The last words he was heard
to say was, *Welcome Life.* So he went his way.

Feeble-
mind
summoned

After this Mr *Feeble-mind* had Tidings brought
him that the Post sounded his Horn at his Chamber-
door. Then he came in and told him, saying, I am
come to tell thee that thy Master has need of thee,
and that in very little time thou must behold his
Face in Brightness. And take this as a Token of
the Truth of my Message, *Those that look out at*
the Windows shall be darkened.

He makes
no will

Then Mr *Feeble-mind* called for his Friends, and
told them what Errand had been brought unto him,
and what Token he had received of the Truth of
the Message. Then he said, Since I have nothing
to bequeath to any, to what purpose should I make
a Will? As for my *feeble mind,* that I will leave
behind me, for that I have no need of that in the
place whither I go. Nor is it worth bestowing upon
the poorest Pilgrim; wherefore when I am gone,
I desire that you, Mr *Valiant,* would bury it in a
Dunghill. This done, and the day being come in
which he was to depart, he entered the River as the

His last
words

rest. His last words were, *Hold out Faith and*
Patience. So he went over to the other side.

Mr
Dispond-
ency's
summons

When days had many of them passed away, Mr
Dispondency was sent for. For a Post was come,
and brought this Message to him, *Trembling man,*
these are to summon thee to be ready with thy
King by the next Lord's day, to shout for Joy for
thy Deliverance from all thy Doubtings.

His
daughter
goes too

And said the Messenger, That my Message is
true take this for a Proof; so he gave him *The*
Grasshopper to be a Burden unto him. Now Mr
Dispondency's Daughter whose name was *Much-*
afraid said when she heard what was done, that
she would go with her Father. Then Mr *Dispond-*
ency said to his Friends, Myself and my Daughter,
you know what we have been, and how trouble-

somely we have behaved ourselves in every Company. My Will and my Daughter's is, that our His will Disponds and slavish Fears be by no man ever received from the day of our Departure for ever, for I know that after my Death they will offer themselves to others. For to be plain with you, they are Ghosts, the which we entertained when we first began to be Pilgrims, and could never shake them off after; and they will walk about and seek entertainment of the Pilgrims, but for our sakes shut ye the doors upon them.

When the time was come for them to depart, they His last went to the Brink of the River. The last words words of Mr *Dispondency* were, *Farewell Night, welcome Day.* His Daughter went through the River singing, but none could understand what she said.

Then it came to pass a while after, that there was Mr a Post in the town that enquired for Mr *Honest.* Honest So he came to his house where he was, and delivered summoned to his hand these lines, *Thou art commanded to be ready against this day seven-night to present thyself before thy Lord at his Father's house.* And for a Token that my Message is true, *All thy Daughters of Musick shall be brought low.* Then Mr *Honest* called for his Friends, and said unto them, I die, but shall make no Will. As for my He makes Honesty, it shall go with me; let him that comes no will after be told of this. When the day that he was to be gone was come, he addressed himself to go over the River. Now the River at that time overflowed the Banks in some places, but Mr *Honest* Good- in his lifetime had spoken to one *Good-conscience* conscience to meet him there, the which he also did, and lent helps Mr him his hand, and so helped him over. The last Honest words of Mr *Honest* were, *Grace reigns.* So he over the left the World. river

After this it was noised abroad that Mr *Valiant-* Mr Valiant *for-truth* was taken with a Summons by the same summoned

Post as the other, and had this for a Token that the Summons was true, *That his Pitcher was broken at the Fountain.* When he understood it, he called for his Friends, and told them of it. Then said he, I am going to my Fathers, and tho' with great diffi-culty I am got hither, yet now I do not repent me of all the Trouble I have been at to arrive where I

His will am. My Sword I give to him that shall succeed me in my Pilgrimage, and my Courage and Skill to him that can get it. My Marks and Scars I carry with me, to be a witness for me that I have fought his Battles who now will be my Rewarder. When the day that he must go hence was come, many accompanied him to the River-side, into which as he went he said, *Death, where is thy Sting?* And

His last as he went down deeper he said, *Grave, where is
words thy Victory?* So he passed over, and all the Trum-pets sounded for him on the other side.

Mr Stand- Then there came forth a Summons for Mr *Stand-*
fast is *fast,* (This Mr *Stand-fast* was he that the rest of
summoned the Pilgrims found upon his Knees in the Inchanted Ground) for the Post brought it him open in his hands. The contents whereof, were, *that he must prepare for a Change of Life, for his Master was not willing that he should be so far from him any longer.* At this Mr *Stand-fast* was put into a muse. Nay, said the Messenger, you need not doubt of the truth of my Message, for here is a Token of the Truth thereof, *Thy Wheel is broken at the Cistern.*

He calls Then he called to him Mr *Great-heart* who was their
for Mr Guide, and said, unto him, Sir, altho' it was not
Great- my hap to be much in your good Company in the
heart days of my Pilgrimage, yet since the time I knew

His speech you, you have been profitable to me. When I came
to him from home, I left behind me a Wife and five small Children, let me entreat you at your return, (for I know that you will go and return to your Master's house, in hopes that you may yet be a Conductor to more of the holy Pilgrims) that you send to my

Family, and let them be acquainted with all that hath and shall happen unto me. Tell them moreover of my happy Arrival to this place, and of the present late blessed condition that I am in. Tell them also of *Christian* and *Christiana* his Wife, and how she and her Children came after her Husband. Tell them also of what a happy end she made, and whither she is gone. I have little or nothing to send to my Family, except it be Prayers and Tears for them; of which it will suffice if thou acquaint them, if peradventure they may prevail.

When Mr *Stand-fast* had thus set things in order, and the time being come for him to haste him away, he also went down to the River. Now there was a great Calm at that time in the River; wherefore Mr *Stand-fast*, when he was about half-way in, he stood awhile, and talked to his Companions that had waited upon him thither. And he said,

This River has been a Terror to many, yea, the thoughts of it also have often frighted me. But now methinks I stand easy, my Foot is fixed upon that upon which the Feet of the Priests that bare the Ark of the Covenant stood, while *Israel* went over this *Jordan*. The Waters indeed are to the Palate bitter and to the Stomach cold, yet the thoughts of what I am going to and of the Conduct that waits for me on the other side, doth lie as a glowing Coal at my Heart.

I see myself now at the end of my Journey, my toilsome days are ended. I am going now to see that Head that was crowned with Thorns, and that Face that was spit upon for me.

I have formerly lived by Hear-say and Faith, but now I go where I shall live by sight, and shall be with him in whose Company I delight myself.

I have loved to hear my Lord spoken of, and wherever I have seen the print of his Shoe in the Earth, there I have coveted to set my Foot too.

His Name has been to me as a Civit-box, yea, sweeter than all Perfumes. His Voice to me has been most sweet, and his Countenance I have more desired than they that have most desired the Light of the Sun. His Word I did use to gather for my Food, and for Antidotes against my Faintings. He has held me, and I have kept me from mine iniquities, yea, my Steps hath he strengthened in his Way.

Now while he was thus in Discourse, his Countenance changed, his strong man bowed under him, and after he had said, *Take me, for I come unto thee,* he ceased to be seen of them.

But glorious it was to see how the open Region was filled with Horses and Chariots, with Trumpeters and Pipers, with Singers and Players on stringed Instruments, to welcome the Pilgrims as they went up, and followed one another in at the beautiful Gate of the City.

As for *Christian's* Children, the four Boys that *Christiana* brought with her, with their Wives and Children, I did not stay where I was till they were gone over. Also since I came away, I heard one say that they were yet alive, and so would be for the Increase of the Church in that place where they were for a time.

Shall it be my Lot to go that way again, I may give those that desire it an account of what I here am silent about; mean-time I bid my Reader *Adieu.*

THE AUTHOR'S VINDICATION

OF HIS PILGRIM

FOUND AT THE END OF HIS "HOLY WAR"

SOME *say the* Pilgrim's Progress *is not mine,*
Insinuating as if I would shine
In name and fame by the worth of another,
Like some made rich by robbing of their Brother.
Or that so fond I am of being Sire,
I'll father Bastards; or if need require,
I'll tell a lye in print to get applause.
I scorn it: John *such dirt-heap never was,*
Since God converted him. Let this suffice
To show why I my Pilgrim patronize.

It came from mine own heart, so to my head,
And thence into my fingers trickled;
Then to my pen, from whence immediately
On paper I did dribble it daintily.

Manner and matter too was all mine own,
Nor was it unto any mortal known,
Till I had done it. Nor did any then
By books, by wits, by tongues, or hand, or pen,
Add five words to it, or write half a line
Thereof: the whole and every whit is mine.

Also, for this thine eye is now upon,
The matter in this manner came from none
But the same heart and head, fingers and pen,
As did the other. Witness all good men;
For none in all the world, without a lye,
Can say that this is mine, excepting I.
I write not this of any ostentation,
Nor 'cause I seek of men their commendation;

I do it to keep them from such surmise,
As tempt them will my name to scandalize.
Witness my name, if anagram'd to thee,
The letters make, Nu hony in a B.

JOHN BUNYAN.

POETRY

GREAT POEMS BY AMERICAN WOMEN: An Anthology, Edited by Susan L. Rattiner. (0-486-40164-2)

FAVORITE POEMS, Henry Wadsworth Longfellow. (0-486-27273-7)

BHAGAVADGITA, Translated by Sir Edwin Arnold. (0-486-27782-8)

ESSAY ON MAN AND OTHER POEMS, Alexander Pope. (0-486-28053-5)

GREAT LOVE POEMS, Edited by Shane Weller. (0-486-27284-2)

DOVER BEACH AND OTHER POEMS, Matthew Arnold. (0-486-28037-3)

THE SHOOTING OF DAN MCGREW AND OTHER POEMS, Robert Service. (0-486-27556-6)

THE BALLAD OF READING GAOL AND OTHER POEMS, Oscar Wilde. (0-486-27072-6)

SELECTED POEMS OF RUMI, Jalalu'l-Din Rumi. (0-486-41583-X)

SELECTED POEMS OF GERARD MANLEY HOPKINS, Gerard Manley Hopkins. Edited and with an Introduction by Bob Blaisdell. (0-486-47867-X)

RENASCENCE AND OTHER POEMS, Edna St. Vincent Millay. (0-486-26873-X)

THE RUBÁIYÁT OF OMAR KHAYYÁM: First and Fifth Editions, Edward FitzGerald. (0-486-26467-X)

TO MY HUSBAND AND OTHER POEMS, Anne Bradstreet. (0-486-41408-6)

LITTLE ORPHANT ANNIE AND OTHER POEMS, James Whitcomb Riley. (0-486-28260-0)

IMAGIST POETRY: AN ANTHOLOGY, Edited by Bob Blaisdell. (0-486-40875-2)

FIRST FIG AND OTHER POEMS, Edna St. Vincent Millay. (0-486-41104-4)

GREAT SHORT POEMS FROM ANTIQUITY TO THE TWENTIETH CENTURY, Edited by Dorothy Belle Pollack. (0-486-47876-9)

THE FLOWERS OF EVIL & PARIS SPLEEN: Selected Poems, Charles Baudelaire. Translated by Wallace Fowlie. (0-486-47545-X)

CIVIL WAR SHORT STORIES AND POEMS, Edited by Bob Blaisdell. (0-486-48226-X)

EARLY POEMS, Edna St. Vincent Millay. (0-486-43672-1)

JABBERWOCKY AND OTHER POEMS, Lewis Carroll. (0-486-41582-1)

THE METAMORPHOSES: Selected Stories in Verse, Ovid. (0-486-42758-7)

IDYLLS OF THE KING, Alfred, Lord Tennyson. Edited by W. J. Rolfe. (0-486-43795-7)

A BOY'S WILL AND NORTH OF BOSTON, Robert Frost. (0-486-26866-7)

100 FAVORITE ENGLISH AND IRISH POEMS, Edited by Clarence C. Strowbridge. (0-486-44429-5)

DOVER THRIFT EDITIONS

POETRY

101 GREAT AMERICAN POEMS, Edited by The American Poetry & Literacy Project. (0-486-40158-8)

100 BEST-LOVED POEMS, Edited by Philip Smith. (0-486-28553-7)

ENGLISH ROMANTIC POETRY: An Anthology, Edited by Stanley Appelbaum. (0-486-29282-7)

THE INFERNO, Dante Alighieri. Translated and with notes by Henry Wadsworth Longfellow. (0-486-44288-8)

PARADISE LOST, John Milton. Introduction and Notes by John A. Himes. (0-486-44287-X)

SPOON RIVER ANTHOLOGY, Edgar Lee Masters. (0-486-27275-3)

SELECTED CANTERBURY TALES, Geoffrey Chaucer. (0-486-28241-4)

SELECTED POEMS, Emily Dickinson. (0-486-26466-1)

LEAVES OF GRASS: The Original 1855 Edition, Walt Whitman. (0-486-45676-5)

COMPLETE SONNETS, William Shakespeare. (0-486-26686-9)

THE RAVEN AND OTHER FAVORITE POEMS, Edgar Allan Poe. (0-486-26685-0)

ENGLISH VICTORIAN POETRY: An Anthology, Edited by Paul Negri. (0-486-40425-0)

SELECTED POEMS, Walt Whitman. (0-486-26878-0)

THE ROAD NOT TAKEN AND OTHER POEMS, Robert Frost. (0-486-27550-7)

AFRICAN-AMERICAN POETRY: An Anthology, 1773-1927, Edited by Joan R. Sherman. (0-486-29604-0)

GREAT SHORT POEMS, Edited by Paul Negri. (0-486-41105-2)

THE RIME OF THE ANCIENT MARINER, Samuel Taylor Coleridge. (0-486-27266-4)

THE WASTE LAND, PRUFROCK AND OTHER POEMS, T. S. Eliot. (0-486-40061-1)

SONG OF MYSELF, Walt Whitman. (0-486-41410-8)

AENEID, Vergil. (0-486-28749-1)

SONGS FOR THE OPEN ROAD: Poems of Travel and Adventure, Edited by The American Poetry & Literacy Project. (0-486-40646-6)

SONGS OF INNOCENCE AND SONGS OF EXPERIENCE, William Blake. (0-486-27051-3)

WORLD WAR ONE BRITISH POETS: Brooke, Owen, Sassoon, Rosenberg and Others, Edited by Candace Ward. (0-486-29568-0)

GREAT SONNETS, Edited by Paul Negri. (0-486-28052-7)

CHRISTMAS CAROLS: Complete Verses, Edited by Shane Weller. (0-486-27397-0)

DOVER THRIFT EDITIONS

NONFICTION

THE DECLARATION OF INDEPENDENCE AND OTHER GREAT DOCUMENTS OF AMERICAN HISTORY: 1775-1865, Edited by John Grafton. (0-486-41124-9)

INCIDENTS IN THE LIFE OF A SLAVE GIRL, Harriet Jacobs. (0-486-41931-2)

GREAT SPEECHES, Abraham Lincoln. (0-486-26872-1)

THE WIT AND WISDOM OF ABRAHAM LINCOLN: A Book of Quotations, Abraham Lincoln. Edited by Bob Blaisdell. (0-486-44097-4)

THE SECOND TREATISE OF GOVERNMENT AND A LETTER CONCERNING TOLERATION, John Locke. (0-486-42464-2)

THE PRINCE, Niccolò Machiavelli. (0-486-27274-5)

MICHEL DE MONTAIGNE: Selected Essays, Michel de Montaigne. Translated by Charles Cotton. Edited by William Carew Hazlitt. (0-486-48603-6)

UTOPIA, Sir Thomas More. (0-486-29583-4)

BEYOND GOOD AND EVIL: Prelude to a Philosophy of the Future, Friedrich Nietzsche. (0-486-29868-X)

TWELVE YEARS A SLAVE, Solomon Northup. (0-486-78962-4)

COMMON SENSE, Thomas Paine. (0-486-29602-4)

BOOK OF AFRICAN-AMERICAN QUOTATIONS, Edited by Joslyn Pine. (0-486-47589-1)

THE TRIAL AND DEATH OF SOCRATES: Four Dialogues, Plato. (0-486-27066-1)

THE REPUBLIC, Plato. (0-486-41121-4)

SIX GREAT DIALOGUES: Apology, Crito, Phaedo, Phaedrus, Symposium, The Republic, Plato. Translated by Benjamin Jowett. (0-486-45465-7)

WOMEN'S WIT AND WISDOM: A Book of Quotations, Edited by Susan L. Rattiner. (0-486-41123-0)

GREAT SPEECHES, Franklin Delano Roosevelt. (0-486-40894-9)

THE CONFESSIONS OF ST. AUGUSTINE, St. Augustine. (0-486-42466-9)

A MODEST PROPOSAL AND OTHER SATIRICAL WORKS, Jonathan Swift. (0-486-28759-9)

THE IMITATION OF CHRIST, Thomas à Kempis. Translated by Aloysius Croft and Harold Bolton. (0-486-43185-1)

CIVIL DISOBEDIENCE AND OTHER ESSAYS, Henry David Thoreau. (0-486-27563-9)

WALDEN; OR, LIFE IN THE WOODS, Henry David Thoreau. (0-486-28495-6)

NARRATIVE OF SOJOURNER TRUTH, Sojourner Truth. (0-486-29899-X)

THE WIT AND WISDOM OF MARK TWAIN: A Book of Quotations, Mark Twain. (0-486-40664-4)

UP FROM SLAVERY, Booker T. Washington. (0-486-28738-6)

A VINDICATION OF THE RIGHTS OF WOMAN, Mary Wollstonecraft. (0-486-29036-0)

FICTION

FLATLAND: A ROMANCE OF MANY DIMENSIONS, Edwin A. Abbott. (0-486-27263-X)

PRIDE AND PREJUDICE, Jane Austen. (0-486-28473-5)

CIVIL WAR SHORT STORIES AND POEMS, Edited by Bob Blaisdell. (0-486-48226-X)

THE DECAMERON: Selected Tales, Giovanni Boccaccio. Edited by Bob Blaisdell. (0-486-41113-3)

JANE EYRE, Charlotte Brontë. (0-486-42449-9)

WUTHERING HEIGHTS, Emily Brontë. (0-486-29256-8)

THE THIRTY-NINE STEPS, John Buchan. (0-486-28201-5)

ALICE'S ADVENTURES IN WONDERLAND, Lewis Carroll. (0-486-27543-4)

MY ÁNTONIA, Willa Cather. (0-486-28240-6)

THE AWAKENING, Kate Chopin. (0-486-27786-0)

HEART OF DARKNESS, Joseph Conrad. (0-486-26464-5)

LORD JIM, Joseph Conrad. (0-486-40650-4)

THE RED BADGE OF COURAGE, Stephen Crane. (0-486-26465-3)

THE WORLD'S GREATEST SHORT STORIES, Edited by James Daley. (0-486-44716-2)

A CHRISTMAS CAROL, Charles Dickens. (0-486-26865-9)

GREAT EXPECTATIONS, Charles Dickens. (0-486-41586-4)

A TALE OF TWO CITIES, Charles Dickens. (0-486-40651-2)

CRIME AND PUNISHMENT, Fyodor Dostoyevsky. Translated by Constance Garnett. (0-486-41587-2)

THE ADVENTURES OF SHERLOCK HOLMES, Sir Arthur Conan Doyle. (0-486-47491-7)

THE HOUND OF THE BASKERVILLES, Sir Arthur Conan Doyle. (0-486-28214-7)

BLAKE: PROPHET AGAINST EMPIRE, David V. Erdman. (0-486-26719-9)

WHERE ANGELS FEAR TO TREAD, E. M. Forster. (0-486-27791-7)

BEOWULF, Translated by R. K. Gordon. (0-486-27264-8)

THE RETURN OF THE NATIVE, Thomas Hardy. (0-486-43165-7)

THE SCARLET LETTER, Nathaniel Hawthorne. (0-486-28048-9)

SIDDHARTHA, Hermann Hesse. (0-486-40653-9)

THE ODYSSEY, Homer. (0-486-40654-7)

THE TURN OF THE SCREW, Henry James. (0-486-26684-2)

DUBLINERS, James Joyce. (0-486-26870-5)